HOSTILE INTENT

This Large Print Book carries the
Seal of Approval of N.A.V.H.

HOSTILE INTENT

MICHAEL WALSH

WHEELER PUBLISHING
A part of Gale, Cengage Learning

GALE
CENGAGE Learning™

Detroit • New York • San Francisco • New Haven, Conn • Waterville, Maine • London

GALE
CENGAGE Learning·

Wheeler Publishing Large Print Hardcover.
The text of this Large Print edition is unabridged.
Other aspects of the book may vary from the original edition.
Set in 16 pt. Plantin.
Printed on permanent paper.

LIBRARY OF CONGRESS CATALOGING-IN-PUBLICATION DATA

Walsh, Michael, 1949–
    Hostile intent / by Michael Walsh. — Large print ed.
      p. cm.
    Originally published: New York : Pinnacle Books, c2009.
    ISBN-13: 978-1-4104-2439-6 (alk. paper)
    ISBN-10: 1-4104-2439-1 (alk. paper)
      1. Terrorism—Prevention—Fiction. 2. Large type books. I.
    Title.
    PS3573.A472242H67 2010
    813'.54—dc22   2009047231

Published in 2010 by arrangement with Pinnacle Books, an imprint of Kensington Publishing Corp.

Printed in the United States of America
1 2 3 4 5 6 7 14 13 12 11 10

For my brother,
Commander Stephen J. Walsh (ret.),
an officer and a gentleman

■ ■ ■ ■

DAY ONE

■ ■ ■ ■

In the life of a man, his time is but a moment, his being an incessant flux, his soul an unquiet eddy, his fortune dark, and his fame doubtful.
— MARCUS AURELIUS, *Meditations,* Book II

CHAPTER ONE

Edwardsville, Illinois

The morning school bell was clattering in the distance as Hope Gardner sandwiched her Volvo station wagon between Mrs. Moscone's Escalade and Janey Eagleton's Prius. She only nicked the Prius's bumper, or rather the plastic piece of junk that passed for a bumper these days, and the gentle thump went unnoticed by her two children in the backseat of her car. She wished she had the guts to ding the Escalade a little, just to make it fair, but the Cadillac belonged to Mrs. Moscone, and nobody wanted Mrs. Moscone mad at them. Her husband was from The Hill in St. Louis, the kind of neighborhood where *The Sopranos* was considered a documentary.

She wondered briefly whether she should leave a note, but that notion flew out of her head as the back door rocketed open.

"Bye, Mom!" shouted Emma, her twelve-year-old. Emma was blond, green-eyed, and filling out with a rapidity that surprised Hope, even though she had gone through the same transformation herself when she was her daughter's age. One moment a skinny kid, the next . . . And if she noticed, how much more quickly the boys noticed too.

More than anything, Emma wanted to grow up to be Gwyneth Paltrow, win an Oscar, and marry a rock star, more or less in that order. Hope didn't have the heart to tell her that the odds were several million to one against any of those things happening. But childhood was for dreaming; Emma would learn about the harsh realities of life soon enough.

Emma was halfway across the schoolyard as Hope turned to Rory. Rory was different. Small for his age, he was skittish, unsure, easily alarmed, especially for a ten-year-old. And right now his nose was running too. "Come on, honey," said Hope, wiping his face with a clean handkerchief and pulling his zipper up tight. "You don't want to be late."

The first snarl of winter had come early to southern Illinois, and there was a stiff, chill breeze blowing into Edwardsville from the

Mississippi, just a few miles to the west. Edwardsville was an exurb of St. Louis, but the big city across the river might as well be in a different country, not just another state. Edwardsville still had an old-fashioned, midwestern small-town feel to it, and that's the way folks liked it.

Nothing ever happened in Edwardsville.

Rory snuffled again and wiped his nose on his sleeve; she could never get him to stop doing that. In the distance, they could both hear the school bell ringing, this time longer and louder.

Hope got out of the car and held out her arms to her son. "Okay, big guy," she said. "Time to go."

"I don't want to go, Mama," Rory said plaintively, not budging.

At times like this, Hope wondered if her son needed some kind of special-ed program. She had talked about it with her husband, Jack, but Jack was a no-nonsense, no-excuses kind of guy, dead set against it. His tech-consulting business did a lot of work with the military all over the Midwest, some of it highly classified, and as far as he was concerned, special-ed programs were for sissies and slackers, and his son was neither. The same went for "conditions" like attention deficit disorder and "diseases"

11

with no physiological symptoms. "Nothing that can't be cured by self-control or a good whack on the ass," Jack would say.

Hope wasn't sure she agreed with him, but there it was. And so Rory sat through class after class, his mind wandering, his grades mediocre, his teachers frustrated.

Oh well, not much could be done about that at the moment. And anyway, Jack was supposed to leave on a business trip to Minneapolis today, so further discussion would have to wait until he got back.

Hope reached in and took her son's hand. It was cold to the touch, clammy, sweaty despite the weather.

Reluctantly, Rory let himself be hoisted up and out of the car. "Can't I stay home today, Mom?" he asked.

In the distance, by the schoolhouse door, Hope could see a man waving at them, telling them to hurry. Later, she would recall that the man was unfamiliar, someone she had never seen before. Ever since Columbine and the other shootings, schools had become much more concerned with security, and strange adults were not allowed to roam the halls. But this man — white, blond, strongly built — was well turned-out in a coat and tie.

Must be a new teacher, Hope thought.

Strange, in the middle of the term. She herself was a substitute teacher at the school, and she thought she knew everybody. In fact, she had a class to teach at noon; well, she'd ask the principal when she saw him.

The bell rang sharply, one last time. No other kids in sight — everyone was in the building. Except Rory, who was still holding on to her hand.

Before she could answer, his hand slipped from hers and he suddenly broke away. "It's okay," he said. "I can handle it."

Hope watched him dash across the dead grass and the new teacher waved him home, like an airplane coming in for a landing. She waved once at Rory's back, but he didn't see her, ducking under the man's arm and through the door just as the bell struck 8:00 A.M.

A brisk gust of wind blew through her, giving her the chills, and it was starting to snow a little. She shook herself to get warm, then walked back toward the car. She made a short detour around the Prius, to see if its bumper was perhaps worse than she'd thought and was surprised to see that it wasn't Janey Eagleton's all, but one with Missouri plates. Now she didn't feel so guilty.

It was not until she was halfway home that she remembered thinking it was odd they were lowering the iron bars on the school windows just as instruction was starting.

CHAPTER TWO

Edwardsville — Jefferson Middle School
Mrs. Braverman's fourth grade arithmetic class opened each school day with a moment of silence. It wasn't exactly a prayer, which the children all knew would be illegal, but neither was it a chance to sneak in a few more winks of sleep before the day began in earnest. Mrs. Braverman saw to that as she patrolled the aisles between the desks.

Rory offered up some quick thoughts in favor of his parents, his dad going away on business, his mom always rushing around in the Volvo, which she treated more like a ferryboat than a car, locked in an eternal game of Cannibals and Missionaries.

Which was, in fact, one of Rory's favorite pastimes: trying to figure out how to get various odd numbers of cannibals and missionaries across a river without ever leaving more man-eaters than men of the cloth on

15

either side. It was a frequent subject of his doodles, but on this morning he tried very hard to visualize the scene: scary dark men with bones in their noses looking hungrily upon pale-faced creatures wearing what seemed to him to be full-length black dresses. You didn't see many holy men around Edwardsville these days, and even though the Gardners were more or less Lutherans, their minister usually wore jeans.

Rory had gotten several moves into his game of mental gymnastics when Mrs. Braverman's midwestern caw brought him out of his reverie and back to attention. He glanced at the clock on the wall and saw that, as usual, only two minutes had passed. Rory didn't like math, and of course wasn't very good at it, but he already had a firm grip on Einstein's theory of relativity: the forty-five minutes between 8:05 and 8:50 A.M. were the Methuselahs of minutes.

Rory knew the drill, and so he flipped his book open to the homework page even before Mrs. Braverman got the words out of her mouth. Except that, on this morning, the words never came out of her mouth. Most of the other kids had done the same thing, but Mrs. Braverman had left her desk and gone over to the classroom door, a wooden one with a large pane of glass in it, the better for the principal, Mr. Nasir-Nassaad, to be able to glance in and give the class one of those looks he was famous for. Which is why, behind his back, the kids all called him Mr. Nasty-Nosy.

Some said Mr. Nasir-Nassaad was from Lebanon, others that he was really from Cleveland, and still others whispered ominously that they knew for a fact that he was a long-lost brother of Osama bin Laden. The funny part was that Mr. Nasir-Nassaad was actually pretty nice, even if he did remind Rory of one of his imaginary cannibals. It was always a disappointment when he opened his mouth and sounded like everybody else in Edwardsville: normal.

It wasn't the principal at the door, however. Rory didn't have a very good view of the door, but from the look on Mrs. Braverman's face, the visitor was somebody she didn't recognize. He could tell, because whenever she was unexpectedly interrupted, unless it was by Nasty-Nosy, she got this how-dare-you look, because as far as Mrs. Braverman was concerned, teaching was the most important thing in the world, and not to be lightly distracted.

She opened the door a crack and stuck her face in the opening. Rory could see only the back of her head. She spoke lowly, inaudibly, then took two steps back and opened the door wide.

A man came in — a man Rory recognized at once. It was the same man who had ushered him through the door as he scooted in. The blond man.

"Children," said Mrs. Braverman. "This is Mr. — what was your name again?"

"Charles," the man replied. He had an accent. He didn't sound like he was normal, or like he was from Edwardsville.

"Charles. He's one of our new substitute teachers, and he's going to be helping out in class today. So let's all give him a big Mississippi River welcome on his first day with us."

The children applauded politely. "I'm just going to run down to the principal's office for a moment," said Mrs. Braverman. "Won't be a minute."

Mrs. Braverman took a step or two out the door, then staggered back inside the classroom as if profoundly puzzled by something that had just happened. There was an extraordinary look on her face as she turned to the class, and then she fell to the floor — sat down, heavily, as if bearing an intolerably heavy burden. She tried to say something, but no sound came out. Instead, blood suddenly poured from her mouth, her head rolled back, and her skull hit the floor with an egg-cracking report that Rory would never forget.

The new teacher, Charles, jumped into action. He leaped over Mrs. Braverman and slammed the door, locking it. Then he turned to the children.

"Everybody down," he said. "Get under your desks and don't look up, no matter what."

Everybody did what he or she was told. Everybody was too shocked to scream. Everybody was real scared.

From under his desk, Rory could hear Mrs. Braverman's labored breathing, growing slower. He knew she'd been shot, but had no idea who shot her. He wondered whether Charles knew first aid or CPR and, if so, when he was going to start helping her.

From outside the door came the sound of screaming and gunfire. Of running feet and the thud of bodies falling. It went on for only a couple of minutes, but childhood minutes are long, and these minutes were as close as youth gets to eternity.

Mrs. Braverman had stopped breathing. From his spot near the back, on the floor, Rory could see a widening puddle of red that had stained her pantsuit and was now spreading across the floor, toward where Annie Applegate and Ehud Aaronson were crouching. He wondered how long it would take for the blood puddle to move through the Bs and Cs and get to the Gs, and whether there would be time for him to find out.

Now it was quiet. Charles's feet moved across the room, stepped over Mrs. Braverman, and stopped in front of the door. The rest of Charles was obviously listening.

"Boys and girls," said Charles after a few long moments. His voice was calm. Rory thought that was cool — that Charles kept it together despite what had just happened. Rory's own heart was pounding like mad. He hoped that when he grew up, he could be cool, like Charles.

"I want you all to stand up, leave your things behind and — very quietly — follow me. Everything is going to be all right. Okay?"

Nobody moved.

"You have to trust me. Stand up, keep silent, and we'll all get out of here."

This time, everybody moved and nobody made a sound. All that fire drill practice was finally paying off. As the children began Indian-filing out of the classroom, Rory noticed that none of the girls looked at Mrs.

Braverman's body through their tears, but the boys each sneaked a peek as they shuffled by. Nobody spoke a word.

"There's a good girl . . . good lad," murmured the man. As Rory approached, the man's free hand reached out and stopped him. "Hold it."

The line stopped; the children froze. It crossed Rory's mind that the man was somehow going to blame him for what happened to Mrs. Braverman. "You were almost late for school," the man said. "What's your name?"

"Rory Gardner."

"Was that your mother dropping you off?"

"Yes, sir." He was close enough to Mrs. Braverman's body that he could have touched her with his foot. He closed his eyes in prayer. He didn't care whether it was illegal. He didn't care if they came to arrest him later. He had a good excuse.

When he opened his eyes, Charles was still looking at him. "It's good to have you on the team, Rory." Charles held out his hand to Rory. "You know what our team's motto is?"

"No, sir."

"Who Dares, Wins."

CHAPTER THREE

St. Louis, Missouri

KXQQ billed itself as "the St. Louis Metro Area's Number One Source for News," but everyone knew that was bullshit. Most of the reporters were fresh out of Penney-Missouri or BU, young kids in their first jobs, ambitious but lazy, fluent in contemporary psychobabble and absolute masters of the jailhouse-jive hand gestures now de rigueur for all TV reporters, but otherwise illiterate, innumerate, and ahistorical. Deep down inside, they really wanted to be cable news anchors or Hollywood screenwriters. By the time any reporters at KXQQ found out about a story, the story was usually over.

Rhonda Gaines-Solomon stared dully at CNN with one ear cocked at the police scanner and the new issue of *Entertainment Weekly* in her hand. She was twenty-four years old, from San Bernardino, California. She hated the Midwest, hated the widebodies who inhabited this part of the country, hated the awful weather, and pretended she was really from Los Angeles, if anybody asked.

"What's hot today, Ms. Solomon?" Mr. Dunkirk always said that, especially when it was she who was hot, which was most days. Like all female on-air talent these days, Rhonda Gaines-Solomon was good looking in that tramp-next-door sort of way that everyone seemed to want lately, and she did the best she could with what God, her parents, and a discreet visit to a plastic surgeon had given her.

Still, she thought, one day she could bust Mr. Dunkirk for sexual harassment if she really set her mind to it. She noticed the way he looked her, had seen his fat wife, and figured him for a possible play if the going got tough, or she wasn't out of this burg in six months, or both.

"All quiet on the midwestern front, chief," she replied, checking out the photo spread on Brad Pitt. It was her standard answer. Nine o'clock in the morning was far too early for St. Louis's usual repertoire of shootings, stabbings, and miscellaneous mayhem to have gotten underway yet. The perps were all still sleeping off their depredations from the previous night.

Casting a quick glance at the bank of TV screens on the newsroom wall, Mr. Dunkirk tacked toward her. "I want something juicy for the four o'clock today," he said, checking out her legs as discreetly as possible.

"I'll see what I can do, chief."

He hated it when she called him "chief." "Who else've we got in the field today?"

"John and Sandy."

That would be Mr. Kelleher and Ms. Gomez. Mr. Dunkirk started to say something, but held his tongue. Young people these days were on a first-name basis with the whole world, as if last names didn't matter, or didn't exist at all. That's why he insisted upon the use of the honorific for himself, and called all his young charges by their last names, just to remind them that they had one.

"See if one of you can get me something better than a weather story, will you?" said Mr. Dunkirk. He looked around the shabby newsroom — the only part of it that shone was the plastic set — and sighed. This was not where he had envisioned himself twenty-five years ago, when he got his first job at a small television station in upstate New York, with dreams of Edward R. Murrow and Walter Cronkite dancing in his head.

And yet here he was, stuck in the dead-end job of news director at the lowest-rated local station in one of the worst television markets in the country. Nothing good was ever going to happen to him again. His life was over.

He wondered if he should make a play for Solomon at some point, just to see what would happen, then decided to table the notion and start thinking about Christmas shopping for his wife.

"How about a cat up a tree? A homeless guy in a cardboard box?" Rhonda shouted after him as he disappeared into his office and closed the door. Every now and then she almost felt sorry for him, if it was possible to feel sorry for somebody that old and hopeless. She would never turn out that way, she promised herself; she'd kill herself long before things came to that.

A crackle on the police scanner seemed promising for a moment but it turned out to be only a hit-and-run with no fatalities.

Then the phone rang. "Newsroom."

A pause, then a voice. Low, modulated, cultivated: a grown-up's voice.

"To whom am I speaking?" There was a hint of an English accent, although truth to tell Rhonda probably couldn't distinguish among English, Australian, New Zealand, or South African if she had a gun at her head. Foreign, in any case.

"Rhonda Gaines-Solomon."

"You will do." A pause. "Do you know what's going on at the school?"

This might be promising. She grabbed a pen, knocked some junk on her desk out of the way, and found a scrap of paper. "What school?"

"Edwardsville Middle School. Jefferson. Do you know what's going on there?"

She glanced at the monitors to see if any of their rivals had anything about Edwardsville: nothing. A glance at the local AP wire on her laptop screen: nothing. "Far as I know, there's nothing going on at the Jefferson Middle School."

A short pause, then a challenge — "What do you know?"

Suddenly, she realized that she'd misunderstood the question. The tipster wasn't *asking* her for information. He was *giving* her information. Rhonda's mind kicked into high gear as the import of what he was saying sank in. Frantically, she waved at Mr. Dunkirk behind the glass, but he was sipping his coffee and reading the paper.

"What is it?" she asked, her voice rising "A school shooting? What is it you're telling me?"

"How fast can you get over here?"

She was out the door so fast that Mr. Dunkirk never even saw her leave. One moment she was there —

And the next moment she was gone.

CHAPTER FOUR

Edwardsville — Jefferson Middle School

The hallway was silent. Unless you looked carefully, you couldn't really tell there was anything wrong, except that the lights were out.

Charles led the children as noiselessly as possible. Rory thought they'd be heading for the front door, but when he pointed in its direction, Charles just shook his head and gestured toward the gym. Rory understood immediately — the gym lay at the rear of the main hallway, and behind it was the loading dock. They'd be able to sneak out that way.

They were about halfway down when a man stepped out of one of the classrooms. He was carrying a gun. Rory didn't know exactly what kind of gun, but it was one of those that you gripped with both hands and shot tons of bullets really fast.

Charles went right after him. They

struggled for a bit, but then the man hit Charles with the butt — at least, that's what it looked like — and Charles went down hard.

This man was quite different. He was funny looking and foreign looking and he was wearing mostly black clothes, like he was some kind of ninja without the sashes and pointed stars. He looked at the children, still standing dutifully in line, and said, "Okay, we go now."

As they walked toward the gym, several other men came out of the shadows. These men were also semi-ninjas, except their faces were covered by ski masks. The man with the rifle barked at them in some strange language — Rory could tell he was the Top Dog, because his face was uncovered and he was holding a cell phone in one hand, and had a pistol stuffed down the front of his pants — and they picked up Charles by the armpits and dragged him along.

The first person Rory spotted upon entering the gym, because he was looking for her, was his sister. Emma was with the other eighth graders, sitting on the bottom bench of the stands. There were tears running down her face. But she was all right; she was alive.

Mr. Nasir-Nassaad was not all right. He was hogtied, lying in the middle of the basketball court, right on the school logo. He was bleeding from his nose and one of his legs was bent back at an impossible angle. He was trying to scream, but there was a dirty, bloody rag stuffed in his mouth.

Rory's eyes drifted from the prone figure of the principal to the nets at either side of the gym. There was something weird hanging from each of them, something heavy and ominous with wires running out of it.

He followed the wires and saw that they ran to one man, another stranger, who was off to the side, near the double fire doors. The wires ran into a doohickey connected to a laptop that was balancing on one of the footstools the cheerleaders used to practice with.

It looked like the whole school was in the gym. Teachers, students, the custodial staff, even Mr. Hebert, the cook, whose family had been in the St. Louis area since it was a French Jesuit trading post and once had owned most of Creve Coeur, or so the story went.

And then there were the strangers, about a dozen, all men, wearing ski masks, all of them armed.

The teachers had already been tied up;

30

the only teacher who wasn't tied up was Charles, but he was still knocked out, and so he lay on one of the benches, unconscious.

But that wasn't the worst part. Several teachers had shotguns wired to their hands, which were bound in front of them, and both their index fingers taped to the triggers. Rory didn't know much about physics yet, but he knew enough to realize that they had to hold their elbows up, the guns pointing directly at their faces. If they got tired, and the guns slipped a bit, the pressure on the triggers would blow their heads off.

Nurse Haskell, he noticed, was having an especially hard time holding her gun up.

Rory submitted without a fuss as one of the bad men — he had already begun to think of them as "cannibals" — roughly bound his hands behind his back with some of that white wire stuff the cops were using now instead of handcuffs and shoved him toward one of the rigged nets.

The Top Dog stepped forward. "Listen to me!" he shouted. He also had a funny accent, but this one was more like what Mr. Nasir-Nassaad should have had but didn't, weird and guttural and scary. "You are all prisoners of war."

Rory expected one of the teachers, maybe

31

Mr. Treadway, who was widely regarded as the meanest man in the school, to say something back. Mr. Treadway was always going on about how America was the worst country in history, which made most people in Edwardsville plenty mad, and how the white man was the worst man in history, but since he taught social studies it was more or less okay. Indeed, Rory had wanted to go find some black people to apologize to, but there weren't all that many of them in Edwardsville, and his parents wouldn't let him go to East St. Louis, where apparently they were pretty easy to find.

With a shotgun taped beneath his chin, though, Mr. Treadway wasn't quite as brave as his reputation.

Rory tried to catch his sister's eye, but as he turned to look her way a blow to the side of his head got his full attention. When the stars stopped shooting, he could see that it was the Top Dog, who had just hit him a glancing blow with the butt of his rifle.

"You don't move! You don't move unless I say so! You hear me?" — he was addressing his remarks to the assembly now. "None of you sons of bitches moves unless I say so. Eyes straight ahead! Eyes straight ahead! Or else!"

Everybody froze. The Top Dog turned

away from Rory.

Now an unusual emotion began to well up inside him. Practically from birth, Rory had been taught to hide his emotions, to conceal them, suppress them, be afraid of them. It wasn't nice to feel bad things, and it was even less nice to express them. Boys, his teachers told him, were different now: they didn't yell, they didn't fight, even when they wanted to, they got along, even when they didn't want to. Not to conform was to risk a trip to Mr. Nasty-Nosy's office or, worse, to the Infirmary, where Nurse Haskell gave you a couple of those pills that supposedly settled you down.

Be nice, they told you. But he didn't want to be nice any more. He didn't want to be afraid any more. He wanted to fight, the way Charles had fought.

"Please, please." It was Nurse Haskell. She was crying, which was making it difficult for her to keep her arms in the right position.

The Top Dog saw her struggles, heard her entreaties. He came over. He took her by the arm and led her toward the center of the gym floor, where Mr. Nasir-Nassaad was lying. He slipped his arms around her waist, propping up her elbows, and waltzed her around a bit.

Then he laughed in her face and released her.

Unsupported, her elbows dropped. She twisted her head just in time — so instead of blowing off the top of her skull, the force of the blast took off the lower half of Nurse Haskell's jaw, sending her teeth showering over those unlucky enough to be close by.

She fell across Mr. Nasir-Nassaad, writhing. Several of the female teachers screamed. But the children were stock-still, as they had been ordered.

The terrorists just laughed. And nobody laughed louder or longer than the Top Dog.

"Okay, okay," he shouted. "Now you see. You see what happens when you fuck with me. Nothing good. But, still — I can be merciful."

Nurse Haskell was still alive, trying to move, trying to moan, even without a mouth. It was hideous. The Top Dog watched her agony for a few moments, then shot her in what remained of her head.

Rory looked across the gym at Emma, who was staring back at him with fear in her eyes. He wanted to rush to her, to protect her. He couldn't do that. But he did know one thing: there was no fear in the glance he shot back at her. Just anger.

The Top Dog put away his gun and looked

at his watch. "Okay, something to do now," he said. "I'll be back."

CHAPTER FIVE

Aboard Air Force One

"Mr. President, I think you'd better look at this."

Augie Willson, the head of President Jeb Tyler's Secret Service detail, was standing in the doorway of the command section with a concerned look on his face. Even at the best of times, Augie had a concerned look on his face, but this look was different. It was even more concerned.

"What is it, Augie?" Tyler and a few other men in suits were sitting around a table, obviously in the middle of an unpleasant conference. "Senator Hartley is trying to explain to me how I could lose the next election, and I'm telling them that's just not going to be possible. You know what a popular guy I am."

President John Edward Bilodeau Tyler smiled that dazzling smile of his, the one that had narrowly won him the presidency the last time out over an older and more experienced opponent, the sitting vice president. A fabulously wealthy trial lawyer, Tyler's political genius was to maintain his image as the champion of the little guy by putting doctors out of business in his home state of Louisiana. Women, especially prochoice women, loved him for his ready wit, his fabulous hair, and the way he could look into their eyes and, as he put it, see their souls. Prolife women, on the other hand, did not exactly appreciate the dearth of ob-gyns that had followed in his meteoric wake.

Men assumed he got laid a lot; there hadn't been a bachelor in the White House since James Buchanan.

Tyler shot a glance at Hartley to see how he was taking the gibe. Despite their many differences, over the years they had bonded over a shared fondness for Maker's Mark bourbon, the novels of John Gregory Dunne and James Ellroy, and the paramount importance of absolute discretion in their personal lives. Often, they got drunk together, swapped stories together, confided in each other. They had few secrets from each other; Bob Hartley was the only man Jeb Tyler could really trust. Even if, given the nature of his office, he couldn't really trust him.

Hartley returned the glance. "I'm just trying to help, Mr. President," he said, but his tone let Tyler know the barb stung a little. "If you don't want to continue to occupy the Oval Office after the next election, there are plenty of people in Washington who would happily take over for you."

Tyler gave Hartley a shot of the famous teeth. "Starting with you, Bob, I imagine," he said, then turned to Augie Willson. Willson didn't much like Hartley, and even with a Secret Service poker face, he was somehow always able to let his personal disdain for the man shine through. "Go ahead, Augie," he said.

"It all started a few minutes ago," the Secret Service man explained, switching on the video screen. The big type at the bottom of the screen was all too familiar:

SCHOOL HOSTAGE SITUATION.
Illinois middle school crisis.

Senator Robert Hartley glanced briefly at the screen, then returned his attention to notes. He was trying to explain to Tyler that his poll numbers were dropping precisely because he was seen as a weak leader by a majority of Americans. The liberal social agenda he had campaigned on — universal health care, hate-crimes legislation, state-sponsored day care for all working mothers — had been largely enacted, and so a fickle country had become restless, which is why it was so difficult to be a two-term president these days: the country craved change, even when it didn't need it. America was an entire nation suffering from attention deficit disorder.

As far as Hartley was concerned, President Tyler was the one who really needed a change: a change of attitude, a change of image. Tyler needed to "rebrand" himself, as the ad men said, as a strong, masculine leader; even the women who had voted him into office and supported his social programs had tired of his metrosexual persona, and were craving something more along the lines of a lumberjack, a biker, or a serial killer.

Truth to tell, Hartley found his own emotions mixed. If Tyler's popularity sank any further, his bid for reelection was going to be in serious trouble, and that left Hartley with both a problem and an opportunity. For President Tyler and Senator Hartley were members of opposite parties, thrown together in an unholy but productive marriage of convenience thanks to Hartley's overweening ambition and Tyler's fetish for bipartisanship. Hartley was intensely disliked within his own party, widely viewed as a weasel who would sell out anybody at any time, and he knew it. Not that it bothered him.

But as Tyler's popularity sank, the chances that Hartley's party had a real shot at the White House increased in lockstep. Like every other senator who looked in the mirror in the morning, Hartley saw a potential president staring back, and as the chairman of the Senate Select Committee on Intelligence, he made sure he was in front of the cameras as often as possible. Indeed, he was so cozy with the media, so happy to leak certain things if it could help his career, that he was known as "Senator Sieve."

So Hartley at first ignored the television. Hostage situations usually played themselves out fairly quickly — half a dozen or so people dead and then the gunman ate his own weapon and that was that. There followed the inevitable suicide note, the video game type revenge You Tube fantasy, the grief counselors, the calls for more gun control, the national navel-gazing about the root causes of violence, etc., etc. Just another day in the USA, especially in the yahoo rural heartland. He was about to urge the president to concentrate on the poll numbers when Tyler turned to Augie Willson and said, "Turn it up, Augie."

Even though the station was a national cable network, the correspondent in front of the locked-down school building was local talent: "Rhonda Gaines-Solomon/ KXQQ/St. Louis."

"She's hot," someone said as Willson cranked up the volume:

". . . happened between eight and nine o'clock this morning, when KXQQ exclusively learned that several armed men, perhaps as many as a dozen, took over the school and have barricaded themselves inside."

The reporter looked both earnest and slightly scared. She kept glancing back over her shoulder, as if expecting someone to emerge from the building at any moment. Overhead, helicopters whirred and there were police cars with flashing lights everywhere. Some of the cops had formed a line, holding back anxious parents from rushing the school.

"The cops can handle this, Jeb," said Hartley. "You've got to look at these polls."

"Shut up, Bob," said the president, irritably. "You know, sometimes you're a real asshole."

"Sometimes?" somebody said.

41

Hartley looked down at the sheaf of papers he was holding in his hand. If the president wasn't going to pay attention to him at a time like this, then when was he? The election was less than a year away, the Iowa caucuses weren't far off, New Hampshire was looming, and Hartley didn't like the looks of his party's guys, not one bit. Even a blow-dried pretty boy like Tyler could lose if he set his mind to it.

"Where are all the other reporters?" asked the man sitting at the president's right hand. He was Lieutenant General Armond "Army" Seelye, the director of the National Security Agency. Hartley despised him, and he knew the feeling was mutual. By law, the DIRNSA had to be at least a three-star flag officer, and although Hartley and others in his party had argued passionately that the nation's most sensitive electronic eavesdropping and communications should not be in the hands of the military, even Tyler had not had the courage to propose any changes in the law. Besides, Hartley suspected, the president probably got a kick out of bossing around the fruit salad.

"What do you mean, Army?" asked Tyler

Seelye shook his head: something was wrong. "Usually there's half a dozen parasites on the scene by now. Local, national.

42

Why just her?"

On the screen, Rhonda answered the question: ". . . have given strict instruction that they will only deal with one representative of the media. Otherwise, they threaten to start killing the hostages, including the children." Rhonda gave a little smile that she hoped came off as concerned, but this was her moment and she was going to milk it for all it was worth. She'd have an offer from a national network before the day was out.

The camera swept the scene — there were plenty of reporters, along with anxious parents, all held back by police SWAT teams and other officials. In the background, an FBI team was moving into place, but nobody dared to approach the school too closely.

At that moment, Senator Hartley had a sudden inspiration: this thing could be just what the doctor ordered if they could spin it to their advantage. He was formulating a new strategy when something small got tossed out of one of the school windows. It hit the ground, bounced a couple of times. And, at that moment, Rhonda's cell phone rang.

The cameraman retrained his focus on Rhonda, who nodded, then walked over, picked up the object, and held it up. Still on her cell phone, she beckoned to the cameraman. As he gingerly moved toward her, everyone could see what she was holding in her hand: a flash drive.

"I've just been instructed by the kidnappers" — she tilted her head in the direction of the building, just as she'd been taught in J-school — "to broadcast this video immediately."

The screen went black for a moment, then the video began.

"Oh, my God," exclaimed the president as he realized what they were looking at. "It's Beslan all over again."

Inside the school gym, where hundreds of kids were gathered, they were yoked together by rope or chain, lying on the floor. Several teachers were bound, with shotguns jammed under their chins. Worse yet were the bombs, wired to the basketball backboards, over the locked and chained doors.

Beslan was the horrific Russian school massacre in 2004, in which hundreds of children and adults had been killed by Chechen separatists and the ineptitude of the Russian security forces. It was the nightmare textbook case of how not to handle a hostage situation.

Inside Air Force One, all hell broke loose.

General Seelye grabbed a secure phone to NSA headquarters in Ft. Meade, Maryland, barked some orders, then rang the secretary of education and told him to order all American public schools into full lockdown mode, and to recommend the same course of action for all private schools. Senator Hartley punched in the number of his party's national committee and told them to stand by to see how this thing played out. The White House press secretary, Pam Dobson, opened her laptop and immediately started pounding out two statements ready for the president to read, depending on what happened.

"How far are we from Washington?" barked President Tyler.

"Half an hour from Andrews," said Augie Willson. "You'll be in the Oval Office in under an hour." As if to underscore, the plane began its descent into the secure air space.

The president turned toward Dobson and shot her a look: double-time. If this thing went south, he was going to need her best efforts.

"Something's happening," said General Seelye. Everyone stared at the screen. Even Hartley had finally shut up.

The door to the school was opening.

Barely visible, in the doorway, was the figure of a man wearing a ski cap pulled down low over his forehead. Still his features were visible. "One of the hostage takers is coming out," whispered Rhonda Gaines-Solomon into her microphone, as if she were covering a golf match. "He's walking toward me now . . . it looks like he wants to talk. Let's get a little closer."

Rhonda moved to meet the man, but instead of responding he raised his right hand and pointed something at her.

She froze. "I think he's got — oh my God. He's got a gun." Not since Jack Ruby had lunged out of the crowd in the Dallas Police garage, brandishing a handgun, and shot Lee Harvey Oswald live on national television, had anyone seen anything like this.

Rhonda stood her ground, scared but professional. She didn't like guns, couldn't understand why some people, mostly right-wing nuts, insisted on having them. The country would be better off without them, she believed, and saw no reason to change her mind now.

As the man drew nigh, she could clearly see the gun in his hand. She couldn't tell what kind it was — some reporters could do that on sight, but she wasn't one of them — but she had to assume it was loaded.

And, to keep her sanity and her wits about her, she had to assume he didn't intend to use it on her. After all, why would he? She was his conduit to the outside world, and he needed her.

"Sir" — she began, extending her microphone toward him — "can you tell us —"

There was the sound of a gunshot, and Rhonda Gaines-Solomon screamed and dropped to the ground.

"Jesus Christ!" exclaimed President Tyler, watching the scene unfold at 24,000 feet.

Rhonda couldn't believe he shot her. He knew she was a reporter, neutral, there to hear his side, and to take it if necessary. But one of her legs hurt like hell.

Without even breaking stride, the man in the ski cap picked up her microphone, looked at her cameraman, and said, "I speak now to the president of the United States. Listen very carefully, everybody, and nobody get hurt no more . . ."

CHAPTER SIX

Los Angeles

"Eddie Bartlett" was out with his eight-year-old daughter, Jade, when his secure cell phone buzzed urgently in his jacket pocket. It was a lovely day in southern California, warm and dry and smog-free. Fire season was just about over and the winter rains hadn't arrived yet. They were hiking together in Griffith Park near the Observatory, high above the city.

"Dad," Jade was saying. "Why do people live in Chicago? Or New York? When they could live here?"

Eddie laughed. It was the kind of question he was used to from Jade: one that came out of the blue. "It sure would be awfully crowded, pumpkin," he replied. From here you see the sweep of the city, from downtown, past the greensward of Hancock Park, to the towers of Century City and all the way to Santa Monica. "Where would we put everybody? Isn't LA traffic bad enough?"

"That's not what I mean," she said, somewhat exasperated with his obtuseness.

"What do you mean, then?"

"I *mean* . . ." she said, choosing her words with great care, "I mean, why would anybody live someplace where the weather is always terrible and the people are always angry?"

The phone buzzed again, and he knew he couldn't ignore it, much as he wanted to. Say what you would about what kind of man Eddie Bartlett was, nobody could say he wasn't a good father. Given the confidential and often clandestine nature of his business, his wife and daughter were everything to him, and he jealously protected his time with them. He even used his real name with them.

"Just a sec', baby," he said. He pulled out the phone and turned away from his little girl as he spoke. Or rather, as he listened. He already knew who it was. Because only one person ever called him on this line.

"It's Tom Powers. Are you watching this?" As usual, the voice was soft, low, scrambled for security.

"No. I'm in the park with my kid."

"Then grab Jade's iPhone and I'll stream it to you."

The phone was a gift from the man who was on the other end of the line. A man whom he'd never met face to face. "Tom Powers" was what he was calling himself today. "Jade — can I borrow your phone?"

Jade looked up from the cactus she was inspecting. "You've already got one, Daddy."

"I need yours, baby. Just for a minute."

Jade fished in her backpack and pulled it out. "How's the reception up here?" Eddie asked her.

"Loud and clear, sir," she replied, handing it to him.

He started the streaming video, and it took only a nanosecond thereafter to realize the purpose of the call. "Is this a go situation?" he asked as, on the screen, a man with heavy Slavic accent rolled off a list of demands: ". . . Abandonment of the Zionist entity. Withdrawal of all forces from the *ummah . . .*"

"Albanian Kosovar, maybe Azerbaijani," said Eddie softly.

". . . The abolition of the North Atlantic Treaty Organization . . . Finally, and most important . . ." With the whole world watching, the camera came in for a tight close-up. Randomly, Eddie Bartlett thought of the last scene of *The Blair Witch Project,* except that movie wasn't scary. "We call upon

President Tyler to publicly embrace and accept Islam on the steps of the Lincoln Memorial no more than twenty-four hours from . . . *now.*"

The camera pulled back. The man's features were very clear: eastern European, unsmiling. His eyes were not the eyes of a fanatic, but rather of a man whose purpose was clear and deadly serious.

"This guy looks familiar. Running face-recognition scan now," said Powers. "The demands are bullshit, of course. What do they really want?"

The terrorist spoke again: "Until then, we demand the removal of all your police forces from this area. No helicopters, no sharpshooters. Turn off all your klieg lights, infrared scopes, electronic surveillance devices. The air space over the school must be kept clear. And we insist that your spies and operatives lay down their arms and identify themselves.

"My comrades and I are not afraid to die. Neither are we afraid to kill all your children. For we have many children each. And you — weak, decadent, intent on your own pleasure — have only one or two. To you, death is an unutterable tragedy. To us, it is the meaning of life." He looked down at the reporter at his feet.

"Got him. Suleyman Drusovic, forty-two, born Kosovo, currently Canadian citizen, resident Montreal."

Rhonda gave him her most pleading look, the kind that would find a target in any man's heart. Her leg hurt like hell but there wasn't much blood; thank God his shot missed the artery. If she could just get out of here, everything was going to be all right.

To her immense relief and astonishment, the man extended his hand to her. As she reached for it, she heard him say, "In the name of Allah, the most merciful, the most compassionate" — as he fired a single shot into her head.

The terrorist leader looked directly into the camera. "No one is to approach the school. Only news crews will be allowed within the perimeter —"

"You got that, Eddie?" said Powers.

"I got it," replied Eddie.

Drusovic continued, "We wish the widest possible international audience. You will deeply regret any violation of these conditions."

"Get ready to hop," said the man on the other line of the line. "Both of you." Abruptly, the connection broke off.

Eddie Bartlett was still staring at the tiny video screen when he heard the helicopter touching down a few hundred yards away. That was for him. A black limo was pulling up near the Observatory. That was for Jade. Tom Powers had already located them and sent their rides.

"Jade, honey," he said. "We have to go now."

CHAPTER SEVEN

Falls Church, Virginia

"Tom Powers" shut down the secure GRID connection to Eddie Bartlett's phone. In sequence, the call had been routed through multiple fake IP/Skype addresses, an Israeli officer's satellite phone, a defunct al-Qaeda cutout in Treviso, and a soon-to-be-deceased Columbian drug dealer's private line in Bogota. It would take Eddie and his team three hours to get to the Xe airfield southeast of St. Louis. They weren't mission operable yet, but there was no point in wasting any time in case the situation went full Branch 4.

The GRID itself was the next-generation Internet, a network of more than 100,000 supercomputers powered by the Large Hadron Collider in Switzerland. Not only was it infinitely faster than the Internet, it could also benignly hijack the computing power of unused personal computers on the network, setting them to work while their owners slept, watched porn, or played video games.

Tom Powers wasn't his real name, of course, any more than Eddie Bartlett was the other man's real name. For this mission, he was using James Cagney characters as rotating aliases; at random intervals, the CSS computers would instruct all Branch 4 ops to re-code and then, by running the Level Six double-blind ciphers through IMDB-Pro, they'd generate a whole new set of operational monikers. And by the time anybody might have the remotest chance in hell of making them, the names would be gone, blown away on the cyber-wind, never to be used again. Tom Powers and Eddie Bartlett would be just as dead as Cagney in *The Public Enemy* and *The Roaring Twenties.*

"Powers" looked at the banks of computers and firearms that lined three of the four walls of his panic room. That's what he called it, even though it wasn't really a panic room. Sure, it could be nearly instantaneously sealed off with halon gas, followed by a lethal jolt of electricity to anyone who touched the descending front wall, but such defensive measures were directed at any unauthorized persons who had managed to get past him and his other defenses first. Which meant, of course, that he was already dead. In which case there was nothing to panic about. The only way around the security settings was to know them.

On his desk, at the exact spot from which he controlled everything, there was a secure telephone. Not a videophone: an old-fashioned black telephone. It looked like the kind of instrument people used in the 1970s, except there were no buttons or dials on it. You couldn't call out with it, and if anyone other than him answered it, the person would hear nothing. Only his voice could activate it through advanced voice-recognition software, but the security didn't stop there. The receiver was a fingerprint reader, so his hand had to be on it for it to function. Finally, he had to look directly into the receiver, which activated a discreet retinal scan. If any of the three elements were not sequenced within five seconds, the phone would self-destruct in a fireball of shrapnel, killing any unauthorized person unlucky enough to have picked it up.

Only three people could reach him via that line: the head of the National Security Agency, the secretary of defense, and the president of the United States. The only three people who were even authorized to know of his existence. Of those three, two knew his permanent operational name, and only one knew his real name.

It was a name he barely remembered, a name from so long ago that it belonged to another person, a boy who'd once had everything a boy should have and then suddenly lost everything. A boy that had been very much like him, until he was gone. All that was left of that boy were a few memories and one indelible moment, a moment he could never get out of his head no matter how much therapy, aversion training, hypnosis, and other, less savory forms of persuasion he underwent.

Idly, his eyes traveled to a photograph that he kept on his desk. It was a picture of him and his parents taken in Rome shortly before Christmas 1985. It was one of the few things he had to remember them by, this fading old Polaroid of two beautiful people and a kid wearing an A. S. Roma football club cap, and carrying a couple of books his father had once given him . . .

One of them was about old movies — his father was a great film buff — and the other was a beginner's guide to ciphers and puzzles and games of logic for the child to read and stretch his brain. "Take these," he said to the boy before going off to meet his colleague on that fateful day. "You'll get a kick out of them someday."

He shook off his reverie and glanced at the phone, which stared back at him silently.

Under normal circumstances, there would be no question of his getting involved. Hostage situations were almost always best left to the local police, or the FBI, unless the hostages were high-value targets. To Powers, hostage situations were just a step up from domestic-violence calls, the kind cops hated most, because there was very little upside, while the downside potential was huge. In the end, there was always a dead husband, a dead wife, or a dead cop. But this was different: these were kids. And he used to be a kid, once.

Tom Powers rippled his fingers across multiple keyboards, calling up everything in the NSA/CSS arsenal: Echelon video feeds, RSS chatter sorters, real-time simultaneous translations of Internet café activity in China, India, Pakistan, Lebanon, Iran, and Saudi Arabia, key-word trigger-coded for instant relay. All conversations could be heard live or as downloaded audio, and read as saved transcriptions in both the original language and in English.

He sampled a few, dipping in and out. He'd lost track of how many languages he spoke fluently, because when you started toting up you had to factor in dialects, sub-dialects, and even random bastardizations like Hawaiian pidgin and Marshallese. Nothing about what was happening in Edwardsville. Plenty of the usual stuff — angry but idle threats against the Great Satan, obscure religious and cultural diatribes, boastful European white supremacist rants, obscure American-sourced swagger — but nothing that stood out. No trip wires. And trip wires were his business.

Nearly a decade after September 11, the American security apparatus had come a long way. Plenty of attacks had been foiled, some — especially early on, when al-Qaeda had the tactical advantage — particularly horrific. There was the Arab cell that had come down from Canada, trying to pass themselves off as American Indians on one of the upstate New York reservations while they waited for the activation codes on a low-yield nuclear device they had smuggled from the former Soviet Union to Halifax, financing the operation by bootlegging cigarettes from the reservation to the outside world and pocketing a fortune in tax avoidance.

The good guys had lucked out on that one: an alert cop in Watertown had noticed the ink on the phony tax stamp rubbing off on his hand, and grabbed the "Indian," who had led him to the other cell members. The cop was shot and killed during the rendezvous, but he had been smart enough to order backup and so the group was rounded up and sent to some especially nasty rendition prisons in Egypt and Slovakia. The cop's widow got a handsome payout from the feds; he got buried at Arlington and the public was never the wiser.

The phone stayed stubbornly silent. Just as well, probably.

Tom Powers stood up and stepped out of the secure room. The rest of his house on North West Street was equally secure, although less dramatically, so he didn't seal the room as he did when he left home.

To enter the front door, for example, he inserted the key into the lock, but rather than aligning a series of tumblers, the key's real work was done by his fresh thumbprint on the head of the key, which was read by the scanner in the door to allow entry.

Once inside, he would glance at the mirror/retinal scanner, which flashed his eyeballs. Anyone who somehow had gained unauthorized entry via the front door — an intruder who forced him to open the door at gunpoint, for example — would miss that beat, with the result that a security gate would descend from the ceiling and trap him in the antechamber, where he could easily be neutralized or dispatched. Video cameras connected directly by dedicated fiber-optic cable to NSA/CSS headquarters in Maryland could be called up on any video screen in the house, and the giant wall-mounted flat screen in the den doubled as a backup, fail-safe control module in a worst-case scenario. Even an EMP (electromagnetic pulse) blast couldn't knock out his communications.

He looked out the window, into his backyard, at one of his favorite sights. From the street, the house was just another postwar brick two-story structure, indistinguishable from thousands of others in this part of northern Virginia. But what almost nobody knew was that, at the edge of the backyard, a small marker, buried in the brush, once marked the southern tip of the District of Columbia. Originally laid out on land ceded by Maryland and Virginia, the District was conceived as a diamond, bisected by the Potomac. Virginia got its land back when the federal district stopped at the river. But there the marker was — a signpost to what might have been — surveyed, the local legend had it, by none other than George

Washington himself.

He looked through the doorway at the black phone and wondered again whether he really wanted to hear it ring.

CHAPTER EIGHT

Washington, D.C.

Marine One had barely hit the South Lawn when President Tyler bounded out. Pam Dobson, Senator Hartley, General Seelye, and Augie Willson bounded behind him in his wake. He really was very fit.

The media jackals were shouting at him — he thought he caught something about "saving kids" and "will you convert to Islam for the children?" — but he ripped a page out of Reagan's playbook and feigned a sudden, inexplicable attack of deafness. Hand cupped behind his ear, pearly whites flashing, Jeb Tyler was the very image of a modern American president: deaf, dumb, and blind to everything he didn't wish to register.

"What's our readiness status?" he snapped at Colonel Al Grizzard, his principal military attaché and the man who controlled the football. Jeb Tyler mistrusted the military and tried to keep "Grizzy" as far away from him as possible and as close to the vice president, Norman Snowden, as constitutionally permissible. Snowden had been a brigadier general in his earlier life, with just enough combat action to make him seems a plausible running mate for a man whose military credentials were, charitably, nonexistent. As far as Tyler was concerned, all military men were trigger-happy maniacs until proven otherwise. He certainly never let the Veep sit in on important affairs of state.

"FBI's in place, sir, and we have special ops airborne now. Delta, Rangers, SEALS, Xe —"

"No Xe," barked the president. "We can't take the hit if this thing goes tits over teacups."

"No Xe," repeated Grizzy, barking into his cell phone.

"And get the FBI and everybody else the hell away. You heard the man."

This time, Colonel Grizzard didn't bark into his cell phone. He couldn't believe his ears: the president of the United States adhering to a terrorist's demand? "Sir?" he said softly.

"You heard me, Colonel. Until we can get a handle on this thing, I'll be goddamned if

I'm going to let these bastards harm a single hair on any child's head."

"Special ops, stand down," said Grizzard into his phone. "All cops, FBI, get well away from the perimeter." Then back to the president, "What now, sir?" His mien and tone of voice both bordered on insubordination.

President Tyler turned to Dobson and held out his hand for his statements as he surveyed the press corps. A sea of anxious faces, mostly female, some with tears already in their eyes. Tears! And nothing bad had really happened yet, if you didn't count that poor reporter. Well, tough luck; he hated the press anyway.

General Seelye spoke up. "Sir, if I may . . ."

The president paid no attention to him. Instead he looked at the two statements she had prepared on the plane, read them both over, then handed one back to her. "This one," he said, crumpling the other up in a ball and letting it fall at his feet.

Pam hopped to, rushing the statement off to key it into the teleprompter. "We'll be live in five, Mr. President," she said.

President Tyler moved smoothly and easily toward the Oval Office, hair and makeup people trailing in his wake.

"Live in two, Mr. President," said Pam Dobson.

"I'm going to reassure the country that everything is under control," Tyler said, as much to himself as to the press secretary.

"Counting down," said Pam Dobson. "Four, three, two — we're live."

The camera light blinked red and the president was on.

"My fellow Americans," he said. "This morning, shortly before nine o'clock Central Standard Time, a group of armed men commandeered a middle school in Edwardsville, Illinois. As soon as I learned of this, I immediately ordered all public schools in the country to be locked down. So far there have been no reports of any other incidents. Mothers and fathers of America, your children are safe."

General Seelye rolled his eyes, but said nothing as the president continued. "As you know, the terrorists — and make no mistake about it, these people, whatever their real or imaginary grievances, *are* terrorists — have murdered a reporter and announced a series of demands. I won't dignify them by repeating them here, but suffice it to say that under no circumstances does the United States government negotiate with terrorists. This has long been the established policy of our country, and it will not be changed on my watch."

The president took a deep breath and smiled. "That said, however —"

"Oh, Jesus," sighed General Seelye to himself. "Here we go . . ."

"We will do everything in our power to ensure the safe release of the some two hundred fifty pupils and teachers at the school."

General Seelye shook his head as inconspicuously as possible.

"I have ordered all our embassies and consulates around the world to be put on the highest alert until this crisis is resolved. The safety of Americans everywhere always has been, and will continue to be, my administration's highest priority."

He misted up for a moment, then regained his composure. It was all an act, but it played well on TV. "One thing I can assure you all — we will bring these men to justice. Thank you, and may God bless America."

The cameras switched off. President Tyler stood up and looked around the Oval Office. His face grew visibly redder, and then he exploded, "God fucking damn it, how the fuck did something like this fucking *happen?*"

CHAPTER NINE

Vaduz, Liechtenstein

Paul Pilier switched off the president of the United States, then laid the remote gently upon the polished-crystal table, next to the vase of white roses, careful not to muss the surface in the slightest. "Sir?" he asked.

The man to whom the question was addressed didn't so much as look up from the banks of laptops purring in front of him. They were neatly arrayed on his teak desk, each one tracking a different international financial market in which he had an interest — which was to say, all of them. As was his habitual wont, he was sipping a glass of Russian tea, the red-hot glass protectively surrounded by a burnished silver holder that was probably worth five thousand American dollars all by itself.

Emanuel Skorzeny was past seventy, but he had the physical vigor of a man half his age and the intellectual firepower of two of them combined. His longstanding talent for multitasking had not deserted him, and so it was that he could listen to the president's speech, monitor its effect on the Nikei, the Dow, the Dax, and the Bourse, make trades, and play a game of simultaneous chess (anonymously, of course) against twelve other players from around the world and still find time to polish his nails. He was very vain about his appearance. "What other news?"

Pilier looked at him from across the room. "May I approach?"

"You may."

The aide placed a sheaf of papers on the desk, printouts of e-mail communications with one of Skorzeny's most trusted lieutenants, being careful not to so much as brush the wood with his fingers or the vase of white roses that adorned the boss's desk as well. Skorzeny had an abhorrence of body oils, and anyone who left so much a trace of his DNA on anything he owned was summarily fired.

Skorzeny glanced through the papers — he was a speed-reader, and could memorize anything on sight. He nodded and then said, "Shred them."

"Yes sir," said Pilier, immediately feeding the documents into an NSA-strength security shredder that sat concealed within a sideboard. He had been with Skorzeny for nearly three years, and was the only one who didn't have to wear gloves at all times. This was a very great sign of trust indeed.

"Have the board members arrived?"

Instinctively, Pilier took three respectful steps backward. "Yes, sir, in the antechamber."

"Show them in, please."

As he awaited his board members, Skorzeny roamed around the room, making sure everything was in its exact place. The furniture, the rugs, and, most important of all, his peerless collection of the art of William Blake that adorned the walls — the finest collection in private hands in the world. Unlike many men of his wealth and taste, Skorzeny was not an indiscriminate buyer; he knew what he liked and what he wanted and he was prepared to pay whatever it took to get it.

Take, for example, the work of Blake's that caught his eye now, his favorite. *The Great Red Dragon and the Woman Clothed with the Sun.* Not the one made famous from that sensational novel in which the psychopath ate it. That painting was still hanging in the Brooklyn Museum: *The Great Red Dragon and the Woman Clothed in Sun.* Different title, different work.

True, his painting was only on loan from the National Gallery of Art in Washington, DC. And the number of chits he had had to call in to get it was almost higher than he was willing to pay. But when it came to Blake, there was almost no such thing as almost. Because Blake understood, as no one else did until Emanuel Skorzeny came along, the misery and mystery of man. That was why his temporary acquisition of it had made headlines around the world. It also reminded people how rich and powerful he was.

Regretfully, his gaze traveled from Blake's masterpiece, out the window and over the mountain-ringed city. Skorzeny International occupied the top three floors of the Tiefenthaler building, which Skorzeny himself owned via one of his many subsidiary companies, and boasted a spectacular view of the Alps in every direction. The boardroom was on the penultimate floor, a state-of-the-art conference chamber from which Skorzeny could rule his vast multinational financial and philanthropic empire. Below were the staff offices. Skorzeny's personal chambers were on the top floor, the penthouse, where only he and a few selected guests were ever allowed *entré.*

Skorzeny moved the short distance from his desk to the chairman's seat, at the head of the mahogany table, which also boasted a crystal vase of white roses — refilled daily, like all the others — as its centerpiece. The table had been a gift from the Sultan of Brunei, in gratitude for some particularly astute investment advice Skorzeny had given him. The rest of the gifts, including the women, Skorzeny had parceled out among his lieutenants: his appetites generally ran to less earthy pleasures.

The board members trooped in and took their seats. No one said a word.

Skorzeny let the silence speak for him. It was, he knew, a subtle but telling way to exercise and display power. No one could speak until he spoke; no one could speak unless spoken to; and every conversation began and ended with Emanuel Skorzeny.

"Gentlemen, thank you for coming. As you know, there's been an incident in America that I believe will affect all of us. It will certainly affect the Skorzeny Foundation, as the New York Stock Exchange is quite sensitive to these sorts of dislocations, especially these days. Monsieur Pilier?"

Pilier snapped on the huge flat-screen television, which instantly divided into multiple quadrants, broadcasting news networks from around the world: CNN, Fox, SKY, BBC1, ARD, ZDF, and others.

"A representative sample," noted Skorzeny who, from time to time glanced at a laptop and tapped a few keys. "Pick one, please."

Pilier turned up the volume on CNN, where the female reporter was busy interviewing some of the parents of the children. Worried, anxious, well-fed midwestern faces filled the screen, their braying American accents falling harshly upon the ears of the sophisticated Europeans watching from thousands of miles away.

Skorzeny gestured to Pilier. The sound was muted.

Skorzeny spoke, "This is the United States of America, Anno Domini 2009. Excuse me, Common Era, 2009. The Lord is not much in our minds these days." A flicker of a smile crossed his lips, signaling to the others that they were permitted a brief display of inaudible mirth. "Not the fearsome warrior it once was. Instead, a country ruled by women and eunuchs. Some call what is happening in Illinois a tragedy. We, however, here at Skorzeny International, call it something else. And what is it that we call it, gentlemen?"

As one: "An *opportunity.*"

"Precisely. An opportunity. After the first

Gulf War, the first President Bush proclaimed the dawn of a New World Order. Even though he was ahead of his time, how right he was. By dint of careful, selected and . . . *targeted* . . . investments, we have been able to treble our operating capital. For you see, gentlemen, it is not true that the race belongs to the swift, or that the future belongs to the strong. Indeed not. The future belongs to the rich and the rich belong to the future. It is a symbiotic relationship, and one that will serve us all very handsomely in the coming days and weeks."

Skorzeny indicated the slender manila folders in front of each board member. On his signal, each man opened his folder, read the contents of the single sheet enclosed therein, then dropped it into the shredder slot next to each seat.

Skorzeny watched them all intently as they digested his action plan. There was one among them who clearly demurred. "Signor Tignanello has a problem," said Skorzeny.

Tignanello was not the man's real name, of course, but was rather his favorite kind of Italian wine. No one but Skorzeny used his real name here; such was the volume of entreaties for foundation support that the board members would never know a moment's peace should their true identities be revealed.

And, of course, Skorzeny's name was not really "Skorzeny," either, but no one needed to know that.

Tignanello looked around the room, trying to avoid Skorzeny's basilisk glare. All eyes turned to him.

"Monsieur Skorzeny," he began, "I have nothing against making money. None of us here does. We are, after all, all rich men." He emitted a brief chuckle, hoping to bring his fellow board members around to his side via a small dollop of humor. In this he was immediately disappointed. "Still, what you are proposing here . . . I cannot, in good conscience . . ."

Skorzeny let Tignanello's words trail off, "conscience" hanging in midair and gradually fading away into silence. It was not a word heard often in this boardroom, and it seemed to foul the air.

"So it's not unanimous then?" asked Skorzeny, although it wasn't a question. "I am disappointed. As you all know, we make no decisions here without complete and utter unanimity."

A glance from Skorzeny to Pilier, and the secretary took up a position just behind the Italian.

"Far be it from me to . . ." Tignanello's head was wrestling with his heart, and his heart was starting to lose when Pilier put his hands on Tignanello's upper trapezius shoulder muscles, the one on either side of the neck, and started massaging them.

"Perhaps you'd like to relax and reconsider," suggested Skorzeny as Pilier's hands moved up the sides of Tignanello's neck. Both his index fingers found the indentation below the Adam's apple and began to press, softly at first, then with increasing pressure.

It was like slow-boiling a frog. Unable to breathe, unable to resist, Tignanello turned the color of his favorite wine. As he lost consciousness, Pilier gently rested the man's head on the table.

"So it is unanimous after all," smiled Skorzeny. "Let the record show that Monsieur Tignanello was unable to vote due to ill health. Thank you, gentlemen. Monsieur Pilier, please inform our supplier in France that we are happy to accept his generous offer. I suggest you contact the HARBOR and the BOREALIS programs to obtain the sort of high-tolerance delivery equipment we need." He turned back to the table. "And now, gentlemen — thank you for your support in this matter. Please calibrate your investments accordingly, and let us plan to rendezvous here in a week's time."

An hour later, the room was cleared, the shredders emptied; it was as if no one had ever been there. At this late hour in central Europe, most of the feeds had been switched to other programming, but CNN International remained focused on the hostage crisis in Illinois.

"Are you thinking about having children with one of your lady friends, Monsieur Pilier?" asked Skorzeny, suddenly. "I wouldn't, if I were you. Better for all to go gently into that good night."

One of Skorzeny's few disconcerting habits was that, while he abhorred being touched, his sense of personal space was almost nil. If he wanted to say something to you directly, something he thought important, he stood so close that you could smell his breath. Pilier chalked it up to Skorzeny's childhood in a special Nazi camp; not a lot of personal space there.

"Children need stability. Security. The knowledge that, in the main, tomorrow is going to be pretty much like today. They're revolutionaries in their minds, but conservatives in their souls. The human condition, writ small." Pilier was on the verge of taking an involuntary step backward when Skorzeny observed, "The situation is ongoing, I see."

Pilier took a silent deep breath. "Yes, sir. The teachers and the pupils are still being held hostage. The authorities have made no moves —"

"Good. The world needs no more Beslans." He reached for and sipped from a small glass of Saint-Geron, as a prophylactic against anemia. It was one of his strictures that his quarters always be outfitted with the distinctive long-necked Alberto Bali-designed bottles, and M. Pilier was diligent in his discharge of that duty. "And yet, given the course of action upon which we have just embarked, this could be a helpful development."

"Helpful, sir?"

"In our business, chaos and uncertainty, while deplorable, can be our friends. Do you disagree?"

Pilier shook his head. "No, sir. Of course not. The vote today was clear, and obviously it's in the best interests of our company. After all —"

"After all," interrupted Skorzeny, "it's the business we're in. Making money. So that the Foundation can tend to the needs of the world's poor. The hungry. The oppressed.

The needy. Doing good by doing well. The bedrock of philanthropy is selfishness — greed, if you will. One of life's petty little oxymorons, but there you are . . . Contact all our sources in America and place our trades accordingly. I want everything in order when the markets open tomorrow morning. We are on a holy crusade."

"Yes, sir."

"And see that my jet is fueled and ready for Paris. We leave immediately."

CHAPTER TEN

Washington, D.C. — The Oval Office
Pam Dobson looked at her watch. She had long, blond hair, which she wore as if she were still twenty-eight, which she wasn't. "We've only got a few hours to get this over with, Mr. President — unless, that is, you want to accept Allah while standing on the steps of the Lincoln Memorial tomorrow morning."

"Have we got a bead on the guy who shot the reporter?" asked Tyler. They were in his private study off the Oval Office, all but Colonel Grizzard, who had been dismissed. The president wanted as few military men in his face as possible, and Seelye was more than enough.

"No sir, no yet," she replied.

"That's not quite right, Mr. President," said Seelye. He pulled out a secure, up-graded version of the civilian BlackBerry and consulted it. "The man has been positively identified as Suleyman Drusovic, a Kosovar Muslim currently resident in Montreal."

"So he's Canadian?" wondered the president. "What would a Canadian have against an American school?"

"With all due respect, Mr. President," said Seelye, trying to conceal his frustration, "he's an ethnic Albanian, a Muslim, who just so happens to hold a Canadian passport at this time. He's no more 'Canadian' than you are." To Seelye, "Canadians" were hockey players and moose hunters, Scottish Presbyterians with names like Maitland and MacGregor, not Balkan Muslims. But what did he know? The world he knew was fast receding, and whatever would replace it fast approaching.

The intercom buzzed. "Secretary Rubin is here, sir," came a female voice. That was Millie Dhouri, a Lebanese Christian from Detroit, who had been with Tyler since the day after September 11, when he suddenly realized his personal staff needed to be more inclusive. The door opened and in walked Howard Rubin, the secretary of defense.

The president addressed him as if he'd been part of the conversation all along. "What else do we know, Howard?"

The SecDef was a mild-mannered intellectual, who had come to government service from the Ivy League. He believed all problems were inherently solvable with enough wit and will; under him, the military had suffered fairly draconian cutbacks. To say he was not particularly popular with the brass would be an understatement. He and Seelye cordially loathed each other, even as they were yoked together in the service of their country.

"Our forces around the world are on high alert, Mr. President," Rubin said. "Keyhole birds report no significant adverse activity in NoKo, Iran, or the breakaway 'stans. We're still watching the Columbia-Venezuela-Bolivia axis, though."

"What about the film the terrorists showed us? What can we tell from that?"

That was Seelye's department. "Being analyzed right now, sir. Results shortly."

The president thought for a moment. "So . . . do we raise the threat level? Get the other agencies involved?"

As far as Seelye was concerned, the second question answered itself. This thing was too urgent to fuck around with the Department of Homeland Security, the CIA, or even the director of National Intelligence. "Not at this time, Mr. President. No sense letting them know they're in our shorts before we get into theirs. As to your second question" — he looked at Rubin, whose face betrayed nothing — "my advice is that we keep this as compartmentalized as possible until we figure out what's going on."

No one dissented. Seelye's BlackBerry buzzed. He hooked it up to a video port and switched on the screen. "NSA has run the tape through advanced face-recog software against all known terrorists in multiple databases, including CIA and FBI. Apologies for the quality, but it's a gen2 beta system that we're still testing."

Everyone watched, fascinated. "As you can see, all of the commandos except Drusovic have some parts of their features obscured, which ordinarily wouldn't be a problem for our equipment, since we can use almost any feature or distinguishing characteristic to —"

"Spare us the details of your wondrous toys, General," ordered Tyler. "What you're saying is, it is a problem."

"In a sense," replied Seelye. "But in an interesting sense. We're drawing a blank on every single one of the commandos. Which means they're all new recruits, fresh blood — or fresh meat — recruited for this specific occasion."

"In other words, you don't have the slightest idea who we're dealing with."

"In other words, we're dealing with rookies," replied Seelye.

Tyler frowned. "Why would this Drusovick —"

"It's pronounced 'Dru-so-vich,' sir —"

"This 'Drusovic' want to show his face?"

Rubin got it in one. "Because whoever's behind him wants us to see it."

The president still didn't get it.

"He's not running the operation," said Seelye. "He's just a patsy, a pawn. A very expendable front man with dreams of martyrdom glory. He —" Seelye looked down at a modified descendant PDA, a special, limited-access, NSA-issued prototype that allowed him full access to just about everything. "Oh, shit."

On the screen now was live coverage from Edwardsville: HOSTAGES SHOT read the graphic.

There were two bodies, lying in front of the main entrance to the school, where they had been dumped. A man and a woman. The woman had half her face blown away, but as soon as the live feed picked her up, it disappeared from the screen. Some details were too gory for the delicate sensibilities of the American public.

"Did I see what I think I just saw?" asked

the president. "Why the hell aren't they showing us what happened? Why did they cut away?"

"The networks don't want to inflame public sentiment," said Secretary Rubin. "And I must say, I don't blame them. All we need now are some gun-toting nuts to jump in their pickup trucks and —"

"And what, Howard?" asked Seelye. "Defend their children?"

"Shut up," barked the president. "He's talking again."

It was Drusovic, sneeringly stepping aside to make sure the bodies would stay in the shot with him.

"These are for you, Mr. President," the man shouted. "And they will keep coming until we get your answer. And when we finish with the teachers . . . we start on the children."

He grinned maliciously. "We want the world to see what you have done, Mr. President. What happens here tonight will make history and we want the world to witness it. Every newspaper, every channel, worldwide. They are welcome. But anybody tries anything and — everybody dies."

Pam Dobson started to cry. The ashen look on the president's face spoke to their common humanity. Tyler may be a fool, thought Seelye, but no one doubted his capacity for empathy or his ability to touch the heart of the average man. It was the quality that had made him such a formidable lawyer and politician.

"Pam, he said, "we're all going to have to be strong now. Strong for each other, strong for the country. So why don't you go back to your office and pull yourself together. I'm going to need your best work."

Dobson rose. "Yes, sir," she said. "Thank you, sir."

Seelye took the opening. "Sir, there's something Secretary Rubin and I need to discuss with you. As you may recall from your briefing —"

Millie's voice wafted over the intercom again: "Senator Hartley is still waiting, Mr. President."

Tyler thought for a moment, then said, "Send him in."

Seelye objected immediately: "Mr. President, I really must object to Senator Hartley's presence in this meeting. He is not authorized to —"

"He's the chairman of the Senate Intelligence Committee, General," replied the president. "Whatever we decide to do, however this plays out, both parties are going to have to be involved."

Seelye glanced over at Rubin, who took the hint. "Sir," he said, "we're not questioning Bob's loyalty or his committee's legitimate legislative oversight. But what we're about to discuss is SCI." Sensitive Compartmented Information, essentially, was above Top Secret.

Tyler shook his head. "I don't care. As the president, I am authorized to release any information to anybody any time I want to, and this is one of those times. I need political backup on this and I also need plausible deniability. Bob Hartley is my friend, even if he is from the other party. So let's get on with it. Hello, Bob . . . take a seat."

Seelye and Rubin nodded in acknowledgment as Hartley entered the room. That was about all the courtesy they were prepared to show him at this moment.

Seelye pretended Hartley wasn't there; not for nothing was "civilian" the dirtiest word in his vocabulary, even if Hartley was a senator. "Under the authority of National Security Decision Memorandum 5100.20, signed by President Nixon on December 23, 1971, and amended by President G. H. W. Bush on June 24, 1991," said General Seelye, "the Sec Def and I believe that you should provisionally authorize a Central Security Service operation to terminate the ongoing incident in Edwardsville."

"Terminate, how?" asked Hartley.

"Shut the fuck up, Bob," said Tyler. "You're here to observe, not talk." Hartley bristled a little. Tyler noticed and didn't care; they had been friends for too long for Hartley to take it personally. "Terminate, how, General?"

"With extreme, exemplary prejudice, sir," replied Seelye.

President Tyler vaguely remembered the CSS, a special division of the National Security Agency that not one American in a million had even heard of, much less understood its function. The CSS had been created originally under the Nixon administration as the "fourth branch" of the armed services, to complement the Army, the Air Force, and the Navy/Marines in the burgeoning field of electronic intelligence and combat. But the traditional-minded put up the predictable bureaucratic fuss, and the CSS was quietly folded in the NSA, authorized to work with each of the individual service branches in capturing and decoding enemy SIGINT. So when, for example, a Navy submarine tapped an undersea Soviet communications cable, or one of the Air Force's many electronic surveillance overflights picked up hostile transmissions, they were relayed to the CSS for evaluation and, if necessary, action.

But the CSS chafed at being a bystander and, using the "No Such Agency" cloak of anonymity, quickly moved into the void, coordinating covert strikes on Soviet assets with the utmost plausible deniability — "accidents" were amazingly common — and establishing its own presence as a service to be reckoned with. Still, resistance from the uniformed services kept it in the shadows of its birth, where it lurked now — the incognito, but highly effective, muscle arm of the NSA.

"Specifically, Section 6.1.21," added Rubin.

"What's that?" interjected Hartley.

"Shut the fuck up, Bob," barked Tyler. "Remind me again what that is," he asked Rubin.

"It's the section of the NSDM that says that the CSS may 'perform such other functions as the Secretary of Defense assigns.' "

"We're talking about a Branch 4 operation, sir," said Seelye. "It's that simple."

"Remind me again what Branch 4 is?"

Seelye ignored the question. "Sir, Branch 4 was established precisely to deal with situations like these, so unless you're prepared to see kiddie corpses start flying out those windows, we strongly advise you to let us get this operation up and running ASAP."

The president's gaze drifted from face to face to the TV set on the other side of the Oval Office, to Edwardsville and the two dead teachers. Finally, it alighted on Rubin. "And your advice is, Howard? Branch 4 or . . . ?"

"Or surrender before anybody else gets killed and run the risk of impeachment from Senator Hartley's party for dereliction of duty. It's that simple."

The president glanced over at Hartley, who silently nodded his assent. "General?"

"I've been involved in counterterrorism since the 1980s," said Seelye, "and if this isn't a job for Branch 4, then nothing is. We need to get in there, take them out, and disappear."

The president was confused but convinced. "So how do we do it?"

"Get 'Devlin.' Now."

"Who's Devlin?" asked Hartley.

"Shut the fuck up, Bob," ordered the president.

"Mr. President, sir," objected Hartley, "you invited me here and —"

Tyler ignored him. "Who's Devlin?" he asked.

" 'Devlin' is the code name for Branch 4's

most trusted and highly skilled operative," explained Seelye, with uncontrolled pride. "He's an expert in cryptology, in electronic surveillance, in marksmanship, and in hand-to-hand combat. In fact, he's the best we've got."

The president's incredulous look begged Seelye to continue. "Nobody knows his real name. If it exists on record at all, it's buried deep in the NSA files. Operationally, however, he used a rotating series of other pseudonyms, never the same one twice. Not even we know what they are when he goes into action."

President Tyler was incredulous. "You mean to tell me that the United States government has an anonymous operative we can't really control?"

"No, sir," replied Seelye. "Not the United States government. We do. The three of us in this room." Seelye caught himself, looked over at Hartley. "And one member of congressional oversight."

If Tyler regretted his decision to let Hartley sit in on the meeting, his face didn't betray him. "Go on," he ordered, glancing over at Hartley with an unspoken warning: *shut the fuck up, Bob.*

"Imagine a platoon of high-tech extermi-nators, who do the job other American agents can't or won't do," explained Rubin. "Each agent has an unbreakable alias or cover. They operate completely off the shelf and under the radar; and they work under pain of death."

"What do you mean, 'pain of death'?" asked the president.

"Operational security is not only everything, it's the only thing," offered Seelye. "The identity of each Branch 4 agent is unknown even to another Branch 4 agent. They put together their own teams, the members of which are unaware for whom they're really working. And should their identities ever become known even to a fellow member of the unit . . ." His voice trailed off, his meaning clear.

"Are you telling me that the United States government employs professional assassins?"

"I wouldn't use that word, Mr. President," replied General Seelye. "More like the business end of our forward defenses. The tip of the tip of the spear."

"Branch 4 is a unit whose very existence — until this moment — is authorized to be known to only three governmental officials: POTUS, the SecDef, and DIRNSA," continued Rubin, turning his attention to Hartley, trying to impress on him the importance of keeping his mouth shut. "Notice I did not use our names. Branch 4 existed before we assumed our offices and it will continue to exist after we leave. No matter who is sitting in our chairs . . ."

The president did a slow burn. "Why is this the first time I'm hearing about it?"

"It's not, sir," said Seelye, quietly. "It's just that you've made domestic considerations the top priority of your administration thus far."

President Tyler was in a box. He hated being in a box. He hated Rubin and Seelye for putting him in a box. When this was over, especially if it ended badly, he was going to have both their heads on pikes, to be displayed in the Rose Garden until the next election. "This Branch 4, this Devlin . . . sounds like God."

"The next best thing," said Seelye. "Plus, Branch 4, you get your prayers answered one hundred percent of the time. Devlin never fails."

The president thought for a moment. "Does this mean I won't have to convert to Islam?" he asked. "I don't think that would go over very well with the folks back home in Lafayette."

"That's exactly what it means," said Seelye.

That seemed to please Jeb Tyler. "Get Devlin," said the president of the United States.

CHAPTER ELEVEN

Leonardo da Vinci Airport, Rome, Christmas, 1985

The man known as "Devlin" was born on December 27, 1985, in Rome, Italy. At the time, he was eight years old.

Survivors of shootings almost always say that, at first, they thought the gunshots were something else. A car backfiring. A man chipping ice off a windshield on a freezing winter's day. Birthday balloons popping. The mind attempts to process what it already knows, and instinctively blocks that which it doesn't wish to recognize. Such things are called "memories."

"Mama, can I have one?" One what? He could only remember the want, not the object. Some trifle for sale in one of the kiosks.

"No," she said.

Far better to remember her, his mother, as she was, young and beautiful, young to him, beautiful to him and at least two others — but that he only found out about later, when he was older, not young.

He and she both knew she didn't mean it. But it was what she had to say. Because her husband, his father, would instantly overrule her had she said yes, that whatever it was he'd wanted would be dismissed as trivial, transient, of no moment. Unworthy. His father always said no.

The boy who would die that day loved his mother. All his childhood memories were of her, because she was the one fixed constant in his life. For as long as he could remember, through all the moves, all the travel, all the strange cities and foreign languages and new friends, there was always his mother there to comfort him, buck him up, and send him back into the fray that he already knew was life.

Civilians always ask service kids whether growing up without a hometown, without old friends, is hard. Absent the familiar anchors, the life that the boy and thousands of others like him lived seemed difficult, intimidating. Better to stay in one place. Better to have a hometown. Nothing ever happens in a hometown.

Harder to grow up without a father or, worse, with an absent father. Devlin's father's business was entirely his own. Later, Devlin understood the nature of that business, perforce embraced it, and took it to lengths his father never could have dreamed. Ironic that he hated his father, hated the business that kept his father away from him, hated the thing that took both his father and his mother away from him, and yet here he was. In it, deeper and darker than dear old Dad ever could have hoped to be. Not by choice, of course.

Until it ended the way it ended, that trip was the happiest memory of his life. Corfu, Biarritz, Palma de Majorca, and finally the Eternal City, where they'd stayed at the Villa Hassler atop the Spanish Steps. How beautiful his mother looked in her bathing suit on the Mediterranean beaches, in her evening dress when they went to the opera performances, in her slacks and blouse, sweater thrown casually over her shoulders, when they threw the petty coins into the Fontana di Trevi, when they stuck their hands in the Bocca della Verita and hoped the Thing inside the Mouth of Truth wouldn't bite them off.

And the best part was, they didn't even have to travel that far. Not one of those long trips that his father took, not one of those overnight airplane flights, the daylong train trips. They were living in Munich, where his father was working at Radio Free Europe, although some of the German kids in his *Grundschule* liked to tease him that RFE really meant CIA. When Devlin would ask his mother where his father was, she would always reply that he was trying to stop some very bad men who were trying to hurt people. Americans, like them.

One night, lying in bed, he managed to overhear a scrap of his parents' conversation. There was somebody else in the room. They were talking in low voices with someone else, switching languages from English to German to Italian to Spanish to Russian to a couple of other tongues that Devlin did not have, practically in midsentence, as they often did.

He was too young to follow everything they spoke about, but he could still catch scraps. At eight, Devlin not only spoke fluent German, but Bavarian as well. From listening to ORF, he had also picked a very fashionable, if slightly goofy, Austrian accent, and could differentiate among Tyrolean, Viennese, and the Italian-inflected *Südtirolisch* of Merano and the *Alto Adige;* his mother loved to ski. Languages were something he didn't even have to think about. They were like listening to music, or working out long division in that particularly German way that so mystified his American-born parents. No "carry-the-anything." Keep the whole thing in your head and just do it.

One of the things they were talking about — no, arguing about — was some kind of animal: a hyena, a dingo, something like that. Devlin had read about beasts like these, opportunistic scavengers that ripped the living flesh from wounded animals, and he wondered why three grown-ups would be discussing creatures from the veldt in the middle of the night.

A burst of Russian followed, and he picked out the word, "Ilyich," and he was proud that he already knew who he was: Vladimir Ilyich Lenin. His father spent a lot of time in the Soviet Union; not that he ever admitted it to Devlin, directly, of course, but from time to time Devlin would find a few unused rubles in the coin cup on his father's dresser and, once in a while, a tin of caviar in the refrigerator. He liked it when his father went to Russia.

Now they were talking about Hungary and Syria and Radio Free Europe. The talk grew louder, more agitated. Somebody yelled something about somebody named Sanchez. Finally, his mother asked for quiet, and the conversation fell back into low murmurs. He listened as long as he could until he drifted off to sleep . . .

Bang. He was in Rome now. In the airport.

No, not bang. *Crack.* That was the sound: *crack.* The sound of the world splintering.

It was a sound he had since made his friend over the intervening years, a sound that at once announced the truth — la Bocca della Verita. Once his enemy, no matter that it became the enemy he loved, the enemy he relied upon, the enemy he could not do without. The friend he could never quite trust.

CRACK.

His father knew that friend immediately.

His mother had been in denial — "No," she was in midsentence — when Dad suddenly shoved her to the ground, knocking her on top of Devlin.

It wasn't the first time his father had pushed his mother, not the first time he'd hit her, struck her, really, a hard blow that sent her to the floor, but it may have been the first and only time such a blow had been delivered out of love instead of anger or jealousy. Devlin himself had been on the receiving end of many such blows, but this was the first and only one that saved his life.

Memories.

Imagine a string of the loudest cherry bombs you ever heard going off. Imagine the branches of every tree in your neighborhood suddenly and simultaneously stripped from their trunks, as if by some sudden ice storm, and sent crashing to the ground. Really fast.

But it wasn't cherry bombs. It wasn't tree branches. It was automatic gunfire, raking the terminal. The sound of bullets chipping marble and plaster, ricocheting off wood and bone. The flash and thunder of hand grenades.

Chunks of flesh, pieces of skull. An arm, severed from its body. A head, rolling. Feet without legs. The dismemberment made more gruesome by the nails, shrapnel, lug nuts, washers, and screws embedded in the ordnance. So many ordinary household objects, so much extraordinary damage. The banality of evil, indeed.

Mother, toppling, catching whatever portion of the ordnance that was meant for him.

They were lying as flat, flattened, her body over his, shielding him. "Stay down, Mama," he begged her, but she was a brave woman, defending her young, and so she raised her head, just a little trying to see the source of danger, trying to make a plan of safety, trying to see if there was any escape from this man-made hell on earth, when something caught in the side of her head and that was that.

It is thankfully not given to many sons to see their mothers die before their eyes, but it was given to Devlin. And at that moment, Devlin learned something extraordinary about himself:

He didn't care.

In retrospect, of course, he did. No boy ever grieved more for this mother than he. But that was later. Not now. Not now, when the bullets and bombs were flying. At that moment — in this moment — Devlin had only one thought:

Self-preservation. He burrowed beneath her still-warm body, waiting for Death to stop.

And he had lived with her death, as the organizing moral principle of his life, ever since. It was what animated him, fueled, propelled him. He was alive because she had died, she who had already given him life once before, and if nothing else he owed it to her to live and keep on living, to kill and keep on killing, until the madness that had engulfed his family either was put to rest, or he was.

The death of his father he witnessed with

more equanimity. He had always known his father was a hero, that his father had accomplished great deeds, which he could never hope to match or equal. For as long as Devlin could remember, he had been aware that his father had sought precisely this life, which meant that he had also sought precisely this death.

Up to this moment, the only grenades Devlin had ever seen were in war movies. German television was full of war movies, in which the good Americans killed the beastly Germans or the even beastlier Japs. For some reasons, Germans enjoyed being the bad guys, and for all Devlin knew maybe they still did, but every movie had a scene in which the Germans tossed one of those funny long skinny grenades, so unlike our grenades, and then their grenades would roll around our trenches until either they exploded, killing at least one of the secondary characters in the movie, or one of our guys picked it up and threw it back at the Germans — we played baseball, so they got it right between their beady little blue eyes — or, best of all, one of our guys fell on the grenade, muffled the explosion with his belly and saved the lives of everybody else in the trench. Even though he died.

Of course, it wasn't like that in real life.

Memories:

Father, pulling his service pistol, trying to return fire. His father was a good shot and Devlin thinks he remembers dad knocking down one of the Arabs with a single shot. True or not, he wants to remember it that way. Otherwise, his father's death was as meaningless as his mother's, and as everyone else's who died that day.

Devlin's last view of him came as he dove onto a rolling grenade. There wasn't much left of him to bury next to his wife, just a bloody trunk and the severed fingers of one hand.

When it was over, when the Israelis guarding the El Al terminal that was the target of the attack had killed three of the four Arabs, eighty people were wounded, and sixteen of them died. A nearly simultaneous attack on Vienna's Schwechat Airport took two more lives, and wounded sixty more, all at the behest of Abu Nidal. The same Abu Nidal who, years later, had turned up mysteriously dead in Baghdad as a guest of Saddam Hussein.

The only surviving Palestinian gunman, Ibrahim Mohammed Khaled — twenty years old at the time of the attack — was given a reduced sentence of thirty years in prison. The defense lawyers had argued for leniency on the grounds of Khaled's youth, his cooperation with the authorities, and the "trauma" of his childhood in a refugee camp. A refugee from Israel, those Nazis . . .

Meanwhile, "Devlin" was one of the survivors who was rushed to the hospital. There, his father's friend, the man in the Munich apartment, told the doctors to stop. He told them the boy was dead. And then he ordered them back to work, saving the lives of those who could be saved.

And so that boy, whatever his name once had been, was no more.

He was adopted into that officer's own family — unofficially, of course — and he changed his name like he changed his socks. At each overseas duty station, and they were all overseas duty stations, he got a new name, a new identity, a new history, a new school transcript, a new life.

Along the way, the boy learned. Blessed with his father's facility for deception and his mother's unerring ear for melody, he learned languages the way other kids learned sports or ate Cracker Jacks. He didn't just learn them, he snacked on them until he had mastered at least as many tongues and dialects as his idol, the great nineteenth-century British explorer and adventurer Sir Richard Francis Burton, including all the major European languages, the Slavic tongues, Hindi, Arabic, Pashtun, Urdu, Japanese, and several dialects of Chinese, including Mandarin and Cantonese. Years later, when a woman asked him how he knew Italian, he replied, "One afternoon it was raining, so I learned Italian." There was no point in exaggerating.

Instead of formal schooling, he studied at the feet of his new father. Boxing and martial arts. Weapons training. He could fight equally well left-handed and right-handed; he could fire two different caliber handguns, one in each hand, and put the bullets in the same spot in the target, whether it was made of paper or, later, flesh and blood. The boy had a head for puzzles, a body for fighting, and a soul for solitude. Not for nothing was his favorite author the Emperor Marcus Aurelius, and he consulted the *Meditations* regularly, always finding inner strength in the *pensées* of the second-century Roman monarch and philosopher.

I do that which it is my duty to do. Nothing else distracts me; for it will be either something that is inanimate and irrational, or somebody who is misled and ignorant of the way.

Other than Marcus, his only boon companion was the movies, which his stepfather took him to as often as possible.

And all of this because his parents had decided to take a Roman holiday. To create the finest intelligence officer in the service of the United States of America. The "Branch 4" prototype. Creation by expiation of a man without a name, without a country, without a native language, without so much as a social security number. A man who, in short, did not officially exist.

The fellow officer's name was Armond Seelye.

The boy's name is Devlin.

CHAPTER TWELVE

Falls Church/Washington, D.C.

At last, the phone rang.

Not the black phone. A nonexistent phone, in fact, one that registered in his consciousness as the sound of chimes, gently clanking in the wind. Except, of course, it wasn't chimes at all, but a distinguishing ring tone that was signaled to him in one of his many compartmentalized capacities and incarnations. He spoke into a Blu-Ray mouthpiece as he answered:

"Mr. Grant's office," he said. Whenever he took a call on this line, his voice was altered to sound like a British woman's — the status symbol of executive assistants in Los Angeles.

Another woman was on the line. "Hello, Helen," she said, "it's Marjorie Takei, just calling to remind Mr. Grant that he's due to speak at RAND the day after tomorrow."

He pretended to consult something on the

computer. Click-clack, click-clack. "Yes," he replied, "I have the appointment in the book. 'Assessing the Threat: The Legal, Practical, and Moral Challenges.' He's very much looking forward to it."

"Good," replied the caller. Her tone changed. "It's terrible, what's going on in St. Louis, isn't it?" "Helen" was silent. "Well, I suppose that makes Mr. Grant's remarks all the more topical, doesn't it?"

"There's a silver lining in everything, I suppose," said Helen, ringing off. British secretaries were nothing if not curt, and nobody, especially in LA, thought them rude.

"Archibald Grant" was one of his favorite identities, yet probably his most dangerous. He was not just an off-the-shelf disposable cover, but an ongoing creation with his own richly imagined life, invented past and borrowed memories. Unlike Devlin's other shades and apparitions, Grant had a continuing existence as one of the RAND Corporation's most important consultants, whose expert exigeses on international terrorism and counterterrorism were delivered at the highest levels of the Santa Monica–based think tank, and under the strictest security guidelines. Not just "Chatham House" rules of nonattribution, but practically pain of death. In fact, over the years he'd had to eliminate one or two loose lips; there was nothing like a watermarked top-security briefing to flush out the traitors. Which, come to think of it, was how he met *her.*

An old-fashioned "ring," just like real phones used to ring before they started playing snatches of 50 Cent, took him out of his reverie and back to reality. The black phone.

His hand picked up the receiver. Fingerprints scanned, the line was uplinked via satphone to one of the NSA's birds, scrambled with level three remodulation logarithms. A stealth-encryption field descended, so that even the most adept or malicious hacker would be left trying to apprehend emptiness.

Now "Tom Powers" looked into the receiver. His iris scan was digitalized, encoded, and flashed over the separate T-3 line to Fort Meade for confirmation.

"Devlin," he said.

He knew who it was right away. "This is DIRNSA," said Seelye. "You're on with POTUS and the SecDef. You're fully up to speed on the sit in Edwardsville." A statement, not a question. Typical Seelye.

"Who else is there with you?" His voice

had an otherworldly quality as it crackled over the hidden speakers.

Seelye looked at Hartley, then to the president, who shook his head. "Nobody," he lied.

"Wrong answer."

"We don't have time for games."

"Neither do I. I'll speak to you, the secretary, and the president. That's the way it is, and it's non-negotiable. You've got ten seconds to get whoever I hear breathing in there the hell out."

Rubin saw that Tyler had that look on his face that he got whenever he was about to blow his stack. He shot him a warning look: *don't do it.* The president controlled his temper. Hartley got the message and slipped out the door.

"This is President Tyler. I'm —"

Devlin didn't care that he was talking to the president of the United States. He interrupted him anyway. "Not recommending direct Branch 4 involvement at this time."

"Why not?" barked Tyler.

"Because something about this stinks, Mr. President."

President Tyler's eyes flashed. "Are you saying we should just sit back and do nothing?"

"No, I'm saying we need to observe."

"Those kids need to be rescued."

"Yes, sir, they do. We know it — and the terrorists know it. But I don't think this is really about the kids."

The president was irritated at this display of independence. Who was commander in chief around here? "Then what do you think it is?"

"Not sure yet. Some kind of feint, or probe, to see how we react."

"You're talking about children's lives," Tyler said.

"If I'm right, sir — and that's what you pay me to be — then we're talking about much more than children's lives. Getting me involved now could potentially make things more difficult for all of us in the end."

"That's a chance I'm willing to take," said the president. "Where are you now?"

"That's classified, sir. And even your authorization doesn't reach that high."

Tyler exploded, "Goddamnit, I'm the fucking president of the United States!"

Even with the electronic scrambling, Devlin's voice came across low and clear and confident. "Yes, sir," he said, "you are. At least until the next election."

Inwardly, General Seelye smiled. Rubin kept a poker face, badly. Devlin paused for a moment, then continued, "I've got your feed on my screen, General. Run the reporter's tape again. I'll show you what I'm talking about."

"Cueing it up now," said Seelye. Once again the tape: the kids, the bombs, the teachers, the shotguns — .

"Hold it. Right there," said Devlin. "See it?" Seelye paused the feed. What was Devlin talking about? "The guy on the bench there, at click 4,156.07." A blond man in a sport coat and tie, lying on the bench with the tied-up teachers, his face only partially visible.

"One of the teachers, obviously," said the president.

"Why, obviously? Look at the way he's dressed. Look at that sport coat — it's an Armani, costs two thousand bucks. Middle school teachers don't wear things like that. General, run an NSA physio scan on this guy. Complete reconstruction —" They could hear the sound of typing. "And match it up with this."

Tapping into the school's internal video feeds, Devlin brought up a shot from inside the school: the main hall, looking toward the front doors. A man in the doorway, holding open the door as a boy rushes in, late.

Zoom. The man up close, from behind.

113

Grainy, but visible.

"Full reconstruction — strip him naked and build him back up again." It wasn't protocol to give orders to the president, but this was no time to stand on ceremony.

Everyone could see, but just barely make out, the man under discussion. Tallish, powerfully built, with his back to the camera. But the back of his head was clearly visible, including one ear. "That ear will be especially helpful," said Devlin.

"We'll get him," said Seelye. "Mag it up — see his hair?" Closer: light hair, maybe blond.

"Not a lot of blond Muslims, Mr. President," observed Rubin.

"Which is why he could be anybody," said General Seelye. "A merc, a Russian speshop, a white South African glory hunter."

"Or a teacher," said the president, stubbornly.

"This guy's no teacher," said Devlin. "He's the ringleader. He just doesn't want us to know it. Once we find out who he is, we'll have some sense of how to handle this thing. Match him with up all NSA motion captures of known terrorists, unrestricted by race, religion, or ethnicity. I don't want any PC bullshit here. Any tics, any gestures. Run video hair-and-fiber infrared analysis,

114

see what you come up with. Got that, General?"

Tyler bristled at Devlin's tone. "Listen, Devlin, I don't think I like your —"

"On it," said Seelye, intervening.

"Overfly ASAP, let's get a radioactivity read, just in case. We don't want any surprises in the basement or the girls' bathroom."

"On that, too . . ."

"And I'll need our best guesstimates of their weaponry, worst-case. Then, I'll call you back."

The president look confused. Was this "Devlin" on the job or not? He wished that America were a kinder, gentler nation, one that didn't need hard, rough men like Devlin to keep the women and children safe from people with legitimate grievances and misunderstood motives. He swallowed his pride. "Are you in or are you out, Devlin?"

"I'm not sure yet. What about chatter?"

"Nothing specific or credible," replied Seelye.

"September eleventh was neither specific nor credible until the first plane hit the World Trade Center," said Devlin.

"So what action do you recommend?" asked Tyler.

"That we await developments. I'll put a

team in place. But things might have to get worse, before I can make them better. As in the level of causalities. It's a risk-reward situation, especially for me, and under the terms of my employment, not even you get to make that call, sir."

"That is unacceptable." Devlin could hear the steam escaping from Tyler's ears. "I will not sacrifice another innocent person."

"Then, with all due respect, sir, let the FBI handle it. Just make sure you have enough body bags when they fuck up and the shit hits the fan. In the meantime, you might want to start learning Arabic."

President Tyler looked over at Seelye and Rubin, absorbing the confident audacity of the man at the other end of the line. A Branch 4 op had every right to refuse a presidential request. With their lives on the line every time, they were the arbiters of their own fate. No choice but to play it his way. "Okay," said Tyler.

"Also, this really is it for me. If we go red zone and score, I'm out. Last job. I disappear, you never hear from me again, and you damn sure never contact me. Yes or no, General?"

The only thing to do was lie. "Agreed," said Seelye. "But —"

"One last thing. If I so much as smell a

116

fart wafting from Langley's direction, I'm gone." And then he really was gone.

At last, Tyler broke the silence. "You're sure nobody else knows about this Branch 4?"

Seelye and Rubin looked at each other. Seelye spoke first, "No one except the three of us and, now, your friend, Senator Hartley."

The president felt the sting. Maybe he had been rash in insisting on political cover. But what was he supposed to do? He was a politician. "But he doesn't know the details. The specifics."

"He knows everything he needs to know to blow Branch 4 sky-high," said Rubin. "And, given his track record, 'Senator Sieve' is just about the last person I'd want entrusted with the combination to my high school locker, much less the national security apparatus of the United States."

"So you're telling me I made a mistake?" The question answered itself. "What do we do about it then?"

"We make it work for us," said Seelye.

The president got up and started pacing around the room. What had he done? "How?" he asked.

Seelye took over. "You heard Devlin himself tell you how, sir," he said. "He smells a rat here. And he's right to do so. Here's why." Seelye opened his laptop, and as it awoke from standby he placed it on the president's desk. The White House wi-fi was as encrypted and as safe as the best minds as the NSA could make it, which didn't preclude an Israeli or Bulgarian teenager from hacking in occasionally. But it was a chance that, for a brief moment, they were going to have to take.

He tapped a couple of keys and an animated dossier sprang onto the screen. Tyler pondered what he was looking at, trying hard to absorb it all, then nodded. Seelye tapped another key sequence and suddenly the electronic version of the dossier was atomized — scattered to the four winds of cyberspace

"The evidence is all circumstantial, but that's not surprising. These forces have been coming together for quite a while, like a perfect storm. But if our suspicions are correct . . ."

The president got it. "If your suspicions are correct, then you've asked me to send our most valuable operative into a situation that might be — no, *is* — a trap."

As Seelye nodded dispassionately, Rubin observed, "A very special kind of trap, sir."

"And you're willing to run that risk?"

"Absolutely we are, yes, Mr. President," said Rubin.

"But why?"

"So we can run the same trap on them."

"Won't they be expecting that?"

"Of course they will, sir," replied Seelye. "Which is why we have to play the hand out. First guy that blinks, loses."

As a candidate, Tyler campaigned against the "wilderness of mirrors" that was the playing field for America's intelligence agencies. He had promised the electorate a new transparency. And yet now here he was, in the fun house with no way out.

"People think intelligence work is complicated, and it is," explained Seelye. "But what it's not, is complex. It's actually very simple. What counts is not what's true, it's what you can make the other guy believe is true. So we play these elaborate games of she-loves-me, she-loves-me-not — or perhaps a two-hand version of musical chairs would be a more apt analogy — and the last man standing wins the pot. To mix a whole bunch of metaphors."

Rubin chimed in. "So they're going to give us a patsy. That's who this Drusovic is. A guy meant to deflect attention from the real bad guys. A poisoned pawn, as it were."

Seelye said: "Which means we have to give

them one in return."

"Who?" Tyler was confused. This was the sort of thing that gave him a headache. He had to think . . . and he kept thinking until he realized that neither Seelye nor Rubin had answered his question. "You're not talking about this 'Devlin' character, are you?" he asked.

Seelye shrugged. "Why don't you let us worry about that, sir?" he said.

"But what if we fail? What if they get Devlin? What if . . . ?"

Seelye smiled a weary smile. "I think you're finally beginning to get the hang of the intel business, sir."

CHAPTER THIRTEEN

Edwardsville — Jefferson Middle School
Rhonda Gaines-Solomon lay where she fell. So did the bodies of the dead teachers. Bodies, beyond indignity, and yet undignified, in impossible postures, with impossible expressions frozen on their faces, terrible and pathetic at the same time. Three people, chosen by death at random, as old as they were ever going to get, lying there, reproachful to the living, for all the world to see. Because all the world was watching.

And now a sense of helplessness began to wash over the country, given voice by the talking heads. How long was this going to go on? Where was the FBI, the National Guard, the Army, Air Force, and Marines? Where was the president of the United States? The head terrorist had spoken directly to him, given him an ultimatum — why wasn't he negotiating? The lives of *children* were at stake, for God's sake.

Hope Gardner learned all this listening to the radio. As soon as the news broke, she had rushed back to the school and found chaos. The main parking lot was blockaded, so she'd pulled around behind the school, on the far side of the athletic field.

At that moment, her cell phone rang. It was Jack. "Hope, what the heck's happening?" His tone was anxious, urgent.

"I don't know, Jack. I'm at the school now. The place is crawling with cops. Where are you?" She could hear crowd noises in the background, and the sound of Wolf Blitzer's voice yipping like a small puppy in his excitement over a big story.

"At the airport. They've got CNN on here, full blast. Are Rory and Emma okay? Are you okay?" He tried hard not to lose it. "Some nut, screaming at the president about Allah . . ."

As Hope sat there, as close as the police would allow any of the parents to get, cell phone to her ear, her children inside a building that had suddenly turned hostile, she found herself surprised by how unhysterical she was. Until something this terrible happened to them, most people in the therapeutic society naturally assumed that they wouldn't be able to handle it — that they would break down almost immediately.

But Hope was learning something about herself she never would have suspected:

She wasn't breaking down. She was getting stronger by the minute.

"Listen, I'm bailing on the meeting. I'll be there as fast as I can."

"Hurry, Jack. Hurry. And be careful." She didn't know why she said that, but it seemed like the right thing to say. There was nothing to do except wait. And pray.

In the interstices between prayers, she thought of her children — of Emma, rushing off, into the arms of danger, and little Rory, hanging back. If only she had heeded him.

She spotted Janey Eagleton and jumped out of her car. They fell into each other's arms. All around them, chaos, uncertainty, fear. "What are we going to do, Hope," cried Janey. "What do they want?"

"Nothing," whispered Hope.

"What do you mean? They must want something — something reasonable."

"They already have what they want, Janey."

Janey recoiled, as if the thought had never actually occurred to her.

"No. They must want something. Something more. Something we can give them."

Until this moment, Hope had never articulated what she was now feeling. She'd been a good American, taught from birth never to resist a mugger, never to defend herself, never to fight back — possessions were just *things,* after all, and while things were replaceable, your life was not — never to assert herself. She'd been taught from birth never to complain, never to raise a ruckus, to accept everything that fate threw her way without complaint. The government will handle it. The police will take care of it. As a midwesterner, too, she was disinclined by nature to outward displays of negative emotion.

And suddenly, in this moment of horror, she knew all that was a lie.

Her children weren't *things.* Her children weren't replaceable. They were *hers.* And she'd be goddamned if she was going to give them up without a fight. Because, as she thought back, she hadn't liked the way that man in the door had looked at her. She began to recall his features, willing herself to conjure up his face, just in case she needed to be able to identify him later, just in case the worst happened.

Now something began to well up inside her — not fear, not horror, not trauma, but an emotion even stronger: hatred. Hatred for the men who could do this to children.

Whatever happened, and however long it took, she would see that they would pay, if it took her the rest of her life. The thought of Emma with their filthy hands on her and of Rory tied up beneath a live bomb unleashed a wellspring of visceral emotion she didn't know she possessed.

She didn't want to be defenseless any more; she didn't want to be weak and passive in the name of "understanding" or "tolerance." She didn't care about their bullshit grievances, or the "root causes" of their behavior. She wanted this to be over, quickly and, if necessarily, lethally.

She wanted them dead.

"Yes, Janey," she said. "There is something we can give them. We can give them hell."

Her cell phone. Jack again. She hugged Janey and got back in the car. "I'm in the taxi, on the way to the school," he said. "Where are you now?"

"Past the sports field."

"Go home. There's nothing you can do there. Go home. Promise."

"Promise," she said.

"I love you, Jack," she said. She flipped her Motorola phone shut and stepped on the accelerator.

The Jefferson Middle School was fairly new, built a little east of town. It was still partly surrounded by farmland, but everybody knew it was just a matter of time before the cornfields turned into subdivisions. Everything was a suburb now — not just of Edwardsville, or St. Louis, but of Washington, New York, and the world.

Still, the old Gondolf farm stood in the cornfields, just beyond to the east. She could park there, hidden from view. It would be dark soon enough, and then she could walk over and see what was happening.

She left the motor running and radio on. Some disembodied voice on NPR was trying to put what was happening in Edwardsville in "context," blathering on about Israel and the Middle East and the Iraq War and the CIA's overthrow of Mossadegh in Iran in the 1950s and —

Suddenly she found herself screaming at the radio, pounding the steering wheel and shouting, "Shut up! We are not the bad guys! *Shut the fuck up!*"

A rap at the window got her attention. A cop. That's when she realized she'd been pounding the horn in her anger and frustration. It was Ernie Dahl, whom she'd known for years, ever since he'd tried to paw her at the junior prom and she'd slapped his face. Just last week he gave her a ticket for ten miles over the posted limit when she had been doing a good twenty-five, rushing to take Rory to hockey practice. He was still feeling guilty about trying to feel her up way back when.

She rolled down the window. "Hi Ernie," she smiled.

"Hope, I think you'd better go home," he said. He took off his police cap and scratched his thinning hair. "There's nothing you can do here right now. So why don't you let us handle this? I'm sure everything's going to be fine."

Hope looked through her open window at Ernie, at the out-of-shape local cop, the hopeless look in his eyes, and knew there was no way this thing was going to have a happy ending.

"My kids are in there."

Visibly, Ernie struggled for words. He never was very good at English. "Hope," he said, "*everybody's* kids are in there. But don't worry — the FBI is here." Like that was supposed to make her feel better. "So go on home now."

Suddenly, a plan occurred to her. It was insane, but it was the only plan she could come up with. "Maybe you're right, Ernie," she lied, in a tone she hoped would pass for sheepish compliance. She put the car in gear and began to back away.

"That's it, Hope," nodded Ernie. "Go along now. I'll make sure nothing happens to Rory or Emma."

Hope could see him in her rearview mirror as she pulled around the corner and away from the school. He was waving goodbye.

CHAPTER FOURTEEN

In the air: Devlin

For operational security, Devlin almost always flew commercial. And that was not all. Unless he was dealing directly through Seelye's office, he paid for everything in cash, including road tolls, and never used a publicly available Web browser. He had no land line that any phone company knew about.

Although he was physically fit, Devlin dressed the part of an average American schlub, in T-shirts and jeans and a baseball cap. To look at him, you would see exactly what he wanted you to see — nothing.

He was the man who wasn't there.

Devlin had long ago learned that hiding in plain sight was the only way to hide. Afflicted with perceptual blindness, people don't notice what they see every day — they only notice its absence or its alteration. You could live on the same street for twenty years and not be able to accurately describe the sequence of houses, but you would notice, briefly, that one of them had been torn down. And once its replacement had stood for six months or so, you would likely never remember what had been there before.

Devlin had to laugh when he read spy novels or went to movie thrillers: the heroes were too chiseled, too toothy, and just too damn conspicuous. Operational security was one thing, but showboating secrecy was entirely another; Jason Bourne might be the closest fictional equivalent to the men and women — were there any women? Even Devlin didn't know — of Branch 4, but Bourne, when you got right down to it, was little more than a homicidal midget with memory troubles. Still, Bourne was lucky — he couldn't remember who he was. Devlin remembered all too well, and it was the toughest thing he did every morning to forget it for one more day.

He let his eyes wander around the interior of the fuselage. Early twenty-first-century *Boobus Americanus* at his finest. Worse dressed than they would have been twenty years ago, stupider, maybe, or at least more ignorant. Forget about getting the Mexicans to speak proper English these days; it was a stroke of pure luck to encounter a twenty-year-old woman who could wrap her lips and tongue around the syllables of the language and pronounce them properly in any place other than her nose.

As the plane descended, he visualized the school plans once more in his mind. It was a fairly standard layout, a typical concrete block standing amid acres of striped parking spaces. He almost wished the terrorists had taken over the other middle school, an older building located in town; infiltration there would have been much easier.

Still, American special ops had gone to school on Beslan, and knew how to avoid most of the mistakes the Russians had made. For one thing, they weren't going to run out of patience and come charging in, shooting indiscriminately. Devlin and his Xe team would invest the battlefield but remain invisible. They would take out the terrorists, not one by one, but all at once. And when they finished, the bad guys would be lying dead — no, not just dead but spectacularly, object-lesson dead — and the team would be gone, a wraith in the night. KRV — kill, rescue, vanish. And no one the wiser. The FBI would take all the credit. As for the media, the press was more lapdog than watchdog. For Devlin understood one big thing about reporters: they might be alcoholic malcontents, frustrated screen-writers, snarky Harvard boys afraid of inanimate objects, and hallucinating politicians-in-waiting, but there was one thing they never wanted to be, and that was reporters. They were always playing another angle.

Wheels down brought Devlin out of his reverie. The flight attendant gave them the obligatory, insincere welcome to St. Louis, where the local time was whatever. He gathered his sports satchel from the over-head compartment, which contained every-thing he needed for an operation like this, and slung it over his shoulder.

There was a full rank of taxis outside, but he passed them by and headed straight to the parking garage. Devlin favored large black SUVs, since their owners should know better than to put such an ungainly, un-wieldy, and unpatriotic vehicle on the road. Besides, the owner would get the insurance money, the plates would disappear from every police registry in the country, and everybody would be happy.

The Escalade was ridiculously easy to jack. The Arch gleamed as he swung over the I-70 bridge. The streets of East St. Louis were dark, dangerous urban prairies. Perfect.

He headed for the intersection of Martin Luther King Drive and North 7th Street. Every American city had a street named after Martin Luther King Jr. North 7th Street was only a few blocks in from the river.

There were six youths standing on the corner, very busy doing nothing. As he approached, he ran a quick scan with the infrared monitor inside his PDA. You never knew who was hiding in the garbage can.

A white man in a cap behind the wheel of an SUV was not exactly an unknown sight in ESL: a transaction was in the offing.

The young men crowded around him as he got out of the jacked wheels. As with every group of young men, there was a Big Dog and a pack. Devlin could always spot the Dawg — the drill sergeant of gangsters, the NCOs of urban crime.

"Yo, check it out," said the Dawg. "I got smoke, coke, coke, smoke."

"I've got an SUV," said Devlin. "You want it or don't you?" Fight or flight, he liked to get it down to basics, to get the bullshit out of the way.

"That piece of shit?"

"Is clean, is worth fifty grand new, twenty

grand chopped, its owner doesn't even know it's gone yet, so I make that at least thirty K profit to you, give or take your paternity payments, asshat." Devlin looked ostentatiously at his watch. "I don't have all day."

Asshat got in his face. "What if we just take it?" The others, the small dogs, began sniffing around.

"You could try," said Devlin.

There was a kind of primitive beauty to every confrontation among men, primates reverting to type. No matter what the PC weenies insisted, might always made right in the end.

"You alone," observed Asshat.

"Sure about that?"

"I don't see nobody else." Not quite as sure now.

"That's different. Would I be dumb enough to come here in a fifty thousand dollar car if somebody didn't have my back?" As Asshat considered this —

"On the other hand, I know you have five homies here and two watching us from that building, plus a lookout kid over there behind the trash pile. I know you're carrying an old .38 that hasn't been cleaned in a year and if you try to fire it you'll blow your balls off. I know that the two guys in the window have machine pistols but from the way they're handling them they probably couldn't hit an elephant in the head if he was standing in front of them. I know your life sucks, and that you think there probably should be more to it than getting high and getting laid, but you don't know what it is. And I know that you could use the money, so let's just make our little transaction now and everybody stays alive."

"You crazy."

"That's the chance you have to take."

Asshat thought for a moment. "What it gonna cost me?"

"That." Devlin pointed to an old Chevy Malibu. "Do we have a deal?"

CHAPTER FIFTEEN

In the air: Bartlett

The Gulfstream was clean and comfortable. On the tarmac at Van Nuys Airport it looked like any of the other corporate jets that allowed the winners of life's lottery to avoid the LAX nightmare. Whether you were flying down to Rio for a climate-change pow-wow, spending the weekend at your ranch in Montana, or just hopping over to Nevada for some stays-in-Vegas fun, the private jet was God's way of telling a sizable number of people in the LA area that they were making just about the right amount of money.

Inside, however, the jet that was ferrying Eddie Bartlett and his friends to Scott Air Force Base near Belleville, Illinois, about twenty miles east of St. Louis, was a little different than, say, the Paramount jet. For one thing, it was a state-of-the-art arsenal, with everything from nonlethal ordnance to armor-penetrating RPGs. Concussion grenades, cluster bombs. Small arms of every description, including the AA-12 automatic shotgun that Xe developed at its training grounds in Moyock, North Carolina. All hidden behind rotating panels that answered only to the team leader's palm prints, retinal scan, and voice register.

The jet was carrying two dozen men, each one of them identified only by a name tag. When he first came to Xe — it was called Blackwater then — the system had been to use only numbers, so as to inhibit the formation of personal relationships and the exchange of confidences. But numbers proved to be too impersonal for the unit's own good; some cohesion was found to be necessary, and so he'd hit upon a rotating, mission-specific structure of common first names — Jim, Fred, Bob, Jose — that could easily be remembered and, later, forgotten. The name tags were worn only during mission prep and needed to be memorized; once in combat they were discarded.

The men — there were no women — were all handpicked for their résumés and their code of silence. Except for the very odd occasion when he needed a woman for camouflage or misdirection, Eddie Bartlett worked exclusively with men. He was old school that way. No sexual jealousy, not protective empathy. Not that Eddie didn't have plenty of the latter — as a husband and father, he was a puddle of protective empathy. But when it came to taking care of business, he was all business.

So his team consisted of Delta, SEALs from Team 6, Green Berets, Rangers, 10th Mountaineers, Specials Operations Command personnel, some retired, some moonlighting, and some just freelancing. Officially, of course, none of them was there.

Once, men like these really were "special ops." The Navy ferried the Marines, the Marines landed, the Army bore the brunt of the fighting and the mopping-up, and special ops were used sparingly, for intel and dirty work. Today, in the wake of the second Iraq War, special ops were the point of the spear — the first resort, not the last — with the regular Army acting in a support capacity. There was a lot of grumbling about it, but this was the brave new world of warfare.

Eddie Bartlett himself cut his teeth with the 160th Special Operations Aviation Regiment (Airborne), 2nd Battalion, at Fort Campbell, Kentucky, better known as the Night Stalkers. Fast in, faster out, wholly lethal, the Night Stalkers were a special helicopter unit, trained to plan and execute the mission and extract everybody in one piece. All of them could fly a chopper between a nun's legs and she'd never even feel the breeze.

Ironically, the unit originated with the failure of Operation Eagle Claw in the desert of Iran, after which President Carter had belatedly ordered up an outfit that could actually have accomplished Desert One. So the Army got its best fliers from the Screaming Eagles and elsewhere, put together the 160th SOAR, and had been doing some serious damage ever since.

One of his three secure, direct-access lines buzzed softly and Bartlett picked it right up. The man on the other end of the line didn't have to identify himself and spoke, as he always did, without preamble or pleasantries:

"Be ready to bubble down the cell phone service for a ten-mile radius, except for our secure network." In tech parlance, "bubbling down" meant to shut down cell towers within a given range. "I also want real-time infrared imaging, 3-D coverage."

"Good idea. The school's out in the middle of a field, surrounded by nothing. Couple of outbuildings, sheds, whatnots."

The voice of "Tom Powers" crackled in

his ear. "That's why they picked it. They think they'll see us coming. But they won't. KRV. No heroes, no medals."

Bartlett nodded to himself. He had the right crew for the job. "KRV. Roger that."

"Got your playbook?"

"Consulting it now," said Eddie. Actually, what he was looking at that precise moment was a computer playing the You Tube video of Miss Teen South Carolina desperately attempting to answer a simple question about Americans and maps, but he knew that "Powers," who had sent him the link via a series of untraceable cut-out gmail addresses from a server in Abu Dhabi, had embedded the tactical plan inside the video; a self-extracting file, good for one use only, would call it up. And then the hard-drive would melt.

Bartlett looked up at the countdown clock located on both front bulkheads: just under an hour to touchdown.

"NSDQ," he said, signing off.

When Miss Teen South Carolina got to her third repetition of "such as," he clocked on the dummy link.

The download was nearly instantaneous. He had just enough time to hit the print button before the hard drive went into its controlled meltdown. The laptop's titanium

140

case would contain the electrical fire. He read the page as it spat from the high-speed laser printer:

"Patriots, Red 54–40." Right. Eddie Bartlett turned to his team. "Lock and load, gentlemen. The zone is hot."

CHAPTER SIXTEEN

In the air: Skorzeny

Skorzeny's Boeing 707 was not immodestly luxurious. This was, after all, a business-man's plane, not a sheik's whorehouse or a rock star's pleasure palace. Tastefully appointed, leather seats, a private sleeping compartment in the back for long trips, it was capable of being refueled while in flight, which meant, as a practical matter, that he could stay airborne for days, even weeks at a time. Rarely were there more than two or three persons aboard, not counting the pilots and the staff.

Flying time to Paris was less than ninety minutes, so there would be no napping on this trip. Skorzeny sat, as he always did, at his built-in computer console, from which he controlled the worldwide activities of Skorzeny International; since he did business in nearly every time zone on earth, sleep was an unprofitable activity.

Skorzeny's plane was equipped with an advanced, satellite-based air-traffic monitoring system, which allowed him to track his corporate fleet, on land, at sea, and in the air. To the naked eye, Skorzeny's screen was an indecipherable series of blips and letter-number combinations, but he could read it the way a great conductor could read a complex symphonic score. Thanks to deals he had struck with just about every air-traffic control system on the planet, and using a sophisticated transponder triangulation system that he himself had modestly conceived and developed, he could keep track of just about everything that belonged to him.

Additionally, it allowed him to monitor, through GPS, the location of every one of his operatives anyplace in the world. Carrying the modified cell- and sat-phones issued by the company, Skorzeny's employees could be instantly traced, located, and, if necessary, recalled or rescued. He trusted this information because it was provided by his own comsat, which he had piggybacked into space aboard one of the French *Ariane* rockets in the nineties. By corporate edict, everyone at a senior or operative level who worked for Skorzeny had to keep his or her GPS device on at all times. The only exception was when you were in duress, in durance, or dead.

"Sir?" Pilier's voice, over his shoulder. "We're approaching Paris."

So engrossed was he that he'd missed the man's approach. Skorzeny made a mental note to see his doctor soon; if this was a sign his senses had started to slip, he wanted to know about it right away. He preferred to think that his inattention was the residue of the excitement he was feeling, and nothing more.

"You've contacted HARBOR and BOREALIS?"

"Yes, sir. Their offices are closed at the moment, due to the lateness of the hour." Given all of Skorzeny's high-tech toys, what the old man wanted with this sort of thing was beyond him. Still, one of the ways Skorzeny was able to keep absolute communications security was through a network of microsatellites, which had been launched into geosynchronous orbit from high-altitude airplanes, so weather balloons probably had some practical use that he could not see. In any case, Pilier's job was to execute, not wonder.

"Thank you."

He tried not to let his excitement show, tried to control his emotions, even when they were responding to the beginning of the realization of his lifelong dream.

Ambition in a child is fueled by many things — parental expectation, want, force majeure, disaster — but Emanuel Skorzeny's ambition was born of *Sippenhaft:* collective responsibility for actions of a family member. In the wake of the failed attempt on Adolf Hitler's life on July 20, 1944, not only the conspirators suffered, so did their families. Some were executed, most were separated and sent to special camps, where the mothers died but where their children's identities were expunged, where all memories of the sins of their fathers were extirpated, where they were allowed to live, albeit with new names and new souls. Emanuel Skorzeny was one of those children.

Skorzeny's father died twisting at the end of some piano wire, but he himself was spared and sent by reason of *Sippenhaft* to purdah or, in his case, a camp near Dresden. On February 13, 1945, the jewel of the Elbe was liberated by "Bomber" Harris of the RAF, with American support, and the camp was demolished. He was in, of all places, the outhouse at the time of the attack and thus survived when the barracks took a direct hit.

There were those who whispered that he was the illegitimate son of Otto Skorzeny himself, the great *Standartenführer* who had rescued Mussolini from the partisans. He let them think that: it made the story of his life so much more . . . redemptive.

Pilier strapped himself into his seat as the plane went into a steep descent. "Sir?" he reminded.

"In a moment, Monsieur Pilier." Skorzeny's fingers flew; for an old man, thought Pilier, he could handle himself around technology like a teenager. As Pilier watched, Skorzeny put on a headset to eliminate the noise of the plane's engines and began to speak softly. Pilier couldn't hear what he was saying, but he knew whom he was talking to: Amanda Harrington, who should be waiting for them in Paris.

Skorzeny finished his conversation and shut down the system. One of the conditions he was forced to accept when he bribed the French minister of the interior was to switch it off in French airspace. No matter how well shielded it was, it would not do to be discovered, and not wishing to annoy a duly appointed official of his host country, especially given his special needs within that host country, Skorzeny had reluctantly agreed. He prided himself on

146

keeping his word.

"Do you read the Bible, Monsieur Pilier?"

Where that question came from, Pilier didn't want to know. He braced himself for a new and strange line of inquiry. "You know I don't, sir," said Pilier. He was a good French Catholic, which meant that he never attended mass.

"What about the *Apocrypha*? The *Gnostic Gospels*? Surely, *Revelation*?"

Where was the crazy old coot going with this? "No, sir."

"The vision of St. John, a masterpiece of speculative superstition that some mistake for dogma. A book of visions, signs, terror, and wonders. Of the End Times. 'And there appeared a great wonder in heaven, a woman clothed with the sun, and the moon under her feet, and upon her head a crown of twelve stars.' Chapter Twelve, Verse One."

Now Pilier understood. It had something to do with Skorzeny's Blake obsession.

"The woman clothed with the sun. The point is, the cartoon versions of reality and history that we see on our so-called 'news' channels are grossly distorted and lacking in specificity. But that, I suppose, is what comes from a century-long assault on western civilization. Don't false dichotomies enrage you? Left, right, communism, na-

147

tional socialism, capitalism?"

Pilier had no idea what Skorzeny was talking about, and wondered whether the old man did, either.

The wheels barely bumped as they landed, which was the way Skorzeny liked it. They were still rolling to a stop when he rose from his seat and let Pilier throw his topcoat around his shoulders. He ran a comb through his hair.

He was first out the door, walking briskly toward the car. Pilier was trailing behind him, carrying their effects. Even though it was dark, he could see her silhouette in the backseat of the Citroën.

CHAPTER SEVENTEEN

Edwardsville — Jefferson Middle School

Emma caught Rory's glance, but tried not to let on. She didn't want any of the bad men to realize they knew each other. She didn't want any harm to come to her brother. If anything happened to him . . .

She wasn't sure how she knew, but at some point before they had dragged his body away she had realized that Mr. Nasir-Nassaad was dead. She had never seen a dead person before, not even in a funeral home, and all of a sudden there had been two of them right in front of her. All four of her grandparents were not only still alive, they were thriving in North Carolina and Florida. Everybody lived forever these days. Except, of course, for Nurse Haskell and Mr. Nasir-Nassaad.

She'd wondered what it felt like to be dead. Wondered if it hurt, the way it hurt when you cut yourself really bad, and

149

whether it kept on hurting even after you were dead. Or if your soul just jumped out of your body and went its merry way up to heaven or wherever, or whether you got to stick around for a while, to see what was happening.

These weren't pleasant thoughts, but under the circumstances, they were the most pleasant thoughts she could muster.

And then doors opened and the man with the funny accent was back again.

He was talking to a few of the other men, like he was the captain of the basketball team calling up a play or something. They broke and the other men went away, out of the gym, carrying their guns. After they'd gone, he started yelling again. "Okay, okay, we don't want no heroes now. Nobody going to get hurt. Everything going to be fine, but now we see if your mother, father love you or not."

Emma had no idea what he meant by that — she was certain that her parents loved her and Rory — but it seemed to amuse him, because he started laughing again, and already she had seen enough of what happened when he started to laugh.

She closed her eyes.

What a difference. It was a world of stillness. But the tranquility had a trade-off: the silence in the gym was not really silence at all, but a mixture of deep breathing, small whimpers and groans, the muttering of bad men.

And the smells. You didn't notice them so much when your eyes were open, but now they jumped right out at you. Many of the children had soiled themselves, and that pungent odor wafted everywhere. Emma hoped she would be able to control her bladder when the time came because she didn't want to embarrass herself and she sure didn't want to ruin her new Citizens of Humanity jeans, which had cost her dad more than a hundred dollars.

A sudden, stinging slap across her face brought her wide awake back to brute reality.

It was him, leering into her face. "No sleeping missy. You wouldn't want to have bad dreams now, would you?"

The smell of his breath made her want to retch, and she fought down the rising bile. He was brown-eyed, with a stubble of scraggly beard and a hawk nose, and he made her even sicker just looking at him. Especially the way he was smiling at her, with his rotten teeth and stinking breath.

"OK pretty missy, brave girl, big hero, huh? When time comes, I think you will be nice date."

He reached out and grabbed one of her breasts and squeezed it —

She said nothing.

He fondled her other breast and then leaned forward and licked the inside of her left ear.

Emma couldn't catch Rory's eye, which she knew was a good thing. The last thing she wanted to do now was to set this animal on her brother. She would just have to take it.

She'd heard some of her older girlfriends talk about kissing and licking and what it felt like when a boy licked your ear, how hot it was, but there was nothing hot about this at all. It was disgusting, and she vowed to herself at this moment that she'd never let another boy do this to her again as long as she lived.

Then he started to laugh again. And lick again.

Nobody said anything. Nobody did anything.

Suddenly, Emma was jerked to her feet, her hands still bound behind her. As she opened her eyes, all she could see was a very large, very sharp knife, which he was holding in front of her face.

"Okay, pretty missy, we go now." And suddenly she was being pulled along by the man, out of the gym, toward the double doors that led into the main hallway and to the front entrance of the school.

Emma could feel her brother's eyes upon her, but there was nothing that either one of them could do. She shot him a quick, discreet, "don't worry" glance. Everything was as it had been before, except — and she only realized this later — the blond teacher who had been lying on one of the benches was gone.

"What do you want?" she said as they passed through the doors. The hallways was dead silent. No lockers slamming, no bells ringing, no voices shrieking, laughing, crying. She couldn't believe she was brave enough to say something, but she did.

The man still had her by the hand. "Nothing much," he said.

Emma couldn't understand what was happening. Edwardsville wasn't one of those faraway places where the houses were made out of dirt, where the soldiers were fighting. This was a place of regular homes and regular families. "Then why are you here?" she asked.

The man stopped abruptly. The knife he'd used to cut her bonds was sticking in his belt. "We do what we are told. Just like you." He smiled. She was afraid he was going to start laughing again, but he didn't. Instead he pulled out a cell phone and pressed the Talk key, redialing the last number he called.

"Ready?" he asked, then nodded. "When? Few minutes? Good."

As scared as she was, Emma couldn't control her curiosity. "What's happening? What do you want?"

He gave her a look, the kind of look she didn't want to see. There was nobody else in the hallway. At this moment, there was nobody else in the world.

"You, pretty missy."

She screamed as he reached for her and dragged her into the closet.

CHAPTER EIGHTEEN

Edwardsville

Thwack thwack thwack . . .

Hope was watching from her hiding place on the Gondolf farm as the helicopter landed on the roof of the school. Her heart leapt — at last, somebody was going to do something about the standoff. She waited for what seemed like ages before she realized that nobody was either leaving it or entering it. It just sat there, its rotors gradually slowing, then stopping. *The escape vehicle,* she finally realized.

Maybe that was a good sign, she told herself. They couldn't possibly take all the children on board, which meant they were going to leave them behind. Then she thought some more, and decided maybe this was not such a good sign after all.

She thought of her children, waiting for someone to come and rescue them. She knew she had no chance against a group of armed and ruthless men. She knew that she was supposed to let the professionals handle it — the hostage negotiators, the SWAT teams.

But what if they failed? Then the other teams would come, the grief counselors, the ministers, the insurance adjustors, the reporters, the lawyers. If she could only get inside, maybe she could do something, maybe she could help in some small way, get them out maybe, but if not then offer herself as a hostage in her children's place, to let them take her instead of them. Because, in the end, she would far rather take her chances with the hard men with knives, bombs, and guns than to see the heralds of the Grief Society show up on her doorstep.

She would, literally, rather be dead.

But how? Ever since the hostage situation had begun, the place had been cordoned off, ringed with cops and emergency services vehicles. The feds were there, too, wearing those silly jackets with "FBI" emblazoned across the back, so they wouldn't shoot each other by mistake.

She slipped out of her car on the passenger's side and closed the door as quietly as she could. She had thought ahead and killed the dome light, and so she didn't need to close it all the way, just enough to make it look normal.

Up ahead, ringed by the lights of the media and the emergency services, the school building had been plunged into complete darkness. There was no chance she'd be able to cross the parking lot without being spotted.

Then she remembered the storage shed.

The storage shed was exactly the kind of place you never noticed. It just stood there, crammed with old tools, cleaning stuff, junk, entered once in a very blue moon when the custodial staff couldn't find something in the main building. She's been in it a couple of times. Even in the dead of winter. Because the shed was connected to the school by an underground tunnel that linked it to the loading dock in the basement.

The shed wasn't that far away. If she ducked and crawled, keeping the shed between her and the main building as much as possible, she could make it. Her teacher's master key would open the door. And the tunnel would get her into the school.

She knew it was crazy, but she didn't care.

She slithered on her hands and knees, across the athletic field and onto the cold blacktop. Thank God she'd worn jeans. The palms of her hands picked up dirt, stray pebbles, squished into something she didn't want to know what. It would wash off later. Or not.

She crept on.

Damn! Her cell phone was ringing. Loudly, of course. Vibrating, too. Hope always kept the ring tone at seven, in case she was singing along to ABBA in the car when Jack or Emma or her mother called.

No way to answer. She thought about stopping to turn it off, but decided instead to keep moving; the sooner she reached the relative safety of the shed, the better. She could turn it off then.

She caught a quick glimpse of the school as she opened the lock and slipped inside the shed. The helicopter was still squatting on the roof, like a giant grasshopper.

Even though the shed was made of corrugated steel, she didn't dare turn the light on. Instead, she felt her way through the darkness to the back, where the tunnel door was. She pushed it open.

Pitch black, but that didn't matter. She fished her cell phone out of her pocket and flipped it open. The dim light was plenty bright enough for her to see by.

The missed call was from Jack. For an instant she thought about calling him back, to let him know she was all right when she realized that she was very far from all right and was even less likely to be all right in a few minutes than she was now.

There — just up ahead: the hydraulic platform where shipments came in. For the first time in her life, Hope Gardner blessed the systemic corruption of the Illinois political system, which siphoned money out of the taxpayers' pocket with the promise of a better tomorrow and passed along the cash to the relatives in the contracting business. Only one problem: the hydraulics made a not so joyful noise as they shuddered to life.

She breathed a short prayer that no one would hear anything as she punched the button on the lift, and ascended toward God only knew what.

CHAPTER NINETEEN

Edwardsville

Devlin's route took him well around the school, which was surrounded by cops, but that suited his purposes just fine. He wasn't going to the school, anyway. His destination was the Community Christian Church, which lay to the east about a mile away. It was the tallest building in the area, and it was perfect for his needs.

He pulled in the parking lot of what looked more like an insurance office building than a church and doused his car's lights. Long ago, somebody had loved this vehicle and babied it, but the car thieves had stripped it of most of its optional accessories, so now it was down to a standard state: a perfectly innocuous American car. Which was just fine with him, because all he needed was a working cigarette lighter.

His field kit consisted of a NSA-level minilaptop, a secure, enhanced BlackBerry, and a micro U3 8-gig smart drive complete with its own security protocols and defense systems; if he had to, he could travel the world with just the drive, and be up and fully operational ten minutes after buying, begging, borrowing, or stealing a laptop. In the intel business, redundancy was a wonderful thing. Untraceable redundancy was even better.

He plugged the laptop into the cigarette lighter and booted it up. The battery was good for at least six hours, but Devlin had learned long ago that to waste not was to want not. Indeed, the older and more experienced he got, the more he realized that nearly every one of the old bromides worked just as well in the twenty-first century as in the eighteenth or nineteenth. Folklore, word of mouth, and old wives' tales, like stereotypes, always contained a generous dollop of truth, especially when it came to human behavior.

As he saw things, the history of the twentieth century — a century that in the name of ideology saw more deaths than all those attributed to religion combined — was a desperate, although often successful attempt to convince otherwise intelligent people that black was white, up was down, inside was outside, right was wrong, and dissent was patriotism. Orwell basically had it right.

Which is why he never felt the slightest twinge of conscience whenever he killed any enemy, foreign or domestic. Unlike most of the recent presidents, Devlin took his oath of office seriously: to protect and defend. He had a job — not a job he might have chosen, a job that had chosen him, but a job that he nevertheless took as seriously as he took his own life — and he had discharged his oath as completely and efficaciously as he could.

To be a CSS officer was an honor vouchsafed to only a few. To be a member of Branch 4, even fewer. He had no regrets about anything he had ever done. No victims stared him in the face as he was falling asleep. Remorse was for the weak, for the shrink-addled and psychologist-oppressed. That a Viennese snake-oil salesman named Freud had been able to convince so many that their imaginations were more powerful in their lives than reality, that their parents had injured them to the point that they were unable to function, that if only lawyers could sue the dead they would be made whole, was a wonder he could never quite grasp. Analysis was for sissies.

Devlin was, to say the least, therapy-adverse. He didn't need counselors, or bartenders, or rabbis, or ministers, or priests. He lived a life without liability, without drugs, without memories. He wanted out for mundane reasons — he wanted to live. And a man in his business who wanted to live had better get out before he got killed.

This was a new emotion to Devlin. Since that terrible day in Rome, there was nothing he cared less for than life. True, the instinct for self-preservation in him was as strong or stronger as it was in every man, but the tribal taboo against death had long ago lost its shamanistic power against him. He'd seen it too many times not to have made it his friend.

And that's why he was quitting. Because he wasn't a real American any more, if indeed he ever was. He was a *beau ideal* from another generation, a throwback, an avatar — not simply the Man Who Wasn't There, but the Man Who Was No Longer Necessary.

Many was the time he'd thought about quitting, about walking away, the way his mom and dad never could have, because they had taken the bullets that might have found him. Which meant that he must now carry on their work, to take the fight to the enemy for them — to bring them back to

163

life. Which so far, he had failed to do.
Which failure had brought him to this
pass.

In a field east of Edwardsville, Illinois. In
a stolen Chevrolet, with his laptop plugged
into an enemy of the people cigarette
lighter, using state-of-the-art technology
authorized, however unknowingly, by face-
less bureaucrats in Washington who not only
had he never met but never would meet,
not if they were both doing their jobs. About
to share an operation with someone to
whom he had only ever spoken on the
telephone, a man whom he counted among
his friends, but a man whom he would have
to kill immediately should "Tom Powers"
ever be made as "Devlin."

One of his secure cell phones buzzed.
Without preamble Eddie said, "You used to
be a tough guy."

The voice analyzed kosher — "You used
to be a big shot."

A pause, as the security check on Eddie's
side went through. Then —

"Find package at 38-36-52-11 by 89-55-
36-37." That would be the Dumpster in the
church parking lot. "On six."

Six beats later — not seconds, but randomly calibrated intervals, visible on their
screens — both men rang off simulta-

neously. It was one last level of security —
any audio eavesdropping would be flagged,
caught, triangulated, located, and eliminated. So far, the system had worked perfectly. It ought to: Devlin himself had
designed it. He retrieved the package.

The church building was deserted.

He counted on two things. First, the in-
nate decency of people in the Midwest, their
trusting nature. In Edwardsville, a lock
wasn't meant to keep people out, it was to
let them know that nobody was home and
that you should call again another time. A
third-rate burglar from the Bronx could
have busted into any of the homes, but this
wasn't the Bronx. It was a nice, decent community that had no idea of the contempt in
which coastal America held it.

Still, there were the security cameras.
Every place had them these days, if only for
insurance purposes; another thing to thank
the lawyers for. Not that anybody actually
live-monitored them, or even bothered to
look at them, unless something happened.
And, until today, nothing ever happened in
Edwardsville.

Which is why he always carried optical
camouflage.

It sounded like something out of science
fiction: a kind of raincoat that he could don

and, essentially, be rendered invisible, especially to the cheap CCTV cameras. But it was real. First developed by the Tachi Lab at Todai, the University of Tokyo, "crystal vision" or, they rendered it, "X'tal vision," it gave the appearance of transparency by using retro-reflective materials and a head-mounted projector. It was a kind of magic trick, but NSA/CSS had quickly taken the technology and improved it. The CCTV feed, which was largely static, he had hacked via Echelon and digitalized on the way over, so it was a simple matter to project it onto his coat as the cameras made their desultory scans. All he needed was screen shots of the hallways and he was in like Flynn. Which he now was. If anybody ever reviewed the tapes, he would see nothing.

A minute later Devlin was on the roof.

Through the scope, he could easily see the school. Washington had allowed the helicopter to land on the roof, just as he'd advised. It was one more indication that the whole "terrorist attack" scenario was crap. Terrorists were ready to die. Somebody in there wanted to live, and get away fast. Still, it made for good theater for the journalists, giving them the impression that, were their demands only satisfied, the bad guys would simply vanish into thin air.

So whose ride was the chopper? Faster almost than the thought was the deed, and he had Seelye on the scrambled cell line. "What about the blond guy video? The teacher?"

"Sent it to you ages ago. Must not have gone through." Even NSA had glitches.

"Resend ASAP."

This time it came through in an instant. Devlin muffled a choice curse under his breath: billions and billions spent on intelligence and here we were, just as susceptible to snafus as the remotest Fourth World shithole.

He brought up a picture of a man's ear. The man he'd spotted immediately, the one he'd made for the guy running the operation. Not Drusovic, but the only guy who planned on getting out of there alive. Devlin punched the ear into the database, and went audio with a Fort Meade tech. "Match me, Sidney."

That was the signal to match the ear to the man, and while the man's face wasn't visible it didn't matter, since no two ear shapes are precisely alike. Using a sophisticated form of the AFIS system that police departments all over the country employed, CSS was able to match the ear to the face of anyone in its vast database, which included not only known hostiles, but all friendlies as well, and a great many — the number at this point ran into the millions — of ordinary civilians, blissfully unaware they had made the National Security Agency's home movies. What that guy did in *Gorky Park,* CSS could do in less than a minute. It was a civil libertarian's nightmare, but an agent's dream.

"Back at ya," said the disembodied voice in his ear as it evaporated.

They were both obeying the first rule of the CSS — that everyone is always listening to you, including your nosy aunt Hilda. The transmitted information that followed was a stream of gibberish to anyone listening in, routed through two other secure cell phones, then decoded and recoded in sequence until finally a single name popped up on Devlin's screen:

Milverton.

Devlin felt a rush of bile. He knew this day was going to have to come, had known it for years, had wondered what took him so long.

Milverton. "The worst man in London." It was his little joke.

For Sherlock Holmes, Charles Augustus Milverton was a blackmailer of society women and all-around dirt bag. For the

CSS, he was the most dangerous rogue agent on earth. Former Special Air Services, discharged under murky circumstances. Where Doyle's Milverton was fiftyish, plump, and hairless, this Milverton was blond, blue-eyed, physically fit, and ruthless — 200 pounds of lethal weapon happily married to killer instinct.

Devlin decided that, for the moment, he'd keep the ID to himself. Milverton and he had a history, and he didn't want anyone thinking this was personal. But his suspicions had been right from the start: Devlin was in mortal danger. Whether Fort Meade or Washington knew that too, and sent him anyway, was a question he didn't even have to ask. Not one pawn in play now, but two. Both poisoned.

Devlin felt his fury rising. This couldn't just be a coincidence. In his line of work, there were no such things as coincidences.

In the eternal game of cross and double-cross that was intelligence work, you had less to worry about from your enemies than your friends. Because while your enemies could always be relied upon for their hostile intent, you could never really trust your friends. In this case, however, both friend and foe had the exact same mission: *they wanted Milverton to find him.*

Devlin took a deep breath, not wishing to confront the implications. His whole purpose in life was to dwell in the shadows, work in the shadows, live in the shadows, and, eventually, die in the shadows. Branch 4 rules were clear: his existence was to stay unknown.

And now Milverton had come looking for him. The past, which for Devlin didn't exist, was about to catch up to him. And however this situation in Edwardsville ended, there would be hell to pay back in Washington.

Very well, then. Time to get it on.

Devlin buzzed Bartlett. Two beeps, followed by a short and a long: "Go on signal." Syllables in reverse. It wasn't a suggestion. No answer was necessary

Devlin called up a three-dimensional map of the school and the surrounding area. Not one of those Google Earth civilian applications, but the latest word in imaging. Every time a certain type of government plane overflew any given ten-square-acre quadrant of the United States of America, a bank of cameras photographed every inch of the target. Those photos were scrambled, encoded, uplinked to a satellite no one had ever heard of, re-encoded, rescrambled and then downlinked to Fort Meade via a series of cutouts in Christchurch, New Zealand; Barrow, Alaska; and Tupelo, Mississippi, the last because a previous administration had been big Elvis fans. Not to mention the new NSA Regional Operations Security Center that had recently come on line in Wahiawa, Oahu.

He flash-memorized the layout, every detail, then rose, ready to act . . .

What was that?

Out on the school grounds, somebody's cell phone was getting a call. Which meant it was punching back GPS coordinates. A parent. An idiot. A hero?

No time to lose. The cell-phone bubble would be in place soon. And then all communications would be cut off, to give Devlin and his men complete communications command of the battlefield.

Most civilians didn't realize this, but their cell phones were the government's best friends. Without any coercion whatsoever, nearly the entire American population had been persuaded to carry around a locating device. You didn't even have to be using your cell phone for someone to track you; it just had to be switched on, sending out those little locating beeps that futzed with your radio if you left it on your bedside table at night, beep-beeping your location to anyone who cared to notice. Might as well wear an ankle bracelet, then paint a bull's eye on your ass.

Devlin fed in the cell phone's information, uplinked, and got back the name of the subscriber: Mrs. Hope Gardner.

He flipped open what looked like a hooded BlackBerry but was in actuality a motion-capture videophone that worked like a TiVo; he could "rewind" to any point in the past hour to see whatever the naked eye had missed: using the field of coverage provided by the school's hidden motion detectors — all newly built schools had them since Beslan, although the public knew nothing about them — he could observe the entire perimeter. He went visual. There:

He could barely make out the blur, but he knew at once it was a human figure, female. Around the back, near the electrical shed. On her hands and knees, disappearing from view just as the chopper settled on the roof. Unfortunately, the video was not real time. The United States had not yet fully descended into Big Brother country, where everything you did was on a live feed, but it was only a matter of time.

He checked the time: four minutes ago. Wherever that woman was, she wasn't there any more.

"Leave your cell phone on, lady," Devlin breathed to himself. "And don't do anything stupid."

He knew that was probably a forlorn hope.

Chapter Twenty

Edwardsville — Jefferson Middle School

Charles Augustus Milverton was sleeping. No, not sleeping — half asleep, almost dreaming. In that special state between wakefulness and slumber, when the mind races, leaps, and makes unique connections between different and disparate people, places, and things. The gym bench was hard, but somehow he managed.

Children. That was the key. Childhood. Think back.

The north of England. Geordie country, Tyneside. The Borders, with the heathen Scots just a stone's throw away. And him a vicar's son. The only son, the eldest child, with one sister, so beautiful, so weak, so helpless in the face of Fate.

Anglo-Catholic. The worst kind. Higher than C of E, lower than the Whore of Rome. All the strictures of the Church of England, but without divorce. No way out. One sin, unconfessed and unrequited, and you were damned to Hell for all eternity. It focused the mind even as it corroded the soul.

The sermons. The lectures, unending. The history lessons, that went on forever. What did he care about history? About England? He had better and bigger places to go. England was nothing to him, a place, a climate, a series of vaguely related accents, a semishared history of conquest and kings. Although sometimes, standing here, near Hadrian's Wall, he could feel himself as one with the Romans and their Anglo-Saxon successors, nervously eyeing the Picts to the north, spears and shields at the ready.

Who dares, wins. That was his motto. Perhaps history had a useful lesson or two after all. That was what his father had tried to impress upon him, anyway. One of the few times in the vicar's life that he had not been cowed by ritual and superstition.

Under normal circumstances, he never would have let that raghead hit him. A savage from the outer limits of Europe, a country so weak it has been easily conquered by Islam and, worse, had stayed conquered. Not like France, under Charles Martel. Not like Spain under Ferdinand and Isabella, who had chucked out the Muslims and the Jews, for good measure, and then had sent Columbus packing across the Atlantic Ocean, pretty much in a single inning. Not like Austria, with Sobieski defending the gates of Vienna.

That Europe was gone now. Even England no longer had to worry about the Picts and the Scots and Irish. There were mosques in Newcastle, and in Leeds, and in York, and in Manchester, Sheffield, Birmingham, and London. England was finished.

And without a fight. That was the bit that still surprised him. When Rhodesia went, he could understand it; Cecil Rhodes was Colonel Blimp, and Ian Smith was a giant pantomime horse for the Fleet Street johnnies of their day, riding high atop their moral dudgeon. He could have sworn South Africa would put up a fight, especially given their nuclear alliance with Israel, but at the end of the day, Johannesburg folded quietly, leaving the Boers and the Huguenots to fend for themselves in the brave new world of Nelson and Winnie Mandela.

He was too young for Rhodesia, but he had fought in South Africa and elsewhere, as a mercenary on the Dark Continent, trying desperately to reclaim not the White Man's Burden but the White Man's Gold; half a century after the end of colonialism, Africa was sliding back into savagery, its infrastructure failing, its farms collapsing, its education and political systems in tat-ters. And now it, and Britain's former colonies in the Middle East and "Asia" — India and Pakistan — were taking their well-deserved revenge on the Mother Country, exporting their charming native pathologies back to Birmingham and Sheffield and Manchester and Newcastle: female circum-cision, "honour killings," stoning homosexu-als, subway bombings, the lot.

He hated them all. He hated them for what they had done to his childhood views of Empire, but most of all he hated them for the lie they had given to what his father had taught him.

And yet he also admired them. Admired them for their audacity to challenge civiliza-tion and dare it to defend itself and its so-called "superiority." Theirs was the rule of the AK-47, not of Article 3, Section 1; the rule of the id, not of the superego. Theirs was the will to power, whether they knew Schopenhauer or not.

And that was the flaw in his father's belief: that he could stand there, watching the oncoming blue-painted Picts and Celts, bones in their noses and the flesh of their enemies between their teeth, with equanim-ity, and see souls to be saved. Even when

177

his sister had died, screaming in pain from a ruptured appendix, begging for help that had never come because their father had had to attend to his superstition, minister to his flock, while she writhed and bled and died, the lesson had not changed. It was God's will . . . and there yet remained souls to be saved.

Whereas Milverton saw not souls but enemies to be slaughtered before they breached the Wall. His father's church was an imaginary refuge, a false castle, a hive of fairy tales about Jesus, the Apostles, the Crusades, Urban II, Bernard of Clairvaux, St. Malachy and his prophecies, St. Louis. The Middle Ages was a nightmare, the Renaissance but a dream, a brief respite before Europe too succumbed and slid back into that endless night that had followed the fall of Rome.

That was why he had joined SAS, the 22s, as soon as he was legally able, that was why he had pushed himself, that was why he had passed all the tests, risen through the ranks, punished England's enemies both at home and abroad, taken the fight to the IRA in Belfast and Gibraltar; and after that operation had gone tits up thanks to the gutter press, had moved into the private sector, working across Europe, Africa, and Asia and now in America. It was hard work but it was good work and it paid very well. In fact, it paid top dollar, as well it should: pound for pound, he was best fighter on the planet.

It was the sound of a female voice that woke him from his reverie. The sound of a little girl screaming. The one sound in the world he could not abide.

Milverton shot off the bench. If he had to break character, if he was no longer "Charles" the teacher, so be it.

Upright now, he tensed for trouble. This hadn't been part of the plan, and he had no idea how the men in the balaclavas were going to react, especially with Drusovic out of the gym.

He walked slowly, unthreateningly, through the ranks of the captive kids and teachers. With the example of Nurse Haskell fresh in everyone's mind, no one dared move his or her head to follow him as he went. Still, Milverton could feel the eyes of the boy, Rory, on him. He felt sorry for the spunky little bugger, but in for a penny, in for a pound.

"Charles," whispered Rory as he walked by him. "He took my sister. He took Emma."

He kept his voice low. "Don't worry, Rory," he said, a thought occurring to him.

"I'll make sure she's safe."

Rory managed a very small smile. "Who dares, wins, right?" the kid asked.

"Absolutely."

Now he noticed the smell. Fear had a stench all its own, and the bodily function by-products were just that, manifestations of the state of mind. He'd had plenty of men beg for their lives before he neutralized them, but this was different. These were children. Not that he cared one way or the other about their fate, but he knew that America was a sentimental country, especially about its kids, and if anything happened to any of them — or worse, a lot of them — the response would be more than they'd bargained for at this point in the operation. The kids were supposed to be very potent and photogenic hostages, nothing more.

That's why he was angry at Drusovic. It was time to sort the bloody fucker out.

And then he heard the girl, Emma, scream again.

The lift shuddered to a stop. Even with no light, Hope more or less knew where she was. Moving carefully so as not to knock anything over, bark her shins, or skin her knees any worse than they already were, she felt her way down the long, rectangular supply room, past the copy machines and the boxes of paper, past the supplies, her eyes and ears straining into the darkness and the silence.

Her heart was pounding. She'd always thought that expression was literary license, but now that it was happening to her, rocketing, sending shock waves soaring throughout the building, she knew it was for real. Breath short, sweat glands fully engaged. But hearing preternatural. Sight, even in this Stygian darkness, supernatural. With her children in danger, Hope Gardner was Superwoman.

A door was just up ahead. In her excitement and confusion, Hope wasn't exactly sure where it led to, but she didn't care. Gingerly, she opened it onto a storage room, which she knew led out into a secondary hallway near the back of the school, one that made a T-intersection with the main hall. The gym was nearby.

She reached for the hallway door, praying that it wouldn't make a sound, that there would be nobody on the other side, that . . .

Then she heard the screams. And she knew, in an instant, the way mothers always do, that it was the voice of her daughter.

The hell with what was on the other side.

The hallway was dark and empty. Only the soft glow of the emergency lights kept it from being completely pitch black. In the distance, at the other end of the long central hallway, she could hear the sound of running footsteps.

Hope hugged the wall as she crept forward. She wanted to run, she wanted to cry out, to tell Emma that Mommy was coming for her, that everything was going to be all right, but she knew a single word from her would probably mean both their deaths.

There were voices, shouting loudly, somewhere beyond the gym. That must be where Emma was.

Hope dropped to her hands and knees, creeping through the darkness. The lights were on in the gym, casting a small patch of light on the hallway floor via the windows. She would have to go right past it.

In the distance, the sound of violence, a body falling. She moved faster, nearing the gym now.

She knew she shouldn't look, shouldn't risk it, but she had to look. Swiftly, she crossed the hall, sidling up to the gym doors, straightening her legs, rising.

She glanced, catching only a glimpse. But what she saw almost made her throw up.

Children, bound; teachers, with guns

trained on them. And explosives everywhere. If the cops or the FBI or whoever tried to rush the school, everyone would die. And Rory was in there, somewhere.

She ducked back down and kept moving.

It didn't take long for Milverton to find Drusovic and Emma. Under any rational circumstance, he'd never take a bollocks crew like this one into battle, but that was the whole point of the exercise: they were all chattel, born to die and, as far he was now concerned, the sooner the better. Well, he could help move the timetable along.

He ripped open the door. Drusovic was where he had expected to find him, on top of the girl. Milverton's left hand shot out, grabbing the Albanian by the scruff of his neck and yanking him backward. As Drusovic fell, Milverton delivered a punch to the man's right cheekbone; a little higher, on the temple, and it would have killed him, but Milverton needed to keep him alive for the moment. A kick to the groin put Drusovic on the floor.

Milverton turned to Emma. Luckily, the savage hadn't tried to undress her; quickly, he restored some semblance of order to her disheveled clothing and looked into her eyes to see if she was all right. The girl was speechless, her eyes wide and her mouth trying to move, but no sound emerging. Milverton swept her up in his arms, carrying her effortlessly under one arm.

With his free hand, he hoisted Drusovic back to his feet. "You sodding arsehole," he said, "I ought to rip your fucking balls off and feed them to the nearest pig. And then you can explain to Allah why you won't be shagging any more virgins." Since he was, in fact, holding Drusovic's balls in his hand, this was not an idle threat. "Now pull your pants up and let's get on with it."

Milverton carried the girl into the darkened hallway. She had fainted, which was good. He opened the door to one of the classrooms and laid her down on a bench. There was a quilt nearby, so he threw it over her. Then he stepped back into the hallway.

Hope saw the door at the far end of the hall open, and she almost screamed when she saw a man emerge with a girl under his arm. Her girl. Her Emma. Unconscious, or . . .

Don't think about it. Calm down. The man carrying Emma was wearing a suit. He wasn't one of *them.* As she watched, they disappeared into a classroom.

She had to get closer. She rose to her feet —

And then the same door opened again and another man tottered out. From the way he was moving, she thought he might be drunk. There was a small alcove with a couple of public telephones in it; she ducked into it, sliding down and beneath the phones. Nobody used them any more — everybody had cell phones now — but no one had gotten around to removing them yet. Thank God.

The man staggered past her, oblivious. She thought she could hear him muttering something, but it was a language she couldn't remotely understand. Hope watched him as he went back into the gym.

Now!

Hope had no idea what she was going to do. She had trusted in God and luck, and so far neither of them had let her down.

She was at the door now, her ear pressed up against it, desperately trying to catch some sort of sound that might tell her that her daughter was still alive, was okay. Nothing. She pressed a little closer, a little harder, straining . . . straining . . .

The door opened so fast she almost fell over.

Hope cursed herself for a fool who thought she could somehow make a difference. She should have listened to her inner voices of reason, the ones who were always telling her that violence never solved anything, that all we had to do to get along was to just give up. It was that simple.

Instead, she had listened to just one inner voice. The voice of Emma and Rory's mother. The voice that understood innately that, no, it was not just that simple.

"It's okay," she said. "I'm a teacher."

"So am I," a man said. The voice wasn't familiar. She peered through the darkness, but couldn't make out his features. Then it hit her — it was the man she'd seen that morning. The "substitute."

"Oh, thank God," she started to say and then his hand was over her mouth and he was lifting her up as if she were made of balsa wood.

"They're my children," she said.

"I know they are," he said.

"What about Emma?"

"She'll be just fine, I promise."

That was when she noticed that he had a gun.

Hope supposed — but not being a firearms expert, didn't really know — that she'd catch the flash of the bullet's charge a nanosecond before it blew through her skull. She wondered whether her last vision would be of her life, or of her children's unlived lives. And suddenly, passionately, she wanted to *know*. Whatever was going to happen, she wanted to witness it. Life or death, win or lose, she wanted to be there, with her children, when it happened.

He pushed her back toward the gym, whose doors she could discern ahead of her in the dim illumination of the emergency lights. From the gym doors, it was a straight shot to the front doors of the building, the doors she had seen this morning and eons ago close behind her two children.

The gym doors opening . . . the noise.

It took her several seconds before she realized it was herself making all the noise. Screaming.

A blow at the back of her head sent her sprawling toward the center of the gym floor. She skidded across something wet and sticky, then realized it was blood. Still viscous and nasty, it clung to her hands and, when she involuntarily wiped her face, to her cheeks. She felt a trickle of something liquid at the base of her skull and didn't have to touch it to know what it was.

She rolled over on her back, uncaring about the blood that was mingling with whatever was on the floor. Almost immediately, her maternal radar located her son. Rory was bound, eyes wide in horror.

"Charles," he shouted, "that's my mom."

"I know," said Milverton. Then he turned to the staggering man, the one Hope had seen coming out of the closet. "It's show-time."

CHAPTER
TWENTY-ONE

Edwardsville

Up on the roof of the Community Christian Church, Devlin assembled the gift that Bartlett had planted for him. It was a bolt-action, single shot Barrett Model 99, chambering a round that flew from the aluminum alloy barrel at 3,250 feet per second. If your enemy was nicely lined up in a row, you could put a single round through twenty skulls seriatim, which is what Devlin called firing for effect.

You could take out a given target from the distance of more than a mile, and put the bullet right on his nose. Even at that distance, the target's head would atomize, which was exactly the point. Better yet, it could punch through a concrete wall three feet thick and kill whoever or whatever was on the other side.

Something was happening at the school. Movement at the front doors. In their heedless lust to cover the story, no matter the consequences, the news crews jostled forward, lights blazing. What did they care if their pressure resulted in more deaths? It all made great video. At least for once they were making themselves useful, because with that much light between him and his targets, there was zero chance he'd be spotted.

Bartlett's men, he knew, would be disguised among them at this point, fanning out, surrounding the building, applying their explosives. As the Israelis had learned at Entebbe and the Germans at Mogadishu, surprise was the attacker's best friend, which meant that in less than ten seconds they would have to blow out the walls and lay down a withering enfilade as the other Xe ops came in with concussion grenades and small arms. Sure, some kids' ear drums would pop, but if all else went well that would be the extent of the injuries. Because, by now, using wall-penetrating radar and the real-time imaging from NSA overflights at 40,000 feet, they would know where every terrorist was.

The bombs didn't worry him much. The Russians had made the mistake of panicking, then charging, giving the Chechens plenty of warning. With nothing to lose, they had popped the bombs and shot the children as they tried to flee. It was a clusterfuck that didn't have to happen; you could take the Russian Federation out of the Soviet Union, but you couldn't take the Soviet mind-set out of the Russian. What had worked for Zhukov in Berlin — raw, brutal power — didn't work in asymmetric warfare.

It was funny, he mused as he took up his firing position: two hundred-plus years after the American Revolution, we were back to square one as far as tactics were concerned. True, the Redcoats didn't come marching down the middle of the field in serried ranks any more, but in many ways the terrorists were their functional equivalent; what they considered hostages, Devlin and his men thought of as anchors that destroyed their mobility and distracted their attention. You couldn't shoot a hostage and defend yourself at the same time, assuming you even had the time to choose.

Terrorists never really changed their methods. By keeping their hostages down, immobilized, they thought they could prevent communication and mutiny. What they were really doing, however, was protecting their captives, keeping them alive during the only moments that mattered, the moments of rescue and revenge.

It was all about the OODA Loop. Observe. Orient. Decide. Act. Rinse, and repeat, until the other guy was dead. About getting inside your opponent's decision loop, staying at least one beat ahead of him, as if you were inside his head. Which is where one or more of Devlin's bullets soon would be. The Barrett fired both the .416 and the .50-caliber round, but he preferred the 400-grain .416 round; wherever he put his shot, the man was going to be very, spectacularly dead.

He checked the computer, streaming the coverage. With GPS coordinates superimposed over the grid, he hardly needed a scope, since he could train on what he was seeing on the screen and calibrate accordingly. But even at this distance, it was more sporting to shoot a man while looking at him.

Via the infrared scans and rad sensors, he'd also located the bomb control — a laptop computer that would sequence the bomb explosions. Like a cell phone, a computer announces its presence through mild radiation and wireless signaling. Taking it out would be a tougher shot, because his second round would have to follow the first by less than a second and he had to hope like hell nobody would touch the machine in the meantime. But, if everything went right, from the same angle he could take out Drusovic and then punch a round through the computer before the terrorists could react. And by then, they'd all be dead.

What about the Gardner woman? He'd almost forgotten about her.

Suddenly the news crews' lights grew brighter. Devlin glanced down at the screen. Someone was coming out, Drusovic probably, to make another statement. Terrorists loved a stage. No time to worry about the woman now.

There were dozens of reporters on the scene. Their trucks kept their distance, but the standup artists were primping and the print johnnies were inching forward, notepads in hand. As he watched, a taxi pulled up on the perimeter, and a man got out. Another civilian, most likely a parent. Just what he needed, another wild card. He lost sight of the man as he was swallowed up by the crowd of cops, firemen, EMS workers, and FBI agents.

Devlin's videophone leapt to life. His heart sank. He was inside the Oval Office, looking at Army Seelye and Secretary Rubin. This was such a breach of security protocol that he wanted to shoot Army on the spot. "Listen up," said his boss. "The president's about to make a statement."

Tyler was sitting behind his desk. "I speak now to Suleyman Drusovic. Yes, we know who you are. And know this as well — we will not let you harm our children."

Devlin closed his eyes so as to skip the look of satisfaction he knew would be on the president's face. He opened them again as Tyler continued. "In our pluralistic society, there is room for all religions — and, indeed, for no religion at all. Therefore, in the name of Allah, the most compassionate, the most merciful —"

Devlin couldn't believe his ears. Couldn't believe the president was actually mouthing these words. Couldn't believe that Seelye and Rubin would stand there, letting him say the Muslim incantation.

"Let it be known that, as president of the United States, I would welcome the visit of an Imam of your choice, here, in Washington, to discuss our differences and hopefully find a way to bridge them. But you must release the innocent hostages at Jefferson School immediately, board your helicopter, and be on your way. You have five minutes."

That's really telling him, thought Devlin. He put down the videophone, picked up the rifle, and looked through the sight.

Drusovic was emerging from the school, with a smirk of triumph on his face. He had heard, and he knew what he had heard: the president of the United States starting to heed the call to Islam. The Infidel-in-Chief of the Great Satan.

Drusovic surveyed the assembled media horde, his satisfaction obvious. Then he clapped his hands. The school doors opened and there was Hope Gardner, a bomb strapped to her body. Drusovic was holding the detonator in the firing position; if he took him out now, the bomb would explode the instant it slipped from his dead hand.

"In the name of Allah and the Prophet, blessings and peace be upon him, I welcome the president's statement. Nevertheless, this unclean woman is an intolerable provocation."

Hope stood there, blinking in the lights. She knew what was happening, and had lost all fear for her own life. But what she had witnessed in the gym cried out to be made public. She could not speak, and she could not move, but she knew inside that she had to warn the president, the country, the world, before anything else happened.

"This spy" — Drusovic shook Hope roughly — "is a pawn in the service of the

United States government. She cannot be acting alone. Therefore, she will meet the fate of all spies under international law and the Geneva Convention. She will be executed."

With a single squeeze of his right index finger, Devlin could blow the man's head off. But Hope had injected a note of instability into his perfect closed system; rather than being inside the terrorists' OODA loop, she had forced him out of his.

And where the hell was Milverton?

Bartlett's voice was soft in his earpiece: "You got him?"

Devlin's reply was a purr. "She's wired. He'll blow her away."

A puzzled pause. "So what? We're good to go."

"Hold off a sec'. Something's happening."

The doors were opening again. At first no one appeared, and then a boy was thrust forward so hard he went sprawling, picked himself up and rushed toward the woman. It was Rory.

Hope turned, instinctively. Rory tried to throw his arms around his mother, but Drusovic shoved him roughly away.

"Come on, Tom." Bartlett's voice.

"She'll take the kid with her."

"But the rest live. I make that trade any day."

The memories were raging in his head. Of a little boy having to watch his mother die.

"Let's hope you never have to."

Drusovic was in the middle of a rant now, working himself up into a photogenic lather. "For too long we have watched our brothers die under the yoke of the Zionist entity. For too long, we have tolerated the intolerable. Let the world know henceforth our tolerance of tolerance is at an end."

"Hurry the fuck up . . ."

"Wait —" said Devlin. Little Rory, dusting himself off, was doing something remarkable.

He was attacking the terrorist.

Rory hit Drusovic from behind, punching, scratching, clawing, and kicking. With the detonator in one hand and Rhonda Gaines-Solomon's mic in the other, Drusovic tried to kick Rory away, but the little kid wouldn't stop even when one of the kicks landed square in his belly.

"Son of a bitch," whispered Eddie. "That kid's got balls."

Devlin saw his play. "Sure your guys can take 'em all?"

"Locked on with penetrating radar. They'll be dead before they can fart."

"How close can you get to Drusovic?"

"Up his ass close enough?"

"It'll have to do. Stand by."

Devlin tapped some coded instructions into the laptop. If NSA was on the ball, and it had better be, in less than ten seconds the news crews' audio would go dead. And then the rest would unfold just like they'd drawn it up on the blackboard.

Another kick from Drusovic and Rory went down hard. Giving Hope an opening. She snatched the mic away —

"It's a trap!" she cried.

Time to act. "I am the Angel of Death," he muttered, and fired.

A .416 round moving at 3,250 feet per second can travel a mile in less than a second and a half. Devlin was nowhere near a mile away.

Drusovic's head evaporated, live, on international television.

As it did, the nearest newsman grabbed the standing corpse's right hand and kept its finger clamped on the trigger. At the same instant, the man drew a Kukri knife and severed Drusovic's right forearm, hand still on the detonator. Hope caught a glimpse of a tattoo, winged centaur holding a sword, and the name DANNY BOY on her savior's arm as he sprinted away, still clutching the severed arm by its hand.

"Good job, Eddie," Devlin thought to himself.

The round, meanwhile, continued on its path of retributive destruction, killing two men standing behind Drusovic.

It was immediately followed by Devlin's second shot, which bisected the terrorist at the computer in the gym, obliterated the machine, punched through the rear wall of the school, demolished the windshield of a parked car, ricocheted, and killed a cow a half-mile away.

Then the gym walls exploded, punched out with Semtex A and RPGs. The terrorists tried to react, but the firing lines coordinated into a killing zone from which no target could escape. Firing on fully automatic, the AA-12 shotguns armed with Frag-12 armor-piercing rounds hit the terrorists at the rate of 120 per minute, and cut them down like God's own scythes.

From the time Devlin squeezed the trigger to the extinction of the terrorists, less than ten seconds had elapsed.

Devlin had no time to celebrate. The instant he fired his second shot, he set the charge on the computer and grabbed the Barrett and took aim at the helicopter.

So he missed Rory, rushing back into the

school to find his sister.

The chopper was rising, its rope ladder dangling. Devlin knew he had to take it down before Milverton could clamber aboard. He took aim —

Fire from an AK-47 kicked up all around him. Instinctively, Devlin dropped. He felt like Cary Grant in *North by Northwest:* a sitting duck, except not quite so good looking.

He rolled, trying to regain the initiative. But the Barrett was a big gun and not easily swung; by the time he got it righted, the helicopter had gained altitude, still spitting fire at him. The rope ladder was no longer dangling. Damn!

Devlin came out of his roll prone, both elbows on the ground. He elevated the barrel. The helicopter was fast but the Barrett was faster.

His third round missed. His fourth penetrated the skin of the Sikorsky and smashed into the engine block. The bird sputtered, then went into a dive.

Devlin was on his feet now, running. His plan had been to leave the Barrett behind, to let Eddie's crew clean it but that was impossible now. He stripped it as he ran down the stairs, jamming pieces into his clothing.

He made the Malibu and stashed the

pieces of the rifle under its backseat. He started the car and floored it.

There was a dirt road through the corn-fields, prepped for a new blacktop that would bisect the farmer's field. It was rough and potholed, but he didn't care. The Malibu's axles had survived worse than this. So had his teeth. He hammered down on the accelerator and roared through the stalks.

He hit the school from the northeast. Cops and ambulances were descending on the scene from all sides. Their attention was on the chopper, now in flames, sputtering one last time and then plunging to earth somewhere near the Mississippi.

Then it hit him. The chopper! What a chump he was.

Devlin didn't have to see the wreckage. He knew that only one body would be found, that of the hapless pilot.

Milverton wasn't on that chopper. All he needed was that one brief instant inside Devlin's OODA loop, one second to regroup, and he'd moved ahead in their chess match.

He'd never intended to get on that chopper.

Which told Devlin everything he needed to know. A brilliant improvisation — a double misdirection.

Redundant systems, just in case.

Devlin, out of the car and sprinting toward the school, just another local Good Samaritan trying to help. He could see Hope, free of the bomb, but Eddie was long gone.

He couldn't see the boy. But he could see the man, rushing into the school, the civilian who had showed up in the taxi. Rushing straight toward —

Oh, Jesus.

Complete chaos had broken out in the building, with police and FBI collapsing on it from all directions. Devlin blended in immediately, ducked inside the school.

Smoke and dust everywhere. Alarms blaring. The freed children, rushing about, nearly blind, nearly mad.

There, the kid. The one shouting, "Emma, Emma!"

Devlin scooped him up under one arm and ran as fast as he could for the back of the building.

"Emma!" the kid shouted.

"Rory!" came a voice in the distance. The man from the taxi.

"Daddy!" cried the kid.

No time. No time. Tough luck about the dad.

The Dumpster would have to do.

The explosion ripped through the gym.

"Are you a cannibal or a missionary?" the

kid asked him as they huddled together in the garbage can, flaming debris raining down around them.

"Neither, kid," he replied. "I'm an angel."

The rain of fiery shit finally stopped. The metal interior was hot to the touch. The boy still lay within the protective embrace of Devlin's arms. "What about my sister?" said the boy, very softly. It was almost as if he knew what must have happened to his father.

"I don't know," whispered Devlin. "I'm not that good of an angel."

"Can't you find out?" said the boy.

"I'll try," said Devlin. He left the boy safely in the Dumpster and slipped away, with a hole in his soul. In Jeb Tyler's America, one dead kid was one too many.

Somebody had set him up — maybe more than one somebody. But who?

He didn't know that, either. But he did know one thing: he knew he was made.

And when a Branch 4 op was made, he was as good as dead. Any time Seelye chose, every intel and special ops agent could be after him. Not to mention Milverton and the forces behind him, whoever they were.

Poison pawn or sacrificial lamb? In the end, it didn't really matter. Friend and foe were the same person.

What was that saying of Bartlett's? The old 160th motto?

"NSDQ." Night Stalkers Don't Quit.

CHAPTER
TWENTY-TWO

Washington, D.C.

There was utter silence for a moment in the Oval Office as the three men watched the school explode. Then Washington exploded.

"GodDAMNit!" exclaimed the president, lunging for the phone. He knew his first thought should be for the people who had just lost their lives, however many of them there were. With any luck, the place was mostly cleared out, but right now he couldn't take that chance. The political fallout, whatever it was going to be, had to be minimized and it had to be minimized fast. "Millie, get the speaker and the majority leader in here, on the double. I don't care if you have to roust them out of bars or beds, but get them in here. Senator Hartley too."

"Yes, sir," said Ms. Dhouri from the outer office.

Rubin, meanwhile, was on the cell phone

with the commanding officer at Scott Air Force Base. If there were going to be any other nasty surprises, the country needed a military presence in Edwardsville pronto. "Make sure you get that wreckage of the helicopter before the cops stomp all over it," he shouted.

Seelye, for his part, did not use the phone. Instead, he was working through a series of cutouts using the NSA's in-house communications system, trying to reach Devlin, and getting no response. He was still trying when the president said, "All right, gentlemen. Now, how do we play this?" His face was red and Seelye knew that Tyler's ultra-political mind was already factoring how this was going to play at the next election.

"The speaker and the leader are on their way, Mr. President," squawked Millie over the intercom. "I can't reach the senator."

"Send them in the minute they get here," said the president, who then turned to Seelye. "Well, Army, looks like your man Devlin just screwed the pooch."

Seelye put down his PDA and looked across the room at Tyler. "With all due respect, sir, he did not. From all the available evidence," he glanced at his PDA in case there was a message, but no light was blinking, "most of the children have been rescued. Under normal circumstances, we would call his mission a brilliant success."

Tyler snorted, and gestured at the television screen. Smoke was still billowing from the wreckage. "You call that a success? Do you have any idea what's going to happen to the markets tomorrow morning unless we get out front on this pretty damn quick? I can see the headlines now — 'AMERICAN BESLAN.' This is just fucking great. I thought you told me this Devlin was the best we've got."

Time to defend the honor of the agency and to protect his turf. "He is sir," said Seelye. "Take a look at that screen — what do you see?"

"I think the pictures pretty well speak for themselves."

"Precisely. Yes, part of the building was destroyed, but all of the terrorists were killed. Sure, it was a nasty surprise, but if you don't think ordinary people all over America weren't cheering when Drusovic caught one in the brain . . . then you're not the politician I thought you were. Sir."

Tyler considered that for a moment. The expression on his face said you might be right. Seelye pressed forward. The earlier you established the "legend," the more likely it was that everyone would believe it. "You see where I'm going with this"

Tyler plainly didn't.

"The point is," explained Seelye, "the bomb detonated *after the operation was over.* Devlin accomplished his mission —"

"But we took some casualties."

"We may have, yes. And, politically, that's bad. Your predecessors have pretty much established a zero-tolerance level for casualties, and I can certainly understand why you'd want to continue their policies. But look at it this way: You have a bunch of dead terrorists, a bunch of rescued kids, and a bunch of happy families. The grief counselors for the few will only add to the poignancy, not detract from it. Surely we still have some friends in the media."

Seelye noticed the president was scribbling notes as he listened. He punched the intercom button again. "Millie, I have some notes here and I want them delivered to Pam Dobson right away." He switched off and addressed Seelye. "What's your point about the bomb going off after the rescue?"

Seelye couldn't believe Tyler couldn't see it. On second thought, yes, he could. "Simple, Mr. President," he said. "We're dealing with *two separate operations.*" He paused to let that sink in. "The first one, the hostages — that was for the cameras. A feint, if you will. The second was a punctuation mark, a way of their letting us know that they got the joke."

Tyler was completely confused by now. He looked at Rubin for guidance.

"I think what Army is saying, sir, is that the hostage situation was a distraction. Whoever set this up couldn't have cared less what happened either to the kids or to the terrorists. But, with the bomb blast, he left his signature."

"Which means . . ." said Tyler, hoping that someone would fill in the blanks. Their job was to figure this out. His job was to play it politically.

"Which means that this is only the beginning," supplied Seelye. "Even worse, it means that someone — a very well-financed and ruthless someone — is testing us, probing us, trying to see how we'd react in a moment of national crisis. After all, there hasn't been a major terrorist incident directed against Americans since September eleventh. Memories fade, emotions jump. What have you done for us lately, you incompetent son of a bitch." He looked right at Tyler. "You take my point."

The PDA buzzed in his left hand. The red light flashed. "Excuse me, sir," Seelye said and called up the message. It was from Devlin:

YOU KNEW, YOU FUCKER, DIDN'T YOU?

The president was nothing if not observant. "What the hell is it, Army?"

YOU SET ME UP, YOU SON OF A BITCH.

The head of the National Security Agency looked at the president of the United States, sitting behind the *Resolute* desk. "We have a problem."

"Can you translate that," asked Tyler.

The intercom buzzed. Millie said, "The speaker and the leader are here, sir."

Tyler caught the warning look in Seelye's eyes. "Ask them to wait a moment." He turned back to Seelye. "Okay, genius, you have the floor for the next fifteen seconds."

"Mr. President," said Seelye, rising. "What just went down in Edwardsville was no ordinary terrorist incident."

"No shit, Sherlock," said Tyler. "What are you — we — going to do about it?"

"Be prepared for more trouble. This was not a one-off. Whoever planned and executed this was playing a double game with his own people. His stooges, if you will. I have no doubt that he and whoever is either working with him or standing behind him

210

has a lot in store for us."

The intercom buzzed again. Tyler ignored it. "So what do we do?"

"Give me twenty-four hours. Not even. Let me debrief Devlin — he understands what's going on. And he's the perfect man for the job."

The president looked dubious. "After what just happened . . ."

Seelye gestured to the door of the Oval Office, beyond which the congressional leaders were cooling their heels. "Remember your public, sir. This was a triumph. The next one, though, will be a tragedy if we don't stop it."

The president rose, signaling the end of the meeting. "From your lips to God's ears," he said, ushering them out. "Just don't fuck up."

CHAPTER
TWENTY-THREE

Paris, France

Pilier switched off the television and turned to Skorzeny, who had already turned his back on the screen and was looking out one of the panoramic display windows. The boss loved to watch the river traffic on the Seine, especially the *bateaux mouches* as they sailed by, lights blazing.

Not that he had much time for movies, since he didn't even watch the ones his movie studio made, even though he was the company's majority silent investor. As far as Skorzeny was concerned, movies were propaganda tools, fairy tales for the masses, and nothing more.

"Horrible," said the factotum.

"Yes," agreed Skorzeny, who had been in a bad mood since they had reached the apartment, and all because of her. "How dare she tell me she had to get back to London? Doesn't she enjoy my company?"

"Of course she does, sir," replied Pilier. "We all do. But I believe she has some preparation to attend to. You can perhaps forgive her . . . anticipation."

Skorzeny kept his gaze focused up the river, toward Notre Dame, defiantly illuminated against the dark European night. From the triplex apartment on the rue Boutarel, you could practically reach out and touch the great cathedral.

"No, it's wonderful," said Skorzeny, answering Pilier's first observation, which meant that the subject of Amanda Harrington was closed for now.

"What dreams they had — dreams that lasted almost a thousand years," mused Skorzeny, looking at the cathedral. "Dreams, and faith, and a belief in themselves. I envy them their certainty. We've lost that today, don't you think, Monsieur Pilier?"

"Yes, sir, I do," Pilier replied and instantly regretted it.

"Which?" inquired Skorzeny. "The certainty? The dreams? The faith?"

He'd walked right into that one. "All of them, sir," replied Pilier quietly. He dreaded it when the boss got into one of his interrogatory moods.

"And why?" Skorzeny turned away from the window and looked his major-domo

213

square in the face. "Without the wherewithal to realize them, dreams are for fools. Certainty rightfully belongs only to the man who can afford it. And as for faith . . ."

"No one worships at Notre Dame anymore," ventured Pilier.

Skorzeny displayed a small smile of half pleasure. "Precisely. The great cathedrals of France are mere tourist attractions now. Soon enough, they'll be nothing but tributes to the nihilistic abyss of infinity. Or mosques."

Pilier waited for a value judgment, which was not forthcoming. But he could guess.

"Empty monuments in stone to a God who has taken up residence elsewhere. The pinnacles of western civilization, now nothing more than curiosities to the Japanese and an offense to the Arabs. What do you make of it?"

Pilier hazarded a guess. "Of Notre Dame, sir?"

A small sigh of exasperation. "Of Edwardsville."

"They're calling it a tragedy."

"I suppose to the Americans, it is. But of course, it's not. Not in the classical sense. There is no protagonist, whose own pride or anger or greed or lust sows the seeds of his own destruction. A random criminal act, now matter how bloody or spectacular, cannot be tragic. You need to reread your Aristotle, Monsieur Pilier. Preferably in the original Greek, not one of those vile French translations."

Pilier issued a small cough of self-deprecation. "My education —"

"Continues with me. Which is why I hired you. You show promise. And at the moment I have no heirs. Only employees. Which is why what happened today —"

Pilier coughed modestly. "Not a tragedy, then?"

"An occurrence." Skorzeny sat down at his desk and contemplated its clean leather surface.

"There were deaths."

"There are deaths every day. Even of school children."

Skorzeny gestured in the direction of Notre Dame. As he did, one of the *bateaux mouches* floated by, casting its Platonic reflections on the walls of Skorzeny's elegant cave. The old man's face danced in and out of the chiaroscuro. "Do you think the God who once resided in that prime piece of Parisian real estate ever murdered a school child? A virgin? A nun? Of course He did. So if what happened today in Edwardsville wasn't a tragedy, then what was it?"

"As you said, sir — an occurrence." He realized that Skorzeny liked to take both sides in an argument, but it was getting late. Even Skorzeny had to sleep some time.

Skorzeny began to move toward the interior stairway, toward his private chambers. It was only at moments like that the man showed even a glimmer of his age. There was the hint of a shuffle in the walk, a *moue* of weariness at the mouth. Both of which would have vanished by morning — which, on Skorzeny's schedule, was only a few hours away. "Really, Monsieur Pilier, you disappoint me."

As Skorzeny passed him, Pilier tried once more: "An opportunity?"

"Precisely," said Skorzeny. "Good night, Monsieur Pilier."

"Good night, sir."

Skorzeny stepped into the hallway. He never took reading to bed. When it was time to sleep, that's what he did. Efficiency above everything. Tonight, however, he had a valedictory. "Do you ever wonder where He went?"

"Who, sir?"

Skorzeny shot him a look. Suddenly, one bony hand shot out, grasping Pilier hard. "Inform our other British member that I expect to receive his report of his American activities at the London board meeting. That is all."

That was his signal. Pilier nodded and went to retrieve a portable basin of water spiced with lemon juice in which Skorzeny ritually washed his hands before retiring, reflecting his absolute abhorrence of dirt. Mentally, Pilier referred to it as the "Pontius Pilate" bowl.

"Thank you," Skorzeny said, wiping his hands on the freshly laundered linen towel draped over Pilier's left forearm, which would go straight to the laundry service in the morning.

Pilier stood motionless as Skorzeny disappeared up the stairs. He had learned from experience not to move until he heard the music — you never knew when Skorzeny would poke his head out one last time with a request or an observation. What would it be tonight? What elegy to accompany Emanuel Skorzeny into slumber?

Sure enough, the voice wafted from above: "Do you remember who St. Bernard was, Monsieur Pilier?"

"Something to do with Clairvaux, sir?" hazarded Pilier, trying not to shout.

"The abbot of the great monastery, to be precise. In the twelfth century, the man who preached the Second Crusade in 1146.

Friend to Saint Malachy, he of the apocalyptic prophecy of papal succession in 1139. Of the 111th Pope, Peter the Roman, and the revenge of the dragon."

Pilier had no idea what he was talking about. When Skorzeny went off on one of these numerological tangents . . .

"Today, their successors will not even use the word, 'crusade,' much less preach one. What do you call that, Monsieur Pilier?"

Pilier thought for a moment. Of course it was a trick question. They were all trick questions. "Prudence, sir?" he replied.

"Cowardice," said Skorzeny, shutting the door again.

Silence for a moment, and then the music: the opening strains of the Elgar cello concerto, first movement. Skorzeny's taste was impeccable, as always.

CHAPTER
TWENTY-FOUR

Lexington, Kentucky

Devlin caught the Greyhound bus from St. Louis to Lexington, Kentucky, where he bought an airplane ticket under the name "Matt Nolan," bound for Reagan International. There, he would pick up a CSS drop car in the long-term parking lot and drive himself home.

Things weren't as bad as he'd feared in Edwardsville. The explosion had demolished the gym, but ironically the fact that Bartlett's team had blown holes in the walls during their assault had dispersed the power of the bomb and saved the rest of the school.

The bad news was there was one child still missing — Emma, the daughter of Hope Gardner, the woman who had so bravely and foolishly penetrated the school, the sister of the boy he had pulled to safety into the Dumpster when Milverton's little going-away present blew. There was no way to tell whether she was alive or dead at this point, but the longer they went without finding her body, the better the chances of finding her were. Unless, of course, she had been blown to bits.

The other bad news was that the hero, the guy he'd seen breaking through the police lines and had gotten himself killed for no reason — that man had been identified as Hope's husband, Jack. That family had really taken a hit.

One part of Devlin admired him. But the time for civilian heroes was when trouble started, not when it was almost over. A civilian hero was the customer sitting munching his Big Mac with a .45 in his pocket when the punks tried to hold up the McDonald's, the man who, seeing a couple of thugs breaking into his neighbor's house, racks up his 12-gauge, blows the perps out of their socks, and then waits for the cops to show up.

Devlin knew all this because had been tracking the aftermath of the school operation via his next-generation iPhone, which after all had been licensed to Apple and AT&T by the NSA in a top-secret agreement that gave the agency discretionary but complete access to all audio and visual files transmitted over the system. Even now, the

NSA computers in Fort Meade and the huge data chompers in Poughkeepsie were busily sorting through teenage pranks, the exotic but enervating sexual practices of random couples, and the idle chatter of millions of cell-phone laundry lists and bitch-out sessions.

Still, the panic that had overtaken the *New York Times* and its fellow travelers when word of the "warrantless wiretapping" program had leaked into print was ridiculous. Nobody, least of all him and the operatives in Branch 4, had the time or the patience to sort through granny's recipes for apple pan dowdy. The vast majority of the intercepts went straight to the data-sifters, churning bytes, megabytes, gigabytes, terabytes, and googlebytes in search of that magic combination of zeros and ones that might signify terrorist buzzwords.

And all thanks to something called the "SKIPJACK" algorithm. First proposed by the Clinton administration as part of something called the "Clipper Chip," the original 80-bit key, 64-bit block, 32-round, unbalanced Feistel network called Skipjack would have placed a chip inside all new communication devices to allow the encryption of private communications. The catch was that, buried deep in the proposal, was an "escrow" proviso that called for a third party to maintain the "keys" to unlock encrypted communications, which government agents could access with court permission. The whole idea being, essentially, to make private data-encryption impossible, as the classified Presidential Decision Directive No. 5, issued by Clinton in 1993, made clear. In other words, like most congressional laws and state referenda, it meant the exact opposite of what it said.

That "third party," of course, was the National Security Agency, which had invented the damn thing in the first place. And it was never very difficult to find a sympathetic judge in Washington, no matter which party was in power.

The NSA had invented the chip's underlying cryptographic algorithm — Skipjack — which the agency promptly classified. When the civil-liberties types started barking, Clinton backed away, leaving the playing field wide open for the NSA to step in and lock the whole thing down. In a fit of false openness, the NSA in 1998 released the Skipjack algorithm to computer security companies wishing to develop off-the-shelf encryption products compatible with federal government communications systems. And so the marriage made in heaven was consummated. Talk about a poisoned pawn: now every American potentially was subject to federal monitoring.

Well, that sure made his job a lot easier. Too bad he didn't have the heart to tell that to Eddie Bartlett's daughter, Jade. Tapped into her iPhone, he could keep tabs on his partner's family, just to be on the safe side.

Devlin's off-market "iPhone" was something else again. It was part of his deal that he had access to beta-plus-one versions of everything. With a few punches of his game console he could slam through into a teenage girl's webcam as she Facebooked some fiftyish dirtbag claiming to be a runaway from Alberta and rat him out to the FBI — anonymously, of course. Echelon had nothing on Skipjack.

"Can I get you something else?" said the cocktail waitress in the Lexington airport lounge. Devlin glanced at his watch: plenty of time. "What do you think . . . Laura?" he replied.

She didn't move. She was about twenty-six, midwestern, tanned — German background, for sure, since Irish and English girls never darkened in the sun like that — small-breasted, nice legs. His type.

The girl smiled. "Do I know you?" Worked every time.

Devlin shot her one of those apparently honest, searching gazes that women loved. Women were like fish; you had to get them to nibble, then bite, but had to reel them in slowly, playing them out just enough to give them the illusion that they could safely swim away at any time. "I'm sorry . . . Courtney?" She dipped a little at the knees, moved in closer, an open invitation if you knew how to read body language.

"Amber," she said. "See?" She pointed to the name tag just above her left breast.

Devlin shook his head. "No, not Amber." The girl looked momentarily puzzled, which is exactly what he expected. "I've met all the girls named Amber and I sure would have remembered you." He was smiling now. "No, I'm pretty sure your name is Destiny."

It took her a couple of seconds to get the joke. She gave him one of those quizzical, excuse-me smiles this generation was so adept at. Instinctively, she moved to the next level, something else he was counting on. "I think it was at Marengo?" The mock-shake of the head, the sarcastic furrowing of the eyebrows. "Remember?"

Devlin pretended to think. This was going to be easier than he thought. Marengo was a nice touch, and out of anybody else's mouth but hers it might have raised a flag or two. "Marengo? Whose side were you on — Napoleon's, the Austrians', or the chicken's?"

She giggled. "You're smart, aren't you? I can tell."

"No one's ever told me that before."

That got her laughing again. "I was talking about the club — you know, the one downtown?"

"Right," he said. "Maybe you could take me there?" He watched her eyes as she was making up her mind. As soon as he saw assent — "What time do you get off?"

"Don't you have somewhere to go?" she smiled. "I mean, you are here at the airport."

"My flight just got canceled."

"Ten o'clock," she said "What did you say your name was?"

Thank God there was a flight to Washington early the next morning. Sometimes the loneliness was crushing.

■ ■ ■ ■

DAY TWO

■ ■ ■ ■

Facts stand wholly outside our gates; they are what they are, and no more; they know nothing about themselves, and they pass no judgment upon themselves. What is it, then, that pronounces the judgment? Our own guide and ruler, reason.

— MARCUS AURELIUS, *Meditations,* Book IX

CHAPTER
TWENTY-FIVE

Washington, D.C.

Senator Robert Hartley kicked off his shoes, poured himself a drink, and looked out the window at the Potomac as it flowed past his apartment in The Watergate. It was after midnight. It had been a very long day and he was looking forward to some well-deserved relaxation.

He liked Washington, he decided, and even though he had promised the people of his state that three terms would be plenty, he had since found ample reason to re-arrange his position on the subject. Seniority, for one thing, which was the only thing on Capitol Hill that outranked sex as a congressional motivating factor. All that was left now was how to pitch his repositioning as high principle, instead of opportunism.

After all, he was an effective pork-barreler — make that "constituent services provider" — and he kept federal dollars flowing into his state far in excess of what they paid out in taxes. Early on, he had learned that pork was a zero-sum contest among the fifty states, and so he'd found himself in complete agreement with Mr. Micawber: that taxes plus one extra dollar back from the feds equaled happiness, and taxes minus one dollar equaled misery. Especially at the ballot box.

Second, he knew his way around the corridors. One thing the Clintons had taught everybody — a lesson they in turn had learned from J. Edgar Hoover — that he who controls the files controls the capital, and Hartley had made it his first order of business upon arrival in the District of Columbia to get to know the men who knew the men who kept the secrets. Although privately he despised the FBI for the life it had forced Hoover and Clyde Tolson to lead, he knew enough to ingratiate himself with the Revolving Door known as the FBI director, as well as with the Empty Seat known as the Director of Central Intelligence. It was amazing how close you could get with somebody once you knew what really motivated him or her. Which was pretty much the same thing that motivated everybody: money, sex, and power.

Third, there was the war chest. So much

cash that Hartley hadn't yet mustered the courage to ask his bundlers where it was all coming from. Small donations, he was assured, all well within the campaign finance limits. Keeping track of stuff like this was beyond anybody's powers except a fleet of high-priced lawyers with unlimited billable hours, but Hartley supposed that was the price you paid for democracy.

Not bad for a boy from the Bronx. As a kid, Hartley had set his cap for a ticket out of the old neighborhood, which in his case lay between Belmont and the Mosholu Parkway. As a teenager, he had started calling himself "Hartley" instead of his real name — it sounded so much tonier — and after a while it had become such second nature that he'd had it legally changed between the time he applied to Harvard Law and when he was accepted. Good-bye Kings College, hello Cambridge, Mass.

After Harvard, he'd clerked for one of the justices for a while, but realized soon enough that the life of a lawyer was not for him, that the law degree was only a means to an end, which was politics. He found he had a real knack for it, so when the time came for him to settle on a base of operations, he picked a state in the upper Midwest where the folks were just as nice as pie, a place where he could rub off the abrasive edges of his native accent and his personality but could still retain a trace of his otherness as he climbed the ladder from the state legislature to the House to the Senate.

He knew that a lot of people considered him a prick — you couldn't rise as high as he had without making plenty of enemies — but his constituents didn't seem to care: he was their prick, and he delivered. And, really, was that so bad? He wanted what everybody else wanted, status, respect, power, and, in those moments when he was truthful with himself, love. Even if he had to look for it in unsavory places sometimes. Oh well, he could live with that. In fact, he had been living with it for most of his life.

Which is why it was strange but true — "ironic," even, in the currently debased usage of that word, which usually signified "coincidental" — that just about the only friend he had in the world was the man who was now sitting in the Oval Office.

But latterly a new element had just been injected into the forthcoming campaign: President Tyler's sagging fortunes. What just happened in Edwardsville wasn't going to help his poll numbers, that was for sure. Despite the false sense of security post–9/11, wouldn't take much to swing the pendulum of fear back into the red zone. Another attack, God forbid, and . . .

Hartley realized in this game of high-low poker, he had a great hand to play. The only question was when to declare.

Declarations were not something politicians instinctively gravitated toward. Like most of his colleagues, Hartley preferred to dither and debate until events or circumstances or fate or whatever finally forced his hand. And then he jumped in the direction of the wind, principles as intact as possible, press releases at the ready.

Hartley didn't live at The Watergate, of course. His residence of record was in Georgetown, like everybody else's. He kept this particular flat rented under an assumed name that was protected by an ironclad confidential understanding with the management, and used it for special occasions.

He was mentally trying on the Oval Office for size when a sound outside in the hallway caught his attention. Sometimes his visitors from the agency were a little shy or inexperienced, and it took a friendly voice of encouragement, or a drink, or something stronger, to put them at ease. Few recognized him — hell, they were barely old enough to vote, most of them. To them, he was just another middle-aged white guy from the hinterland, come to the great city to stroll on what passed for the wild side on the banks of the Potomac.

He peered through the security peephole, but saw nothing. He put his ear against the door, but heard nothing. Hartley was no longer paranoid — liberation was a wonderful thing — but discretion was still part of his implicit deal with the voters and there was no point in pushing his luck.

He glanced at his watch and made a mental note to discuss tardiness with the manager of the service, the next time he encountered him in one of the District's discreet watering holes that catered to powerful men with his tastes.

This time, the knock was unmistakable. Hartley turned back to the door, and yanked it open —

Nobody.

"Goddamnit —"

The man he didn't see blew past him before he knew what was happening. Grabbed Hartley by the arm and pulled him inside. Closed the door behind them softly and said, "Ready?"

Hartley looked his unexpected visitor over. The fellow certainly didn't look like he was from A Current Affair, the name of the escort service he regularly employed. Even were he into fetishes, this get-up — a good-looking blond hunk in a suit — wasn't what he had ordered at all. "Who are you?"

"Right," said the visitor, and the next thing Hartley knew he was on the floor, blood gushing from his nose. Just as he hadn't seen the man, he hadn't seen the punch either.

"I'm a United States senator!" he protested, fumbling for his handkerchief. He hated to ruin an Egyptian-cotton present from one of his admirers, but he really had no other choice.

"Don't try to impress me," said the man, settling into Hartley's best chair. "I've met lepers with a better pedigree, and hookers with more taste."

Hartley didn't see why his unexpected visitor had to add insult to injury. He had not requested any role-playing this evening, and rough stuff was almost never on his agenda, but the lad was big and strapping and very good looking. . . .

"I suppose you'll want cash up front," he said, wiping away the blood. "It's in my bedroom."

"Stay put, pops, it's not your money I want." The man had some kind of accent Hartley couldn't quite place, but then he never was very good at languages. He was an American.

Hartley was about to inquire what he meant when the doorbell rang. He glanced at his visitor for instructions. "It's for you," the man said. Hartley wiped his face with what remained of his clean handkerchief and opened the door.

The boy was young, just old enough, which was the way he liked them, and dressed as he had requested, like a pizza delivery man. "Come in," said Senator Hartley, turning back toward his guest. He just had time to breathe a small sigh of relief, thankful that there was somebody else in the apartment, a witness, to spare him from further trouble when he noticed that the blond man was no longer there.

"Um, mister . . ." said the boy, which was too bad, because they were his last words. In retrospect, thought Hartley, all of us would like a proper valedictory.

The .22 slug entered the boy's head and bounced around his skull for less than a second, killing him without so much as a sigh. He fell, the empty pizza box with the hole punched in its bottom floating lightly on the air for a moment before it joined the lifeless body on the floor. Then the man put another bullet into his head, for good measure.

"Jesus —" was all Hartley could muster before he too landed on the floor, knocked unconscious, from a tremendous blow to his head.

Hartley awoke a few minutes later, in bed, naked, with the late pizza boy for a companion. His visitor sat opposite, watching CNN on the bedroom television, unruffled by the commotion. "You know what they used to say in the old South? That a politician couldn't get reelected if he was caught in bed with a dead girl or a live boy. Well, we're about to go one step further."

The BlackBerry camera flashed. Hartley was still stunned by the blow but he was tech-savvy enough to know that the photograph was already being uplinked somewhere, and that he was, basically, fucked. "What do you want?" he croaked.

"Now you're making sense," said the man. "The first order of business is you're working for me. The second is this." He handed Hartley a small slip of paper, upon which was printed a local Washington telephone number. "Memorize it."

Hartley stared at the number, numb. "I think I have it."

"Brilliant," said the man. "Now, eat it." Hartley realized he wasn't kidding. He ate it. "Now dial it." For encouragement, he pointed the gun at Hartley's head. He dialed it, let it ring until the man disconnected the call. "Good. You passed the first test."

He reached into his pocket and took out what looked like a minicomputer and fired it up. Hartley blanched when he saw the Web site, but there wasn't much he could do about it. "Now, Mr. Chairman," the man said, "let's get started. We've got some hacking to do."

CHAPTER
TWENTY-SIX

Falls Church

There were no visible televisions in the public rooms of Devlin's home. No radios, either. A visitor would surely remark their absence, if he ever had visitors. The only rooms with what might be called "normal" furniture were those that, by chance, could be glimpsed from the outside in the evening, before the curtains were automatically drawn, but those rooms were just for show. There was only one wing of the house that mattered, one room where he spent the bulk of his time.

In which he now sat still, a spider at the center of his vast sigint web. On his main monitor, he could track all incoming calls by signal origin; those he wished to answer could be rerouted to a dead-zone mailbox for later retrieval. Random incoming calls were ignored. Those deemed suspicious or hostile were eliminated by sending back a retro-virus that fried the bounce-back receptors and eliminated the phone numbers from active use for at least forty-eight hours, by which time they had been reassigned to someone else.

He felt a twinge about the girl in Kentucky. Not about what they had done — that was natural, if slightly furtive and definitely transitory. And the emotions he felt for her at the moment were certainly genuine. One would have thought he'd long gotten over the lying that was a necessary part of the seduction, but what came naturally to other men in their endless, restless pursuit of conquest was the one element in his life that he preferred to keep separate from his day job.

He couldn't, of course. He knew that the life of others was not the life given to him. And now that Milverton had reappeared on the scene, any hope he might have had of getting out after Edwardsville was long gone. He couldn't just walk away now, not with the most dangerous man on the planet looking for him, his life forfeit to any other Branch 4 op any time the president or Seelye decided to punch his ticket. They had him by the balls.

Which is why he sat here, in the safe room of his house in the Virginia suburbs, surrounded by computers and keyboards, electronically connected anywhere in the world and yet absolutely alone.

To look at this room one might be surprised at its simplicity. Not for him were the vast NSA bullpens of Fort Meade, where the donkey work of electronic surveillance was carried out. If he wanted or needed access to anything in the great black box off the Baltimore-Washington Parkway he needed only to get in his car and drive there, less than an hour away, Beltway traffic willing, where he parked his car and entered the building as part of the custodial staff.

Devlin believed in hiding in plain sight. Devlin believed that naked is the best disguise. Which was why he lived here, alone, on North West Street. Once, Falls Church was a sleepy suburb, the smallest incorporated city in America, equally balanced between government time-servers and what was left of the Virginia gentry who first occupied the place. In recent years, however, Falls Church had undergone a dramatic ethnic shift. Illegal Mexicans clustered on street corners in the old downtown section, and mosques now stood where defunct businesses once had been. Ten miles from the nation's capital, Arabic and Spanish jostled English as the lingua franca of the new, emergent United States.

Just as Jaguars had no visible radio antennas that would mar the sleek lines of the expensive automobiles, neither did Devlin's house have any visible external indication of his profession, aside from a small satellite dish easily mistaken for a TV receiver but was in reality a beta-testing uplink that he had devised himself. Only the canniest of observers would have noticed that it was directed not toward the southern sky, where the television satellites were located, but to the southwest, where the secret comsats were.

Arrayed in a row on his desk were three laptops, each with a different operating system and a different web browser. Double-blind passwords, proprietary encryption algorithms. Each of the machines running DB2 and Intelligent Miner and hotlinked separately to the three parallel mainframe servers at the IBM RS/6000 Teraplex Integration Center in Poughkeepsie — the RS/6000 SP, the S/390, and the AS/400. Predictive and descriptive modes, depending on what he was looking for.

He was running Sharpreader on Windows, NetNewsWire on the Mac, Straw on Linux: his inbox was RSS-updated on a minute-by-minute basis, with real-time news and stories of interest on preselected topics. Level Five NSA firewall security, updated regularly. Complete virus, trojan, and spyware projection, automatically updated every twenty-four hours. His best friends. His data miners.

One of the flaws in the government's security apparatus, he had long realized, was its very nature as a governmental organization. Although he tried to stay off the grid as much as possible, NSA/CSS could not avoid some of the oversight that came with taxpayer funds, and as a result they were blinkered and inhibited, like other governmental agencies. Not to the same extent, of course, or else they could not have functioned, and many of their activities were unfortunately but necessarily devoted to pretense, to the appearance of compliance, just to keep the bean-counters, the bluenoses, the civil-libertarians, and the recrudescent communists as pacified as possible.

But just as war was too important to be left to the generals, the business of national security was too vital to be left to the elected representatives of the people. So there had to be work-arounds, and open-source data mining was one of them.

Some of his fellow professionals scoffed at the notion. To them, "open-source" was synonymous with "amateur," but amateurs had been responsible for many of the significant breakthroughs in almost every field, and even — perhaps especially — in today's over-credentialed society they had their manifest uses.

Take, for example, something as simple as a relationship chart, generated by a global search; for any given name, the program could quickly extract all known personal and institutional associates and rank-order them by their proximity to the subject's name in any news story, video clip, press release, bank record, money-transfer order, e-mail address book, iPhone, or PDA database, Yahoo, Gmail and Hotmail accounts, etc. In a few seconds, the printer would spit out a chart graphically displaying the links and degrees of separation. It was often both amazing and instructive to see, visually, who was doing what to whom, and it helped him to make connections that otherwise might have slid by unnoticed.

Take Ali Abu-al-Hamza al-Saleh, for example. One of the problems with Arabic names was that practically every Arab male had more than one "real" name, all of them multiple variations on a relatively small pool of names that could be either patronymic, geographic, or descriptive. Thus, to express it in English, Tom the Fat Man could also be Thomas son of Walter or Tommy the Yemeni, depending. This particular dirtbag, an Israeli Arab, had used his twelve-year-old daughter as a human mule, packed her suitcase chock full of explosives, and put her on a bus bound for Haifa, where she took out an Israeli high-school soccer team that was going to spend the day at the shore.

Saleh had covered his tracks very well, but when the same thing happened a year later, involving an eight-year-old boy detonating amidst some German tourists near the Pyramids, Devlin opened up a file and began watching and linking anything remotely similar. The Case of the Incredible Exploding Children, he referred to it in his own mind, and it didn't take long before he realized that what seemed frighteningly like a deadly new, inhuman, form of terrorism turned out to be limited to one very fecund and productive male, operating under multiple identities in multiple countries, who had devoted his life to siring as many expendable progeny as possible.

Devlin embedded the information in the infamous look-ma-no-undies Britney Spears video and sent it to a friend at the Jonathan Institute in Tel Aviv, who relayed it to the wet-work boys at Shin Bet, who acted appropriately when Saleh returned to Israel from a "vacation" to Turkey. Devlin was pleased to read press accounts of various body parts washing up on various Mediterranean beaches over a six-week period, until all the limbs, the torso, and finally the head of Mr. Saleh were accounted for. Case closed.

The thought had occurred to him to run a relationship chart on Seelye, but for some reason he hadn't yet done so. Six degrees of Kevin Bacon was fun with your friends, less fun with your professional relationships. And not at all fun with the man who was, for all practical purposes, his father. O brave new world, where every man is both king and couch potato.

He wasn't surprised when the first ping came through. In the aftermath of Edwardsville, his first thought was clearing the battlefield as quickly as possible, just in case Milverton's trap was more complex than it first appeared. The night with the waitress in Lexington was as much for operational security as carnal pleasure, or so he told himself.

The header flashed top-secret, urgent, national-security. By law, he was supposed to answer it unless he was dead, incapacitated, or held under duress. Devlin hit the translator button, to view the content of Seelye's pings. WHAT FUCKING HAPPENED BACK THERE? Pretty much as he thought, except the message was obviously coming from President Tyler, since Seelye never swore.

HELLO, MR. PRESIDENT, he responded, his reply thoroughly scrambled even over the dedicated fiber-optic line.

HOW DID YOU KNOW? He tried to get a read on where the president was — with Seelye somewhere, certainly.

YOUR ELOQUENCE IS UNMISTAKEABLE. That was sure to piss Tyler off.

Sure enough: LISTEN UP YOU ASSHOLE. I NEED TO KNOW IF THE SITUATION IS UNDER CONTROL. I CANNOT AFFORD ANY POLITICAL BLOWBACK FROM THIS.

I BELIEVE IT IS, YES, SIR. Only a white lie at this point, but . . .

CAN YOU GUARANTEE THAT?

WITH ALL RESPECT, SIR, PERHAPS YOU'D BETTER ASK GENERAL SEELYE ABOUT GUARANTEES. That would piss Seelye off for sure.

A longer pause: MY OFFICE IN FOUR HOURS. CAMP DAVID.

Not good. Camp David was very private.

Asses got chewed off and spit out at Camp David.

DON'T WORRY I'M NOT GOING TO CHEW YOUR ASS OFF. Tyler was quite the mind-reader.

ROGER THAT, SIR.

GET MOVING. The line went dead.

He didn't like it. No matter how complete his report, he had no intention at this time of mentioning his suspicion, no, make that his absolute dead-solid certainty, that Milverton had made him. That was his problem; no sense adding to it by begging for Branch 4 to be out looking for him as well. Besides, if someone high up was collaborating with Milverton and whoever was running him, compartmentalization was the order of the day.

Which meant that he was in no position to guarantee anything to anybody. And without 100 percent certainty and deniability, the whole purpose of Branch 4 — Devlin's very existence — was pretty much moot. Tyler was facing a tough reelection campaign, and sharks in both parties — like that creepazoid Hartley — were already sniffing blood in the water. An inquiry into Edwardsville, a leak or two, and suddenly one of the most closely guarded secrets in the American intelligence community was blown to hell and gone.

Which meant that Camp David could be a termination meeting.

It wasn't that Devlin didn't trust the president of the United States, it's that he didn't trust anybody, and so the president of the United States was as good a person to start with as anybody.

CHAPTER
TWENTY-SEVEN

Edwardsville

Since the rescue, Hope and Rory had been inundated by the moral detritus of modern America. They had surrounded her and Rory so fast that she only realized later that she never had time to thank the man who had saved both their lives. The "reporter" with the knife, who had lopped off that awful man's arm with the utmost ease. Hope didn't get a real good look at him, but she did catch his eyes and what she saw in them both thrilled and scared her.

She didn't see fear. She didn't see anger. She saw *confidence.* A sense of purpose, a sense of . . . professionalism.

The police, the FBI, the doctors, and the news crews had left. The grief counselors and social services people and "caregivers" she wouldn't let in. There was nothing to say. Hope and Rory sat looking at each other across a half-empty dinner table. The silence in the house was both comforting and almost unendurable.

From time to time the phone rang, but she didn't answer it. There was nothing to say to anybody, and nothing that could be said to her to make her feel any better.

They had found Jack's body almost immediately. It wasn't the blast itself that had killed him; he had been hit by a tiny shard of glass that had punctured his eyeball and penetrated his brain. When they found him, it was almost as if he'd lain down to take a short nap.

There was still no sign of Emma. The rescue workers had tried to tell her that that was a good sign, that maybe she somehow got out, and would turn up tomorrow, wandering dazed somewhere. But they'd also admitted that it might take them days to identify any remains at the blast site. Hope had tried to use her woman's intuition, to look into her own heart, to listen very carefully to the small voice within and hear what it was saying, that either her daughter was still alive, or she wasn't. But the voice was as silent as the rest of the house.

Oh well, she could make her peace with that. Plenty of families had gone through the same thing, military families, crime-victim families, and they somehow managed. Until today, Hope was like most of her neighbors; she never really gave much thought to whether her country was actually at war, or whether the whole thing was some fraud cooked up in Texas and Washington and Baghdad and God knows where else, a scam like "Remember the Maine" and "54-40 or Fight," designed to separate the American people from their money and their children, to enrich men elsewhere.

Hope and Rory looked at each other over a cold meal, neither wishing to break the silence.

"I tried to save her, Mom," Rory said, after a while.

"I know you did, Rory."

"And I would have, too. If I'd a found her . . ."

The memory of him attacking that filthy animal washed over her — her little son, doing something that so many Americans were loath to do: fighting back.

Once more, she remembered how the man's head had suddenly exploded and how another man suddenly had come out of nowhere and chopped off the arm that held her life in its now lifeless hand. She remembered the gratified look in his eyes when he realized that he had saved both her and her son.

And then she remember something else: the tattoo on his forearm of the winged centaur holding a sword, and a name: DANNY BOY. And, at that moment, she knew that she could not rest until she met him again, spoke with him, thanked him — and begged him to help her take her revenge on whoever had killed Jack and Emma. In his business, Jack had lots of military friends and she'd seen the tattoos on their arms, could tell military tattoos from the civilian ones that had popped up on everybody's son's and daughter's body in the past decade. With some phone calls, she could probably find out what the centaur with the sword represented. Just get Rory to bed first.

She was lost in her thoughts until Rory again broke the awful silence. "What're we going to do, Mom?" he asked.

"We'll be okay," she said, meaning it but not knowing how.

"Yeah, but . . . what're we going to do?"

Hope looked at her son: "I don't know yet. But we're going to do something." The phone rang again, but she let it go. She'd already spoken with her parents and with Jack's mother, and there was nobody else she wanted to hear from right now. Least of all the media vultures. How could these people live with themselves?

It was just a matter of time, she knew, before the numbness and the grief wore off. The disbelief. They would go to bed tonight, she knew, telling themselves that Jack was out of town and Emma was away at a sleepover, and they might even believe it, for a minute. But when they woke up, there would be that gnawing hole in their souls. They were just going to have to live with it for a while. And then the blame would begin.

Mentally, she replayed the day. Jack had to go out of town. She had to take the kids to school. Nothing either of them had done was wrong, and Hope's attempted rescue and Jack's impetuous bravery, in the end, hadn't affected the outcome one way or the other. In fact, she was lucky she hadn't got both herself and Rory killed. What happened, happened.

But now, somehow, some way, she wanted payback. Payback for what these people — who had come to her town, to her school, unbidden, and foisted their grievances upon an innocent and unsuspecting community — had done to her and her family. She may not have wanted to be at war with them, but somebody was surely at war with her.

"What you did," she said at last, "was amazing." Immediately, she hated herself for using such a cheap, modish word. There had been nothing amazing about it. Rory's actions had been simply stone-cold brave, the lion cub defending his mother.

"I wasn't brave, Mom," he said. "I was scared."

"Sometimes they're the same thing."

Rory picked up a cold pea and ate it. "That man, the one with the sword, he was brave." He pushed his plate away.

"There's still a chance, Rory," she said. "I heard her voice."

"I heard it, too. She's still alive, Mom. I know it."

Hope swallowed hard. "I do too."

"So what are we going to do about it?"

The look on his face made her so proud so could cry. But she had to hold back the tears. "We're going to find out the truth," she said at last, "and if Emma is still alive, we're going to find her."

Rory managed to muster the simulacrum of a smile. "Promise?"

"Double-dog-dare-ya promise," she replied, trying to put on a brave face. And then it hit her. What if they did find Emma's body tonight? Hope was a midwestern girl, not given to strong emotions. Emotions were for easterners, ethnics, southerners. The people of Edwardsville prided themselves on their equanimity, on their ability to get along and go along, and while they might harbor private anger, private grudges, they would be damned if they would ever let such emotions show.

But now, she was not so sure. Now she was becoming ever more sure that, somehow, if she ever found the men responsible for what had happened, she would kill them with her bare hands.

She caught herself. That was the kind of thing hillbillies did, folks from Cairo and the Ozarks in Missouri, and farther south. Guys who secreted handguns in their pants and blew away the defendant as he sat at the lawyers' table or, better, in the witness box. The kind of people she had instinctively recoiled from, but whose ranks she now, goddammit, all of a sudden very much wanted to join.

Kill them. And keep killing them until they stopped. Stopped coming to her country, stopped shouting, stopped gesticulating, stop firing weapons into the air, stopped making those ungodly noises, stopped killing our soldiers, stopped. Wrapped up in her private emotions, she swept her arm and the butter dish fell to the floor, shattered.

"He took her with him. Charles. I know he did." Rory was talking to her. Hope's eyes gleamed as she saw so clearly what she so desperately wanted to believe. "He got away and he took her with him," he said. "And then the helicopter crashed —"

"And they said they found only one body, the pilot. So what? Remember when that Muslim from Canada turned up dead at that political convention in Denver with a suitcase full of cyanide? No link to terrorism, they said. Remember when that Arab kid crashed his plane into that building in Florida? No link to terrorism, they said. Remember when those two Arabs turned up in North Carolina or wherever it was with bomb stuff in their cars and claimed they were joyriding around to set off some fireworks? No link to terrorism, they said. No link, no link, no link." She pounded the table at its iteration of the word, "link."

"Our own government is lying to us. Lying to us all the time. What is it they don't want us to know? What kind of fools do they take us for, us hicks out here in flyover country? They take our tax money and they buy our votes and then they treat us like idiot children. They fly over us and they laugh at us on their way to Malibu or the Hamptons. Well, I'm not going to take it any more."

"Mom, who was that man?" At first Hope thought Rory meant the man with the tattoo, but he continued, "The man who saved me. The man who grabbed me — he came out of nowhere and we jumped into the Dumpster. I thought he was a missionary."

That caught her up short — something she hadn't thought about. It was so hard to concentrate at a time like this, but yes . . . who was that man? She had assumed he was a rescue worker. "A missionary?" she asked. "What are you talking about?"

"Like cannibals and missionaries. You know, the game? I asked him if he was a missionary, and he said, 'No, kid, I'm an angel.' "

"An angel?"

"That's what he said, Mom."

Hope thought for a moment: not one but two mystery men. She wondered if they had anything to do with each other. "Try to get some sleep, Rory," she said at last.

"I'm not sleepy."

"No, you're not sleepy — you're exhausted." Finally, she broke down and started to cry. Rory rushed to her and held his mother. Then they both cried.

"I miss Dad," he sobbed. "Why did it have to be him? Why, Mom, why?"

Hope brushed away her tears and tried to comfort her son. "I don't know, Rory," she said, letting the boy cry himself out. "It's just part of God's plan."

"Well — it's a sucky plan."

"Shhh . . ." she said. "Try to get some sleep now."

She led him into his bedroom and got him under the covers. He fell asleep before she even turned out the light.

Hope sat in the living room, trying to get ahold of herself. Her family may have been struck by unimaginable tragedy, but maybe there was something she could do about it. Some way she could fight back.

She knew exactly what she was going to do: find the man with the tattoo and hire him to find Emma. And maybe find the angel too.

She picked up the phone.

CHAPTER
TWENTY-EIGHT

Los Angeles

"Daddy!"

Jade jumped into his arms, and Eddie hugged her tight. He hated leaving his daughter, hated even more leaving his wife, hated in fact everything about his job except the job itself. He was also bone tired, happy that he had been able to rescue that woman and her son, and profoundly pissed off that the job had gone so wrong at the end. That had never happened with a "Tom Powers" job before . . .

"How was your ride in the chopper?"

Eddie Bartlett put his daughter down on the ground, stepped back, and then kissed her again. His wife, Diane, beamed from the kitchen doorway. Eddie was never quite sure what if anything Diane knew about what he did, but one of the reasons he had married her was that she was smart and she was discreet, and so he never asked and she never told.

"Lots of fun."

"Will you take me with you the next time?"

"You bet, pumpkin."

Jade pulled a face. "That's what you always say."

"And that's what I always mean. So there we have it — means, motive . . . now all we need is the opportunity —"

"Which I hope to God never comes," said Diane. She wrapped herself around him, kissing him as passionately as propriety permitted.

"Get a room, you two," observed Jade.

"We've already got one," said Eddie. "In fact, we've got a whole house. A bedroom, too. How do you think you got here?"

"Awww . . ."

"What do they teach you in that expensive private school of yours, anyway?"

Jade took a step back and smiled that knowing smile of hers, so much wiser and older than her eight years. "You don't want to know."

Eddie was about to say something when Diane stepped between them. "All right, you two, enough of this banter. You and I have some serious shopping to do, young

261

lady, and I know just where we're going to do it."

So did Jade: "The Grove?" The Grove was a kind of Disneyland for shoppers adjacent to the old Farmer's Market at Fairfax and Third, turning a forlorn corner of the old Kosher Canyon into one of the most successful outdoor malls and entertainment complexes in America.

As Diane nodded, Jade let out what sounded like a series of war whoops, which was the way young girls expressed enthusiasm these days. Then she turned to Eddie, "Are you coming, too, Daddy?"

Eddie shook his head. "I think I'm going to catch a little shut-eye, pumpkin," he said. "If you don't mind."

Jade seemed a little disappointed, but Diane took her by the hand. "Your father's been working hard and he needs a little nap, just like you do sometimes. By the time we get back, he'll be tanned, rested, and ready — and then we'll all go to Fat Fish for sushi. Okay?"

More war whoops. If there was anything Jade loved more than shopping at the Grove with her mom, it was sushi at Fat Fish, in West Hollywood.

"What are you spending my hard-earned money on today?" he asked, as a wave of exhaustion washed over him.

"Duh — a new MacBook? Can I get anything for you, Daddy?" asked Jade

Eddie looked at Diane and smiled. "Just bring your mommy home safe to me and we'll call it even," he said.

Diane kissed him on her way out the door. "Good-bye, Danny," she said.

Danny Impellatieri was "Eddie Bartlett's" real name, and the Impellatieri family lived quietly and unostentatiously in one of those houses in Los Feliz that most Angelenos never knew existed. Built by a random scion of the Chandler family in the mid-1920s, the house lay sheltered away on Hobart Street in the flats between Franklin Street and Los Feliz Boulevard, just west of Loughlin Park, the gated neighborhood where Hollywood had set down temporary roots between its founding in Echo Park and its later incarnation in Hancock Park, Beverly Hills, Brentwood, Bel-Air, and Pacific Palisades.

The great March to the Sea, however, was now over and many of the young Hollywood stars were now rediscovering the joys of living off the Wilshire-Beverly-Sunset grid and finding that they could somehow survive without getting shot in neighborhoods close to, you know, where "they" lived. "They" being LA PC–speak for People of Color.

The Impellatieri home boasted five bedrooms, a den, a swimming pool, a cabana, a billiards room, a formal dining room with fireplace and an elegant living room, all of which he bought half a dozen years ago for less than half a million. That was the beauty of LA, he thought: letting other people's prejudices make you a fortune in real estate. The next thing you knew, houses in Echo Park would be hot again.

What a world, thought Eddie, kicking off his shoes and stumbling into bed. From Edwardsville he had traveled by car to a private airfield near Springfield, then flew to North Carolina to file his report with Xe and fill out the paperwork to get his men paid directly into their offshore bank accounts. He had caught the first commercial flight out this morning and so was back in LA by noon and home by one.

The pillow still smelled like Diane.

He grabbed the remote, to see what the cables were saying about Edwardsville. Sure enough, they were still running with the "Aftermath of the Tragedy" logos — these days, direct, murderous assaults on Americans were called "tragedies" instead of "acts of war" — interviews with the parents of the school kids, the local cops, even a clown or two from the FBI, whose pride was mixed with the egg on their faces from the explosion. He punched up the volume a couple of notches:

"We believe these were home-grown terrorists," said a man identified as Leslie P. Waters, the special agent-in-charge for the St. Louis area. "Notwithstanding the allusions to Allah, etcetera, at this time there is no evidence that this was anything other than a . . ."

Right, thought Eddie, hitting the mute button. He supposed that the ability to make asinine weasel statements were part of the training at Quantico these days, but in this case he could cut Leslie P. Waters some slack, since there was no way anybody associated with "Tom Powers" was going to get fingered. Operational security in a Powers operation came before everything.

Although Eddie worked at his instruction, he had complete latitude in putting together his team. He had a few rules: no two men from the same past military unit at the same time, no two men with the same specialty, nobody except service members or those who had passed through Xe's rigorous training program in North Carolina. Xe had come in for a lot of heat since the Iraq War, but it was still the go-to protective service of choice for Republicans, Democrats, and journalists alike — those who wanted to live, anyway.

Still, there was something about the Edwardsville operation that was nagging him. He couldn't quite put his finger on it, but the very fact that the operation had not been a complete success very nearly meant that it was a total failure. Not only in his eyes but, he was sure, in Tom Powers's eyes as well. It wasn't that the school assault itself was that surprising — hell, the government had been worrying about a Beslan copycat for years. It was that everything had gone so well, and yet ended so badly. He had never known Powers to fuck up like that, and it made him wonder. Wonder if Powers was slipping, wonder if their team somehow got compromised, wonder if something else, something he couldn't see but only sense, was going on beneath the surface of an apparent terrorist operation.

Oh, well, plenty of time to hash that over when he was rested . . .

Sometimes, just before he fell asleep, he would think back to his days with the 160th. Although he rarely got behind the controls of a chopper these days, the gift of flight was still in his fingertips, and no matter how much the technology changed and evolved, his natural affinity for the soaring birds had not.

He left the tube on as he soared over, not rafted down, the River Lethe. His last memory was kissing Diane and Jade a little harder than normal, which hours later after uneasy slumber, he realized was just about the only thing he had done right.

CHAPTER TWENTY-NINE

Camp David, Maryland

If you were going to liquidate somebody, reflected Devlin, you couldn't pick a better place than Camp David. For one thing, despite its deceptively idyllic mountain location in the Catoctins, its real name was Naval Support Facility Thurmont, with every sailor in the place, including the kitchen staff, boasting a "Yankee White" DoD security clearance — the highest available for this kind of duty. What happened at Camp David stayed at Camp David.

For another, it was guarded by an elite unit that even Devlin had to admire, the MSC-CD. This unit, whose acronym stood for Marine Security Company — Camp David, was the best the Corps had to offer, highly screened infantrymen hand-picked for training at the Marine Corps Security Forces School in Chesapeake, Virginia. Camp David was 125 lethal acres of high-security rustication. FDR had dubbed it "Shangri-La," a name later downgraded to Camp David by Ike, in honor of his grandson.

Devlin had forsaken all thoughts of monkey business straightaway. You came to Camp David and you took your medicine like a man. With Seelye, he normally insisted on as many security protocols as possible, but in a rural retreat with a handful of cabins and a whole lot of patrolled woods, there really wasn't any place for him to hide.

He entered the camp using one of his false identities, this one proclaiming him to be a ship's carpenter with a "Yankee White" clearance, which Seelye had determined was one of the two job openings on the base at the moment, the other being a gardener. As he passed through the gates, his practiced eye took in the myriad security cameras and other surveillance devices, not to mention the camouflaged Marines lurking just beyond the visible perimeter. Camp David was only sixty miles from Washington, not far from Gettysburg, and not exactly the biggest secret in the world, so many were the nutbags who packed their cars full of ammo and explosives and motored on up to see if the POTUS hunting was good that day. Some of them were detained until they sobered up, some of them arrested, and the worst of them sent off to prisons in Colorado and North Carolina for a very long time. A few of them were even shot, although their death certificates later read "automobile crash" or "hunting accident" or, his favorite, "domestic altercation."

In the past decade, since September 11, security had been ratcheted up to a whole new level. It took only a couple of would-be car bombers for the government to revamp its watch list from "good ole boys with a snootful" to "armed moonbats/wingnuts" and "full-throttle jihadis." While there was still a certain amount of on-site triangulation, nobody thought a goober with a gun was particularly funny any more, and as for Dinesh from Dearborn, he quickly found himself on a plane to a very nasty Egyptian prison, or pushing up daisies, or both.

The thermal scanners, both ground-based and aerial, were just the beginning. The one at the main gate, whose presence was obvious to anybody, also doubled as an X-ray machine with the power of a CAT scanner. Radiation detectors were stationed at viable intervals along every roadway and pathway; a miscreant didn't actually have to have anything nuclear on his person for him to be detected, he just had to have been, once upon a time, within kissing distance of any such device, whether suitcase-nuke or dirty bomb. The Marine guards surveyed everyone with the same dead-eyed suspicion, their trigger fingers transparently itchy (to him, at least), which is something he understood; if you were going to catch this shit-ass bucolic duty, waiting for the president to kick back or, worse, entertain some scum-sucking bottom-feeder of a foreign potentate, you might as well be ready to party if and when the time came.

Seelye was waiting for him just beyond the main gate. "Trouble?"

"Not today, thanks," he replied, trying to sort out his feelings.

They rarely saw each other, which was fine by both of them. If Seelye had drawn this up on the blackboard back in 1985, it couldn't have turned out better for him, or worse for Devlin. The man who had made a whore of his mother and a cuckold out of his father, and who had inadvertently gotten both of them killed. The man who had brought Devlin back to life as someone he was not, re-created him, trained him to become . . .

To become what he was. Whatever that was.

Many were the times he'd thought of

simply killing Seelye and getting the whole farce over with. With a gun, a knife, an ashtray, a fireplace poker, a shattered beer bottle, his bare hands, Colonel Mustard in the Parlor with the Lead Pipe. The thing could be done in moments, and either he would die in a hail of retaliatory gunfire, or be beaten into submission and arrested, or be given a medal and sent into well-deserved retirement. It didn't matter. It was a way out.

"The president's very much looking forward to meeting you," Seelye was saying.

"Unfortunately, the feeling is very much not mutual."

"Come on, he's the president."

"Which means he's the guy I don't want to meet. I don't serve the man, Army, I serve the office. Better to imagine an empty suit than a man. Less disgusting too considering some of the men."

Army smiled inwardly; Devlin had not lost his edge. "And an empty suit is precisely who you're about to meet. So keep a civil tongue in your head, answer his questions, take your orders, and leave."

"This was never part of our deal, Army. No face-to-face. Bulletproof deniability. What does he want?"

Seelye didn't look at him. He hardly ever

looked at him, even when Devlin was a kid. "He wants to see the man who saved all those middle-American schoolchildren from a bunch of ruthless terrorists. After all, 'the children' —"

" '— are our future.' "

"Something like that. Hey, it wins elections."

"Is it going to win the next election?"

"Here we are."

They were at Aspen Lodge, the presidential retreat. Dogwood, Maple, Holly, Birch, Rosebud — they were for visitors. Aspen was where the Big He lived.

"I don't like it."

"Then that makes you a minority of one," said Seelye, ushering him through the door. "Churchill sure did. Sadat as well."

"Look what happened to him," said Devlin.

"Through those doors," said Seelye, pointing ahead.

It was just cool enough outside for the walk-in fireplace to be roaring, consuming vast quantities of maple, birch, holly, dogwood, and aspen. Jeb Tyler was wearing a cardigan and an ascot. He was standing, framed against the fireplace, as they entered. "This must be —"

He caught himself and didn't mention

Devlin's name, as he'd been briefed by Seelye not to do. "I thought you'd be taller." The president didn't offer his hand and neither did Devlin.

"I try to be, sir," replied Devlin.

Tyler didn't get the joke or the reference, as his expression showed.

"Doghouse Reilly. You know, Bogart? *The Big Sleep?*"

"The president doesn't waste his time with movies —" suggested Seelye, throwing Tyler a lifeline.

He didn't take it. "Loved that new *Batman* movie. Why doesn't NSA have gadgets and gizmos like that?"

"It's an honor to meet you, sir," lied Devlin. "I'm sure the affairs of state must keep you very busy, so we should be brief."

Tyler stood there with his famous smile frozen on his face. He thought he'd just been insulted, but he wasn't sure. "Please sit down. Drink?"

"No thank you, sir," replied Devlin, hitting the cushions. He figured that the faster he sat the quicker he could get up and out again, if he played his cards right. Unfortunately, he was holding a busted flush, nine-high. Still, he'd won with worse.

"I gather that there's only one child missing —"

Tyler got that look on his face that he saved for all discussions of dead or dying kids. "And feared dead. The blast —"

"The blast didn't kill her, sir." You weren't supposed to interrupt the president, but Devlin didn't see what he had to lose, and pressed his advantage. "We tracked all the warm bodies with infrared before the assault, and only one kid was moved into the school proper. If she was there, she'd still be alive."

Tyler was knocked off his game, but only just a little. He was, after all, a politician. "Cleanup teams scoured the place. No sign of her."

"Then he took her with him. I don't know why and I don't want to think about why, but —"

"Who's 'he'? The man who tried to get away in the chopper?" Nice — Tyler was smarter than Devlin had expected.

"Which I shot down, yes, sir."

"Then you might have killed her."

"I might have, but I didn't."

"How do you know? The helicopter went down, killing the —"

"Killing the pilot, yes, sir. Who was expendable."

"So how did —"

"Milverton, sir."

275

Devlin heard Seelye gasp. Just a brief intake of breath, but as telling as if he'd just socked him in the gut. There — that cat was out of the bag and pissing on the table.

"I don't understand," said President Tyler, but Seelye was already punching up Milverton on his PDA.

"Charles Augustus Milverton, Mr. President," said Seelye. "Not his real name, of course. 'The most dangerous man in London,' he likes to call himself. Most dangerous man in the world, or one of them, is more like it."

"I don't care what he calls himself. I call him dead," said President Tyler.

"Working on it, sir," said Devlin, realizing he'd just been handed a stay of execution, thanks to a little girl.

"Do it," said Tyler. He got up and threw another log on the fire. One of the Marine sergeants would have done it, but the famously populist president snatched the birch log away from him and did the deed himself. "I don't give a shit how you do it. Just get him."

"It will be a real pleasure," said Devlin.

Tyler turned, offering his hands to the Marine sergeant to wipe them off with a clean handkerchief. "Mr. Devlin, you said something to me over the phone about this being a misdirection. A feint, you called it. Is that still your considered opinion?"

"Yes, sir, it is."

"So you think there's more to come?"

"I don't see why not. Even if we take what happened at face value, which we shouldn't —"

"Tell that to the people of Edwardsville —"

"Yes, sir. But even if we do, then they didn't get a thing that they ostensibly wanted. Unless Edwardsville was a very elaborate way of snatching one kid, which is obviously ridiculous. Which means either they'll try again to get what they say they want, or — and this is what I've thought all along — it was a probe, to test our defenses. Which is why, one way or another, something else wicked this way comes."

President Tyler thought for a moment. "How much time have we got?"

Devlin answered: "Assume none, if they're doing it right."

The president turned to Seelye. "Army, I want you to give Devlin all assistance, carte fucking blanche, to get this Milverton. No matter where the trail leads, no matter whose dicks get caught in the wringer, I want this man found, braced, grilled. I want his fucking head on a pike, and I want it

ASAP. Top priority."

"Yes, sir," said Seelye.

"Failure is not an option. I want to know everything about this guy, including the names of his twelve best friends. I want to know whether this goes higher up the food chain, and if it does who's the son of a bitch behind this whole thing. Fail me, and it's your ass." He looked at Devlin, as if for the first time. "You read me?"

Devlin decided to play his wild card. "I can name at least one of them for you right now. But you might not want to hear it."

Tyler was fast and he was sharp. "Do you suspect someone in my administration?" Devlin's estimation of him improved on the spot.

"Mr. President, I'd be lying to you if I didn't say that I'm more than a little disturbed that knowledge of my existence has leaked beyond the inner circle. Especially since you're the leak."

Devlin waited for the nearly obligatory "how dare you?" speech as Tyler's famously short fuse went off. But it never came. Devlin glanced over at Seelye, who wasn't going to like this part. "On my own initiative, I cast a wide-net intercept flag in the Washington area on the telephones lines, cell and hard, all e-mail, text, and other PDA traffic as well."

"And what did you find?" asked the President, impatiently.

"I found exactly one anomaly. The chairman of the Senate Intelligence Committee —"

"Bob Hartley?" exclaimed the president.

"Yes, sir. The man who was in the Oval Office with you yesterday when my name came up. That's who it was, wasn't it?" The president chose not to answer, so Devlin took that as a yes and continued. "Last night, he made a call to a local number —"

"So?" Tyler was starting to lose it.

"— to a Washington number that does not exist. It's a cutout, with how many bounces I don't know yet. I've traced it as far as Los Angeles, but it may not end there. Whoever gave him that number thinks his secret is safe, but he doesn't know that we're smarter than he is."

"What was this call about?"

"Nothing. No connection was made. I think it was a dry run."

"Why? Do you think the next attack could come in LA?"

"I have no idea. But it's a good place to start."

"Dismissed, sailor," said the president.

There was an unmarked car waiting at the

gate. Seelye nodded in its direction. "Can I give you a lift?"

"I had a car here somewhere," said Devlin.

" 'I had to crash that Honda, honey,' " replied Seelye, doing a passable imitation of Bruce Willis's character Butch in *Pulp Fiction.* "In fact, it's already pulped. It's sleeping peacefully with Jimmy Hoffa somewhere in Pennsylvania. Just in case Milverton is in your shorts."

Did he suspect something? Did he know something? Seelye knew perfectly well that made Branch 4 agents were soon dead Branch 4 agents, and the thought had occurred to Devlin that Seelye's life would be so much easier once he was finally rid of his long-ago lover's inconvenient son.

Seelye closed the door and pounded on the trunk twice, the signal for the driver to get a move on. Then he changed his mind, rapped on the window. Devlin rolled down his window, making sure that the partition between him and the driver was securely in place.

Seelye leaned through the window and asked, "How come you never call me 'Dad'?"

CHAPTER
THIRTY

Washington, D.C.

Hartley lay on his bed, shaking. He couldn't believe what had happened, couldn't believe what was about to happen. He had to get control of himself, calm down. Nothing was ever quite as bad as it seemed, not even this.

Well, maybe this.

Thank God the phone stopped ringing. The damn thing had been ringing all morning, his cell phone too. He knew it was the White House, which meant it was the president, which meant that sooner or later he was going to have to answer or else they'd send the Secret Service over to his flat to find out if he was okay. And, at this point, he was very fucking far from okay, and the Secret Service were the last people who needed to know just how far from okay everything really was.

The pizza boy was still there. That poor fellow wasn't going anywhere, not of his own volition, and part of Senator Hartley's problem at this moment was to figure just how and when to make him disappear. His unwelcome visitor had gone through the boy's pockets after the murder and told him that the escort service had deliberately set Hartley up and would have exposed him to one of the supermarket tabloids or cable TV, so in a sense the stranger had done him a favor. Still, the corpse in his flat was the least of his worries right now; his nocturnal visitor was going to help Hartley with that, assuming he played ball on the main request.

Which had been, for him, relatively easy. Thank God and the Founding Fathers for civilian oversight of the military. And for access to certain files.

As Balzac once said, behind every great fortune is a great crime, and if Hartley played his cards right, he could wind up with everything — money, power, glory. Already there were stocks, rather a lot of them, that he was to sell short today, very short, and he was encouraged to spread the word to select individuals, corporate managers, defense contractors, and pension-fund bosses of his acquaintance — very discreetly — that rolling back their exposure to certain things, immediately if not sooner, would pay huge dividends. Besides, the man had assured him that no one would be thinking about insider trading in twenty-four hours, but that the political opportunities that were about to open up for a man of Senator Hartley's perspicacity and intelligence were, literally, invaluable.

So Hartley had made all the phone calls, placed all the bets. The man had given him the number of what he said was a Swiss bank account to finance his transactions, and sure enough they had all gone through smoothly. Now it was time to make that one last phone call, to the number the man had given him, and the die was cast.

He dialed it.

Instead of an answer, he heard a series of clicks, like back in the old days when phones clicked instead of beeped as they ordered up a connection. The clicks stopped, replaced temporarily by silence, then a loud buzzing sound, as if a fax machine had picked up the line. He hung up. What the hell was going on?

He rose and looked out the window. He needed some air, so he stepped onto the balcony. Almost immediately, he was sorry he did. He could hear police sirens, approaching.

Hartley darted back inside, closed the

plate-glass picture window, and pulled the curtains. His nerves were shot. Police sirens were always sounding in Washington, as in any big city. He thought about pouring himself a drink, but decided against it.

He padded back over to the window, parted the curtains, and looked down at the street. Nothing. See? He was letting his imagination run away with him. He looked at the phone in his hand and hit redial.

No clicks or noises — the connection went straight through. This time, a voice answered. It may or may not have been the same as his visitor's, he couldn't tell.

Hartley gave the man the information his visitor had demanded.

"I'm glad you're seeing things . . . our way, Senator," said the voice. Hartley realized that it was scrambled, disguising both the timbre and the accent of the speaker; that was why he couldn't recognize it. "Look out the window."

Two police cars were pulling up to the building's service entrance.

"Don't worry about the police, Senator. As long as you cooperate with us, they'll sit tight. But if you fuck up, they'll be at your door to investigate a report of a murder, and the next call you make will be to your lawyer. Understand?"

Hartley nodded dumbly.

"I can't hear you."

"Yes, I understand."

"Well done," the voice at the other end of the line said. "Now sit tight and await further instructions." The fax-machine blast again, followed by the clicks. In his surprise and fear, Hartley dropped the phone, which bounced and settled on the sofa. He was still wondering what to do when there was a knock on the door.

He practically sprinted over and peered through the peephole. Two men in business suits. Hotel security. "What do you want?" he croaked.

"Routine security check," came a voice from the other side. Hartley glanced behind him to make sure the bedroom door was closed and nothing untoward or suspicious was visible.

He opened the door a crack. No sooner had he done so when one of the men flashed a badge and pushed his way past him, followed by his partner, who shut the door and locked it.

"Who are you?" gasped Hartley.

"Don't worry," said the lead man. "We're from the government, and we're here to help."

One of them — the bigger, beefier fellow

285

— headed straight for the bedroom, while his smaller partner, a whippet, just stood there, staring at him.

"Nice," said the voice from the bedroom. "Houston, I would say we have a situation here."

The Whippet smiled. "Ain't that a kick in the head." He looked at Hartley. "Sit down, Senator. The president's been worried about you."

"And now we know why," said the Refrigerator behind him.

Hartley sat, his mind racing. He knew he was in a lot of trouble, but after all he hadn't killed the pizza boy. They could take paraffin tests or whatever more sophisticated procedures they were using these days, which would surely show he hadn't fired a weapon. He could explain everything.

"Two pops in the head with this baby." Hartley turned to see the Refrigerator holding up the gun. "Pro job — nice shooting, Senator."

"Senator Hartley," said Whippet. "I'm not going to fuck around with you. Unless you play ball with us, not only is your political career over, not only are you going to jail for the rest of your life, but your good friend from across the aisle, Jeb Tyler, is going to be heartbroken. At a time of national crisis and peril, to lose one of his closest and most trusted advisors, with an election coming up . . . well, I'm sure you agree that this unfortunate incident couldn't possibly have come at a worse time. Which is why he'll feed you to the dogs."

Hartley nodded dully. "Am I under arrest?" he asked.

"I wouldn't exactly call it arrest," said the Refrigerator.

"More like day care," said the Whippet.

"It'll be fun," said the Refrigerator. "We can bunk down out here."

"Just the three of us," said the Whippet.

"Four of us," reminded the Refrigerator. "Until your playmate gets back in touch with you or the Boss says otherwise."

"No, you can't mean . . ." shouted Hartley as the implications sank in. "Not that."

The Whippet smiled. "I'd think about it twice if I were you," he said.

Hartley was about to protest that he *was* thinking about it when he felt the snub nose of the .22 pressed up against the back of his head.

"In fact," said the Refrigerator behind him, "I'd think about it twenty-two times."

CHAPTER
THIRTY-ONE

Falls Church

They were waiting for him by the time he got back from Camp David. The unmarked government car had dropped him at a Washington Metro station, and he had made it home from there, covering the last bit on foot.

From the outside, everything seemed all right. But Devlin knew it wasn't. To a man living in the shadows, the smallest speck of light is like a laser beam: the front curtains were ever so slightly wrong.

Devlin had multiple ways into his house, but he needed to know the right one.

He took out his car keys, held down the alarm button, and punched the unlock button. That relayed the house's interior security CCTV feed to his BlackBerry.

Front hall, side hall, LR, DR . . . empty. So far so good. But he still didn't like it. Second floor. Empty BR. His private study was locked and unmolested. That told him something right there: *these guys know enough not to touch it.*

He had no idea who they were, but it almost didn't matter: two makes in two days was double-plus ungood. Somehow, somebody had gotten hold of his private address. Or somebody with access had leaked it. Same difference.

He punched another button — the trunk lock, followed in quick succession by two clicks on the lock button. That activated the 180-degree infrared scanner, which would give him a rough look at the interior. If their hearts were beating, he'd see them.

There — three of them, one on the first floor and two on the second. Under the circumstances, the cellar door was the best way. He pressed the code on his house keys and it silently slid aside. There was a pair of infra-red goggles hanging on a hook in the darkness by the door. He grabbed them and put them on. He also took off his shoes.

Weapons: inside each of his back pockets he slipped throwing knives, and slid a K-Bar knife in its scabbard down the back of his jeans. Under each armpit he placed twin Glock 37s, with a pair of Colt .38s revolvers in special pockets sewn into the front of his jeans. A concussion grenade rounded out his ensemble.

There was what looked like a light switch at the top of the basement stairs. And it was. But if you moved it from side to side in a Morse Code pattern that spelled out his real middle name, it opened the door into the interior of the house. And then it temporarily disabled every electrical system except those on batteries.

He was inside, in the dark, where only he could see.

The man on the ground floor had his back to him, and that's the way he died, Devlin's K-Bar slipping easily between his ribs and puncturing his heart. It was a nice, clean kill, no sound, only instant death. Devlin wondered briefly if he knew the guy; he cared not at all whether he had a family. Everybody had a family, except for him.

Now — *fast.* Up the stairs, pulling the grenade, arming it, tossing it. The phosphorescent flash would temporarily blind them. He was, once more, the Angel of Death, deputized by God to decide which of his two visitors would live, however temporarily, and which would die.

As every soldier knew, time slows down in hand-to-hand combat even as it moves at warp speed. Man One had fallen to his knees, grabbing his eyes, so Devlin shot him in the head — no sense wasting a bullet on a Kevlar vest — and moved on to Man Two.

Not immediately visible, but it didn't matter. He'd be where, for some reason, they always tried to hide. The bathroom. Pressing another button on his keys, Devlin activated all the interior door locks. Then he hit the gas. Each of the rooms in the house was equipped with nerve gas, hidden behind the green eye of the smoke detectors. It disabled the person but kept him alive and conscious, and able to talk. Most of the time.

He heard the sound of a body falling. Gun drawn, he unlocked and opened the door and shot the person inside through both legs.

There was no sense of triumph, or even of exhilaration, as he stepped through the doorway. If you had measured his pulse and heart rate, they would both have been near normal. Emotionally, he was entirely unaffected. He was just doing what they had trained him to do. What Seelye had trained him to do.

Even before he got the mask off her, Devlin knew it was a woman. There was political correctness for you — putting a woman on a clean team. Somebody's daughter for sure; somebody's sister, very likely; maybe even somebody's mother.

"Who are you?" she gasped through her pain. The question caught him up short. If this were a team from CSS, they would have known.

"How did you get in?" he asked, lowering his weapon. Instead of answering, she went for her gun. This time, he shot her in both forearms. A spunky little thing, he had to give her that, and putting up a better fight than her dead male colleagues. "How?"

The pain must have been excruciating, but she wasn't letting on. Instead, she was fading out, and Devlin hoped he hadn't hit an artery. "FBI," she said. "You're under arrest."

He ripped open her vest and found her badge. It was real. Then he saw all the blood, pooling under her body. It too was real, and as he'd feared: one of his leg shots had severed a femoral artery.

"On suspicion . . ." Her eyes started to roll. He was losing her.

He cradled her head in his arms. "Okay, you got me," he said. "I'm your prisoner. What's the charge?"

"Terrorism," she whispered.

"I confess. Who ratted me out?"

She smiled at him, grateful. "That's classified," she said, and died.

He laid her to rest gently on the bathroom floor. His mind raced, trying to come up with a working hypothesis. A Branch 4 op would have just taken him out, not tried to arrest him. But the FBI — what the hell did they have to do with this? And how did they get into his house, or even know where it was?

The female special agent's last word: terrorism. Somebody had fingered him for Edwardsville. There was only one person who knew him by sight at Edwardsville: Milverton. Somebody had hacked his file at NSA. There were only a handful of people who could do that. One of them he knew personally. Two of them he knew by sight. Three of them he knew by their offices. Which left one more person: Hartley. Devlin was suddenly glad he had dropped the dime on him to the president. He wasn't authorized to conduct assassinations of duly elected American officials, and he hoped to hell his newfound respect for Tyler extended to the man's sense of political self-preservation. Tyler may or may not be the secular saint or the blithering idiot his friends and foes made him out to be, but he was one very smart politician, and he hadn't come this far because his instincts were mostly wrong.

Of course, just because Hartley had been

added to the loop didn't actually rule out any of the others. There might be a connection elsewhere. And if there was, then everything was a lie — the law, the Congress, the president, the whole damn United States of America. Everything that he had been raised to believe in, to live for, to fight for, to die for . . . a lie. A fixed fight, a gambler's racket, a sucker's game.

He sent the computers into lockdown/self-destruct mode; if anyone tried to access them, all data, right down to the keystroke loggers, would be destroyed. It would not be lost — he had mirrored sites at Internet dead drops all over the world, but he would not have the same ease of access to the material. Still, it would have to do for now.

He grabbed only what was necessary: the books his father gave him and the picture of himself and his parents in Rome.

He set the charges on the house. If anyone besides himself tried to enter, the whole place would implode in a controlled demolition. If the clean team really was FBI, he might be able to get Seelye to make sure everybody left the site alone, and down the institutional memory hole it would go. Still, he'd probably never go back there to live again.

If he was going to put a full-court press

on Milverton, he needed help. He needed somebody he could trust to do the job right. There was only one such person he trusted. Maybe the time had come at last for a meeting. For he was already formulating a hypothesis. That the Edwardsville school operation had been a feint he had long been certain. It was a jab, a softening blow, to set up the knockout punch that would come at the end of a series of combinations, each of which would stagger the country a little more until finally it fell over.

Devlin punched up Eddie's number, and waited. The cutouts worked smoothly, the line rang. And rang. And rang. No answer. Damn.

He knew Eddie had a family, had a little girl he adored, supposed he was out right this minute with her and her mother, doing the things family men who could afford to turn off their cell phones actually did. Sometimes, in fact, he wondered why Eddie stayed on this job, in this racket, when he had so much more to live for than, say, Devlin himself did. A little girl . . .

He wondered what it felt like to have a little girl. To have a creature he could unconditionally love, and who would love him back because she didn't know any better, who didn't ask anything from him except unconditional love. He probably would never know.

He tried again, this time on Eddie's secure hot line. Family or no family, this was no time for fucking around.

Same result: no answer. Where the hell was he, anyway? He decided to leave a message: "Whaddya know, whaddya say?" Eddie would know what it meant, what level of security he would need to use to get in touch with Devlin and, most important of all, just how damn urgent this thing was getting.

There was a flight leaving from Dulles to LA soon, and he was already booked on it. He'd dispose of the bodies along the way. He felt bad about the woman, but she was part of the job.

CHAPTER
THIRTY-TWO

Los Angeles

The fountain was dancing and Dean Martin was singing about the moon hitting your eye like a big pizza pie. The Asian tourists were cell-phoning photos of themselves back to Taipei and Tokyo. The chubby Latina girls with the tramp stamps above their ample muffin tops pretended not to notice as the rich Iranian girls — some of them headscarved, most not — waltzed by in wolf packs, radiating fuck-you wealthy. The trolley line was returning to the station, over by Abercrombie and Fitch. Diane and Jade were in the Apple store when it happened.

Later, investigators determined that the device had been hidden at the bottom of the fountain pool, with a trigger mechanism set to blow on the thirteenth time Dino sang the words "that's *amore.*" It was the most popular song at the busiest time of day, and the perps were practically guaranteed a large audience, nearly all of whom were facing the waving fountains, delighting in the synchronicity of the music, the water, and the perfect southern California weather.

The bomb was a fairly typical, albeit extremely powerful IED, a roadside bomb from Baghdad with a college degree. It had also been packed with shrapnel of almost every kind that could be purchased in any hardware store: nails, ball bearings, broken glass, screws, which caused the initial fatalities at the blast site. Worse, it had been augmented with radioactive hospital waste in an attempt to fashion a crude "dirty bomb."

The shock waves and debris radiated out, accompanied by a wall of contaminated water, tearing through the giant movie theater, blowing Nordstrom's to rubble, imploding the plate-glass windows of the Apple Store and the Barnes & Noble bookstore, splashing across Third Street to contaminate Park La Brea and the Palazzo, demolishing the Farmer's Market to the west and pancaking the huge parking structure directly to the north. In the aftermath, about the only thing left within the blast radius relatively unscathed was the Pan-Pacific Park to the east, and that only because much of it was below street level.

Diane and Jade were at the back of the store, on the upper level, when the blast hit. They had just bought Jade's new laptop and were getting her old files transferred at the geek desk when it happened.

The plate-glass windows at the front of the store blew inward, killing or maiming almost everybody. The upper floor was better sheltered, especially at the back. The tech guy was decapitated by a window shard, but Jade was short, and Diane had just bent down to pick her change purse off the floor when suddenly she was slammed against the side of the counter, then propelled through it.

Jade was slammed back into the counter as well, but the impact of her mother's body had torn it from its moorings, and so Jade was shoved along by the shock wave, through the space where the counter had stood and into the wall. Shelving came crashing down around her, and then a body, which is what saved her life. When they found her, unconscious but still alive, the shelves surrounding her were tattooed with shrapnel.

Diane was not so lucky. Even though she had taken the brunt of the blast, even with her skull fractured, she was able to reach for her daughter, grasp her hand, and then collapse on top of her as the wave of metal ripped through what was left of the store. Each screw, each nail tore through her body in that painless way that only the most grievous wounds can inflict, and she might even have survived had she not turned her head toward Jade one last time, as a ball bearing took out her left eye and exploded through the back of her head.

Diane was already dead when she fell across her daughter, still shielding her in death, her body warm as her child embraced it, but lying still, so very still, as the building collapsed around them. Jade couldn't move, and couldn't see much. Just the headless body of the tech guy, as the world went to hell and the fountains stopped dancing and Dino stopped singing and the moon hit your eye . . .

The head was staring right at her, the eyes wide open in the astonishment of sudden death. She had just enough strength to reach out and brush it away; it wobbled like a pumpkin on a splayed, bloody axis, then spun, rolled and tipped over.

"Mom?" she said. "Mama?"

Everything was really quiet. Those might be screams in the distance, and those might be moans closer by, but she couldn't tell;

her ears were still ringing. After what seemed forever, she realized that the distant screams were sirens, and that the sirens were getting louder.

There was something heavy and unmoving lying across her. Her mother, she knew, was also nearby. It took her a while to figure out that the two things were one and same.

Jade struggled a bit, then managed to slip out from beneath Diane. Death has no emotional meaning to a child of Jade's age, other than as an abstract concept, and so in her mind it was perfectly possible for her mother to be both dead and with her at the same time. Diane's face was turned away from Jade, but the back of her head was missing. That was the worst part. That was how, in her stunned and bloody state, she knew.

"Mama," she said trying to turn her mother's face to hers. "Mama?"

Aside from the missing eye, it was her mother's face, the face she knew and loved so well and so much. Whatever the wounds Diane had endured — the autopsy report would later show that she was hit by eighteen separate pieces of bomb shrapnel, shattered glass, and assorted other objects demolished in the blast's progression from fountain to store — they had come so fast and so furiously that she would have had almost no time to really suffer. She would have died knowing that she still held her little girl in her arms, that she could still protect her, and that, no matter the evil that men could fashion, she was still her mother.

CHAPTER
THIRTY-THREE

London, England

Emanuel Skorzeny and Paul Pilier had checked into the same hotel, the Savoy, but under different pseudonyms. In general, Skorzeny preferred never to alert either the authorities or the media to his presence in their countries. In the U.K., there had been that little bother over some insider-trading allegations a few years back, which had engendered a considerable amount of ill-will toward him until the Skorzeny Foundation suddenly found several high-profile projects on which to lavish equally high-profile support, and then the prime minister had embraced him on camera.

Still, to avoid the undue scrutiny of the Fleet Street paparazzi, they had taken the Chunnel, where they could spend the half-hour trip under the English Channel in the comfort of Skorzeny's new Jaguar XJ Portfolio, then motor their way to London from

Folkestone.

The Skorzeny Foundation could be found in the forefront of nearly every fashionable cause; from Darfur to land mines to female genital circumcision, there was hardly a position it took that did not meet with the enthusiastic approval of the editorial board of the *New York Times.* It supported renewable resources, delivered home heating oil to the poor at affordable prices, and generously funded medical research.

Through its Skorzeny Fellowships, the Foundation observed, monitored, and selected for advancement the brightest young minds in the countries — mostly the United States and Europe — where it bestowed its largesse. Without ever learning the source of their good fortune, since the scholarships were administered through a silent network of culturally sympathetic operatives, each supported by the Foundation in their roles as talent scouts, the young people "won" scholarships to the best prep schools and/or top universities in their respective countries. It was a little like the MacArthur Foundation's "genius" grants, but with an entirely different purpose in mind: not the advancement of art, but the advancement of a certain political point of view, one long and fervently held since the appearance of *Das*

Kapital: social justice.

Finally, but equally important, the Foundation actively supported politicians it found praiseworthy, funneling the money through a series of cut-outs and 527s, bundling where appropriate; in short, doing whatever it took to maintain its tax-exempt status in the United States while still affecting the outcome of every election that it possibly could.

Although the Foundation was headquartered in London, the United States was the principal focus of its activities. Emanuel Skorzeny had long taken a keen interest in the world's largest economy and even after the advent of the European Union and its currency, the euro, he maintained his fixation on America.

Not that he would ever live there, of course. He found the people too common; he found the pop culture too vulgar when it was not downright disgusting; he found the food unhealthy, hormonal, and inedible. True, Old Europe was not what it used to be, but that was one of the things that Skorzeny liked about it. It was changing, right before his eyes and under the noses of everyone living there, a boiling frog happily swimming in a lukewarm bath that would slowly and very surely gradually grow warmer and warmer. He both mourned and celebrated its oncoming demise, determined both to hasten it and to profit from it before he too had to shuffle off the stage and into infinite blackness.

It was the task for which he had been chosen.

Emanuel Skorzeny had seen and experienced too much of life either to believe or disbelieve in God, and he was pleased and proud that so many others were beginning to see it his way. There had been a raft of books and television programs not only proclaiming the death of God but disputing whether he even existed at all; agnosticism was the way forward, not atheism. Skorzeny believe in hedging his bets when necessary.

Many of these books and programs were published by publishing houses in which Skorzeny maintained a sizable equity position. Some of the television programs had been underwritten by the Foundation via various ad hoc production companies. The empty cathedrals of France, the abandoned churches of Britain — these things were testimonials to the power of his ideas. He was, in his own mind, the modern incarnation of both Voltaire and Louis XV.

One of the phone extensions in the fifth-floor river suite buzzed. "Sir?" said Pilier, "your guest is here."

Skorzeny rose and pulled on a smoking jacket. He didn't smoke, but it was the sort of thing one wore in the Savoy when receiving visitors. As he moved toward the door he switched on the television and saw that the New York Stock Exchange was cratering. Then he opened the door.

It was she. "Good day, Miss Harrington," he said, ushering her in.

Amanda Harrington kissed him lightly on both cheeks as she breezed past him in a rustle of silk and a zephyr of expensive perfume. There was, alas, nothing overtly affectionate about her greeting, just good manners and good breeding. After all, they had seen each other last night and had much urgent business to discuss.

"I thought you'd never ask," she said, reclining unbidden on the sofa in the suite's plush living room.

Skorzeny forgave Amanda sins that others would have to pay for. He walked to the bar, which was always stocked to his order, and poured Amanda a drink. It was one of the many ways in which this impossibly poised woman was a throwback to the great beauties of the 1940s and 1950s. Unless she was swimming, riding, or playing tennis, she never wore anything other than dresses and proper shoes. She had her hair immaculately done up every day. She never used a four-letter word, nor suffered one to be used in her presence. There was not a single tattoo on her glorious body. She would, he knew, have one drink and then get down to business, or brass tacks, depending.

Indeed, Skorzeny knew, the only flaw in her life was her inability to have a child. In that respect, she resembled the majority of her European sisters: resigned to sacrificing the Continent's future to the immigrant hordes, in order to savor their Pyrrhic victory over the patriarchy.

Skorzeny handed her a shaken, ice-cold gin martini and stepped back to admire her as she took the first sip. Really, she was magnificent. She was the only woman in the world on whom he would gladly wait.

"When did you hear?" she asked.

"Just now," he said.

"Luckily," she said, "I've come prepared."

One of Amanda's few concessions to modernity was the array of electronic gadgets she habitually carried with her. As one of London's most successful stockbrokers, she had worked her way to the top of the heap at the firm of Islay Partnership, Ltd., living proof that London's reclaiming the title of the world's financial capital was no mere jingoistic, John Bull dream. She worked all of the hours that she was not sleeping, but she did so without ever calling attention to the fact. In her professional life, as in everything else, she was the very soul of discretion.

That was why he had snatched her away from Islay and made her as chairman of the board of Skorzeny Foundation. That, and one other thing: her impossible beauty. Amanda Harrington was the kind of woman that not even his money could buy, which was why he kept trying. Emanuel Skorzeny had never met anyone he couldn't purchase, or at least lease, and he was not about to break his unblemished record now.

She laid the instruments out on the table, occasionally flicking an eye at the running stock tables on the Sky News ticker. Still sipping on her martini, she punched in instructions on her battery of BlackBerrys, and at one point had not one but two cell phones working; there was something distinctly comic about her holding each of them to a separate ear as she talked, but Skorzeny was too much of a gentleman to laugh.

"Hand me the remote, would you, please?" she said, snapping both phones shut and putting the BlackBerrys on "silent." Dutifully, he handed it over. No one who knew him would believe that the great Emanuel Skorzeny would heed a woman, even one as spectacular as Amanda Harrington, but there you were.

She turned up the sound and changed channels. It didn't matter where she landed, the coverage from Los Angeles was everywhere. "Good God," was all she said, looking at an aerial shot of the blast radius.

The Grove lay near the city's geographic heart, and so its destruction affected the freedom of movement of all Angelenos. With both Third Street and Beverly Boulevard knocked out, two of the city's most important east-west arteries had been cut; the north-south streets of Fairfax and La Brea were similarly affected. Gridlock was expanding outward, a ripple effect that would soon engulf Beverly Hills to the west, Hollywood to the north, and Los Feliz to the northeast.

That, however, was the least of the city's problems. The Grove itself was a complete loss, and the historic Farmer's Market as well. The CBS broadcast center was a smoking ruin and had temporarily knocked the network off the air. American networks were notoriously squeamish about showing dead bodies, but the Europeans felt no such Puritan compunctions, and even from this height, one could see that body parts were liberally strewn over a quarter-mile radius.

"Horrible," said Amanda.

"Yes," said Skorzeny softly. "We have to do something."

"Already underway," said Amanda briskly, knocking back the last of her martini. "I've rearranged our positions on the New York Stock Exchange in order to limit our exposure to —"

"That's not what I mean, Miss Harrington," said Skorzeny. "I mean, we have to help these poor people. *Now.*"

Amanda caught the shift in tone, but kept her voice level. "I've anticipated that, sir. At your word, I'm prepared to go public with a variety of Skorzeny Foundation initiatives, depending on the reaction of the American government. We can immediately make large cash donations to local hospitals and charities and, through our contacts in various European governments, we are also in a position to offer official aid if the Americans request or accept it. Further, our supply ships —"

"Yes, yes," said Skorzeny softly. "I mean we also have to act politically, through our contacts in America, to ensure that the government of the United States is as good as its people. I'm afraid President Tyler has been something of a disappointment."

"Yes, sir," she said, making a note. "There are several senators and congressmen who benefit handsomely from our largesse, and I'm sure —"

A knock at the door. "You may enter, Monsieur Pilier," said Skorzeny.

Paul Pilier stood in the doorway; his imperturbable face showed no emotions. "I was wondering if you had any instructions for me, sir?" he said.

"Who do we have on the ground in Los Angeles?" he asked, pronouncing the name of the city the old-fashioned way, with a hard "g."

"The usual complement, sir," replied Pilier.

"And what do they have to say?"

"Reports are just now coming in, sir. Many dead, many more wounded —"

"I can see that on television," said Skorzeny impatiently.

"The freeways are at a standstill, the Red Line has been shut down as a security precaution . . ."

"Call a press conference at once," said Skorzeny, decisively.

"A press conference, sir?" asked Pilier, but

Skorzeny was already up and off the couch, pacing, thinking.

"A press conference announcing that the entire worldwide resources of the Skorzeny Foundation, Emanuel Skorzeny Enterprises, and ancillary businesses are hereby devoted to aiding and assisting the government of the United States of America in any way or capacity within our power. That I will shortly be contacting President Tyler to make this offer to him personally, and that, furthermore, we will be happy to assist the Central Intelligence Agency or any other agency of the U.S. government in identifying, locating, tracking down, capturing, and handing over to the proper authorities the person or persons responsible for this civilizational outrage." He looked at Pilier. "Did you get all that down?"

"Of course, sir."

"And you, Miss Harrington," said Skorzeny, turning to Amanda. "This is a challenge for you as well."

Amanda leaned forward. There were times that Skorzeny wished she wouldn't do that, not attired as she was, and this was most definitely one of them.

"And you, Miss Harrington," he began again. "While it is of the utmost urgency that we respond to this tragedy with all our humanitarian impulses, we must also make certain that we continue to have the delivery mechanism to do so. Do I make myself clear?"

Amanda was already punching her Black-Berrys. "Perfectly, sir."

Skorzeny permitted himself the luxury of a small smile. "Very good. Now . . ." He went to the window and gazed out at London. That was the signal for Pilier to leave. He left.

"And now," said Amanda, exploding the awkward silence, "I really must get things in order for your press conference."

That caught him a little short. "Aren't you accompanying me to dinner?" he inquired.

"I think you will find your dinner date both attractive and accommodating," said Amanda.

"That was not what I had in —"

"There are arrangements to be made, and quickly. And if we're to have all of our positions in place before the worldwide markets open . . . you do the math."

She turned and smiled. "The sun never sets on the Skorzeny Empire."

"Miss Harrington . . ."

She pulled a face. "You old goat," she said. "Now get ready. You don't want to be late.

I'm told that she's a lovely girl who finds older men fascinating."

CHAPTER
THIRTY-FOUR

Washington, D.C.
Upon learning the news of Los Angeles, the president helicoptered aboard Marine One directly to the White House lawn, where he held an impromptu press conference. Even his worst enemies and most ardent critics had to admit that Jeb Tyler was made for moments like these. His natural empathy, his good looks, his unforced air of concern — these were some of the qualities that had gotten him elected and today was his finest hour.

Across from him, the usual assemblage of preening White House correspondents, augmented by the network anchors, had their microphones and notebooks at the ready, itching to shout their questions. But right now, the president had the floor:

"My fellow Americans," Tyler began, with just the right quiver of rage in his voice. Dobson had whipped up the speech on the short chopper ride from Camp David, and it was probably the best thing she'd ever done. Did half the country think him a wimp? Very well then, he would show them. "Today, our country was attacked by wanton, vicious murdering scum."

A ripple ran through the press corps. Scum? Several reporters made a mental note to contact . . . well, somebody . . . to see if any group could possibly take offense at such an un-PC characterization. So far, there had been no terrorist statement that anyone had heard, but it would surely come, and then the great national game of recriminating moral equivalence could begin in earnest. In the meantime, the president was still speaking:

"Many of our fellow citizens are dead. Many more lie dying. A significant portion of Los Angeles has been destroyed by a very powerful bomb. But it could have been worse. Reports are still fragmentary and preliminary, but it appears that the terrorists' attempt to construct a so-called dirty bomb has largely failed. With the gracious acquiescence of Mayor Gonzales of Los Angeles, federal FEMA, Hazmat, and SWAT teams are either already on site or underway. We'll have no Katrina here."

He took a breath, but continued to look

steadily and calmly into the TV cameras. "As of this moment, we have not received any communication from the people who have done this reprehensible deed. But let me assure you that we will find them, and we will bring them to swift and sure justice.

"I gather there already has been speculation that this attack was in retaliation for the foiling of the plot in Edwardsville yesterday. I have conferred with my senior national security staff, and they assure me that such a thing would be impossible. This operation was too well planned for it to be a simple act of revenge. No matter how Edwardsville had played out, no matter whether we had acceded to all their demands, it wouldn't have mattered one whit. The attack on Los Angeles would have happened anyway. So if and when we hear from them, please keep that in mind. There is simply no grievance, whether real or imaginary, that justifies this cowardly and despicable act."

The president paused. Something caught his eye: Pam Dobson, gesturing discreetly but urgently and pointing to her iPhone.

As President Tyler turned back to the cameras and the press corps he saw that they too were consulting their wireless devices. Pam Dobson walked over and showed him her screen. Tyler blanched, then made a command decision: show it.

"Are you sure?" whispered Pam.

"Sunlight is the best disinfectant," said Tyler. "My fellow Americans," said President Tyler, "behold our enemy." And so the nation's television feeds cut away from the White House lawn to the face of a terrorist in a ski mask. Tyler signaled for the audio feed to begin:

". . . cowardly attack on our forces yesterday cried out to Heaven above for revenge," the masked man was saying in a muffled and electronically scrambled voice. "And so has it been done. Let there be no mistake about our resolve. Unless the American government immediately and completely capitulates to our demands, these attacks will continue in ever-increasing ferocity until America and the West are destroyed in a holy rain of fire."

The terrorist looked directly at the cameras. "And that day of reckoning will be the most terrible in the history of the world." The video was shot in some empty room, blank white walls, no music. "You have had your chance. From this moment on, there will be no further communications, no negotiating. We made our justifiable demands and our reward was death. Now, we will visit death upon you. No justice, no peace, no surrender."

The masked man stopped, looked at the camera. "Have a nice day."

The president came back on, calm, unruffled, not a perfect hair on his perfect head out of place. Even the half of the country who hadn't voted for him, who in fact despised him, had to admit that he was pretty damn impressive at this moment.

"My fellow Americans, everything you have just heard is a lie. You have just seen the hooded face of evil. I realize that some members of both parties have tried to tell you that the threat from beyond our shores is not real. That if we would just be nice to them, if we would just address their 'legitimate grievances,' all would be well.

"But let me tell you something. Yesterday's events in Edwardsville opened my eyes. I too thought that health care and the capital gains tax were the issues most important to you, my fellow countrymen. How wrong I was. And I stand before you now, humbled and contrite of heart, and pledge to you that we will not rest, we will not falter, until we have eliminated this threat to the Republic, and our families can once again sleep soundly in their beds at night — secure in the knowledge that we employ rough men ready to do our enemies grievous harm for the actions they have taken against us today. My fellow Americans — we will not fail."

It was a lucky thing that the cameras were on Tyler and not his group of advisors behind him; flies would have found comfortable nesting places in their mouths as he continued.

"This very day, I have ordered the leader of one of the most secret, the most elite units in the American intelligence hierarchy to stop at nothing to remove this threat. From this moment on, we will hunt down these folks and terminate them with the most extreme prejudice America has ever brought to bear on an enemy, and that includes Tojo's Japan and Hitler's Nazi Germany."

One last pause. "Thank you, good night, and may God bless America."

Several of the reporters — the Fox News correspondent most visibly — applauded as the president finished speaking. The ranks of advisors stepped forward to congratulate him. Pam Dobson beamed. As Rubin stepped forward to shake his hand, the president said, "How's the market doing?"

Rubin glanced at his BlackBerry — the Dow had already lost another 800 points. "We might have to close the Street if things keep going south."

Seelye was next in line. Before he could open his mouth — "Where's Devlin?" the President asked.

Seelye thought twice before replying. The president of the United States had just blown one of the nation's top secrets, and just condemned to death the man Seelye had guiltily raised as a foster son. "In the air, I believe, sir, just as you ordered. Bound for Los Angeles."

Tyler gripped his hand a little longer than protocol demanded. "Well," he said, "that's a lucky break. Now just make sure that cocksucker doesn't make a liar out of me."

CHAPTER
THIRTY-FIVE

In the air: Devlin

In the window seat, Devlin was in the middle of a vigorous game of Spades with two morons and a blithering idiot when the president came on the air with the news of the Los Angeles bombing. The video on the screen remained the Spades game, but the audio came directly from the White House's internal transmission system, which Devlin had taken the liberty of tapping into via Fort Meade the day Tyler was inaugurated.

His blood ran cold as he absorbed the awful news. Although the extent of the bombing in central Los Angeles was not yet clear, there were obviously going to be many, many casualties. Casualties were part of war, and this was a war, no matter whether half his countrymen felt otherwise. The thing that really raised his hackles was the President's statement:

This very day I have ordered the leader of one of the most secret, the most elite units in the American intelligence hierarchy to stop at nothing to remove this threat. From this moment on, this individual will hunt down these folks and terminate them with the most extreme prejudice America has ever brought to bear on an enemy, and that includes Tojo's Japan and Hitler's Nazi Germany.

As he listened to the president's words over his earbuds, rerouted through the "zone.com" link, the president's challenge to him personally, he heard one thing and one thing only: *his execution order.*

Again the thought came to mind that someone was deliberately trying to get him killed — that there was some kind of mole inside NSA/CSS, maybe even inside Branch 4 itself, someone who had twigged Milverton to him in advance of Edwardsville. Who could it be?

There weren't many suspects. If he had to bet, he'd bet on Seelye; when the day came that Devlin had outlived his usefulness to either the country or, more likely, the general, he would be left out in the cold. Seelye certainly didn't need a living recrimination, proof of his sins, walking around in public.

This scenario assumed that someone in Washington bore him ill. But, to turn it around and look at it from their perspective, the "mole" could just as easily turn out to be Devlin himself, working in some strange consort with Milverton in order to . . . what? The best he could come up with was that he'd be running a sting operation against whoever was behind Milverton. A double flush-out, and the first guy whose head pops up above the underbrush gets it blown off.

Well, he was not that smart, or that daring, or that desperate. And Tyler was certainly stupid and boastful enough to have semi-blown Devlin's cover out of sheer braggadocio. Which left the possibility that either Milverton or the man behind him already knew about Devlin, knew that this kind of operation was almost certain to bring him into the mix, after which Milverton could either kill Devlin himself or, better yet, have one of the other Branch 4 ops take him out.

He stayed calm; panic was for lesser men, and Devlin had long ago made fear his friend. It was true: nothing did concentrate the mind like the prospect of being hanged in the morning. There had to be some way for him to turn this chain of events into an advantage, but until he could, one thing was clear: Milverton was already inside his OODA loop. Devlin was heading out to LA, and already Milverton was one step ahead of him.

Devlin looked around the aircraft: no sign that anybody knew anything yet. Luckily, the equipment was an older plane on a budget airline, the kind with TV screens over every third or fourth row, and they were all showing the same movie. Still, it was only a matter of time until some wise-ass disobeying the cell phone restrictions would start shouting the news. Only one thing to do.

Viciously, he wiped out a stupid, first-position double-nil with a three of clubs. His partner, a Hungarian, flashed him a sarcastic "good job" and disappeared into cyberspace. "What an asshole," he thought to himself as he slammed his laptop shut.

"Hey, mister, are you okay?"

The kid next to him, in the middle seat. A boy, about the same age as the one he'd rescued in Edwardsville. A typical innocent American kid, who had every right to believe that the world he knew now was going to be the world he would find himself in when he was a man. A poor, deluded, lied-to kid who at this moment had no clue about the Grove. Another act of war, a war that had been being waged asymmetrically against the United States since Sirhan Sirhan shot Bobby Kennedy.

His heart went out to the kid and his mother — the forty-something blonde in the aisle seat reading *People*. He looked her over. Not bad. Another time, another place . . . another lonely woman. He hated himself for the predatory thought.

"Gotta use the head," he lied.

Gingerly, Devlin stepped over the boy. The blond smiled at him as she discreetly raised her gaze from *People* to his rear end and then, demurely, back to her magazine. "Excuse me, Missus . . ." he said.

"It's 'Ms.,' " she smiled invitingly. "I'm divorced." Of course she was. He moved forward, toward business class.

Where he was stopped by one of the flight attendants. He flashed a badge at her — the genuine badge of a federal air marshal — and she moved aside. He took her by the arm and whispered into her ear: "I need to speak with the pilot immediately," he said.

As if to emphasize the situation, a couple of cell phones started ringing. Nobody answered them. Good, obedient sheeple.

The stew walked him to the front of the plane. He paid no attention to any of the passengers, and hoped like hell none of them paid him any mind.

She pulled him into the front galley while she phoned the pilot. Even the air marshals weren't allowed inside the cockpit unless they were retaking it by force. Devlin waited as she spoke, then hung up. "He'll be right out," she said.

"Kill the video feeds. Do it now." His tone and mien brooked no argument.

"This doesn't have anything to do with the lady in 4A does it?" she asked.

"What about her?" asked Devlin. He hadn't noticed anybody in particular on his way up front.

"Well . . ." the flight attendant lowered her voice, "she's one of *them.* I mean, just look at her. And I heard her talking in some foreign language on her cell phone just before we took off."

"What's this all about?" barked the captain, emerging from the flight deck.

Devlin flashed his badge again. "Rocky Sullivan," he said. He waited until the stewardess took the hint and left. "Captain, I assume you've heard about Los Angeles."

The pilot's stoic look, followed by concern, told him he had. "There's been some kind of explosion at the Grove, near the Farmer's Market. There are deaths, but we don't know how many yet."

Devlin took a deep breath. "Do you think they'll close the airports in southern California?"

The man — his name tag read, "WILKINSON" — thought for a moment. "Maybe. Probably. We're awaiting word now."

"Then what? Where do we land?"

"Vegas, depending. Maybe John Wayne, but if this is as bad as . . . as bad as it could be, they'll probably shut down the whole southland."

"That's what I figured," said Devlin. "Which is why I need you to ignore any redirection order."

Captain Wilkinson looked at Devlin like he was nuts. "Negative. That would cost me my wings."

"Not if national security is at stake." Devlin vamped, trying to come up with a plausible scenario. What was it the flight attendant had said about the woman in 4A. Devlin lowered his voice to a whisper. "There's someone we're watching on board this flight. She doesn't know she's being surveilled, but it's imperative that I get her to Los Angeles."

The captain thought for a moment. He

seemed to know what Devlin was talking about. "Does she have anything to do with what just happened?"

"I can't tell you that," said Devlin, honestly, "but it's crucial that we land in LA."

A pause, and then — "Sorry, but I can't. They'll shoot us down. If we go Code Red, they'll scramble at Edwards and you'll have put 150 people in the Pacific."

"We won't go Code Red," said Devlin. "I'll guarantee it."

"Then it'll be a general aviation order."

"And you can beat that, can't you?"

At that moment, the cockpit door opened and the co-pilot stuck his head out. "Captain," he began, eyeballing Devlin.

"It's okay," said Wilkinson. "Have they closed LAX?

The co-pilot was smart enough not to ask who Devlin was. "Affirmative, sir. We're being diverted to Vegas."

"Thanks, Ben," said the captain. "I'll be right in." He turned back to Devlin. "Rocky, ol' buddy, you'd better give me a goddamn good reason to even think about what you're suggesting."

Only one play left. Whoever the unlucky lady in 4A was, she was now going to be the goddamn good reason. He could take her into custody in a second, and then figure out how to frame her for something as they headed to LA.

"I'll make the bust right now. Then you'll have a high-value federal prisoner who must be delivered to LA without delay. I'll get you all the CYA authorization you need. Deal?"

Captain Wilkinson thought for a moment. "That is one good-looking federal prisoner," he said, shaking Devlin's hand. "I'll have the flight attendant ask the man in the seat next to her to come up front for a moment, for some bullshit message. Then you swap seats and do your thing. But try to keep the fireworks to a minimum, will ya?"

Devlin nodded. "Thanks," he said. "One more thing — land in Burbank."

The stew went to get the man in 4B. As he came forward, Devlin slipped past him and walked calmly but purposefully, head down, toward the empty aisle seat. He hated to burn one of his covers, hated to have spent as much time with the captain as he'd had to, but that's the way it was.

The face of the woman in 4A was buried in a copy of Paris *Vogue* as he took the seat. She didn't bother to look over, or acknowledge his presence, or absence, in any way. Under other circumstances, the perfect seat mate.

Then his world turned upside down.

Maybe it was the perfume, that magical *madeleine* that triggered involuntary memory. Maybe the shape of the left forearm. Maybe a sixth sense. It didn't matter. They both knew immediately when she lowered the magazine and looked at him.

"Hello, Frank," she said evenly. "Long time no see."

It was a good thing he didn't have a heart. "Hello, Maryam," he said. "You're under arrest."

CHAPTER
THIRTY-SIX

Paris — seven years earlier

He was in the city on a RAND clean-up operation. He was dressed as a Frenchman, loitering around the stage entrance of the Olympia waiting for his mark — a British SAS officer, who'd come over to Santa Monica with an MI-6 vet stamp in his dossier, but who was now suspected of running his own sideline business in sensitive SIGINT cables, hawking them to the Israelis, the Palestinians, the Egyptians, the Georgians, whoever came firstest with the mostest. Even a "22" couldn't be allowed to get away with that. He was about to become, what they called in the trade, an exemplar. An object lesson. A warning.

Normally on a job like this, Devlin blended into the scenery and, whenever possible, the furniture. But only an idiot who was trying to attract attention would try not to attract attention in Paris. Every

Frenchman considered himself the second coming of Yves Montand, and peacockery was de rigueur, and among the *beures,* the immigrants from north Africa and the Middle East, it was practically religious doctrine. So he was dressed well, in the current mode, and smoking a cigarette as he loitered and cast admiring glances at the young ladies passing by — who, after all, both expected and deserved nothing less.

She blindsided him. His French was excellent; hers was perfect. So when she somehow snuck up on him as he was checking out the derriere on a particularly good-looking Anamese *salope* and asked him for a light, he fumbled a vowel and she busted him on the spot.

"American, huh?" she said. She must have come out of the club, while his eyes were on Little Miss Saigon's bum. Why she'd approached him, he had no idea. She spoke softly, so as not to embarrass him. "You can always tell. Match me."

She produced an unlighted cigarette, leaned forward, and lit hers from his. The tips glowed as they met.

Now he looked at her, really looked at her. Middle Eastern, short, slender, very fashionably dressed. She filled it out nicely too without any hint of the future rotundity that almost invariably accompanied girls of her tribe. But it was the big, liquid brown eyes, the hint of olive in the skin, that really blew her cover.

"Persian, huh?" he retorted. "You can always tell. Especially when you're trying to pass for French."

"Touché, monsieur."

"Frank."

"Maryam."

"Assalmu' Alayki Maryam."

She crinkled her nose and laughed. "Your Arabic is even worse than your French . . . although they're both okay." He caught her eyes and held them until she looked away. "But I'm Iranian, remember?"

"Wanna go for Farsi too?" he said. "With three, you get egg roll."

Now she laughed heartily, and he knew he had her, if he wanted her. And want her he did. Too bad he was on duty.

"Seriously," she said. "What are you doing here?"

He glanced across the street. So far, nothing. "Waiting for a friend."

"Dressed like a Marseilles pimp?"

"He's a whore, so it's okay."

"Can I watch?"

"No, but you can have a rain check."

"What's a rain check?"

"I thought you said you spoke English."

She made a *moue.* "I don't think I like you any more."

"Who said you ever did?" Movement in the doorway across the street. "I gotta go now, baby."

"Don't call me baby. I hate when men call me baby."

He was moving now and so was she, tagging along. He either had to ditch her, kill her, or let her come. He didn't like either of the first two choices, so he might as well make use of the cover. He took her by the hand. "Where are we going?" she asked.

"I don't know," he said, "but you seem like a fun girl, so you're getting your rain check right now."

She had to hurry to keep up, her feet clattering her impossibly high heels on the Paris sidewalks.

The man he was trailing stopped, his keen ears tuned to the slightest discrepancy in his environment, visual or aural. In a flash, Devlin had pulled Maryam into the shadows of a nearby doorway and kissed her as hard as he could. He caught sight of the man turning and he knew he was, for the moment, safe. He kept kissing Maryam long after the man had started back along his way. She tasted that good.

At last, he let her up for air. "What was that for?"

"For saving my ass."

"It's a nice ass," she said.

He waltzed her out onto the sidewalk. He stepped in some dog shit but he didn't care. Dog shit was as much a part of the romance of Paris as the Seine, as the shellfish spilling out from their ice beds on the sidewalks, as the whiffs of perfume and body odor coming off the ugly but sexy women, as the sight of Notre Dame by night, as the Pont des Arts in late afternoon, and the Sacre-Coeuer against the morning sun.

The man ahead had stopped again. Did he sense something?

"Slap me," he whispered. "Really, do it. Now."

She learned fast. She slapped him hard. Harder, in fact, than he expected. Good. That meant she liked him.

"Encule de son père!" he shouted.

She came right back at him:

"Sale fils de pute enculée par un gros connard de pede!"

That hurt. So would this: *"J'aurais te donner un coup de pied dans la choune, mais ça degueulasserais trop mon godasse!"* He couldn't believe the vile things that were coming from his mouth. Neither could she:

"Boro gomsho pedear soukteh, jakesh!" It was the choicest Tehran invective he had heard in years.

As he'd hoped, a crowd gathered around them, hoping for some action and blocking them from the sight of his quarry. Silently, he started counting down to ten, which was exactly how long he was going to let this little piece of street theater last.

"Goh bokhor!" he cried and pulled her close again.

"That was pretty good," she said. "For an American."

"Let's go."

They pushed their way through the crowd. The man Devlin was following was still in sight, but moving faster now, his wind up a bit, but not so much that he would disappear. To vanish would be to admit guilt to any pursuer. And then it would be war.

"Who is he?" she said.

"Somebody I want to talk to."

"Just talk?" She grabbed him and whirled him around. "Enough to kill him?" She patted the gun under his left armpit, the one that was so well concealed that not even a drunken *flic* with a grudge against Americans would have noticed it on a first patdown. Or even a second . . .

The sudden rush of emotion he was feel-

338

ing was something new, unexpected. He'd spent his life after Rome living within a carefully constructed iron box that the world couldn't dent, and now this girl comes along and cracks it right down the middle with one kiss.

He made a snap decision. The first rule of snap decisions was never to make them. The second rule was to make one exception. "You'd better leave now. Things could get ugly."

Big brown eyes, looking right into his. "I'm from Shiraz. You think I haven't seen ugly things?" She took off her heels, ready to run. Maybe the second rule was right after all.

Third rule: never underestimate a woman. Not her brains, not her heart, not her soul.

The man was heading toward the Seine. Inwardly, Devlin smiled; that's where he would head at this point in the game too — someplace open, with a clear shot in every direction, one with plenty of shadows among the closed kiosks, lovers galore, bridge abutments. Open spaces could be killing fields, but only when the battlefield had already been prepped; otherwise, they were observation posts.

Okay, they could play it either way. "This could get rough," he said. "And I want to see you again, after this is over."

"I'll have to think about it."

"Make it snappy."

"What's your name?"

"Frank Ross," he lied.

"Okay, Frank Ross," she said with a hint of entirely accurate suspicion, "I'll meet you at the Café de la Paix."

"When?"

"I'll be there all night. I'll be the girl with a broken heart, playing 'Hearts and Flowers' on my violin, if you don't show up."

He kissed her again, for absolute real this time. "I'll see you there."

"Try not to get yourself killed, Frank Ross," she whispered. Before she could say anything else, he was gone.

He hit the Seine across from Notre Dame. The man ahead of him was jogging now, down the left bank of the river along the Quai Malaquais, heading for the safety of the crowds at St.-Michel.

Devlin trailed him along the various quays. There could be no doubt now that the man was guilty. Or that he was good. Or that he was very dangerous. He had played the pickup just the way Devlin would have, sensing, sorting, then heading for safety, which meant that he had sized up his pursuer and would be ready for him.

It was a cliché, but it was also true: Paris really was for lovers. In the heart of one of the world's greatest cities, his race along the Seine was run nearly alone, the auto-tunnels buried beneath him, the river quiet except for the passing barge or tourist boat, but everywhere, mostly unseen but never unsensed, in the shadows, were the lovers.

He realized with a start that, for the first time in his life, he had just joined their ranks.

The man tossed a glance over his left shoulder. Devlin peeled off near the rue de Seine, heading south, where he could cross the rue Mazarine and then cut back into the warren of streets in the Latin Quarter. He had a pretty good idea where the man was heading: the rue Galande.

Charles Augustus Milverton. At one time, "Milverton" had been one of the finest operatives in Britain's most elite fighting force, a leader of the 22nd Regiment Special Air Service at Credenhill. Later, he moved on to "deep battle-space" assignment.

The best part of an SAS posting was that absolute anonymity prevailed, even when operating at home. SAS officers were not required to identify themselves either to police or civilian agencies; in effect, there was no bothersome review authority over them, which meant that Milverton was pretty much free to operate as he saw fit, even after he left the Two-Two's Mobility Troop and had moved closer to home in the Artists Rifles reserve, in Regent's Park. He had spent the past few years roaming the wreckage of the old Soviet Union as a kind of hired gun, sorting out communists and capitalists alike and burnishing his reputation for sudden, violent lethality. Milverton could kill you in dozens of different ways, but so could a lot of guys. What made him special is that he could kill you and be gone before you even knew you were dead.

Devlin passed south of the Place St.-Michel and turned left on the rue St.-Séverin, across the rue St.-Jacques. There it was, up ahead — the place he was looking for: 42 rue Galande.

Devlin moved slowly now, down the crowded street. This part of the Quarter was always packed with young humanity, pretty girls and phony-tough boys, the Arabs jostling their way in packs over and through the French, who still had not quite grasped the extent to which they were becoming strangers in their own capital city.

The spires of Notre Dame shone brightly just off the west: from the sacred to the profane in five minutes, and all you had to do was cross the Pont St.-Michel. It was as if the great cathedral had deliberately faced west, down the Seine, turning its back on the sin and sacrilege behind it.

He took a spot in a darkened doorway and waited. Mentally, he reviewed the intelligence. It was all NSA stuff, nothing from Langley, which meant that on a scale of one to ten it scored about a six, as opposed to a one. The rue Galande was where Milverton kept a safe house, a flat, in one of the last places in Paris that anyone would ever think to look for such a thing.

Maryam wandered briefly into his thoughts, but he cast her aside. He had her parting promise to meet him at the Café de la Paix, near the Opéra, and if she was true to her word, so would he be. He had no intention of getting killed by Milverton. He was there as judge, jury, and hooded executioner.

"I am the Angel of Death," he said, under his breath.

There was no chance that Milverton would go through the front entrance. But he didn't want him to. That was the way he was going to go in. And so he bought a ticket and entered the building.

Everybody was dressed for the occasion except him. Men in bustiers, fishnet stockings, and high heels. Women dressed as virginal brides, but wearing no underwear. Mock-hunchbacks. Vampirish whores. All there for *The Rocky Horror Picture Show.*

The cult movie had been playing at the Studio Galande since forever. It had taken the French a few years to catch on to the fact that the Tim Curry movie was not just a movie but an audience-participation extravaganza, but once they got the hang of it, they showed up with the same fervid and flamboyant enthusiasm as their counterparts in Boston, New York, and elsewhere.

Devlin had long since memorized the layout as he took a seat near the back of the auditorium. Thanks to NSA, liaising with DARPA (Defense Advanced Research Projects Agency, run out of the DoD), he knew that Milverton's lair lay to the rear of the screen and just above, on the first floor, in Euro-speak. He gave Milverton about fifteen minutes to get comfortable, to feel safe. The audience was in the middle of "Let's Do the Time Warp Again" when he made his move.

There was a conga line up on the stage in front of the screen. As he rose, several girls cheered him, got out of their seats, and sandwiched him as they propelled Devlin toward the stage. The girl behind him put her hands on his ass and squeezed it tight, while the one in front reached back and grabbed his balls.

And then they were up on the stage. The audience was screaming with delight and shouting encouragement.

Hands on hips, knees in tight . . .

The girls were very sexy. He found his thoughts flashing back to Maryam. No — get her out of your mind. Stay focused on the job.

The wings beckoned. He wasn't the first *Rocky Horror* virgin to feel embarrassment and flee the stage.

Even behind the screen and the loud-speakers, the music was deafening.

He drew his silenced SigSauer and fired nine shots in quick succession, punching a perfect circle in the ceiling above. As the plaster showered down, he took out something that looked like a dart gun and fired.

The metal claw expanded as it hit the ceiling, grabbed a purchase on the floor above. He hit the retractor and the ceiling fell in.

Milverton came down at the speed of gravity, firing all the way. He was that good — better than Devlin even had thought. Faster too.

His first few shots shredded the screen from behind. Tim Curry took a bullet through the groin. Richard O'Brien, one through the hump. And Susan Sarandon, right in the titties.

Milverton continued firing as he hit the floor, rolling. The fall must have hurt like hell, if it didn't actually break anything, but he didn't seem to care. Devlin respected that; unless he had been killed by the plunge, he wouldn't have cared about the pain either. All that mattered at this point was the job.

Shots splintered everything around him as he rammed another clip into the SigSauer. But he was bound by the rules of engagement: he couldn't fire toward the audience.

Milverton rose and charged toward the screen from behind.

It's just like *Point Blank,* though Devlin, trying both to stay hidden and get a clear shot. Observe, orient, decide —

There he was, outlined and back-lit against what was left of the screen.

Act.

Devlin held up. He couldn't risk missing Milverton and hitting some poor kid. Milverton burst through the screen, firing back at Devlin, then dropping off the proscenium and into the first row of seats.

Devlin realized it was useless. He had to get up, expose himself, if he had any hope.

He couldn't believe how badly this operation had gone. And all because of the girl.

No, check that — all because him. Because of his weakness. Because of his need.

Devlin broke through the remains of the screen. Barry Bostwick and Little Nell were still singing on the soundtrack, but the picture was long gone. People were screaming and shoving each other to get out as Milverton bulled his way toward the front exit. He was holding the two girls who had sandwiched Devlin. Hostages now.

From his angle, he didn't have a clear shot. Milverton raised his gun —

Then a shot, from somewhere in the auditorium. Milverton stumbled, lost his grip on the girls, who tore away from him and dove for cover. Another shot, which splintered the wall behind Milverton, who was already returning fire. He emptied a clip into the darkened auditorium, and a woman's voice cried out in pain.

This was his chance. At full speed, Devlin leapt from the stage.

He landed on Milverton square, raining punches as they went down. The body blows didn't do much damage. It was like socking steel.

Milverton's first punch caught Devlin behind the neck, stunning him. He knew what was coming next, even as the SAS fighter pulled his knife and slashed at the back of Devlin's knee. Had it landed, the knife thrust would have been a crippling, then a killing blow. Devlin would have been a marionette whose strings had just been cut, and lying there helpless, he would have been ripe for the final plunge into the neck.

But Milverton missed. He missed because everything in Devlin's training had prepared him for moments like these and while someday he might meet a better shot than himself, he was not going to meet a better street fighter.

He blocked the blow with a forearm, then threw the other forearm at Milverton's head. It caught him flush on the ear. He brought the butt of his gun down across the bridge of Milverton's nose.

Devlin spun, grabbing Milverton's wrist. With a sharp yank, he disarmed him, the knife clattering to the ground. His eyes briefly followed the knife —

"Look out!" A woman's voice. He glanced left, just in time to see the shiv that had been yanked from Milverton's boot heel heading for his face. He could feel the air as it missed.

"Drop it!" shouted the woman's voice and now Devlin understood who she was.

Maryam held her Lady Glock steady on Milverton. She was a pro, but she wasn't as good as he was.

Instead of breaking his motion, Milverton transferred the arc of the shiv in her direction and let it fly, like a dart. She tried to control the shock and the pain, but Devlin heard the breath punch out of her as she fell.

In a flash Milverton was up on his feet and running for the door. Devlin rolled and brought his pistol up, but it was too late.

Milverton was gone.

He found her slumped on the floor between a row of seats. He could hear the sirens, rapidly approaching. Leave her, shoot her, or fall in love with her, once and for all. Observe, orient, decide.

Act.

He picked her up. There was a side exit that led into a noxious Parisian alley. The kind of street where lovely ladies with blackened teeth and hairy armpits used to empty the contents of their chamber pots on the heads of peasants even blacker of tooth and hairier of body back in the seventeenth century.

No chamber pots tonight. He kept his pistol ready, just in case Milverton was waiting for him.

She was losing blood, going into shock now. A hospital was out of the question; too much curiosity. The agency had doctors here in Paris. It also had nurses, spies, whores, safe houses, safe cars, bought cops, cooperative members of the *Deuxième Bureau,* the works. They'd be here within minutes.

"Hold on, Maryam," he said, punching a couple tones on his cell phone.

"Who are you?" she whispered as he carried her down the alley, her voice fading.

"Your guardian angel," he said.

Paris was for lovers.

CHAPTER
THIRTY-SEVEN

Los Angeles

Danny Impellatieri's first inkling that anything was amiss came as he gradually awoke to the soft, almost sexy, buzz of his secure cell phone, which he always slept with, under his pillow, right alongside his pistol. Swimming back to consciousness, he became aware of a symphony of sirens wailing somewhere to the south and west. At first he mistook them for the sounds of the radio, or perhaps a television commercial; the TV was still on, although he couldn't see it from this angle. He was trying to synthesize this random information when he realized he had the phone in his hand. "Hello?"

Stupid. That hadn't been a standard ring tone — it was his private message ring tone, the overture to *Zampa,* just energetic enough to be motivating, and clichéd enough to be comical. No answer was necessary. There was a crackle and a beep and he realized

351

this was a message from "Tom Powers." He punched his access code and waited for the clearance to go through. Then he saw it.

"Whaddya know, whaddya say?" That got him awake.

That was what he used to say when he was commanding his unit of the 160th, the Night Stalkers. Powers had asked him for a private phrase, one that only the two of them shared. Thus they learned that they both shared a love for Cagney movies, loved the way the banty little rooster from hell moved as he chomped through the scenery. Cagney just didn't stand there, he vibrated. He didn't just do nothing when he had nothing to do; he did something: flashed his devilish eyes, shot a leering grin, balanced expertly on the balls of his feet, ready for anything, ready to make love to a girl or punch a guy's lights out. Cagney, they decided, was their role model.

So this message was not good. Danny had expected the small pleasures of homecoming and sleep, and then a significant rise in one of his off-shore bank accounts, the ones that, despite his overwhelming love for her — or perhaps because of it — he had never breathed a word of to Diane, but had put in her name in case anything happened to him. It was meant as a warning, to be ready;

worse, it meant that something really nasty had come up.

Ready for what? What could have been worse than what they'd just gone through?

Normally, the first thing Danny would do was sit down at his computer in his secure room, boot it up, and do a quick scan of all available feeds, official, semiofficial, open source, and absolute bullshit. You could learn a lot from the first three, but sometimes you could learn even more from absolute bullshit, since it afforded you a window onto the thinking of the wingnuts, basket cases, moonbats, psychos, and all the other flotsam and jetsam of the human race, weightless amid the rapidly expanding junk of cyberspace.

That kind of war was not for him. Danny preferred a sidearm or a knife and an enemy, face to face, up close and personal. Like that Drusovic asshole. Danny was a good Catholic, but the thought that religion could compel a man to murder — no, to slaughter — was beyond him. He would have made a lousy Crusader, *Deus lo vult* and all that; he needed to know who he was killing and why. For Danny Impellatieri, it was always personal.

The phone rang again — this time the tone was the *William Tell Overture.* Another

Devlin ring tone. He wasn't sure if he wanted to answer it. If Devlin really had wanted to communicate something to him, he could have done it with his first message. If he just wanted to shoot the shit, well, there was plenty of time for that later. Maybe he should check his bank account first; it was a cardinal rule that "Eddie" never took on a new job before he got paid for the last. Anyway, he had to take a pee that would make Austin Powers proud.

He ignored the phone and staggered to the bathroom. Let the son of a bitch leave a proper message.

There it was, on the bathroom counter: Jade's iPhone. Just like her to get so excited that she'd walked out the door without it. He had to laugh: the stuff kids had today would have made intel pros twenty years ago weep with envy; hell, he thought, we could have brought down the Soviet Union with two iPods and a set of steak knives if we had had this stuff back in 1989.

Then the iPhone rang. The *William Tell Overture.*

What the hell?

For a moment, Danny just stared at it dully. The chance that Jade had Rossini as one of her ring tones was impossible; she'd never even heard of Rossini. But the chance that Tom Powers would try to communicate with him via his kid's phone was equally impossible. Their working agreement was founded on the bedrock principle that no way would Danny's family ever get involved with business. Families were off-limits, sacrosanct.

Danny could feel his anger rising, his explosive temper boiling over. He couldn't imagine what possessed Powers to do such a thing. Didn't he realize how dangerous it was? And dragging his daughter, Jade, into this, was totally unconscionable. He'd better have a pretty goddamn good excuse for calling his daughter —

Just before he opened his mouth, Danny glanced over at the television set, which was still on. Then, unprofessionally but understandably, he dropped the phone and started screaming.

CHAPTER
THIRTY-EIGHT

Los Angeles

Danny made the short distance from Hobart Street to the Kaiser-Permanente hospital on Sunset and Edgemont in record time. Speeding east on Franklin, weaving in and out of traffic like an ace pilot, his mind raced faster than his car. Surely, Powers must have known what was coming — why else would he have called? Worse, Powers had had him and his family under surveillance — through his kid, for chrissakes! — the whole time, ever since the poisoned gift had arrived.

That fucking Skipjack. How could he have been so stupid? He had trusted this guy, bonded with him — insofar as you could bond with a man you'd never actually met face to face. But they'd been on a half a dozen missions together, and each one had ended in success and, even better, anonymity. He'd made a lot of money from Powers, and so had his men. They'd lost damn few Night Stalkers. But now . . .

Danny wasn't pretending to think logically as he raced around a Mexican in a Ford pickup hauling three lawn mowers. There, up ahead — Edgemont Avenue, a sharp, screaming right. He didn't quite beat the light at Hollywood Boulevard, but didn't give a shit, didn't even bother parking his car properly; such was his rage and grief that had any LAPD cop popped his head up, he would have blown it off on the spot and dealt with the consequences later.

After he saw his baby girl. After he'd made sure she was going to make it, no matter what it took. After he'd mourned her mother. If they wanted to fuck with him then, so be it. First things first.

He raced past the nurses, heading directly for the floor where his sources had told him his daughter was lying. The security scanners went nuclear as he blew past the metal detector, but that was another thing that would just have to be sorted out later. Besides, the city of Los Angeles had bigger problems at the moment than one grieving father with a weapon or two.

Into the elevator, where he frightened an old Chinese lady in a wheelchair surrounded by four or five members of family banging away in Cantonese. His Cantonese was rusty, but he could have told them to go fuck themselves had they given him any grief. Instead, they just cowered and complained as he barged into the lift, and then spewed some Chinese venom at him as he barreled out. Like he cared.

There was the room. Jade's room.

Eddie Bartlett had seen a lot of things in his time. With the 160th, he'd seen men blown apart, men shredded by chopper blades, men decapitated in training accidents, men with their heads shattered as they smashed through the cockpit glass, men defenestrated, whether accidentally or, in combat, intentionally. He knew what a body looked like after it had fallen from a few thousand feet, knew what a hostile looked like after he'd been riddled with automatic weapons fire in a strafing run, knew what was left after man, woman, or child was hit by a cluster bomb or a missile.

His mind raced. His memory slowed.

The road to Baghdad, 2003. No matter what anybody said about who was responsible for 9/11, for the men on the ground it was payback time for the sand monkeys. Leading a SOAR team, in close air support of a forward Marine unit. Knife through rancid butter until one of the damned sandstorms appeared out of nowhere, a whirling, desert dervish like something out of *The Mummy*.

The Marine column was caught out in the open. Not so bad for them; they could hunker down, even under fire. He and his choppers were up in the air, with sand blasting through their rotors, enfilading their engines. If he didn't get them down, they would all crash in the desert, like the ill-fated Carter mission, the one that had given birth to the SOARs in the first place.

The enemy was dug in at a village just up ahead. A few of Saddam's inept Republican Guard's wasted tanks were blocking the Marines' way into the village. The dirty little secret of desert fighting was that the Iraqis didn't like the sand any better than the Americans did; as a natural resource, it was a lousy ally. They would be having just as much trouble with their rifles and small arms as anybody else, just as little freedom of movement. The Arab response to almost any kind of adverse combat situation was to hunker down, lie low, and either turn tail — their ordinary course of action — or dig in, camouflaged, and then shoot their opponents in the back as they passed by.

If the Night Stalkers bailed now, the Iraqis would become emboldened by what they viewed as American cowardice. Although they thought nothing of abject surrender and honored what the West considered treachery, the Arabs preferred sure suicide to perceived dishonor, and they could pin the Marines down. The jarheads' lifeline was Danny's Black Hawks, and Danny would be damned if he was going to deny them that.

Was the situation dangerous? Damn straight. But that's what the 160th was invented for in the first place.

"Captain?" The voice of one of his officers crackled in his ear. He had ten seconds to make up his mind.

Danny glanced at the radar — no letup in sight. The MH-60/DAP (Direct Action Penetrator) Black Hawks boasted state-of-the-art navigation systems, in addition to their airborne refueling capabilities, their infrared sensors, "disco light" IR jammers, SATCOM, and M-134 Miniguns, all bringing death at a top speed of 178 knots, but now it was time to shit or get off the pot. No amount of technology was going to get them through this. It was classic decision time.

Now or never, and now was always better than never.

They flew those babies in, right over the

top of the village, hovering ten feet off the ground as their four-man crews scrambled down and opened fire. The Iraqis were astonished to see the Americans materialize from nowhere and in their seconds of hesitation, the SOARs' infrared goggles and automatic weapons took them apart.

Danny stayed in the chopper, working the machine guns as his men went house to house, cleaning out the nests. The weather wasn't getting any better. If they were going to get out, they had to do it now.

The hell with it. They'd leave when they were damn good and ready.

They took one casualty that day. The Iraqis lost every single fighter. In the morning, when the storm had cleared, they left a pile of bodies in the middle of the village, with one of the corpses holding a big sign: KILROY WAS HERE, for the Marines to find. They ought to shut their mouths for a while. And then they were gone.

And now he was here. With his daughter. Looking at her lying there, bandages everywhere, tubes everywhere, her eyes closed, hooked up to various machines, her chest rising and falling rhythmically but otherwise showing no signs of life. His beautiful little girl, Jade, whose only crime was going to the Apple store with her mother.

"Sir?" He turned to see a nurse with a couple of security men behind her, two men and a woman. "Would you please accompany these gentlemen downstairs?"

One of the security men laid a hand on his shoulder. Big mistake.

Danny wheeled and punched the man in the stomach. The second man he bounced off a wall. Then he held up his hands. "It's okay, I'm leaving. I'm just a little overwrought, is all."

On an ordinary day, they might have called the cops. Not today. There were no cops. They were all at the Grove.

The security guys glared at him. The hospital staff let him go.

He got into his car. Not even a ticket. He drove off.

There was only one man he knew who could have known about the Grove bomb in advance. The same man who had let the bomb go off in Edwardsville, after the mission was already accomplished.

The same man responsible for his wife's body, lying in the downtown morgue, one of the hundreds of victims of his callousness.

"Tom Powers."

He had to find him. But how? Their deal was that Powers had to initiate the contact.

He had no number for him, nothing. He didn't even know his real name.

Sort of made a mockery of his motto, NSDQ. Night Stalkers Don't Quit.

For the first time in a very long time, Danny started to pray.

CHAPTER
THIRTY-NINE

Los Angeles

Traffic in central Los Angeles was at a standstill, and so they made their way over the hill from Burbank, avoiding the freeways, cutting around Griffith Park on San Fernando, crossing the LA River and darting down Glendale Boulevard and into Echo Park.

Deliberately, he kept a house in one of the most unfashionable neighborhoods in the city. The home on Laveta Terrace in once-fashionable Sunset Heights had been built in 1921 by a rich man, a member of the city's prestigious Jonathan Club, but had slid downhill in the early 1930s once W. C. Fields, whose house was just three doors down, moved west to Los Feliz. It was a perfect place for him to live as anonymously as the nature of his job demanded.

Echo Park was the Greenwich Village of Los Angeles, a longstanding hotbed of radicals, gays, commies, lefties, greens, Latinos, and once upon a time, Aimee Semple McPherson herself. Indeed, her Angelus Temple lay just down the hill to the west, at the northern end of the Echo Park Lake. True, there was the occasional gunshot that broke the stillness of the night, but the view of downtown from his second-floor terrace was nothing short of spectacular, and on game nights, the lights of Chavez Ravine stabbed the night sky like some kind of secular cathedral.

"Am I still under arrest?" she asked. "That was cute."

"No, it was clever."

"We'd better get to work," she said.

That was it. No mention of the Studio Galande and its aftermath, no reference to the last time they saw each other, no hint of her feelings when, after weeks of nursing her back to health at a safe house in Neuilly, he had suddenly and completely vanished from her life. She just picked up right where they'd left off.

"Don't you want to know why —"

She held up a hand. "No. We don't have time for that."

"I'm sorry," he said.

"I know you are, Frank," she replied.

"My name's not Frank," he admitted.

"I know it isn't," she said, moving toward him. "Everything you've told me since the day we met was a lie, but I accepted it."

"Because you were lying too."

"Because I accepted it."

Observe, orient . . . fuck it. "Follow me."

He led her into a tiny hallway that separated the west wing from the east wing, and then into what was once was, charmingly, the 1920s "telephone room," a cubbyhole about the size of an old-fashioned phone booth under the central stairway that still had the hook for the home's original telephone. The proper combination dialed on the reproduction wall phone he'd had installed would slide open to allow passage to the inner sanctum. The wrong combination would result in a slam-shut on the hallway side and the controlled explosion of a cyanide gas bomb in the enclosed space, followed by a trapdoor release of the corpse into a pit below. Nothing personal.

He dialed all the right numbers, shielding the combination from Maryam. "Still don't trust me, do you?" she said, as the false wall slid open.

"I love you," he said. "I loved you from that first kiss in Paris —"

"*Our* first kiss," she said. "It takes two to tango."

"From *our* first kiss in Paris. When you saved my life at the Studio Galande."

She grew somber at the memory. "Like I said, it takes two to —"

"Love comes first. Trust comes later."

The door slid open. The basement stairs beckoned. She grabbed his arm.

"It can't be this easy, can it? People like us . . ."

"Even people like us get lucky, once in a while."

Most people in LA not only didn't have basements, they had never even heard of them. But his house, located on top of a hill, had what was known locally as a "California basement," a half-cellar tucked beneath the living room on the downward slope, maybe eight by ten. Plenty of room for his needs: the inner sanctum of Devlin West.

He ran the video of the president's news conference. There was the terrorist:

Unless the American government immediately and completely capitulates to our demands, these attacks will continue in ever-increasing ferocity until America and the West is destroyed in a holy rain of fire . . . And that day of reckoning will be the most terrible in the history of the world . . . We made our justifiable demands and our reward was death. Now, we will visit death upon you.

Devlin checked all lines of secure communication. Nothing from Seelye, or Rubin or, worse, Tyler. Didn't matter — he's already gotten his assignment from the president on national television. It would be good to keep a little radio silence for a while.

Now he knew he was absolutely right not to have bought the Muslim terrorist line. Everybody expected "terrorists" to be Muslims these days, especially the media. They were the politically incorrect bogeymen with incendiary "sensibilities." They were also a singularly inept group of adversaries from cultures that could not build a flush toilet or maintain an electrical grid.

Real terrorists wouldn't have shot that poor reporter — hell, the press was usually their most ardent sympathizer, ever ready to "understand" them. Plus, real terrorists wouldn't have had such an absurd list of demands. The quick succession of new attacks also spoke against the conventional terrorist angle, since it took Muslim terrorists months or years to conceive, plan, mount, and execute their operations, most of which were half-baked and technically unfeasible anyway; that was one of the reasons why the United States had been able to roll up so many of their networks after September 11.

Even their vaunted Internet cadres had been busted down to buck private, thanks to NSA/CSS. This wasn't Devlin's department, but he was well aware of the extraordinary battle that had been waged, and now basically won, against Al-Qaeda in cyberspace. On September 19, 2008, the NSA warriors had taken down four of the five principal jihad sites, DSA'ed them to death, then poisoned them; what the Romans had done to Carthage, Fort Meade had done to what was left of bin Laden's network. It was the kind of victory that should have been hailed on the editorial pages of every major newspaper, but of course wasn't.

He tried Eddie Bartlett again. Nothing, not even a ring — straight to voice mail. Ditto for his satphone and the iPhone. Nix.

Worse than nix. For security reasons, if Eddie didn't pick up on three secure lines, Devlin was supposed to drop him. It was his own rule, because Devlin had learned the hard way over the years that there was a penalty for breaking even arbitrary, self-imposed rules. Still . . .

"What?"

"I can't raise my partner, the guy I was on my way out here to see when it happened. That's never happened before."

"And you think something happened to him."

"I never think, until I know."

"Let me work with you." There, she said it.

He turned away from his computers and looked at her. "I guess we're either going to have to trust each other or we're going to have to kill each other, so why don't we decide right now? Why did you follow me in Paris?"

"I wasn't following you. I was there *for* you."

"Who sent you?"

"That's classified."

"Do you know who I am?"

"Yes. You're Frank Ross."

"And do you know who Frank Ross was?"

"Yes."

"Tell me."

"He was a reporter who got framed and sent to jail. James Cagney played him in *Each Dawn I Die*."

It was getting clearer now. "NCRI?" The National Council of Resistance of Iran. The great Iranian diaspora had put many of the richest Persians in America, a lot of them burning with desire to see the last of the mullahs.

She didn't answer. "It's my turn now. Why did you leave me?"

"How about a drink?"

"I'm Muslim, remember?"

"Not a Mormon?"

"No."

"So . . . how about a drink?"

"I thought you'd never ask."

They took the private lift up to the second floor and stepped out onto the terrace. The lights of downtown Los Angeles were still on. Hundreds of people had just died to the west, and the city had a big hole in its heart, but life went on. That was the thing about tragedies: they were only tragic to the dead, who didn't care, and those relatively few who cared for them. To the rest of humanity, tragedies were fodder for Oprah.

He kept a bar sheltered under the eaves. He poured them both a single malt Islay with a couple of ice cubes. They had their drinks in happy silence, with only the lights of downtown to accompany their thoughts.

Back to work. Devlin pulled out his PDA and ran the cutout number that Hartley had dialed from the Watergate. The one he had traced as far as LA. It was easier from here to tap into the LA phone system without attracting attention. He had no intention of dialing the number himself, only tracing the bounce-on from this point.

The first thing he did was to match the number to a subscriber who, of course, turned out to be a Mr. Henry A. Wong of Rancho Park, recently deceased. The second thing was to use the system's internal assignment logarithm to freeze it and take it off the grid for another few days. It was like isolating a virus in a lab dish: now he could play with it.

The first bounce-on didn't surprise him in the least. It was the private, unlisted telephone number of Senator Robert Hartley in Georgetown; that was a nice touch. The second bounce was the main switchboard at NSA headquarters in Fort Meade. OK, that told him something too. But it was the third and final bounce that he was really looking for: central London, somewhere between Highgate and Islington. Milverton just couldn't resist showing off and now he just made the biggest mistake of his life. He let out a shout of triumph.

"Are you okay?" She'd finished her scotch.

"Never better." So had he.

The master bedroom lay on the west side of the house, with a view toward Silverlake, Los Feliz, the Observatory, the Hollywood sign. The bed was up on a short pedestal, his closet just off to the right, the master bath to the south. He slipped out of his clothes and into bed. She was warm and smooth next to him.

"Why?" he asked, reaching for her.

"Why not?" she said, reaching for him.

■ ■ ■ ■

Day Three

■ ■ ■ ■

When men are inhuman, take care not to feel towards them as they do towards other humans.
— MARCUS AURELIUS, *Meditations,* Book VII

CHAPTER
FORTY

Camden Town, London

Charles Augustus Milverton checked his chronometer. He loved modern technology. He didn't believe in God, but if he were to believe in any kind of a god, he would imagine one that was half — or perhaps entirely — electronic. A kind of virtual Shiva, warlike and bloodthirsty and able to strike down his enemies from any distance. That was what really put fear into people: not the act of violence that they could see, but the act of violence whose arrival they dreaded and which, when it came, even when it was expected, came *ex machina,* like something out of a Handel opera — God from the skies, except this god was all Zeus and thunderbolts, not Danae's rain of gold.

The rain of gold was his department. His specialty. His reward.

He punched up his computers, waking them from hibernation. While he was gone, they had been churning the data he had sent back from Edwardsville, especially what had happened at the end. Thank God for the Wiki-share, the DARPAs, the SETIs. Unused computing power no longer had to go unused. We were all linked now, even if we didn't know it.

There it was. Him in the helicopter, and his antagonist below. This, after all, had been the primary attraction of the mission all along, to flush that man out from the dark hiding place where Milverton had long suspected he dwelled. And while he had not really got a good look at him, not while lifting off, and readying for the jump he knew must come upon impact of the Barrett's speeding round into the engine block of the chopper, his video apparatus had. No matter how poor the quality, the computers would be able to extract an image, extrapolate concealed features simply from the shape of the chin or the earlobe.

On television, meanwhile, there was Skorzeny, front and center, framed by the giant Ferris wheel everybody called the "London Eye." The old phony could really snow them. All that aid, rushing to Los Angeles, surplus crap he had no use for in the first place. Free turkeys for the poor, and more, all obscuring the real reason the ship had put into port, which was safely tucked away in the hold and buried on the manifest as "scientific experiment materials."

Barnum, or Mencken, or somebody, almost had it right: no one ever went broke underestimating the sentimentality of the American public. The greatest country on earth, a country (it pained him to admit) even more powerful than the Empire at its zenith, was being brought low by its sappy Victorian fondness for morally uplifting "narratives." Triumph and tragedy. Hope rising from the ashes. Smiling through the tears. Well, soon enough they would have something to smile about.

Damn it, but the old man loved the spotlight. Well, he supposed that had he had the upbringing Skorzeny did, he'd want to shine on as long as possible. To pay the world back in Christian coin for the wrongs it had visited upon him — that surely was the mark of the secular saint these days. Still, business was business, and his job was to follow instructions.

He punched a code on his BlackBerry and turned up the sound. All these years in the Anglosphere and the old fart still sounded like Dr. Strangelove.

"And so, ladies and gentlemen, please allow me to thank you from the bottom of my heart for offering me this platform today. A boy born in Germany, who grew up when our two countries were bitter enemies, when there was suffering and dying beyond compare. . . ." The faker choked up briefly, then continued.

"Thus, I do what I can in return. Already, our ship the *Stella Maris* is in port in Los Angeles, along with our prayers. She is one of the most advanced ships on the seas, with a state-of-the-art navigation system and a titanium-hardened cargo hold. What we have for the people of California cannot be compromised or damaged in any way. It will be delivered. For we cannot wait for governments to act. Another Skorzeny humanitarian vessel, the *Clara Vallis,* will make port in Baltimore in three days. As you know, it is my fondest dream to see a new world order emerge before I die, one in which we all are citizens of the world, not simply citizens of whatever nation in which we happen to have been born. As the poet said, 'No man is an island.' "

Skorzeny stopped. The "London Eye" turned. Behind them, the Thames flowed, as it had for thousands of years, since before the Romans settled the place and called it Londinium, and as it would after the Britons finally gave up and abandoned the place to its new fate of Londonistan. Too bad, thought Milverton. He was a native Londoner. He liked the place, and he would miss it, but there were plenty of other places in the world, and with better weather too. Might as well start the ball rolling toward the transition.

John Donne was his cue. He started the countdown. Three . . . two . . . one.

He'd run the simulation a dozen times. The reality was almost exactly as he'd planned.

Somewhere just off the southeast coast of England, a Tomahawk missile blasted out of the hold of a Liberian tanker and sped toward London at subsonic speed.

Skorzeny's entourage had just left the area when the missile slammed into the Eye.

Milverton had charged the Tomahawk with just enough explosive power to take down the Eye. Naturally, given the velocity, there would be some collateral damage, but it was the visual he was after, the image of the Eye collapsing, and it was the visual he got.

Twisted, burning metal flew in all directions. Some cars, wholly intact, went flying; several landed in the Thames and sank straightaway. Other cars had their bottoms blown away, the passengers plunging screaming 443 feet to their deaths. At ground zero, vehicles exploded, or were tossed skyward.

A second set of codes and the hidden charges in the ship sent the tanker to the bottom. That part he had neglected to mention to the captain when he hired the vessel.

Message delivered, COD — not just to the United States this time, but to the West.

In the distance, he heard the front door open, then close again. No alarms went off. He didn't even turn around as she entered the room.

He could hear the thunk of her shoes as she kicked them off, the rustle of her clothes as they fell to the floor. Her soft footpads as she made her way toward him. In his old SAS days, he might have killed her anyway, so thoroughly reflexive was his training. Maybe he was getting sloppy; maybe he was just getting old. Maybe he really wasn't as controlled as he thought he was. And maybe he was in love with her — not just to guy the old man, but because he really was.

In any case, he knew who was behind him. And despite her inarguable beauty and indisputable nakedness, what was in front of him was even more interesting. A face, re-created by the computers. The face of the man he sought. The face of an old enemy, brought to him courtesy of the very latest in facial-recognition software.

"He got away OK?" she asked.

"That was the idea, wasn't it?"

"Still, seemed a little close."

Milverton tried not to let his irritation show. Everything had worked perfectly. The panic-driven restrictive policies instituted after September 11th had long since been sloughed away, like a snake shedding old skin. Keeping the shipping lanes open had proven more important than inspecting every piece of cargo in their holds. After today, that would all change, of course, but it didn't really matter. What was in port was already in port.

"The idea was to make him look both heroic and like a victim simultaneously, just the way he likes it. It is an unfortunate fact of life, however, tragic accidents do happen."

She gave Milverton a long look. "I didn't think you cared," she said.

"Why don't you pour us both a drink?" he said over his shoulder.

She slipped her bare arms around his neck and set down two martinis in front of them on the desk. *"Voilà,"* she said.

He took a sip, then spun in his chair. Her breasts were already in his face. "It's not nice to keep a lady waiting," said Amanda Harrington.

"What about your daughter?" he asked as she wrapped her legs around his waist.

"I got a sitter," she said.

CHAPTER
FORTY-ONE

Washington, D.C.

The president was on the transatlantic hotline when Seelye entered the Oval Office. He expected a crowd, and was surprised to see that the president was alone.

Tyler motioned for Seelye to sit down as he continued his conversation; on the television, the markets were tanking. After three successive shocks, the Dow had lost more than half its value, and the bottom was nowhere to be seen.

"Annabel," he was saying. "I can assure you that we had no inkling, none at all, that this . . . outrage, as you put it, was about to happen. Yes. Yes. No, I don't care what the 'chatter' is. It's not true. It's simply not true." He held the phone away from his ear and shot his visitor an exasperated glance; even from across the room they could hear the British prime minister's voice, shouting angrily.

"Annabel — Madame Prime Minister — please be careful with your accusations. Do you think for a moment that if we had specific and credible evidence of a terrorist plot on British soil we would not have alerted you? Come on —"

Whatever he was about to say was cut off in a controlled explosion on the other end of the line. Annabel Macombie, the new British PM, was renowned for her Celtic temper. Seelye almost felt sorry for Tyler. Almost.

"Let me just say — excuse me, may I speak? The Dow is below 4,000, my approval numbers are in the toilet, and unless we can nail whoever is behind these outrages, I am not going to be reelected president of the United States next year. So I have a lot more to lose than you. Let me just say that we have our top people working on this. In fact, the director of the NSA has just walked into my office and I'll get back to you as soon as I've had a chance to hear his report. Yes. Yes. Thank you. Yes, you too."

He hung up. Seelye braced himself for what he knew was coming: Mount Tyler, exploding in a fiery shower of profanities. Which blew, right on schedule. "This is war," said the president, after the volcano had subsided. "Flat-out war."

"Yes, sir," said Seelye. "But against whom?"

"That's what you're supposed to tell me. You and the rest of that useless bunch: Rubin, DHS, my national security advisor, what's-her-name, and that fuckwit at CIA. Christ! How many intelligence agencies does a country have to have before one of them gets one fucking thing right?"

"Secretary Rubin's a good man, sir, even if I personally don't care for him."

"What about the others?"

Seelye had no comment.

"Right. So what are he, and you, and I . . . what the fuck are we going to do?"

Seelye knew what that question meant. It didn't mean, "What are we going to do?" It meant, "What can I tell the American people we are already doing and, if it goes wrong, put your head up on a pike and parade it down Constitution Avenue?"

"The first thing we need to do," said Seelye, choosing his words carefully, "we've already done. The next-generation SDI shields are now fully operational on both coasts. Nobody's gonna sneak a missile into New York or San Francisco."

"If Congress knew, they'd have a cow," said the president. "What about ships already in port?"

"The sensors have been in place for a while. So far, so good. No system is completely foolproof. But we believe we have enough safeguards. The real question is, why London?"

Tyler stepped eagerly up to the plate. This was something he could address. "Easy — because they're not as ready as we are. They weren't attacked in 2001, and when they finally were, the attack came on the buses and the subways. Because of the Special Relationship. Because the Brits are our friends, our allies. Our partners. Hell, they do what we tell 'em, no questions asked, if they know what's good for them."

Seelye shook his head. "With all . . . due respect, sir, I think not. Whoever just hit London doesn't care a fig about the 'special relationship.' There's a pattern here, if you can see it."

Tyler couldn't see it.

"Whiplash," said Seelye, after a decent interval. "They're trying to give us whiplash. Spinning us like a top. Or, to put it bluntly, fucking us up, down, and sideways until our eyeballs pop."

That was something this president could understand. "Why?" he said.

"Because they want to. Because they can.

Or, worst of all, because they're about to ram it right up our ass." He enjoyed putting complex ideas into terms the president could readily grasp.

"I thought you assured me Devlin was on this case."

"He's only one man, sir. He's —"

Tyler smashed his fist down on the *Resolute* desk. "Goddamnit, Army, this is no time for pettifogging bullshit." Only Jeb Tyler could yoke together two words like "pettifogging bullshit." That was part of what made him so presidential. "Can he do the job or do I have to call in the Marines?"

"I believe he can, yes sir. Which is why —"

"But can he do it in time? I need you to lay all the cards on the table, right the hell now, so we're both singing from the same choir book." And only Jeb Tyler could shotgun-marry those two metaphors. Which is what made him an asshole. "Why what?"

"Which is why somebody is whipsawing him from coast to coast. Find out who that someone is and you've got your culprit."

"I thought we decided it was this Milverton character."

Seelye shook his head. "Milverton's a hired gun, a soldier of fortune. We need to find out whom he's working for. And, no

389

offense, sir, but you've just made Devlin's job a lot more difficult."

"What do you mean?" asked Tyler, who hated criticism.

"Well, sir, insofar as 'Branch 4' is concerned . . ." he had to choose his words very carefully, "insofar as Branch 4 is concerned, you pretty much blew its existence at the press conference. I'm sure you had a good reason, but right now every foreign intelligence service, both friendly and hostile, will be working that out right now. And let me tell you, they'll be plenty pissed that we haven't been leveling with them about this. The friendlies, I mean."

"Fuck 'em," said President Tyler.

"Now, as far as Devlin is concerned, he's is in California, and" — Seelye pretended to look at his watch — "is in no position at the moment to get to London, if that's what you're asking."

"Send somebody else, then," said Tyler. "One of the other Branch 4's."

"There are —" began Seelye, and then stopped to rephrase. "Branch 4 ops work alone. They cannot be identified, even to members of their own service. You know that, sir."

"Yes," said Tyler, reddening, "but I don't give a damn. I want results, not —"

"Not pettifogging bullshit," supplied Seelye.

"Precisely."

Seelye took a deep breath. Damage control, above all, damage control. "I'll do what I can do, sir . . . without harming operational security, of course."

The president's secretary, Millie Dhouri, was at the doorway. "Mr. President," she said, "I think you should take this call."

"Not now, Millie," said Tyler, but the look on her face bespoke worry, and she had very sharp political instincts. For the call to have bumped its way up to her desk must mean something.

"It's evil, sir," she said softly, shaking. "What he's saying."

The president motioned for her to put the call through on speaker phone. The Oval Office speaker phone was not one of those tinny contraptions that sounded as if you were connected with a wire tied between two hamsters. Instead, it sounded like you were having a private conversation, which is exactly what it was intended to sound like.

"Okay," said Tyler, signaling for her to trace the call. The White House number was in the phone book, and any idiot could call the switchboard. It was a democratic holdover from the days when John Quincy Adams used to go swimming nude in the Potomac, when Andy Jackson let the great unwashed troop through the White House, stealing everything they could lay their hands on, when Truman used to play poker with the press corps and fleece them out of their paltry weekly salaries and make them feel good about it. It was one of the things Tyler had decided he was going to have to change after his reelection.

Tyler picked up the phone. "This is the president of the United States. To whom am I speaking?"

"Mr. President," said the ghostly voice at the other end of the ether, scrambled and opaque. "You are badly trying our patience."

Seelye was already in action, punching in instructions to NSA headquarters. He knew they wouldn't have much time, but at least the call was already being digitally recorded and analyzed. He wanted a full report on his PDA pdq, and made that quite clear as he listened to the conversation.

"We have given you clear instructions and an even clearer timeline. Because we are merciful, we spared the lives of the children in Illinois . . . most of them, anyway."

Seelye was already relaying the conversation capture straight to Devlin. Seelye's BlackBerry lit up as Devlin punched in.

"If anything, we should have thought that the incident in Los Angeles —"

HE'S BRITISH popped up on DIRNSA's screen. KEEP HIM TALKING. Seelye had noticed that too: the pronunciation of "anything" — *en-a-thing.* The use of the word, "should." Not to mention: "Loss ANGE-e-leese."

"— focused your minds, but it appears that such was not the case. It appears that many more deaths will be required. Not just in America, as you have just seen, but all over the Christian West. The stakes have been raised. It is now immaterial whether you accept Allah. You are all doomed."

THIS IS BULLSHIT.

"Therefore rejoice, ye heavens, and ye that dwell in them. Woe to the inhabiters of the earth and of the sea! for the devil is come down unto you, having great wrath, because he knoweth that he hath *but* a short time."

AND THIS IS NOT. IT'S "REVELA-TION."

The line went dead.

Seelye's other BlackBerry buzzed. NSA, with the trace: the technology had been developed at Fort Meade using a fifth-generation network-centric system based on a Rijndael block cipher.

The call was coming from inside the White

House. Which left only two possible conclusions: either the call really was coming from inside the White House, which was impossible, or whoever was making it had cracked the NSA defenses. Seelye decided the president didn't need to know that yet.

"That was this Milverton, wasn't it?"

Seelye had left the scrambled audio feed on, so Devlin could hear every word. "It may well be, yes, sir," he said.

"Get Devlin on this immediately."

I HEARD THAT. Then Devlin punched through another text message. Seelye read it and blanched.

Seelye's perturbed look caught the president's attention. "What's he saying?" asked Tyler.

"He says to say thank you, sir."

"Thank me for what?"

"I'm not sure you want to know, sir," replied Seelye.

"I'm a big boy — let me see it."

Seelye handed the president his Black-Berry: THANK YOU FOR BLOWING ME BEFORE YOU FUCKED ME.

Chapter
Forty-Two

Los Angeles

Devlin switched off his secure PDA and tried to figure out what to do next. It was time for a new game plan. Telling the president of the United States to go fuck himself was as good a place as any to start.

Milverton, he was sure, was back in London; everything pointed to it, including the London Eye attack. But he was just the conductor; someone else had written this symphony and the tempo was going to keep picking up until they got to the climax. Which wasn't going to be pretty, that was for sure. Already the American economy had been rocked back on its heels, and if this didn't stop, and fast, the pieces of it that remained would hardly be worth picking up, although some vulture was sure to do so. And if the government of the United States had been parliamentary instead of republican, it might have already fallen.

But here he was in LA, thousands of miles from the action, with the clock ticking on his own personal presidential directive. What had seemed a good idea — to enlist Eddie Bartlett and mount a counteroperation — was already out of date. Eddie was AWOL, Milverton was too far up his decision loop, and he was getting outmaneuvered at each term. Once Milverton had him in his sights, Devlin knew, he would be a sitting duck for the kill shot.

Think: try to fit the pieces together.

The attack on Edwardsville made some sense, if testing the American defenses had been the point of the exercise. The quick and lethal response had made a point. But what if that was exactly beside the point? Seen in this light, the Grove attack made some sense as a follow-up. It got him pinned down in the wrong direction at the same time it pulled him in further, escalated the terror quotient, and hung him out to dry so that Milverton could execute the third leg of this triad, the attack in London. When you looked at the sequence that way, there was one conclusion: this was all about him.

Which was ridiculous. Why would Milverton, why would anybody, go to all this trouble just to flush Devlin out? Even the highly freighted, emotional angle — middle

America, kids in peril — was no guarantee the president would order a Branch 4 operation. In fact, the opposite. Unless somebody in Washington was risking burning him for a higher purpose — or, worse, didn't mind burning him at all.

If they had wanted to fire a missile at London, Milverton could have done that without Edwardsville and Los Angeles. For another, the damage there, while terrible, was not as extensive as in Los Angeles. It too was still a feint. Milverton was being used, just as Devlin was being used.

Unfortunately, that brought him back to where he started — that this really was all about him. What were the chances that he would get ordered into an operation, and at the presidential level no less, involving Milverton? Milverton, who had never shown any overt or covert connections to the various terrorist factions that had been floating around Europe since the 1980s. Who had always been a rogue freelancer.

What would Marcus Aurelius do? Marcus would let reason rule. Very well, then.

There were only three players involved in this drama that he could see: himself, Milverton, and whoever was paying him. Four, if you counted the possible mole in Washington, whose presence he sensed rather than saw at this point, like Pluto's gravitational effect on Uranus's orbit. Devlin, however, was a great believer in Occam's Razor, which literally posited that beings should not be multiplied except out of necessity — meaning that the mole, if he or she existed, could also be the person running Milverton. So we were back to the triangle — the worst geometry in both love and intelligence work.

"What's wrong?" Maryam joined him on the terrace. She was wearing one of his dress shirts. Possibly the sexiest outfit a woman could wear, but then she knew that already.

"London is what's wrong."

Her face fell, the joy draining out of it. "What is it now?"

"About forty dead," he said. He handed her a small video screen and replayed the whole scene at the London Eye: Skorzeny's press conference, the attack, the aftermath. "Could have been worse. The Brit papers have gone wall-to-wall, of course. Aunty, too. 'Terrorism Strikes Britain Again.' "

Her first observation surprised him: "Funny name for a ship, isn't it?" she said. That was something he hadn't thought of. "*Stella Maris* is one of the Virgin's titles," she continued. "*Star of the Sea*. It's one of the first things you learn when you're named after her. Even in Iran. In this day and age, nobody names ships after religious figures. It's too . . . politically incorrect. Besides," she asked, "who uses a Tomahawk for an assassination attempt? It's like using a mallet to swat a fly."

"We do," he replied. "We tried to get bin Laden with something similar, and the Israelis enjoy nailing whoever's warming the chair marked 'Hamas leader' with one as often as possible —"

He stopped in midsentence. *Assassination* attempt? Put the pieces together. Milverton was whipsawing him. Somebody was running Milverton. The latest attack had come in London . . . had almost killed Skorzeny. And now the *Stella Maris* just so happened to be anchored in Long Beach Harbor. What were the odds?

Maryam was still talking. "It's right here, don't you see? The strike came just as Emanuel Skorzeny was leaving his press conference. It missed him by a matter of minutes. Not to mention half the London press corps."

"Too bad," said Devlin. "A bunch of reporters at the bottom of the Thames is almost as good a start as a bunch of lawyers at the bottom of the Thames."

Maryam ignored the joke, if she even got

it. "Why would anyone want to kill Emanuel Skorzeny?" she went on. "He's one of the most respected, powerful men in Europe, maybe the world."

"Is he?" asked Devlin, noncommittally, seeking to draw her out, play for time while he thought the sequence through, and what he had to do about it.

"You know he is. His foundation has helped more people internationally than most governments ever do. Look how he helped Zimbabwe, post-Mugabe. When that earthquake hit in China last year, his relief teams were some of the first on the scene. It's only natural that he might be a target for . . ."

"For whom?"

"I don't know. Some nuts. Some renegades — you know how many missiles are floating around. The old Soviet satellites. The North Koreans. The —"

"The mullahs?"

"The point is," Maryam said, "Skorzeny is a saint. You heard what he just said. One of his company's ships is in Long Beach Harbor right now, helping out with —"

One of Skorzeny's ships.

He grabbed her by both shoulders and kissed her. "We have to go," he said.

"To London — right?"

"Santa Monica for me, LAX for you. I'll explain later."

He rushed her into the guest room at the east end of the house. Yanked open the door to the closet —

Two rows of men's clothes, in varying sizes, colors, and fashions. She didn't ask; he didn't explain. And one other thing — a single dress. Size 2. Bought in Paris, just before he left, in the hope for the day when he'd see her again. Her gaze traveled from the dress to his eyes. There was nothing to say.

He was already pulling "Mr. Grant's" clothes. "Grant" was taller (lifts), fatter (thank you, Universal Studios prop department), slouchier, and sported a very unfashionable mustache and a set of discolored teeth. In the end, there really wasn't much to the art of disguise. It was like caricature in reverse: you obscured your salient features and made people concentrate on the things that weren't important. The rest could be done with voice, accent, and mien; after all, with the passage of time people often didn't recognize their own relatives, so why should a total stranger be any different.

As he pulled on the fake midsection, he thought once more of Occam's Razor: *Entia*

non sunt multiplicanda praeter necessitatem.
Easy for William of Ockham to say, hard for
Devlin to live by.

She dropped his shirt to the floor and
slipped on the dress. It fit her perfectly.

"Let's go."

CHAPTER
FORTY-THREE

Santa Monica/Long Beach, California
The RAND Corporation building stood out among the buildings in "downtown" Santa Monica like the proverbial sore thumb — but only if you were already aware that you had just struck your opposable digit with a hammer. Located south of the Third Street Promenade, across Main Street from city hall and the courthouse, it was well away from the congeries of bums and winos — the "homeless" — who had transformed what was once LA's foremost beach community into Berkeley South. Near RAND, however, there were no homeless to be seen: they didn't have the requisite security clearance. Few did, homeless or not.

He did.

Devlin glanced at his watch. It was more than a watch, of course. The team leader could text him at any time, over a secure uplink, and his message would appear nearly instantly on the watch's face.

He looked out at his audience in the small auditorium. Some of the faces — he never forgot a face, because that was how he'd been trained — were familiar. He smiled as he took inventory; to judge from the haircuts and the clothes, mostly Americans. A couple of MI-6 Brits in ill-fitting suits from the Savoy Tailors Guild. Members of the German Federal Intelligence Service, the *Bundesnachrichtendient,* in their motley. Queens-born Mossad and Shin Bet, at home in both worlds. Three or four Chinese, whose bona fides he immediately discounted by 50 percent; unlike the Russians, they were still new at this game, and incredibly obvious. He'd get the security report later, but already he was tailoring his remarks. The key to one of these speeches was to balance genuine information with even better disinformation, and he was more than up to the task.

"Let me be blunt," he began without preamble. "In the years since September 11, despite all our intelligence triumphs — necessarily recondite — we as a society have grown complacent. Comfortable. Therefore, I hope and trust that the events of the past two days might serve as a wake-up call for all of us. For, whatever our political differences, we are all civilized men and women here." There were very few women present, but linguistically he felt compelled to maintain the egalitarian fiction in case somehow his remarks got leaked to the *Los Angeles Times* Web site; even though the physical newspaper was dying, the handful of reporters tied in to the blogs and RSS and Twitter feeds could still make plenty of trouble. Loose lips still sank ships.

"I refer not only to the events of the past two days in Edwardsville and here in Los Angeles, but to the ongoing series of cyber-attacks on our mainframes at the Pentagon, in Langley, in Fort Meade, in Washington, and elsewhere. Forget everything you think you know about contemporary terrorism. We are no longer up against a nation-state, or even a stateless group of like-minded individuals motivated by ideology, such as al-Qaeda. That, as they say, is so yesterday."

Murmurs and polite chuckles ripped through his select audience as he reached for the glass of water. Which enabled him to see what was going on in Long Beach via secure video feed in real time . . .

The *Stella Maris* was a magnificent vessel. Displacing nearly 200,000 metric tons, the big cargo ship was riding low in the water, preparing to get her cargo offloaded. The dock was a hive of activity as the longshoremen got ready to unload her, but in fact security forces were everywhere, disguised a teamsters, sailors, even casual passersby.

The red-zone call-in had pretty much confirmed that. Since September 11, every major American port was equipped with the latest radiation-detection devices. On three separate occasions, Middle Eastern terrorists had tried to smuggle in a suitcase nuke, but each time they had been tripped up by the detection devices on the docks.

But what if the docks were too late a line of defense? That was what the drone overflights were for. Except they didn't look like drones. Not the kind that had struck fear into the hearts of late *mujahedin* in Iraq and Afghanistan, anyway. They looked like kites.

No California beach was complete without its complement of kites. It was amazing how high you could get some of them, and how sensitive the radiation sensors were these days. No matter how strong the ocean breeze, all they needed was a clear line of sight to their target, and the DHS agents who were lucky enough to draw beach duty could take their readings from the comfort of their beach blankets, while ogling the rear ends of the teenage girls wiggling by.

Devlin had the readings on his special PDA before he left the house, which triggered his "go" order to the SEAL team standing by in a sub off the coast of Huntington Beach on a training exercise. The SDVs were already launched and away by the time he got to Santa Monica.

"As you know, the National Security Research Division's International Security and Defense Policy Center, based in Arlington, exists on the leading edge of threat assessment. Together with our governmental and NGO colleagues around the world, it is our duty to constantly evaluate and extrapolate, not simply from 'known knowns' to 'known unknowns,' but into the realm of 'unknown unknowns' as well. As the United States Marine Corps likes to say, 'the difficult we do right away. The impossible takes a little longer.' But let me assure you — since our national wake-up call on the morning of September 11, 2001, the impossible is not only what we seek to do, it is, in many respects, what we have already done."

A small ripple of applause.

"The Marines have another saying, less widely known but, for our purposes, even more apposite. 'Don't worry about what your enemy might do. Worry about what he

407

can do, and plan accordingly.'

"About our enemy's intention, there can be no doubt. It is nothing less than the destruction of western civilization. By that, I don't just mean the current American administration, or Israel, or global warming, or world hunger. We could dismantle the Cathedral of Notre Dame, obliterate Tel Aviv, reduce our carbon emissions to zero, return to the Stone Age, and starve ourselves to death, and that still would not be enough.

"Many of you have perhaps seen the motion picture, *Independence Day.* In it, the president of the United States confronts a captured alien invader and asks whether our two species might live in peace. 'No peace,' replies the alien. 'What do you want us to do, then?' inquires the president. 'Die,' replies the alien. That, in a nutshell, sums up our enemy's demands. No amount of appeasement, short of suicide, will satisfy him. Ladies and gentlemen, we are not fighting a twenty-first-century war. We are fighting a nineteenth-century war — not so much against zealotry, but against Nietzschean nihilism, masked by religious doctrine, enervation, and anomie."

As he expected, this did not go over well with some of those in attendance. Probably half the members of his audience were "root cause" types; the idea that sheer nihilism might lay at the dark heart of society's enemies was something they were not prepared to admit. As they muttered among themselves, "Mr. Grant" took the opportunity to glance at his watch.

Seal Delivery Vehicles were the latest thing in delivering death to your ocean-borne doorstep. A kind of minisubmarine, they carried a six-man team consisting of a pilot, co-pilot, and combat swimmers. The SDV Devlin's team was using was a Mark 8 Model 1, which ran on lithium-ion batteries and came fully equipped with its own navigation and communications systems. In other words, it was totally silent.

The radiation detectors had come back negative, which was exactly what he had expected. What also was expected was the dead zone in the center of the ship's cargo hold, the lead-lined "scientific" area. Everything, even people, emit some sort of radiation, but not this blank space; using imaging radar, he had run the image through every NSA analytical program he could think of, but all that computing power had only served to confirm his suspicions. There was something there that Skorzeny didn't want anybody to see.

Prior to arriving in Santa Monica, Devlin had taken a crash course on Emanuel Skorzeny. Aside from his well-publicized forays in international finance and philanthropy, he was not the sort of man to come across the CSS radar screens. He was immensely rich and powerful, of course, but the occasional indictment for insider trading notwithstanding — inevitable in his line of work — there was nothing criminal about the man. Indeed, there was much that was admirable, including his well-publicized personal story and his generous philanthropy.

Still, there was a strain of misanthropy running through Skorzeny's tangled skein that bothered Devlin. He would have to spend a lot more time with the files, of course, but the outlines of a very disturbed individual were there to be seen. The childhood alone — the DP camps — would be enough to affect even the sanest boy. But the closer he had looked at Skorzeny, the stranger the man became.

Take his charitable causes, an odd mixture of cultural conservatism — through the Skorzeny Foundation, run by a British woman named Amanda Harrington, he lavishly funded orchestras and opera houses

410

around the world — and political radical-
ism. There wasn't a Green Party in Europe
he didn't donate generously to, and there
was considerable evidence that, through
cutouts, shells, dummies, and nonprofits, he
was injecting vast sums of money into the
American political process, no matter how
illegal it was.

At home in Echo Park, Devlin had har-
nessed all the computing power at NSA,
CIA, and Poughkeepsie to search every
existing database — closed- and open-
source — for a police record and had come
up with nothing. About the only negative
thing he could find was the sudden death of
one of Skorzeny International's board
members, but strokes could happen to anybody.

As Devlin had learned from long experience in the trenches of classified material,
nobody was clean. It was part of the human
condition. Everybody had skeletons, past
activities, furtive desires, illicit relationships,
occasions of sin both venial and mortal. In
the great court of law in the sky, everybody
was guilty, especially in the age of computers and the Internet. The only question was,
how you dealt with it: fake it, lie about it,
cop a plea, or brazen it out. With the abolition of sin, the last option had become more

and more attractive.

"Brazen" might let you skate in the court-room, but the rules of evidence in the Moral Court were much less restrictive; there, anything went. So the smart play was to admit almost everything. Blow your own cover if you had to, give up your best friend, plead out to almost every charge. Toss them fish. But save the last minnow, the one part of your cover story that didn't pass the smell test, until they pried it from your cold, dead hands.

But Skorzeny wasn't just clean; he was scrubbed — scrubbed in a way only money and access could buy.

"In position," crackled the voice in his hidden earpiece.

"And so the question arises, how do we fight back? Do we, in fact, even bother to fight back at all, or do we allow ourselves to succumb to the false dichotomy between the rule of law and the right of self-preservation? These are questions that each of us, each country, each society, must answer for itself. I imagine these are the same questions that the fifth-century poets of the Roman Empire asked themselves, just before the Vandals sacked their city. Perhaps from their example, we can glean the answer. Or at least understand what *not* to do."

"Dr. Grant," said one of the Germans, "I have a question . . ."

Devlin's eyes, a nameless Navy SEAL, was standing in Angel's Gate Park, overlooking the harbor to the east and the Pacific Ocean to the south.

They had caught one big break. The *Stella Maris* was not truly in port. Instead, she had dropped anchor in deeper waters outside the Los Angeles Main Channel. That in itself was only slightly suspicious — the urgency of offloading the supplies was the stated reason — but taken together with everything else, made Devlin sure he was doing the right thing.

Everybody had heard of the SEALs, but few Americans actually knew who they were, or what they did. The SEALs — SEa, Air, and Land forces — had grown out of the old Underwater Demolition Teams (UDT). Basically they were waterborne commandos who could slip into an enemy port, blow shit up, and retire without a trace.

Most people forgot that President Kennedy, in his famous 1961 speech about putting a man on the moon within the decade, had thrown the lamb chop past the wolf by strengthening the Special Ops in Vietnam at the same time. Not wanting to play second fiddle to the Army Rangers, the Navy got into the act, establishing Team One in Coronado and Team Two in Virginia. This is where it got serious. In addition to underwater demolition, the UDT lads got training in sabotage, hand-to-hand combat, even parachuting. Languages became a must; any SEAL who couldn't pass for native in at least three languages washed out before the end of the training period. They were men after his own heart.

"Go," he said, over the wallawalla.

"Roger that," said the voice in his ear.

"It seems to me," said the German, "that without the law, we have no society. So I am perhaps a bit confused by your implication that there might be, shall we say, a higher law than the law itself. Can you please clarify?"

Devlin resisted the temptation to reply in German. Schopenhauerian questions were best answered in the tongue whose syntax gave them birth, but "Mr. Grant's" German was not totally fluent, and he didn't feel like dumbing himself down at this point. Not with what was happening in Long Beach.

"Thank you, Dr. Hesse, for your most astute and provocative question. I think that what I am trying to say, in essence, is this — what we are up against is not something new. There have been forces of savagery antithetical to our culture since its beginning. Since the Irish monks salvaged the detritus of Roman civilization and retreated to the rocky western shores of Eire. Since St. Malachy mentored Bernard of Clairvaux. This savagery — I'm sorry, but there is really no other word to describe it — must be fought with both understanding and resolve and even, at times, utter ruthlessness. Fortunately we in the United States are blessed with some of the finest intelligence and security operatives in the world."

The BND man pondered this for a moment. "But, if what you said about the nature of the threat is true, doesn't that give these 'operatives' extraordinary executive authority with very little accountability?"

Inwardly, Devlin smiled. "The best way I can answer that question is to quote Wendell Phillips, in a speech before the Massachusetts Antislavery Society in 1852. 'Eternal vigilance is the price of liberty,' he said. I really can't improve on that."

■ ■ ■ ■

Half an hour later the news was on the radio, on television, and on the Web sites:

"*Stella Maris* Sinks at Long Beach." By the time she sank, imploded from the bottom with limpet mines, placed with the aid of radar-and-ELINT-surveillance jammers, the SEALs had retrieved whatever had been in the dead zone, and would let him know sooner than ASAP; if his hunch was right, this was a major national-security issue now.

And by the time they did, he'd be on an airplane. Long Beach Airport was only ten minutes away and he'd booked a seat for himself on a flight to Baltimore. Maryam was already in the air.

■ ■ ■ ■

DAY FOUR

■ ■ ■ ■

Take no enterprise in hand at haphazard, or without regard to the principles governing its proper execution.

— MARCUS AURELIUS, *Meditations,* Book IV

CHAPTER
FORTY-FOUR

London

It was a shaken Emanuel Skorzeny who absorbed the shock of the sinking of the *Stella Maris* just after midnight in his suite at the Savoy. It was all over Sky News by the time Amanda Harrington reached the fifth floor. The river and the lights of the South Bank held no charm either for her or her boss at this moment. "Mr. Skorzeny," she began. "I'm so —"

Skorzeny gave her his best basilisk glare. "This is war," he said, "Someone is at war with us, Miss Harrington."

"Sir, there's no evidence —"

"Evidence is for lawyers. I am interested in reality. And the reality is, someone is waging war against me, and I want something done about it."

"Yes, sir." As usual, she was juggling a brace of cell phones. "I've already —"

"Please sit down. Turn those things off

and put them away. Sit here, by me." He patted the empty space on the sofa next to him. Lying on the coffee table was one of the Savoy's Victorian signatures: a three-button panel with which one could summon the maid, room service, or the valet. The help.

Warily, she crossed the room and sat. The TV was still on, flashing its silent images. "I gather they're saying it was some kind of accident, an explosion in the ship's —"

"Let me be blunt. I believe the U.S. government was involved in this. In fact, I am certain of it. I want my protestations to reach the ear of the president, with the understanding that I will go public with them if I do not receive some sort of satisfaction. Is that clear?"

"Yes, sir."

"We have many people in Washington on our payroll, including several congressmen and senators. I am thinking of one senator in particular who has long been a friend to us and, I am given to believe, is now even more sympathetic. Despite their political differences, he is a friend to the current president and has his ear. He is the chairman of a powerful committee. He knows things."

Amanda wasn't quite sure where Skorzeny

was going with this. "What is it, exactly, that you wish me to do, Mr. Skorzeny?" she asked.

Skorzeny leveled his gaze at her. It always made her flesh crawl, they way he looked at her. "I want the man behind this punished."

How she was supposed to accomplish that was beyond her. "Sir, the United States is a sovereign country. Even assuming that you're right and for some reason an American operative was involved, what can we do about it?"

"This American operative," said Skorzeny levelly, "is a devil, whose very existence is an affront to me and everything I hold dear. He must be terminated."

Amanda gasped. "Are you asking me to kill him? You . . . I don't —"

Skorzeny waved away her objection. "No. I am saying *they* can kill him. And that is what I want Senator Hartley to effect."

"And just how am I supposed to convince him to do that?"

"You aren't. That is a job for your boyfriend. Your job is to make sure he carries it out."

Her heart nearly stopped. Had he been following them? Monitoring them? Had Milverton blabbed? They had been as discreet as possible, which was to say very. Or was he just guessing?

"Boyfriend? I'm sure I don't know what you mean, sir. My duties as a mother preclude . . ."

He reached out and stroked her hair. "There, there," he purred. "You look tired, stressed out."

She tried to relax a little. "It's been a very bad day all around."

"I should say so. I was nearly killed." Another dig, another suspicion?

"Mr. Skorzeny," she said. "Milverton calibrated the missile strike exactly, to the second. As we all agreed. It was meant to be close, to make you look good. Heroic. A victim, in the modern fashion." She was glad that Milverton had already prepped her.

"I've already been a victim," he said, "many times over . . . and yet something went wrong."

"Nothing went wrong, Mr. Skorzeny. You are here." She reached out and took his hand away from her hair, but continued to hold it. "*We* are here. Together."

That was all the encouragement he needed. He tugged her hand closer, pulling her toward him. And then he lunged for her, throwing his arms around her, kissing her, his mouth seeking hers.

She knew that to pull away now was to risk everything. She had seen, so often, the side of Emanuel Skorzeny few others had: the Caligula-side, in which the slightest frustration of his will to power was met with instant punishment. The uncontrollable, raging man-child, bearing the hurt of generations in his breast and the vengeance of centuries in his heart.

And so, despite her loathing, she kissed him back, stroked him, and kept stroking him. At this moment she wished him dead, wished the missile strike had hit him, that they had gone ahead and done the deed and rid themselves and the world of this monster. But now it was too late.

At last, she felt him softening, relaxing, withdrawing. When at last he subsided, she pulled herself away, smoothing her skirt. "There," she said soothingly. "There . . ."

Gradually, his breathing returned to normal. If he felt any shame, it was not reflected in his face. "Do you know what Blake said, Miss Harrington? He said, 'Those who restrain desire do so because theirs is weak enough to be restrained.' I could not agree more."

He looked at her with that reptilian, penetrating, blinkless gaze he could always muster when he needed to stare down an opponent. There was no way to beat him, no way to insult him, no way to fight back. He was impervious to normal human emotions. All except one.

"Are *you* my enemy, Amanda?" he said. It was the first time he had used her Christian name.

"No, sir. I am not your enemy."

"Then carry out my wishes."

"Yes, sir."

"You do love me, don't you, Miss Harrington?" he said as he reached for her again. She had just enough time to be amazed that he could recover this quickly when he was on her again, like an old tiger leaping upon a piece of helpless prey and tearing it limb from limb.

I hate you, she thought as he ripped her clothes away. *I hate you and I wish you were dead.*

As she fell backward on the couch, her eye caught the three-button panel lying on the coffee table, and thought about reaching out, pressing, calling for help. But she knew if she did that, she'd never leave the Savoy alive. And there was a little girl at home who needed her.

"Do not fail me," he said as she closed her eyes and thought of England.

CHAPTER
FORTY-FIVE

Eastern Shore of Maryland

President Jeb Tyler looked toward the west over the Chesapeake Bay and took a deep breath. Either this gamble would pay off or it wouldn't. It wasn't just his job on the line, it was the fate of the entire country. Even for an experienced and avid poker player like himself, this was the biggest gamble of his life.

Nothing — no advisors, no campaign managers, no public relations assholes — prepared you for this. All his life he'd been a politician, and to him "politician" wasn't a dirty word. Sure it was sometimes mean, sure you had to associate with some pretty unsavory characters and, most of all, you had to forgo the notion that the ends never justified the means. That was for sissies and nuns: in politics, the ends were the only thing that could possibly justify the means. And if you believed in those ends, believed in the rightness and the justice of them, then you were in it to win it by any means necessary short of murder. And, sometimes, not even that, if some of the tales told of his predecessors were to be believed.

Still, Jeb Tyler never thought it would happen to him. He'd led a charmed life, a golden boy life, a life too good to willingly change. When he'd first announced that he was running for president, his friends told him he was insane to subject his life to the kind of scrutiny he had been able to avoid during his single term as a senator. Politics, he reflected, was like a love affair, and at the right time, he had been Mr. Right.

But this . . . this was different. He had never expected to be a war president, not like his predecessors, never expected to have an atrocity like this happen on his watch. And while Louisiana's politics were plenty dirty, they were nothing like what he was about to go through. What he was about to do.

Betray his only friend in the capital. Not "betray" exactly — the betrayal had already occurred — but certainly destroy. At last he understood the old joke; if you want a friend in Washington, get a dog.

"May I get you something, sir?" asked his orderly, Manuel. Manuel Concepcion was a

Filipino, like many of the servants in the White House. Twenty years ago, he would have been black.

"What about a Labrador Retriever?"

Manuel was used to the president's jokes, but he didn't get this one. "Excuse me, sir?"

"A joke, Manny . . . how's the market doing?" He knew the answer was going to be bad, the only question was how bad.

Manuel glanced away. "Down another six hundred points or so," he said.

After three straight incidents, the shock to the world's stock markets had been devastating. He might have to shut the markets down by early this afternoon.

"On second thought, I'll have a gin and tonic. And a whiskey neat for my guest."

"Yes, sir," said Manuel, withdrawing for real this time.

Jeb Tyler sighed. He'd only been president for three years and already the demands of the office were wearing him down. He hated looking in the mirror any more; every year in the White House added at least four years to his face and took a decade off his ticker. Nobody got out alive from this gilded cage, nobody's reputation survived unsavaged, and, as he often did, he wondered why he had spent so much time and money and love and friendship attaining the office. Far better, he sometimes thought, to just . . .

To just what? This is what he lived for. Elections. Campaigns. Votes. He really didn't want to do anything else, but he was surprised when he walked into the Oval Office on the first day and realized he didn't have the slightest idea what to do. Somehow, it looked easier from the outside. He felt like Robert Redford in *The Candidate,* at the end, just after he wins the senate race, asking his strategist, "What do we do now?"

So not only was it time for results, it was time for a political play, a game-changer. It was time for him to start acting like a president instead of a politician.

In the distance, he could hear the car pulling up, doors opening, feet hitting the gravel; for him, the rubber meeting the road.

Manuel materialized at his side, the drinks ready on a silver tray, which he set down on a small table. "Would you kindly ask the senator to meet me down here, at the dock. No SS either. I cannot think with their earpieces up my ass. Besides, this is just between us girls."

Manuel looked dubious. "But, sir, Mr. Willson —"

"Works for me and the American people, Manuel," said the president. "So, if he gives you any shit, tell him to go fuck himself and tell him I said so."

"Yes, Mr. President," said Manuel.

Jeb Tyler plucked a skimmer out of his pocket and sent it sailing across the water on a six-bounce on the Chesapeake. A minor river suddenly turned into a mighty bay, surging its way toward the Atlantic. Nothing, abruptly becoming something. Just like a politician. Just like a president.

The Senate, on the other hand, had become a hotbed of blow-dried, Botoxed seditionists, each one plotting to succeed him, if and when they got their chance. His visitor was no exception — friend or no friend.

"Hello, Bob," he said, turning around at the footfalls. "You look like shit."

Hartley was a mess. There was blood all over his shirtfront and the lapels of his suit. His hair was mussed. He looked like he hadn't slept for a month. He was dazed, disoriented, and right where Tyler wanted him.

Hartley tried to speak, but couldn't. He couldn't believe what was happening to him. In just a couple of days his entire world had been turned upside down. And now here he was, at the president's private retreat on Maryland's eastern shore. Tyler liked to come here to crab and fish and be alone. Even members of his inner circle rarely got an invitation.

Tyler took one of the drinks and, tantalizingly, left the other sitting on the tray.

Hartley wanted a drink. Even more, he wanted a hot shower and a change of clothes, but that apparently was not on the agenda today. "I gather you're thinking of running against me," said Tyler. "Even for an opportunistic asshole like you, Bob, the audacity is breathtaking. But I guess that's what I get for reaching across the aisle. I guess that's what I get for considering you a friend."

He sipped, savoring his gin and tonic. "But what the hell, go ahead. Run. I want you to do it. I want you to give me the fight of my life. I want you to tear me a new one. In fact, let's drink to it."

Tyler handed Hartley his whiskey: "To an honorable campaign," the president said. They didn't clink glasses.

Hartley took a long draught of his whiskey. He was trying to wrap his mind around what the president was saying to him, and why. There was no way Jeb Tyler didn't still want to be president. It had to be a trap.

Hartley wiped his bloody nose on his sleeve and mustered as much dignity as possible. "Why are you doing this to me?"

"Good question. I could ask you the same

thing. Complicated answers to both. Right?" Tyler looked at the steward, who hovered back into view. "Manuel?"

Carefully, Manuel laid two dossiers on the table. Even in his condition, Hartley could see that one was marked HARTLEY and the other, SCI.

"Which one am I supposed to look at?"

"You're the guest — you choose."

Gingerly, Hartley set his drink down and took the one marked SCI. He knew it had to be dynamite. "I want you to make a big stink about this — a very big stink," the president said. "About how I haven't been fully leveling with the American people in this time of crisis. That you have somehow gotten your hands on this explosive information and, given this grave threat to our national security, you feel compelled to share it with your fellow citizens. And you'll do it exactly when I tell you."

This was crazy. Hartley's mind reeled as he tried to glean Tyler's angle. "But, Jeb — Mr. President — this doesn't make any sense. I can't. This is a matter of national security. I won't."

"Have it your way, Bob," said Tyler, pushing the other dossier toward him.

Somehow, Hartley knew what was in there even before he opened it. Probably the photos of himself and the dead boy. Probably the photos that awful man had taken of him, after he'd knocked Hartley out. Not just career-ending pictures, but life-ending pictures. If these ever got out, he'd just have to kill himself. "Where did you get these?" he stammered.

Tyler laughed. "Over the e-transom, as it were. They were delivered embedded in the Paris Hilton blowjob video. I guess somebody out there has a sense of humor, eh?"

"And you'll release these if I don't —"

"Ain't bipartisanship grand?"

A new thought hit Hartley just before a wave of nausea swept over him. Suddenly, the whiskey didn't taste so great any more and he just had time to turn away from the president and his valet before he hurled. Neither of them made a move to help him or offer him a towel. Hartley wiped his frothing mouth on his sleeve and tried to compose himself as much as possible under the circumstances. "What if I win?" he croaked

The president didn't have to answer that question and, after a moment, even Hartley understood: he was damned if he did and damned if he didn't and finished politically either way. Tyler would take a scurrilous beating while he presented himself to the

American people as their savior. And then this stuff would come out, and Tyler would win in a walk. It was brilliant politics. Hartley nodded mutely, defeated.

Tyler slapped him, hard, on the back. A cold, hard slap, with the none of the affectionate bonhomie he was used to. Jeb Tyler had changed.

"I'm glad that's settled, Bob. Here — take your file with you. There's plenty of copies where that came from." He turned to the Filipino steward. "Manuel, burn the other one."

"Yes, Mr. President," said Manuel.

He motioned toward the house and a few seconds later Hartley could see the Whippet and the Refrigerator marching toward them. He'd never liked Augie Willson, the head of the Secret Service presidential detail, and assumed they were Willson's way of telling him the feeling was mutual.

Hartley had nothing left to lose. "Why Jeb?" he asked. "Why are you doing this to me? I've always been your —"

"My what?" Tyler shot back. "You've always been your own best friend, Bob, until you got yourself a new little playmate. Well, we found out about him, and now I'm going to fuck him up and fuck up everybody else involved with this . . . with this clusterfuck." Hartley couldn't help but thinking that, for the first time in his presidency, Jeb Tyler was actually acting like a president. Even if it was at his expense.

"The other day, a very wise and brave man said something to me. Okay, not said. He texted it to me. Wanna know what he said?"

The Whippet and the Refrigerator were almost upon them now.

" 'THANK YOU FOR BLOWING ME BEFORE YOU FUCKED ME.' That's what he said to me. What do you supposed he meant by that, Bob? I mean, I figured you might be able to translate."

The two goons flanked him, side by side. "I believe you've already made the acquaintance of two of the best members of my Secret Service detail," said Tyler. "They're going to be your new best friends for the duration of this situation. They're going to make sure you do exactly as you're told. And if you don't, they're going to help you meet with a very unfortunate and painful accident. Are we clear about this, Bob?"

"Yes, sir." Hartley started to add something, but Tyler cut him off.

"And don't even think about asking me if you can clean up. You're going to stay in those clothes until you get back to the Watergate and then, if you're a good boy, your new roomies may think about letting you have some shower time before you announce. Which, by the way, will be when you drop your first bombshell about that rogue intelligence operation that the American people need to know about. Understood?"

Hartley nodded, but his eyes were vacant.

"Good. Now get out of here. You disgust me." Tyler signaled to Hartley's babysitters. As they led him away —

"Oh, and Bob — one more thing." He paused for effect, then fired. "Don't drop the soap." Tyler watched as the two Secret Service men led Hartley away. One chess piece in motion, another couple to go.

"Did you catch most of that, Army?" said Tyler to General Seelye, emerging from the woods.

"Yes, sir," Seelye had never been here before, to the president's private retreat, so close to the White House and yet worlds away.

"Army, what I'm doing may seem strange, but I need you to trust me." Usually, Tyler indulged in some small talk, especially after a snort, but today he was all business. "I know you and some of the others think I'm weak, that I'm a sob sister, a weenie — hell, I know half the country does too. And these last three days haven't been good ones, to say the least. But now I need you to do something for me, even if it doesn't seem at first glance the right thing to do."

Seelye studied Tyler carefully. For the first time since he became president, Tyler actually seemed like a human being instead of a politician. "You're the president. You give me an order, my job is to execute." He decided not to say a word about Hartley's appearance, or what the president had just asked him to do. It was none of his business unless Tyler brought it up.

"Good," said Tyler. "I want you to suspend Devlin's operation, effective immediately."

That was something completely unexpected. "Suspend, Mr. President?"

"As in, terminate."

General Armond Seelye took a step back from the president of the United States. "You do understand the implications of that order, sir?"

"You and Rubin explained them to me all too well during the Edwardsville thing. About Branch 4 and its internal rules."

"Senator Hartley was present too as I recall." It was as gentle a remonstrance as he could manage under the circumstances.

"Yes, he was . . . well, as the lawyers like to say, you can't unring the bell. So why don't you let me deal with Bob Hartley."

Now Seelye got it. "The phone tap that Devlin put on him. That's what this is about, isn't it?" Jesus Christ, was Tyler running his own operation now?

"Bob was in contact today with someone claiming to represent Emanuel Skorzeny, the owner of the *Stella Maria*."

"The ship that sank yesterday at Long Beach."

"Yes. Skorzeny is convinced that we did it."

"Of course we did. Devlin did. You authorized him to take any measures that —"

"Well, now I'm un-authorizing him. Turns out there was nothing on that ship, just humanitarian supplies and some equipment that one of Skorzeny's companies was going to use for some high-atmosphere ecological experiments. I gather that, because of the sensitivity of the instruments, they kept it in a shielded vault in the hold."

That was just great. Seelye tried his best to put a good face on Devlin's actions. "Which obviously aroused his suspicions."

"Which just as obviously were ill-founded," snapped Tyler. "Then there's the little matter of an FBI team that ended up dead in NoVa. We found three bodies in a van parked in Tyson's Corners. They were all laid out neat; a phone tip told the Director where to find them. Any guesses?"

There was nothing to say. The president went on. "It's clear to me that Devlin has been blown, and that his usefulness to us is now at an end. Hell, he practically said it himself."

A cold chill was dancing up and down Seelye's spine, the hand of a long-dead ghost passing over him. "You realize what you're saying?"

Tyler turned and looked Seelye square in the eye, as if he were trying to press a particularly crucial point home in a closing argument.

"All I know is what you've told me about Branch 4. Your procedures are your procedures. Do I make myself clear?"

At first, Seelye was not sure he did. "Yes, sir. According to the rules, any Branch 4 operative who is publicly —"

"As I said," said Tyler, turning away. "Your rules are your rules. Now, I suggest you get back to Fort Meade and act accordingly."

"Yes, Mr. President."

"Oh, and Army . . ." Seelye looked at his commander in chief. "You were right. I am getting the hang of this intel business."

CHAPTER
FORTY-SIX

Fort Meade, Maryland

Weather balloons?

That was what was in the hold of the *Stella Maris*. A couple of fucking weather balloons.

Devlin switched off his PDA, atomizing the confidential report sent to him anonymously by his SEAL buddies in San Diego. He parked his car in the far lot and made his way toward the big black building. Even though it was his home office, so to speak, he hardly ever came here. When he did, he came as he did now, as a custodian in overalls, a nonentity who would blend in with the rest of the night staff, and nobody the wiser. It was, he reflected, a fitting metaphor for his life.

Who was he, really? Everything else flowed from that, including the reason that somebody was trying to flush him out, humiliate him, and kill him.

He came in via one of the service entrances, where his low-level security pass would gain him admission. At this hour, late afternoon, most of the salaried workers were on their way out the door, heading for the Baltimore-Washington parkway and the comforts of spousal, suburban Maryland and Virginia.

"Hey, Brick," said one old hand to Devlin as he shuffled toward the front of the building. That was how he was known here. "Brick" Davis. Nobody got the joke.

Brick wasn't very bright and sure wasn't very threatening. In fact, unlike his Cagney namesake, he wasn't much of anything at all, which is why hardly anybody ever noticed him. Just the way Devlin liked things.

"Hey, Jake," he mumbled, not looking up.

Just off the main hall, he slipped into a custodial room. Like everything at Fort Meade, this room too demanded a level of operational security. There was too much access to the building's support systems, its wiring, its air ducts, its ventilation, its electronic infrastructure, which was why he had chosen to put his office here.

The station included several rooms, including a locker room, a bathroom, and a room in which all the tools of the janitor's trade were kept. Devlin headed straight for the bathroom.

Inside, he closed the door. He moved toward the sink and stared at it hard for the retinal scan. He placed his left hand at a certain spot on the mirrored glass and with his right hand, flushed the toilet. The back of the medicine cabinet slid open, revealing the control panel behind it. As he began punching in the codes that only he knew —

A banging on the door. The jiggling of the doorknob. A desperate voice. "Anybody in there?"

No time to close the back of the medicine chest. He shut the mirror as quietly as he could. "I'm on the john," he croaked. "Gonna be a while."

"Yeah, well hurry it up will ya? I got a four-alarm fire going here."

He recognized the voice. It was Jasper Reddiwood, the old Baltimorean who had worked here for years, knew every square inch of the building, and never opened his mouth about anything. He flushed and ran the sink. "Be right out, Jasper."

"Brick, is that you?" came the voice from the other side of the door. "Jesus, man, I'm sorry, but —"

"No sweat, Jasper." The codes were already activated, but there was no way he could close the panel without aborting the sequence. The way he'd designed it, an abort and reset meant that he would have to wait at least one hour before reinitializing the sequence. He didn't have an hour.

Even worse, he still had to punch in the finishing sequence codes, otherwise . . . well, there was no otherwise. A powerful plastic explosive would rip through the room and kill them both. He had twelve minutes.

He opened the door. Jasper looked like he was about to have a brown cow. "Thanks, man," gulped Jasper, heading for the can. But Devlin made no move to leave. Instead, he went back to the sink and proceeded to wash his hands, slowly and carefully. Jasper looked at him like he was nuts.

"Be my guest," said Devlin, looking away. Jasper had no choice. He dropped his drawers and did his business with an explosive, audible sense of relief. Devlin kept washing his hands.

Jasper finished up and moved toward the sink. Devlin was still washing. He moved aside to let Jasper clean himself, but still made no move to leave. Jasper ran the hot water over his soapy hands without saying a word, then turned to the blow dryer, and dried himself off. Devlin moved back to the sink and started washing up again.

"What's wrong with you man?"

"Not feeling too well myself, Jasper," he replied, still facing away.

"Brick, you are one weird dude," said Jasper.

"That's what everybody says," said Devlin, still washing. "Thick as a brick."

Jasper edged out the door. "You have yourself a nice night, Brick, you hear?"

"I got a lot of work to do, Jasper," he said. "Cleaning up and all. Cleaning up."

"Right," said Jasper, and then he was gone.

Devlin whipped open the medicine chest door and finished the sequence with less than two minutes to spare.

The back wall of the bathroom slid open and he stepped into the next room. His office.

Not even Seelye's office was this well equipped. It was a mirror of his Falls Church home, but with the added advantage of zero possible security leaks; everything was wired directly into NSA's main system; whatever No Such Agency was watching and listening to, so was he.

There was a message waiting for him as he logged in. It was from Seelye: ABORT A/P POTUS DIRECTIVE THIS DAY.

He sat there for a moment, absorbing the import. That was it, then. He was well and truly fucked. The president of the United States had compromised operation security, hung him out to dry, and signed his death warrant. The sinking of the *Stella Maris* had just clobbered him with blowback. It was time to get out, and fast. But not before he got what he came here for.

Think.

Everything had a pattern — that was the entire basis of cryptography. Even the most of basic of codes — a simple substitution cipher, like his father had taught him when he was a kid — had some sort of pattern, and where there was a pattern, there was a key.

Edwardsville brought him into the game, got him spinning toward Los Angeles. The Grove turned him around again, looking at London after the missile attack. Milverton, Skorzeny, the *Stella Maris* . . . misdirection everywhere he looked.

There was an old Sherlock Holmes story — "The Adventure of the Dancing Men" — that he'd first read when he was a child; it was in that book of codes that his dad had given him, the book that had survived the Rome Airport massacre, the book that he hadn't cracked since that awful day, not wanting to sully the memory of his parents with the blood of his mother that was still on the book.

Dancing men, each one standing for a letter of the alphabet. A substitution cipher, whose message gradually became clear as Holmes filled in the missing letters. Filled in the blanks. Time to do the same thing.

He ran a full sequencing deep drill on his keywords. Concentric relationship patterns. Google and other search engines, including NSA's own. All levels of security clearances, including Seelye's. Local, global, and universal. Leave nothing to chance:

His father and mother's full names, plus his own real first name. No one ever called him by that name, and hadn't since his mother died in his arms, but he still remembered it. Compartmentalization was the name of the game. In "real life," he couldn't remember anything about his past, but at the mighty Wurlitzer, he remembered everything.

He threw in Seelye's name, too. And now he added "MILVERTON, CHARLES A." and "SKORZENY, EMANUEL."

The full search would take awhile, even at the speed at which the NSA mainframes operated. No matter how fast they were, though, real time was always faster. Civil libertarians might quail, but the fact was that SIGINT and ELINT were always going to be a step or two behind reality. NSA officers were like those people who went to Disney World and recorded everything they did and saw, then replayed it when they got back home. It took them the same amount of time to relive the experience as to actually have the experience, which meant that they had not only lost one day to the blandishments of the Walt Disney Co., they had lost two.

Devlin rose and, securing the door to his inner sanctum, stepped through the bathroom and out into the main hall. There was something he had to see while the hamsters churned.

Near the front of the NSA building, there is a long hallway, adorned with photographs. At first glance, it might seem like the foyer of the CIA in Langley, whose ostentatious wall of anonymity commemorates the Company operatives who died in the line of duty. Heroes all. But the NSA hall was different.

At first glance, nothing special about the wall. Quintessential NSA guys, smiling white men in suits mostly, family men, all of whom had one thing in common: they were traitors.

Devlin had been down this hallway many times before, but this time he scrutinized each face as if he'd never seen it before.

Somewhere on this wall lay the clue to his past, the missing link, the man or (in very rare cases) the woman who could provide the missing cipher code to the mystery of his past.

"G-night, Brick." More of the staff, heading home.

"Haven't seen you around much lately, Brick — you okay?"

"Retard." This last muttered sotto voce.

Dancing men, all of them, dancing men. He pushed his mop past the ranks of photos methodically. He had walked past their ranks many times, but now he put his photographic memory to good use, scrutinizing every face, filing it away for future reference. It could be a useless exercise in memorization, but in his line of work there were no useless exercises in memorization.

There she was. His mother. Give her a name.

Carol Telemacher, née Cunningham. Code name, Polly. It wasn't until many years after her death that Devlin knew his mother had worked for NSA. She had started in the 1970s with the top-secret NRO, the National Reconnaissance Office, which together with its sister service, the National Reconnaissance Program, had been founded in 1961 to coordinate the aerial surveillance activities of the CIA and the Air Force. Nobody could read a map like his mother, and even on that final, fatal trip, she had guided through the labyrinthine streets of the Italian cities with ease.

Her presence here was Seelye's revenge. Or maybe homage. What difference did it make?

There she was, so close to him, so near, and yet so very, very impossibly far. Put there by the man who had used her and then betrayed her, exhibited like a traitor, to cover his own shame and complicity in her death. One thing was clear though; no matter how many years had passed, Army Seelye was still in love with his mother. That was why her picture was up on the wall, where he could walk by it every day. Devlin could respect, even admire, him for that.

His brain formed the sentence, but his lips didn't move. "I love you." A sentiment he could never give voice to, for fear of certain discovery; in this place, the walls not only had eyes, they had ears too. But one that was always in his heart. Right alongside the anger and thirst for vengeance, which was growing with each passing day.

Devlin rolled his mop and bucket back toward the custodial room. The computers would be finished by now.

One of the programs he had run, called PHIZREC — some in-house geek had a sense of humor — accessed the records of all the faces on the wall. Not just their pictures, but their entire dossiers, including the crimes they had committed that had gotten them on the Wall of Shame in the first place.

He was under no illusions that his presence in NSA would go undetected for long. He was smart, but Army Seelye was at least as smart as he was. In the game of cat and mouse that had evolved between them, they were fully equals.

Hurry. Think. Sequence.

Concentric circles, flowing outward, like the ripple of a stone in the middle of a pond. No one went through life leaving no traces, even a spook. You always affected someone else's orbit.

He had programmed his search to a Level 10 sensibility, to trigger anything, no matter how small.

Misdirection. That had to be the key. The old magic trick — focusing attention on the irrelevant while the trick was worked practically in plain sight. Or what would have been plain sight, if not for —

His screen blipped amber. His program was set to detect roaming spybots, and it had just found one.

Spybots were protective pawns that could be set to detect any untoward inquiries, especially at his level of security clearance. Devlin had to identify the 'bot without giving away his position or, indeed, letting the drone know he was even there.

Follow the drone.

It was pointing to his personal file. Above top secret. Above SCI. So secret, in fact, that only he and Seelye even knew it existed.

Holy shit. It wasn't a spybot, it was a guide dog, pointing for him to look at something. An embed message. He clicked on it:

"ABORT A/P POTUS DIRECTIVE THIS DAY." Abort the mission as per today's presidential directive — that much he already knew. But this time there was an addendum. It read, AND I QUOTE: "YOUR RULES ARE YOUR RULES. ACT ACCORDINGLY."

Both a reprieve and a misdirection. He was officially off the case, but unofficially on it. He had no idea whether the president or Seelye was playing him, but at this point it didn't matter. Time to get what he was coming for and get the hell out.

The screen flashed: BOT APPROACH. A real 'bot this time. A small red light began flashing, at first slowly and then with increasing rapidity. It meant that his probe had been spotted but not yet ID'ed: full red would be confirmation, but he didn't intended to wait around that long.

His fingers flew: FALSNEGS TIL MIS/ACC.

There were workarounds against even the most sophisticated 'bots. He knew, because he had developed half of them. He could feed the crawler a steady diet of false negatives, contradictory instructions that would cause it to lose valuable time sorting through the mutual impossibilities, until his mission was accomplished.

He had taken something of a risk by his blunt, frontal assault on the databases, but it would still take counterintel a while to find a single command in a nearly infinite series of code lines. But it could be done.

One more thing: SEELYE SKORZENY MILVERTON POLLY CUNNINGHAM.

The 'bot's red light was still flashing, steadily. Then — something he didn't expect.

PRIOR ACCESS DETECTED. CONT? Y/N?

Somebody else, some other fox, had been in the hen house. The one who had set the

FBI team on him. Hartley's cutout: Milverton.

YES

WORKING. The fastest artificial brains in the NSA server rooms whirred. A green light popped up.

MISACC read the screen. Mission accomplished.

DOWNLOAD. A flash drive, no bigger than his thumb, blinked as it absorbed the data.

DONE.

Quickly, Devlin shut down his terminal, using an extraction route that passed him through multiple, routine, authorized identities; it would take a little longer but it would cover his tracks.

He put the thumbnail drive into his pocket. Already, however, he'd learned enough.

He was off the case, but he wasn't.

He was marked for termination. Maybe Seelye would protect him as long as he could, and maybe he wouldn't.

He had to sort this out as quickly as possible if he was to have any chance at survival.

London, the terminus for Hartley's mysterious caller.

Milverton.

Ships. Something tugged at his memory.

Something Skorzeny had said at his press conference, just before the missile struck. The name of his other ship, which was . . . on its way to Baltimore. The *Clara Vallis.*

Weather balloons.

The *Stella Maris.*

Dancing Men.

Misdirection.

The *Clara Vallis.*

Oh, Jesus.

France.

■ ■ ■ ■

DAY FIVE

■ ■ ■ ■

How ridiculous not to flee from one's own wickedness, which is possible, yet endeavor to flee from another's, which is not.
— MARCUS AURELIUS, *Meditations,* Book VII

CHAPTER
FORTY-SEVEN

London

It was well after midnight by the time Amanda Harrington unlocked the door to No. 4 Kensington Park Gardens. The big house yawned, silent, nearly empty. She liked it that way, which was why she had lied about the sitter.

"I'm home, darling!" she shouted up the stairs; despite what had just happened, the humiliation she felt, she tried to sound cheery, motherly. The past few days had been very difficult, with the traveling and the treatments. Sometimes she wondered whether it was worth all the trouble. And then she remembered the look in the girl's eyes, and realized that the question had answered itself.

Not for nothing was No. 4 known as one of the finest private homes in London. Backing up onto the park, with a stunning solarium parkside, four spacious, elegant floors of living space, plus a basement and an attic, it had been featured in every social and architectural magazine in Britain over the past quarter of a century. And it was hers, all hers.

The first thing she did was take a shower, to wash every trace of him off her and out of her.

She was still shaking as she wrapped herself in her bathrobe and padded into the parlor. A 1927 Hamburg Steinway was the featured attraction, along with the collection of first editions, many of them signed, by Graham Greene, T. E. Lawrence, Virginia Woolf, Evelyn Waugh, and T. S. Elliot.

There was a bar on a side shelf near the piano, well stocked, and she poured herself a whiskey before sitting down at the keyboard. Even if she only played ten minutes a day, it was better than all the therapy in the world. She choose something from memory, one of the Brahms Op. 116 piano pieces, the soulful and autumnal A minor intermezzo, because that was the way she was feeling right now.

This couldn't go on much longer.

Amanda Harrington was thirty-nine years old, unmarried, and had lived alone since her parents died.

Her hands sank into the keys. You couldn't

play Brahms by pounding the keyboard. Instead, you had to become one with it, ease into it, practically have sex with it, so that the tips of your fingers touched the strings, atomizing the keys and hammers and dampers and flanges and whatever else Cristofori had devised to come between the player and the played.

She wasn't sure if she really liked Milverton, or whatever his name really was. SAS men, she had found, rarely made good boyfriends, much less husband material, and at her age a girl had to think ahead. Especially now, in modern Britain, where the native population would be a minority in its own country in less than two generations unless the women of England stepped up to the wicket. At least she was doing her part.

Still, the more she thought about it, the more useful Milverton became. He had been freelancing, or perhaps just testing the waters, at the London Eye, but . . . there was always a next time.

She caught herself. Skorzeny, she was quite sure, had bugged her house, maybe even her brain. Despite what he had done for her and her daughter, there was no plumbing the depths of his malevolence.

She finished the piece and looked around

the room, at the books on the bookshelves, at the names of long-dead authors who had believed in Britain, who thought its ideals would never die, who had lived, and sometimes fought and even died through the first and second Somme, and Dunkirk, and Singapore. And what had they given their lives for? New Labour? Posh and Beck? The Finsbury Park mosque?

She closed the keyboard, protectively. There was something about the purity of the ivories — ivories that were now illegal, perhaps even a hanging offense, in modern Britain. The country of Burton and Speke and Stanley, of the greatest hunters and explorers and scientists, had become a nasty little island of guilt, shame, and political correctness.

Fuck them, the sob sisters and the nancy boys and the chinless wonders who nattered about morality while they rutted with the commonest whores of the old Empire. Fuck the politicians who sold out their old constituencies in anticipation of the constituencies to come. This instrument was hers. This house was hers. The child upstairs was *hers.* She tossed back her whiskey and headed upstairs, to check on her daughter.

The girl was lying in her bed, where Amanda had left her. She didn't believe in nannies or any of that claptrap. Besides, the bindings were not too onerous and hardly left a mark.

The drugs were wearing off, but still working. Good. That made things easier, just the way the doctors had said they would.

"I'm home, darling," she whispered, brushing the girl's fevered brow. "It's all right now."

"Mama?" muttered the girl from her deep sleep.

"I'm here."

"I want to go home."

"You are home. This *is* your home. You're safe here. Safe in my arms." How she loved her, despite all the adoption troubles.

The girl's eyes fluttered open briefly. But they were still blank stares, wide pupils, unfocused irises. The doctors had told her that this was natural, that after the shock and the trauma, it would take time. Days, a week, maybe a little more.

Amanda loosened the restraints, which were for the girl's own good. They left no visible marks. "I'm hungry," the girl said.

"Dinner's on its way." Thank God she had called ahead for delivery. Sometimes, without meaning to, she forgot. A lot had been going on this week. "Indian, just the way you like it."

One of her phones buzzed. She glanced over: him. She decided not to take the call.

"Mama," whispered the girl, "I'm scared."

"Mummy's right here," she said, stroking her daughter's hair.

"What happened?" said the girl, her voice still weak.

"Nothing, darling," soothed Amanda. "Nothing."

"There was a man. He hurt me. Then fire . . ." Totally normal post-traumatic stress reaction; at least that was what the shrinks had said.

"There was no man, and no fire, my darling," she said. "It's all in your head." She wondered if she should call Dr. Knightley, just in case a needle was needed, instead of the array of pills he had prescribed. But her soothing hand quickly had the desired calming effect, and the girl fell back asleep. Once again, the combination of Morpheus and morphine was irresistible.

The phone buzzed again. Milverton, this time. Once more, she didn't answer. Everybody had down time, even her. She'd call him back later, when she had poured herself another whiskey, when she got downstairs, when she had slipped out of her clothes and stood naked in the solarium, with all the lights out, staring into the darkness of Kensington Park, stripped bare and alone not with her thoughts, which were for sale, but with her emotions, which weren't. She might even invite him over, but she wasn't sure if she wanted another man's hands on her just now. Better to keep him on the hook, interested, pliable . . . useful.

Amanda rose and tiptoed away from the bed. She didn't want to risk the chance of waking the girl. The phone buzzed once more. It wasn't a call, it was a text message, from Skorzeny. She ignored it for now. The girl stirred. She must have heard the buzz. "What is it?" she said in her sleep.

"Nothing, darling," replied Amanda.

The girl might have smiled. "Are we going home?"

"We are home," replied Amanda. "Remember?"

"Is everything okay?"

"Never better. Now go back to sleep."

"Good night, Mom," said the girl.

"Good night, Emma."

Her phone buzzed once more. She let it ring and turned on the telly. The president of the United States was announcing that he had closed down the stock and commodities markets until further notice. Betting on the bears, the Foundation had just made another 40 million pounds sterling.

Maybe, for once in her life, everything really was right with the world. Maybe she had done her job well. Maybe she had finally got her reward.

She turned off all her phones. Beeb-2 was rerunning highlights of *Beyond the Fringe*. The world could wait, for a change.

Chapter
Forty-Eight

Los Angeles

The taxi pulled into the parking lot of the Griffith Park Observatory and a woman and a boy got out. "Eddie Bartlett" had been watching them all the way up the hill, to make sure they weren't being followed, but the cab checked out and there was no tail. He put away his binoculars and sprinted down the steps from the roof to meet them at the entrance.

What he was about to do he would never have done under ordinary circumstances. But these times were hardly ordinary. Since the nightmare at the Grove, his world had been turned upside down, and he knew that for this woman, this Hope Gardner, the nightmare had started a day earlier, and had been even worse. At least Jade was going to make it.

Still, he was going to have to turn her down.

They were standing on the outside steps as he walked right past them, heading for his car. He eyeballed them both and the woman's visual matched up to her driver's license photo. He started his car and pulled around toward the front. The radio was still nattering on about the *Stella Maris,* the ship that had gone to the bottom in Long Beach Harbor. Danny didn't buy any of the bullshit story they were putting out, about how some explosive gases had reached critical mass in one of the compartmentalized holds, and had ignited with a random spark. Somebody had put that ship down, and part of him wished that he had been in on the operation. But he was still too wrapped up in his own grief. Maybe that — his grief — was why he had agreed to this meeting. To assuage his own by imbibing somebody else's.

The woman and the boy were mesmerized by the view, as all tourists were. Back in the days before smog, this had been one of the great observation posts in southern California, not Mt. Palomar caliber, but close. California must have been something back then.

"Mrs. Gardner?" he called out. She turned. "Get in, please. You in the front, Rory in the back." They got in. He drove off quickly.

At first nobody said anything. She had already told him plenty on the phone. He knew the story, she knew the drill.

"Where are we going?" she finally asked. Brave woman — getting in a car with a total stranger. Brave him, opening up to a civilian. But he felt guilty — he had been ready to sacrifice her and the boy and now here they both were, no thanks to his judgment. He and Devlin had saved them both, but had cost Diane her life.

They were heading deep into the park, over the crest and onto the side that looked toward Glendale and Burbank. There were riding trails and golf courses and the Los Angeles Zoo on this side, but plenty of solitude as well.

There was a fire trail he knew, one of the roads the fire department used as access in case of trouble. A few years ago, there had been a big fire up here and even at a distance you could easily see which parts of the park had burned and which hadn't.

He ignored the warning sign to keep out and entered the access trail. If any cops bothered them, well, he knew all the cops from Hollywood Station. It was little more than a dirt road and the car bumped heavily. Sometimes dirtbags hid up here, kids fucked in their cars, illegals hid out, and the occasional dump job wound up under six inches of dirt. Those were the chances he had to take.

He found a clearing and parked. They were hemmed in all sides by pine trees; the only thing he could see was the sky.

"Rory, you stay inside for now," he said, leaving the air conditioner on. It was blazing hot, still fire season, and the pine needles cracked under his feet as he and Hope got out of the car.

"All right, Mrs. Gardner," he said. "It's your meeting."

At first, she didn't know what he meant. That was what he got for using Hollywood-speak; even if you weren't in the Industry out here, you talked like you were. "I mean, you asked to see me."

Hope nodded. It looked like she hadn't slept a wink in three days. "Yes. Thank you for agreeing to see me on such short notice." She took a deep breath. "As I said on the phone, I want to hire you."

"And as I told you, you can't afford me," he replied.

"I don't care. Jack had a sizable insurance policy, with a rider for accidental death, and I'm prepared to spend every penny of it if you can help me find my daughter."

"I told you. She's probably dead."

"Probably is not good enough for me."

Danny kicked some dirt. "Ordinarily, I would never have taken your call. Never agreed to see you. Never would have invited you out here. But I cremated my wife this morning and . . ."

"We had our service yesterday," she said, simply. "Then we got on the plane."

"I'm sorry. Sorry for your loss, sorry for your trouble. But I don't see how I can help you. Why don't you take your kid and go home. Start over. Rebuild your life. That's what I'm going to do."

Hope was surprised that it was so easy to hold her emotions in check. She was so much stronger than she ever would have thought, before all this happened. She had come all this way. And she wasn't about to take no for an answer.

"You're a liar," she said. "That's not at all what you're going to do. You're never going to rest until you get revenge."

She was uncomfortably under his skin. "What makes you say that?"

"Because I saw you chop that man's arm off . . . with a smile. You're a killer, so don't try to pretend otherwise."

Danny felt his heart racing. This little woman had just rocked him back on his heels in a way no man could. "Like I said, it's your meeting."

"The 160th. You guys are supposed to be the best."

He looked back at the car. There was a video player built into the backseats, and he had put a movie on for Rory. "We're pretty good."

She took that as a yes. "So's Xe, I hear."

Danny was impressed; this lady had done her homework. "We try. We take a lot of bum raps, but whenever any Congress critter or media nitwit needs to keep his ass safe, we keep his ass safe. Not that we get any thanks for it."

"I know she's alive."

"I already told you —"

"I don't care. A mother knows these things . . . Besides — I know about the other man. And I want to hire him too."

"What did you say? About another man?" That part she hadn't mentioned on the phone. She had his full attention now.

"The man who saved Rory's life when the bomb went off. An angel, he called himself."

"Can Rory describe him?"

Hope was confused. "I thought you might know him."

"I might," said Danny. "But I need to hear from Rory first."

"Okay." Hope had thought to keep Rory out of this, but she realized that would be impossible. They walked back to the car. As they did, she said, "So does this mean you'll help us?"

"I haven't decided yet," said Danny.

They got into the car, feeling relief from the heat, dry or otherwise. Danny glanced at the temperature gauge on the dashboard — well over 90. A red-flag day. "Tell me about the man you saw, Rory," he said. "The angel."

Rory threw his mother a look and she nodded: go ahead. "I didn't get a real good look at him," he began. "All of a sudden, he just grabbed me and we both dove in the big trash can. I was scared — you know . . ."

"But he said he was an angel. What kind of angel?"

Rory shrugged. "I asked him if he was a missionary. Like in cannibals and missionaries. I like to play that game. Do you?"

Danny looked at Hope and Rory, a woman and a child. Not helpless, exactly, but as vulnerable as the missionaries to the cannibals. "Looks like I'm going to have to," he said.

He knew what he had to do.

He had to keep them safe.

He had to help Hope find her daughter.

He had to avenge Diane and give himself and Jade something to live for.

How he was going to do all this, he had no idea. He'd already missed three calls from "Tom Powers," but somehow he had to track him down.

"Are you in or are you out?" Hope asked him. An hour in LA and she was already speaking the local lingo.

"Let's go," he said, slamming the car into gear and roaring down the dusty trail toward Hollywood.

Twenty minutes later they were flying down Highland Avenue. The Kodak Center was the new fresh underbelly of the entertainment beast, where the Oscars were now held, a vast, sprawling complex that took in everything from the intersection of Hollywood and Highland, west to what used to be Grauman's Chinese Theater, now owned by the Mann group. The one with the hand- and footprints.

Just before the intersection of Hollywood Boulevard, Danny turned right into the parking garage and headed to the lowest level.

There wasn't much to subterranean Los Angeles, not like New York or even Seattle, but he had a small piece of it. The Red Line ran right under the complex and where subways traveled, so also did clandestine offices flourish.

Instead of punching the button, Danny slapped an ID card up against a plate on the elevator bank. The doors opened. Then he pushed a key into the console. "Security code, please," said an electronic woman's voice. Using the floor keys, he punched in a five-digit number. "Going down," said the synthesized voice, even though there were no "down" floors visible.

After what seemed an eternity, the doors slowly slid open. Even three stories beneath Hollywood Boulevard, it looked like a normal office floor in anybuilding, anywhere, USA.

Danny led them down a private hallway. Hope caught a glimpse of people in some of the offices — cops, guys in suits talking quietly into telephones. He unlocked a door and ushered them into a small office. At once, Danny set to work, firing up computers, flicking switches, checking voice mails. Video screens flickered to life, audio streams came online; from a tomb, the room was suddenly alive with activity.

Furiously, he punched numbers into a keyboard, from time to time consulting old-fashioned black loose-leaf code binders, flipping through pages of what to her eye looked like gibberish. It wasn't gibberish to Danny. Every keystroke, every glance, had a purpose.

Nothing. He had mined every database, run every kind of tracking software, done a dozen concentric-circle relationship charts, and he still couldn't find out who the hell Tom Powers was, or how to contact him. One-way streets were a bitch, especially when they were blind alleys.

He was about to turn to Hope and tell her that he was sorry, that he couldn't help her after all, when suddenly Rory said — "Cool. An iPhone."

There it was, in his bag. It had been there all along.

Fucking Skipjack. *That* was how he was going to get in touch with Powers, whether he liked it or not. Walk the dog backward . . .

Its contract with the U.S. government stipulated that Xe had to be ready to put a team on the ground anywhere within twenty-four hours. Sub rosa, untraceable. Just enough men to do the job, but not one more than necessary. He couldn't roll without the kind of authorization that Powers could pull, but with it, in a heartbeat, he could have a full complement of men who had served in the 160th: in, up somebody's ass, out. The Night Stalkers.

The *Stella Maris.* That had to be what "Powers" had been calling him about. Somehow, it must be related to what had happened at the Grove. And, in his grief, he had blown the assignment. Nobody could blame him for that, but —

Thank God Jade was going to make it. When he'd visited her today, she was awake, barely. Her eyes had lit up at the sight of him, and for a long time he said nothing. He just sat there, stroking his little girl's hair and telling her everything was going to be okay. He didn't say anything about Diane. He didn't know whether she knew, whether she remembered. She'd learn soon enough.

He thought of Diane and all the pain and rage and guilt and blame came flooding back. And yet, she was gone and no amount of remembrance could bring her back. It could only honor her, passively —

"Stay a little longer, Daddy," came a weak little voice. Danny looked down at Jade and squeezed her hand.

"I'll be back as soon as I can and not one second less. And then we'll go for that chopper ride . . . all of us."

But maybe it was more appropriate to honor her memory actively. Proactively.

What the hell was Powers up to? Whatever

it was, it was big. Whatever had started in Edwardsville, it was time to finish it. For the sake of his family — for the sake of all their families — he had to be a part of it.

Well, that was what he had this office for. Up to now, he had abided by Powers's rules. But this was no time to stand on ceremony.

It wasn't simply a matter of a last-number call-back. Powers's contacts went through multiple cutouts. But however many there were, in the end his call would have to be vetted by the Skipjack chip embedded in Jade's iPhone, a chip that Powers himself had placed there. He could reverse-engineer the sequence, and one of those cutouts, no matter how many there were, would have to be real, and would accept the handshake from its very own mole, inside a little girl's cell phone. He had no idea how long it would take, but there was no time like the present to start.

He said a silent prayer. The hamsters started spinning.

He was in luck.

The last call had been recent, fresh. The sequencing logarithms weren't that old, and he was high on Powers's priority list.

He didn't get a ring-through, but he got a punch-through. Good enough for government work.

As he waited for the response, he realized that he was biting his own tongue.

Come on, damn it . . . come on . . .

There —

HOW'S YOUR FRENCH?

UP TO SNUFF.

SOAR, CLARA VALLIS, SOAR.

He got it. NSDQ.

Danny turned to Hope. "We've got a plane to catch."

That brought a smile to Rory's face. "Where are we going?" he cried.

"Van Nuys, for starters," said Danny, shutting down the office and gathering up his stuff, as if that explained everything.

CHAPTER
FORTY-NINE

Vaduz

With stock and property markets around the world collapsing in fear, Emanuel Skorzeny doubled down on his bets, short-selling like mad, snapping up whole companies for ten cents on the dollar. Through a series of shells, he had already taken a majority position in General Electric, whose stock price was at a depression-era level. He worked the phones, ordering shipments of relief supplies to Illinois, Los Angeles, London. He even gave interviews to selected friendly media, by Internet video. Four days after Edwardsville, Skorzeny International was nearly ten billion dollars richer than it had been a week earlier. One more disaster and he would practically own the U.S. Treasury.

"What news of Miss Harrington?" Skorzeny inquired of Pilier. "I have not heard from her in several hours. I suspect alienation of affection."

Inwardly, Pilier frowned. The old man was already besotted; now, he was bordering on obsession. The Harrington woman, while spectacular, was young enough to be his daughter.

"Busy, sir," replied Pilier. "Making a fortune for us. For the Foundation. That is her brief, I believe."

"A woman of many and variegated talents," observed Skorzeny. He was standing by his desk, staring at the Alps in the fading light. "And no less than what I expect of her. Still, I am distressed that she hasn't called."

Typical Skorzeny, thought Pilier: no matter what the situation, it was always about him. And yet that selfishness, often masked as selflessness, was what made him great. And richer every day. Not bad for a boy who started with nothing.

His back to Pilier, Skorzeny said, "What of the news?"

"Im Westen nichts neues," said Pilier, in German. *All Quiet on the Western Front.* It was, he knew, one of Skorzeny's favorite books and motion pictures.

Skorzeny looked at his watch and raised an eyebrow. "Really?" he said. "I have found throughout my life that bad news begets more bad news. The panic of the mob. The extraordinary madness of crowds. In the country of the blind, the one-eyed man is king. And in times of mass hysteria —"

"*If,* sir," observed Pilier. "If you keep your head when all about —"

"You dare quote Kipling to me?" he said.

Pilier backtracked as fast as he could. "Purely for referential purposes, sir," he said. "After all, Kipling is —"

"An imperialist and an Englishman," said Skorzeny. "As the Americans say, that is two strikes against him."

"Yes, sir," admitted Pilier in defeat. Best not to try and trade literary witticisms with his superior.

"This woman . . ." mused Skorzeny.

Oh, no, thought Pilier.

"She is remarkable, is she not?" inquired Skorzeny.

"Are you soliciting my opinion, sir, or merely stating a fact?"

"Both, I should say."

"Then I absolutely agree."

The Glare, for just a fleeting moment. Then, "When the American markets re-open," said Skorzeny, blessedly changing the subject, "what will be our position?"

"Aggressive, sir. Stocks, commodities, real estate. We also snap up the ancillaries —

tech stocks, defense industries, shipping, the lot."

"Good. What about the public utilities? The banks?"

"The utilities can wait a bit, but we will be taking a very strong position in Bank of America and Citicorp and I expect we should be able to push that toward majority status should we wish to. In fact, with any luck, we can own them outright tomorrow."

"What about Credit Suisse? J.P. Morgan Chase?"

"Proxies will take care of both of them. Also Barclay's. And, of course, Société Générale we already own. Last but not least, we've taken a very bearish stance against both the dollar and the euro, and I believe events are bearing out our wisdom of the plan adopted by the board at your suggestion."

"Sell our holdings in Universal and Paramount. Parent companies too. Might as well make a clean divestiture. Clear out the rot and start over."

"What 'rot' might that be, sir?" wondered Pilier. "The company has done very well with its Hollywood investments. Not to mention by its friends in the industry."

Skorzeny shot him an irritated glance, a warning that he was overstepping his servile boundary. "I am bored with movies about comic books," he said. "What is this world coming to? Jejune juvenilia, elevated to the level of art. What would Shakespeare say? Goethe? Rimbaud? Tolstoy? *Ne kulturny.* Given the demographics, we will first run out of children and then run out of comic books . . . Now, what of our ship?"

Pilier wondered whether the old man was going senile. "Sir, you know that the *Stella Maris* sank two days ago under mysterious circumstances in Long Beach Harbor. And despite our protestations, the United States government has not yet seen fit to —"

"I am not interested in old news, Monsieur Pilier," said Skorzeny coolly. "I am referring to the *Clara Vallis.* How is she making?"

"On schedule."

"And our experiments?"

"Ready to launch."

"Good." Skorzeny glanced over at the eternal television screen. "Shut that infernal thing off and sit down so we can have a proper talk."

Pilier clicked the remote and the TV winked off. He took the nearest chair and sat. It wasn't very comfortable, but that was the way the boss liked it. The only congenial chair in the room was Skorzeny's; everybody else had to suffer. It was like being at Bayreuth without Wagner's music. Death without Transfiguration. Skorzeny stared at Pilier for an uncomfortably long time before he spoke.

"There is a mighty wind coming, Monsieur Pilier. Perhaps you have not noticed it, but rest assured that I have. For years, decades, I have felt its approach, smelt its dragon breath. And when it blows through, when it has wrought what it was sent to wreak, who will be left to mourn what it leaves in its wake?"

Pilier had no idea what the old man was talking about. He almost wished he was still on the subject of the lovely Amanda Harrington — a woman, he had to confess to his inner chaplain, who had often figured in his erotic fantasies, some of them quite exotic. She embodied, he supposed, what the late Roman Catholic Church meant by "an occasion of sin."

"I'm sure I don't know, sir."

"I will. I and those closest to me."

Skorzeny fell silent for a while, contemplating the art on the walls, from time to time humming some small snatch of music to himself. To Pilier, he seemed in the grip of a great agitation, which even his iron will could not quite control.

"I have not been able to reach her by telephone or text."

So it was back to Amanda again. "Sir, you saw her last night, in London."

Skorzeny seemed to struggle back to his senses. "Yes," he said. "London. The last piece of our little puzzle. What of our representative there?"

Pilier checked the time. "He is due to report in to you by teleconference shortly. I am led to believe that you will be very happy with his report, sir."

Skorzeny folded his hands together. "Then everything is in order. And now it is in the hands of God, if He has any interest in us left . . . One last thing. Please make ready our holiday home for occupancy."

That caught Pilier by surprise. Although he had multiple residences in many of the world's garden spots, Skorzeny only ever used that phrase, "holiday home" to refer to one place in particular. "Yes, sir."

Skorzeny reached for one of the remotes and switched on some music. Usually, he waited until he had retired for the evening's concert, but on this night it was as if he wanted to share it with Pilier, with the world.

The music sounded. A soft, mournful, cello line above a contemplative piano ac-

484

companiment, slow, very slow, but steady, like the beating of a broken heart. Pilier was about to ask what it was, but Skorzeny anticipated his question and held up his hand peremptorily for silence. Pilier obeyed.

For more than eight and a half eternal minutes, the music continued, unchanging on its infinitely slow, ecstatic course.

"Do you know what that was, Monsieur Pilier?" asked Skorzeny, when the last, dying note could no longer be heard.

"No, sir," he replied, truthfully.

"And yet you are a graduate of the Sorbonne. Amazing. You might as well have attended Harvard and emerged no less an ignorant, though perhaps more ideologically blinkered, savage."

Skorzeny signaled for the ablution bowl. " *'I saw a mighty Angel descending from heaven . . . and the Angel swore by Him who lives forever and ever, saying: there will be no more Time . . . the mystery of God will be completed.'* The Book of Revelation, written by John the Evangelist on Patmos, as the Christians believe. Now can you tell me what that music was?"

Inwardly, Pilier seethed. Outwardly, he remained as placid as the music had been. "No, sir," he said.

" 'Praise Eternity.' The fifth movement of

Messiaen's *Quatour pour le fin du temps.* 'The Quartet for the End of Time.' Written in seven movements and an interlude, and premiered by its composer in a Nazi prison camp at Görlitz during the winter of 1940–41, for the instruments he had on hand: piano, violin, cello, and clarinet. Do you know what Messiaen said about it?"

The shame of ignorance was burning Pilier's cheeks. He couldn't compete with Skorzeny's all-embracing, omniscient *Weltanschauung.*

"Of course you don't. He said, 'Never have I been heard with as much attention and understanding.' In a concentration camp. Thus focusing the mind and concentration wonderfully. As I know from bitter experience."

"It's beautiful, sir," mustered Pilier.

"It's not beautiful," barked Skorzeny. "It's *radiant.* 'Seven is the perfect number.' But he wrote one extra movement, the interlude, so as not to compete with Creation. *Le 7 de ce repos se prolonge dans l'éternité de devient le 8 de la lumière indéfectible, de l'inaltérable paix.* 'The seventh of his day of repose prolongs itself into eternity and becomes the eighth, of unfailing light, of immutable peace.' Do you understand that? *Unfailing light. Immutable peace.*"

"Yes, sir. No, sir." Pilier had no idea which the correct answer was, so he tried them both. How he wished the old man would just go to bed one night, and never wake up. All this blather about useless culture gave him a migraine.

"Messiaen believed it was his faith that got him safely through the camps, and made him one of the greatest composers of the benighted twentieth century. Do you agree, Monsieur Pilier?"

That was no way to answer that question, except honestly. "No, sir. I don't. Religion is superstition, dressed up in vestments and perfumed with incense."

Skorzeny contemplated him for a long time before he spoke. "We are, all of us, in need of salvation, Monsieur Pilier," he said at last.

The huge video screen suddenly flickered to life; despite his fashionable atheism, Pilier breathed a silent prayer of relief, for having spared him whatever was to have followed. "That would be our London member, sir," he said, switching on the private video feed.

The face of Charles Augustus Milverton filled the screen. Skorzeny contemplated it with equanimity; this was no time to give voice to his suspicions, nor let them color the business they needed to transact. There would be plenty of time for that later, after the great event. "Report," he said.

"Our Washington friend has been most helpful — I got the final confirmation yesterday. Not in so many words, of course, but in actions. Hidden signals. Emanations of penumbras. He's the one you've been looking for. And, sir —"

"What's his name?" Skorzeny could hardly contain his excitement.

"And may I say that he's the one I've been looking for as well. Ever since that night in Paris —"

"What's his name?"

"He doesn't have a name, sir."

"Then how do you know it's him?"

"I know."

This was the moment Emanuel Skorzeny had been waiting for nearly a quarter of a century. The one thing, the one man, that could interrupt his plans, the one person who could link him to that unholy triangle, to the days when he learned firsthand how deadly the female of the species could be, how the weakness of men would always be their undoing, how the passions of the moment always trumped reason. As Blake had foretold.

The thing that had first put fear into him. Love.

He had vowed then that he would not become what he had beheld. He had failed.

But perhaps it was not too late. A moment of vengeance, and t'were best done, especially t'were it done quickly.

"Kill him. Launch the experiment."

Milverton paused. He was used to impossible missions. But this . . .

Skorzeny heard, no, make that sensed, his hesitation — "You know who he is?"

"I only caught a glimpse of him in Edwardsville."

Skorzeny saw his play. It was perfect. Solved all his problems at one stroke. "And did he see you?"

Milverton's face betrayed no emotion. There was no right answer. "I don't know."

"A profession of ignorance is not an answer."

"Perhaps. I think so."

Skorzeny smiled and reached once more for the ablution bowl. If it worked once, it would work twice, even in one night. "Then let him come to you. *Make* him come to you. Draw him to your home turf and kill him. What could be easier? You have the defender's advantage."

For once, there was silence at the other end of the line. Milverton's face betrayed no emotion, but nothing came out of his mouth.

"It's perfect, don't you see?" said Skorzeny, pausing a little longer than necessary for effect. "One last misdirection, while the real work occurs elsewhere." Milverton wasn't sure if he liked this idea, but stayed silent. "While you two settle an old score . . . In the meantime, if by any chance you should see Miss Harrington, please ask her to call me immediately. I require her presence tomorrow at the country house in France."

Amanda. So that was what this was all about. The old bastard was on to them. Had he wrung a confession out of her when he was in London? Milverton realized that he hadn't been able to get ahold of Amanda, either, that she hadn't answered his calls. "The country house?"

"Yes. With the insurance policy."

The insurance policy. This was getting worse by the second.

"I'm not sure I understand, Mr. Skorzeny."

Milverton knew that, had they been face to face, Skorzeny would have looked upon him as if he were an idiot child. Or worse, that iron mannequin holding out the begging bowl on Regent Street with the sign saying SUPPORT YOUR LOCAL SPASTIC, or whatever politically correct thing it said these days.

Skorzeny chuckled. "Of course you do."

He was being set up. Even at this distance, Milverton could smell the stench of desperation on Skorzeny, even as he could smell the scent of Amanda Harrington on him. That was what this was all about.

Her. With the biggest, most audacious play of his life right in front of him, Emanuel Skorzeny was losing focus over a woman.

So unimportant to a man of Milverton's age and experience. So vitally important to a man of Skorzeny's age and experience. And he never saw it coming. What a fool he had been.

"It's him, isn't it? The man whom I seek."

"Yes, sir, it is."

Milverton could feel the excitement radiating from the other end of the continental trunk line. Skorzeny had overplayed his hand. He had given something away. His *need.* He had never seen that before. His lust — for money, power, women — of course. But never need. Never desperation. Skorzeny's need, if Milverton played his cards right, would be the thing that kept him alive.

"Then make us both happy. Draw him to

491

you and kill him."

Even though he knew it was a trap, even though he knew that Skorzeny was setting him up, even though he knew that it didn't matter to the old man which of them killed the other — because in the aftermath it wouldn't really matter — Milverton could feel his own excitement rising. His own lust for combat. His own need to pay back this man for the indignity he had inflicted on him in Paris, and for the countless other frustrations he had had to endure during their long cold war in the darkest shadows of cyberspace.

Which meant that he would get to face him. The shadow. The man who wasn't there. This child whom Skorzeny sought. Protected by the NSA. Given up by Hartley. Very well, then. Bring him on.

And bring on Skorzeny too. He had put up with Caligula long enough, with his barely disguised contempt, with the way he had treated Amanda. He had not survived the training camps of the SAS, not run to ground the deadly operatives of the Provos in Spain, not cut the throats of the IRA men on the streets of Belfast and Londonderry, not dealt with the worst Soviet Georgian, Armenian, Azerbaijani, and Jewish gangsters to kowtow to a man whose only real claim to fame was that he was a victim. He would show Skorzeny what the word *victim* really meant.

Not a symbolic victim.

Not a possible victim.

Not a putative victim.

Not a potential victim.

A real victim.

A dead victim.

"Yes, sir," he said, hanging up.

Nobody hung up on Emanuel Skorzeny.

Milverton didn't care. He called Amanda Harrington again.

■ ■ ■ ■

DAY SIX

■ ■ ■ ■

Ask yourself, what is this thing in itself, by its own special constitution? What is it in substance, and in form, and in matter? What is its function in the world? For how long does it subsist?
— MARCUS AURELIUS, *Meditations, Book VIII*

CHAPTER
FIFTY

Rosslyn, Virginia

Senator Robert Hartley strode to the podium at his hastily called press conference. He was clean, shaved, and sober, and was glad that everybody could tell.

"Ladies and gentlemen," he said, beaming at the cameras, "I have an important announcement."

A modest hubbub ran through the modest crowd. Hartley's staffers had done the best they could on short notice, but their IMs were only just beginning to pull in the public. Right now, it was mostly media.

"As you all know," he continued, "I have spent my career in the Senate, reaching across the aisle, striving for bipartisanship to solve the issues that divide us as Americans. To that end, I have work assiduously with this president, Jeb Tyler, in an effort to protect and serve the American people." He made what is called a pregnant pause.

"I am sorry to tell you today that that effort — has failed."

Gasps, especially from what was left of the once-formidable Washington press corps, now reduced through the collapse of most of the major newspapers in the country, to a few pool reporters and a host of cable-TV cameramen and producers. If there was one thing that Americans — at least, Ivy League-educated Americans — believed in more than God, it was bipartisanship. Except when they didn't.

"After all, President Tyler was elected on just such a platform. And after the toxic partisanship of the past sixteen years, we all could see why. But now, certain documents have come to light —"

A buzz ran through the older members of the crowd. It was like a live baby seal thrown to the sharks. "Certain documents" could mean only one thing. The maleficent corpse of Senator Joe McCarthy was about to be exhumed and resurrected once more.

The newsies leaned forward, hanging on every word. Even though Hartley was a bona fide idiot, renowned as a human gaffe machine, called behind his back — and sometimes to his face — the "Senator from the Bar Association" — this was sure to be the lead national story in about two minutes.

And, three minutes from now, bloggers from Indiana to India would be writing about What It All Meant.

Hartley beamed at the audience. It was great to see all the gray hair, the ponytails, the facial hair, the Botox, the hair plugs. One particularly ugly old crone in the front row shouted, "Does this mean somebody's finally gonna put the son of a bitch in his place?"

Hartley held up his hands for calm. This was getting out of hand. Television, or what was left of it, was a cool medium. Plus, more and more people were streaming onto the shopping-mall plaza.

"Ladies and gentlemen," said Hartley, "ours is a democracy." Cheers. "A representative, republican democracy." Boos. "Which is why — which is why — although it pains me to my core — I feel I must come before you today and share what I have learned. For it has come to my attention —"

Quiet, leading to silence.

"— that the events of the past few days . . ." He paused again. In high school, he had always wanted to play Hamlet, and now he was getting his chance, on a bigger stage than he had ever imagined.

"That the horrible, unconscionable events

of the past few years — unprecedented as they are in American history, a history that stretches back to Washington, Jefferson, Lincoln and FDR . . ." Maybe that was going too far. No matter — he plunged on:

"Have revealed the most monstrous . . . conspiracy is not too strong a word . . . against the American people. A conspiracy so vast . . ."

The cheering of the crowd, especially the reporters, was almost too much for him to continue. But he managed.

"Ladies and gentlemen, let me be the first to tell you — no secret, no e-mail, no conversation, almost no private thought, has been safe from your government. The National Security Agency — the one they used to laughingly call 'No Such Agency' — has been spying on you, all of you, for decades. Since long before September 11."

He held up his hands for calm.

"Yes, each and every one of you. Every one of you who owns an iPod. Or a Black-Berry. A cell phone. Maybe even a land line. Every one of your conversations has been grist for their evil mill, everyone one of your conversations — yes, even those with your Tante Emma, Grandma Mary, or Bubbi Sadie in Florida — has been intercepted, decoded, digested, logged, and analyzed by a sinister branch of the NSA called the Central Security Service."

A ripple of outrage ran through the crowd. No one had ever heard of the Central Security Service, but they sure didn't like the sound of it.

"So that's why, today, I'm announcing the formation of an exploratory committee for a possible presidential run for the nomination of my party against my great and good friend, President Tyler. Because, friendship aside, we can't afford politics as usual. We can't afford the 'system.' We need action — and we need it now!"

The place erupted in cheers. Viewers watching at home were impressed by Hartley's sheer, brave honesty. Bloggers pounded their keyboards. Internet servers hummed. Half the nation, watching at home, seethed.

"Are you aware?" Hartley shouted. Shouting was too hot for Marshall McLuhan's cool medium, but luckily nobody knew who Marshall McLuhan was any more. "Are you aware that the entire 'War on Terror' has been a sham? A way to divest you of your civil liberties? A way to penetrate your most intimate conversations, your homes, your hearths, yes, even your bedrooms?

"We can't afford four more years of the same failed Jeb Tyler policies. Because we can't afford any change in the tax system, any change in our military preparedness, any change in our relationship with our allies overseas, any change in the polar ice caps, we have to maintain the status quo — and then make it better!"

The crowd lapped up the nonsense and the non sequiturs. Hartley took a deep breath.

"And that's why, even at this late date, I'm asking for your support. I need money and I need your vote. To turn Jeb Tyler out of office, and take back our country!"

Apeshit was not too mild a word to describe the reaction. He was riding the wave now. He held up the folder that Tyler had given him.

"I have here in my hand" — he waved the folder, like the red flag before the bull — "proof positive that our government has been lying to us all along. Their promises of transparency were worthless. That there exists, at the deepest and most hidden levels of the NSA, a rogue agency devoted to the subversion of everything we hold dear as Americans. And personally authorized by President Jeb Tyler to carry out its mission."

A gasp ran through the crowd. Shouts of "Impeach him!" were heard.

Hartley held up his hands again for quiet.

"We don't have to impeach him. We just have to beat him. And when I'm president, you can bet your bottom dollar that I'm going to unleash a full-scale investigation and those responsible will get what's coming to them! Thank you, and may God bless America!"

For a brief, exhilarating moment, he actually believed his own bullshit, until he caught sight of the Whippet and the Refrigerator standing off to one side, out of the view of the cameras. Then he remembered where he was, what was happening, and where this was all likely to end.

"Good job, Bob," said the Whippet as the Refrigerator fell in behind them. They were both dressed in black, just like real Secret Service agents now.

The Refrigerator handed him a secure cell phone. "You've got a phone call from the Big Guy."

"Nice work," came Tyler's voice. "You actually sounded like you meant what you were saying out there."

"Thank you, Mr. President. But there's one thing I just don't understand —"

Tyler knew where he was going with the question. "Why I'm doing this to myself, right? Simple. In order for me to deal with whatever the hell is going on here, I need to throw the jackals in the press some red meat. You know how they are, Bob. Basically, there's room for only one story at a time in their precious little airheads. And now, thanks to you, the story today is that I'm a dirty low-down, double-dealing, malfeasant skunk who ought to be strung up on the Mall. Which is just fine with me at the moment."

Hartley swallowed hard. "And I'm the red meat."

"You more or less nominated yourself, didn't you, Bob?"

"Who dropped the dime on me? I have to know?"

The president ignored the question. "Play this out until further notice and when we're done, then you and I will call it even. The only acceptable answer is yes, sir."

"Yes, sir."

"Have a nice day," said Jeb Tyler, ringing off.

They rode back to the Watergate in silence.

Hartley was alone in his bedroom. His babysitters were in the front room. They'd sealed the windows so he couldn't jump out. They'd taken everything sharp away from him. The only shoes he had were loafers.

Hartley lit a cigarette. A plan was forming

in his mind — a way for him to get out of this mess with his dignity intact. Sure, he was a douchebag, like almost everybody in Congress, a corrupt hypocrite who preached one thing and did another; a man who constantly brayed about his devotion to his constituents as he went about screwing them as hard as he could. But maybe now he could make up for it in some small way.

He dug the folder marked HARTLEY out of his briefcase and put it in the trash can. Too bad nobody used metal trash cans more, but the gray plastic one would have to do. He opened it up so that there was plenty of air around the pictures and then set fire to it.

It took a few minutes for the smoke detectors to kick in, setting off a screech. Hartley wasn't sure whether alarms would ring all over the complex, but it didn't matter; a localized ruckus would be just fine. As the alarms shrieked, he moved behind the bedroom door and waited.

He'd kept himself in good physical shape for a man of his age and he realized with grim irony that his fitness was finally going to come in handy for something other than a barroom pickup. Well, better late than never. He picked up one of his bookends, a heavy reproduction of the Maltese Falcon that he'd found in Provincetown one summer.

It was the Whippet first through the door, gun drawn, just as Hartley had hoped. He hit him square on the back of his head with the Falcon, fracturing his skull. As the man fell, Hartley quickly slammed the door and locked it. He knew the Refrigerator would burst though, but he only needed a few seconds. He grabbed the gun.

The Refrigerator didn't bother with a knock. Hurling his weight he burst through the door. Hartley shot him three times, once in the chest, once in the groin, and once in the head, just for fun.

The trash can fire was still burning merrily. Hartley ran to the bathroom and sprinkled some aftershave on it, which caused the flames to leap higher. Then he wadded as much paper as could — the *Washington Post* came in handy — and finally the sprinklers went off.

Outside, in the hallway, he could hear shouting, running. Alarms started to whoop everywhere.

He sat on the bed, the water from the sprinklers pouring over him. He hadn't prayed since he was a kid, but it was funny how the prayers came back to you when you needed them most.

His last thought was, *This will really give them something to write about tomorrow.* Then he put the Whippet's gun in his mouth.

"Have a nice day, Jeb," was his last thought before he pulled the trigger.

CHAPTER
FIFTY-ONE

London/Washington, D.C.

Milverton picked up Hartley's presser halfway through. He couldn't believe his luck. Things were going just as they had planned. The bit about running for president was, he thought, inspired. He wondered if Hartley had thought of it all by himself.

Flush him out and kill him. That's what Skorzeny wanted. Mission half-accomplished. If the FBI team he had sicced on his nemesis hadn't succeeded, well, so what? He was better suited to do the job himself, right here in Blighty. Milverton had no idea why the old man was so keen on getting Devlin, but in this case business and pleasure were mixing admirably.

From the beginning, Skorzeny must have known, somehow, that they'd send Devlin to Edwardsville, must have known that Devlin's catching sight of Milverton would only whet his appetite for score-settling, must have known that Devlin would then be a human yo-yo, shuttling back and forth between the coasts, trying to conceal his identity while wondering who the hell was doing this to him.

Milverton never made the mistake of underestimating an adversary, and he had learned the hard way that Devlin was every bit his equal in tradecraft. Hartley's access, as head of the Senate Intelligence Committee, had been solid gold, but Devlin had outwitted him in the battle of Fort Meade. Who knew, maybe he was on to him, on his way to him, and all Milverton had to do was sit back and await developments.

Hartley — now there was a good little boy. Milverton had to admit that Skorzeny's Hoover-like collection of the personal peccadilloes of nearly every major political figure in Europe, China, Japan, and the United States was second to none. It was like acupressure — you didn't need an MRI of the whole body to know what would happen to it if pressure were applied just so and to just the right place. And it was so easy — with the intrusive scope of information technology today, nobody in his right mind would run for office except sociopaths, who either didn't care who knew about their manifold skeletons (several U.S. Congressmen came immediately to mind) or who felt they were smarter than everybody else (more than one American president). A more singular collection of intellectually mediocre, greedy psychopaths he had not encountered outside of a banana republic or sub-Saharan Africa or the city council of Milton Keynes.

What was it Ben Franklin once said about the American government? "A republic, if you can keep it." Well, that question was fast being answered. America's chickens were coming home to roost. It couldn't happen to a worse country.

There was only one problem, from Milverton's point of view: What if all this effort had been for naught, and Devlin would not engage in time? The clock was ticking, especially with Skorzeny's demand that Amanda Harrington take the insurance policy to the country house in France.

That policy had been a tricky proposition, both in obtaining it and getting it conveyed to the proper place. It had cost him, personally, a lot, and the fact that Skorzeny suddenly wanted to shove his nose into what should have been a private — intimate, even — transaction between two consenting parties very definitely complicated matters. But then, when it came to affairs of Skorzeny's heart, everything was unpredictable.

He rang Amanda's number, but there was no answer. Ditto her mobile. Not a good sign.

Milverton had learned from long experience that when things went wrong, they went wrong in spades. And spades was his short suit at the moment. He didn't have time for spades.

He rang Amanda again. No answer. Damn it!

OK, now he was officially worried. It made him hate Skorzeny all the more. It put him at a disadvantage, on the defensive, which was never a place he wanted to be. He was frozen in place, tethered to the timing of the "scientific experiment" off the coast of Baltimore, tomorrow. As the *Clara Vallis* approached port.

The weather balloon experiment. With nothing else to do at the moment, he decided to run through the codes, protocols, and security measures one more time.

Blowing operational security — the ultimate poisoned pawn gambit — was something only the best intelligence operatives could get away with. It was the *ne plus ultra* of the intel biz, beyond which there was nothing — only triumph or disaster. To blow one agent might look like a tragedy, but to blow an entire operation had damn well better look like carelessness, or you were well and truly fucked. Oscar Wilde would have understood the concept, if not the call letters: EMP. Electro-Magnetic Pulse. That was the genius of the thing.

Simplicity. First principles, as Hannibal Lecter or somebody once said, *What is this thing in itself, by its own special constitution? What is it in substance, and in form, and in matter? What is its function in the world?*

Since Reagan, the Americans had been obsessed with their SDI, the Strategic Defense Initiative, or "Star Wars." Friends in the American media — paid operatives, fellow travelers, Harvard-educated idiots — had done their best to mock it as an old cowboy's fantasy, a pipe dream, something that, because it was not and could not be 100 percent fool-proof, was therefore, QED, zero percent effective.

And yet, in the end, it was the thing that had brought down the Soviet Union. Milverton had been there, in Dresden, on that freezing cold night in 1985, when Erich Honecker, the last dictator of the late German Democratic Republic, had stood in forty-below-zero weather (no matter whether it was measured in Celsius or Fahrenheit, forty-below was the sole point of agreement on the two scales) and railed against the *Stern-kriege*. Five years later, he was gone, and the East Germans would be scarfing up bananas and porn and west-marks as the Wall came down. Whether SDI worked or not, it didn't matter. Reagan had bluffed his ass off, and the Soviet communists, used to chess and not poker, toppled their king and walked away from the board.

And yet the movement had lived on, in men like Emanuel Skorzeny, who realized that true communism was capitalism by other means. There was no communist quite like a guilty plutocratic manipulator of the capitalist system. And, to paraphrase Baudelaire, Satan's greatest accomplishment was to make the West believe that the two systems were fundamentally incompatible, when, in fact, they were the same thing, if only you know how to play the angles.

EMP.

After the fall of the Soviet Union, everything was for sale. Firearms, art, icons, women — it was a giant going-out-of-business fire sale. Seeing an opportunity where the hapless American administration had not, Skorzeny had swooped in, buying them all, and more. True, he had his setbacks; when "Captain Bob" Maxwell mysteriously went overboard on his yacht . . . well that was a deal gone wrong. But a lot of deals went right.

And now Emanuel Skorzeny had the ordnance to prove it.

Because missiles and missile shields were all beside the point. Like all right-thinking people, he had mourned the demise of the USSR as a noble experiment gone wrong. But the impulse that had given it birth, to control everything and everybody for their own good, was a fundamental human impulse. And so the Soviet Union had never really died; it had simply molted, mutated, gone both underground and above board — especially in the United States.

President Carter had cautioned Americans against their "inordinate fear of communism." Stout fellow, laying the ground. The ongoing vilification of Joe McCarthy — never mind that the sainted Bobby Kennedy was his right-hand man — the destruction of Hoover's posthumous reputation, the penetration of the American universities, political parties and media by brave men and women dedicated to the ideals of Marxism-Leninism — all this was at last bearing fruit.

Perhaps the most ambitious, and ultimately successful, operation had been the

Soviet "illegals" program. This involved the expenditure of vast sums of cash — some of it financed by Skorzeny himself — in order to identify, indoctrinate, train and promote the careers of bright young things sympathetic to the Cause. Men and women who would benefit from fortunate and fortuitous scholarships to elite prep schools and universities, who would be mentored by former "radicals" turned "distinguished professors," who relied on the short, indeed nonexistent, historical memories of their fellow countrymen; who would be taken in hand by powerful politicians in need of an infusion of cash.

It took a little longer than "direct action," but the result was the same. And men like Emanuel Skorzeny could beam with pride at what they had wrought.

In a way, he thought, it was like the nexus of the Pill, the Sexual Revolution, and *Roe v. Wade.* Disrupt the understanding that had obtained between men and women for eons: that there were consequences to choice. Convince the women that they were being "liberated" from their bodies: sex without consequences. Convince the men that their dreams had come true: sex without consequences. Convince society that the "choice" was not between keeping the baby or giving it up for adoption, but between having the baby and killing the baby.

Win-win-win for everybody but the baby. Sheer genius.

And then, in two generations, suddenly there were no more generations.

Bereft of progeny, the insurance systems would collapse. Then the private pensions. Finally the government pensions. The end would come quickly, in mutual recriminations and, with any luck, civil war as the Party of Take battled the Party of Give.

But, for Skorzeny, time was running out. Even the election of an "illegal" president of the United States could not come quickly enough for him. Like all secular saints, he needed to hasten the day of his investiture into the pantheon. Needed to see his icon. If the world began the day he was born, then it must end the day he died.

EMP.

This was where al-Qaeda and the raggedy-ass terrorists had got it all wrong. You didn't have to nuke New York or Los Angeles. You didn't have to try a dirty bomb in the subways or in the cargo hold of a container ship.

Weather balloons.

They could easily launch to 95,000 feet. Near space. And, thanks to "global warming," as pure and innocent as radiation-free snow. Off-shore, from ships beyond the twenty-mile limit. A scientific experiment, to gauge the ice-melt of the permafrost of Tucson, Arizona, since the arrival of the first SUVs from Britain in 1492. Whatever.

No worries about a weather balloon. No detection of a payload hovering in the semidarkness of the ionosphere. After all, a panel truck packed with explosives nearly took down the World Trade Center the first time. A couple of airplanes did the trick the second time.

And now a weather balloon. Asymmetrical warfare at its finest.

When the device went off, at his electronic signal, sent from the comfort of his study in Camden Town, the following would happen:

Every electrical system on the East Coast of the United States would immediately fail.

Telephone service would terminate. All cell phones would go out.

Nothing electrical would operate. Not ATMs, not gas pumps, not computers, not the Internet.

The United States would be blind, deaf, and dumb.

NSA would be dead.

SDI would be dead.

America would be vulnerable to every kind of threat. Fortress America, once so secure between her two vast oceans, would now be Sitting Duck America, a pincushion for every two-bit throw-weight power including France, Israel, and South Africa. She would be like one of those pathetic water buffaloes in the veldt, food for the lions, and then carrion for the jackals.

And yet, some would profit handsomely, Skorzeny foremost among them. There was a fortune to be made in catastrophe, as there had been ever since the year 410, Common Era. Just ask Alaric the Visigoth

Only this time, if he understood the man correctly, Skorzeny would be left to pick up the pieces, preserve what was left of the civilization, to be the Irish monks of his own time: the Saint Malachy, the Bernard of Clairvaux . . .

Clairvaux.

He punched back into the NSA net, using the codes that Hartley had given him. Thank God the Americans cared about security clearances for everybody but their elected officials.

The codes were still working.

One 'bot to another. Devlin, he was sure, would get the message, and come running to him. Back into his loving arms.

Right here, on Buck Street. Number 22. Camden Town.

EMP, baby. Have a nice day.

He thought up the simplest message he could think of and sent it off to Devlin. Three little stick-figure drawings. There would be multiple security cutouts, redirects, 'bots warring against 'bots, it didn't matter. The more security protocols the better. He'd get it. He was that good. And he wouldn't be able to resist.

Amanda's life depended on it.

For the first time in his life, Milverton realized that he actually cared about somebody other than himself.

Better late than never.

CHAPTER
FIFTY-TWO

Waynesboro, Pennsylvania

Not one American in a million had ever heard of Site R, better known as the Raven Rock Mountain Complex, or the RRMC. Located about six miles north of Camp David, it was one of the country's most formidable centers of electronic intelligence, home to the Defense Threat Reduction Agency, a separate office for the secretary of defense, and the Joint Staff Support Center, among other things. With nearly forty separate communications systems, it was the nerve center of America's ELINT apparatus, as well as the emergency operations center for the uniformed services. Not for nothing did its denizens refer to it as the "Underground Pentagon."

Everything about Site R was classified. In fact, it was against DoD policy to take any pictures or make any drawings or maps of the complex without prior permission. It was at once a refuge and a command center for the highest-ranking officials in the U.S. government, the first and best "undisclosed location."

It was also the perfect place for the meeting Devlin was about to call.

Wearing an Army uniform, "Lieutenant Colonel Dan Quigley" was on time for his appointment with Secretary Rubin. Civilians getting a tour of the Pentagon were always amazed at the relative informality of the secretary of defense's Pentagon office: third floor, E-ring, between the eighth and ninth corridors. This office was similar, with the secretary's private office just an antechamber away from the main hallway.

The orderly saluted him and waved him through. "The Secretary is expecting you, Colonel," he said, and saluted.

Devlin returned the salute and walked to the open doorway. "Come in, Colonel Quigley," said Rubin's voice. "And please shut the door behind you."

Rubin was a mild-mannered, soft-spoken man, not given to Tyler's fierce fits of temper. But to say he was unhappy about this meeting was to say the least. "We meet at last. The most troublesome man in the service of the United States. There's a dead FBI team in northern Virginia that I bet you know something about."

Devlin didn't have time either for apologies or pleasantries. "There will be a lot more dead people if you don't listen to what I have to say and then do exactly what I tell you."

Rubin bristled. Devlin was Seelye's boy. He didn't have to take this kind of lip. "Watch your tone with me, Colonel," he said.

Devlin stood in the doorway, trying to decide whether to stay or to go. He believed in protocol, in playing by the rules, until he didn't, and this was one of those times.

"Mr. Secretary, I can walk out of here right now and take what I know with me. You can either let me go or have me arrested, imprisoned, and killed, but none of those courses of actions will do you any good, because you'll never get the contents of my head onto your desk until it's far too late. And by then you'll either be dead or most definitely out of a job. So why don't you drop the attitude and listen to what I have to say? Sir."

For just a moment, Rubin was tempted to tell this man where to go. And for another moment, even more chilling, he realized the Devlin could kill him right here in his office, in the safest place in America, and probably get away with it. That is what Seelye, and by extension the U.S. government, had raised him to do, trained him to do, rewarded him for doing. "It's your meeting," Rubin finally admitted.

"We've been penetrated. Somebody sent that FBI team to my home. Where I live is absolutely beyond top secret, which means it's far, far beyond the capacity of the FBI to get its hands on that information. So if it was you, say your prayers right now, because no matter how fast you are, I'm faster, and you'll be dead before you can pick up the phone. You're alive only at my forbearance, so don't push your luck." He watched as the blood drained out of Rubin's face, then continued.

"Luckily for you, I don't suspect you. It's either Seelye or Hartley —"

"Bob Hartley is dead," said Rubin. "Nobody knows it yet, but he apparently shot himself and a couple of other people at the Watergate earlier today."

"A couple of other people? Who?"

Rubin mulled whether to tell the truth or lie, but decided in favor of the former. Even without the scope on a Barrett, Devlin could spot a liar a mile away. "Secret Service agents. Members of the president's own personal detail. They were, um, protecting the senator —"

"Son of a bitch," exclaimed Devlin. "Tyler's been running his own sting operation and didn't tell anybody?" He thought things over for a moment. It was a smart play, a real smart play.

"So Hartley was your man," said Rubin: a statement, not a question. "Let's move on."

"Let's not and say we did. Hartley may well have been involved and, given his predilections, he probably was being blackmailed."

"That is an accurate statement," said the Secretary.

"But a dupe like Hartley is a two-way street of disinformation," said Devlin. He placed his PDA on the desk in front of Rubin so that the secretary could see the screen. "This just came in," he said.

Rubin looked at the message. Gibberish, in the middle of which he could just barely discern what might be three stick figures, each one of them waving a little flag. "What is this supposed to mean?" he asked.

"Other than illiteracy, do you have any other qualifications for your job, Mr. Secretary?" said Devlin, deliberately being provocative. He wanted to get a rise out of Rubin, to get his blood flowing, if he had any, if they hadn't sucked it all out of him at Columbia, to make him understand the seriousness of the situation emotionally, not just intellectually.

Contemptuously, Rubin spun the PDA back around so that it was facing Devlin. "This is kids' stuff," he spat.

Devlin was on him so fast the last "f" wasn't out of his mouth. He slapped the secretary of defense as hard as he could, right across the face. "This 'kids' stuff' spells the end of the United States, you fool," he said, "unless you listen to me, and do exactly what I tell you."

Rubin's face was red where Devlin had slapped him, but the other side was reddening almost as fast. Devlin continued as if nothing had happened —

"Ever since Edwardsville, I've believed that this whole thing, the school hostage situation, the bombing, everything — even the *Stella Maris* — has been a coordinated series of feints and misdirections, designed to sap our strength and our will, softening us up for the real blow — the one that we might have prevented were our attention not directed elsewhere."

"Do you know how ridiculous that sounds?" said Rubin, trying to regain his dignity.

"But it wasn't a simple misdirection after

all — getting me involved so that they could set off the bomb in Los Angeles, and then the missile in London. It's a *double* misdirection. A Trojan horse. Somebody — not Milverton, he's not that smart — is inside our OODA loop, making us dance. I've been a puppet on a string, yo-yoing between the coasts, while very powerful forces have been having their way with us. Edwardsville was never about the school or the kids. It was about me." There, he said it. "But this is where it stops."

The orderly's voice came over the intercom. "General Seelye is here, Mr. Secretary."

Rubin shot a glance at Devlin, if only just to keep an eye on him. He nodded. "Send the general in, please."

The door opened and in came Seelye. He started to speak, then did a double take when he saw Devlin standing there in the uniform of an Army officer. Devlin watched his eyes carefully for any sign of untoward suspicion.

"Hi, Dad," he said. Rubin looked like he might topple out of his chair. "What the hell is going on here?" he barked.

Devlin looked at Seelye but spoke to Rubin, "General Seelye here is going to give us a little dog-and-pony show. Isn't that right, Pops?"

Seelye thought seriously about trying to bluff his way through this, even as the look in Devlin's eyes told him not even to think about it.

Devlin reached in his military attaché case and took out two books, their covers still stained, the stains a dark brown now instead of blood-red.

And then Seelye knew that the game was not only afoot, it was up.

Devlin didn't wait for Seelye to sit down. "The answer was in here all along. I don't know why he did it. Maybe to leave a clue. Maybe for me to find some day. Maybe to show both of us that he's the smartest guy in the room, the smartest guy on the planet. And maybe, Army, he did it to fuck you over, the way you fucked him over. The way you fucked my mother, over, under, and sideways. The way you wrecked my family."

Devlin spoke very softly, his body coiled. Army Seelye understood that if he so much as moved, tried to call for help, or worse, attack, Devlin would kill him on the spot and take his chances with Rubin later. Wisely, he did nothing.

Devlin opened one of the books. The pages groaned and cracked. "When you grow up the way I did, without parents, well . . . you don't have many friends either. But I had these, books my father had given to me in Rome, and one of them was about the movies. So I became a movie fan. They were my escape. They were my family. And those characters played by Cagney and Bogart and Brando became more real to me than anybody real . . . including you, Dad."

"Why do you keep —" interjected Rubin, but Devlin paid him no attention.

"So this book of movie stories was a boon companion. But an even greater boon companion was this." He opened the other book, bloodier, more worn, and flipped it opened. It was covered in symbols, which zigged and zagged their way across the pages — the same dancing men as the symbols on Devlin's BlackBerry.

"Kids' stuff," blurted Seelye.

"Right," said Devlin. "Childish markings, the kind of basic substitution cipher that a father might teach his son, especially a father in our business. Except you forgot something. You forgot where my father gave me this book."

"Italy," muttered Seelye.

"Correctamundo," said Devlin, his voice mirthless. "Italy. The home of some of the greatest minds western civilization ever produced. Machiavelli — I bet he was one of your special favorites. Michelangelo. And Leonardo."

There was a mirror on one wall. Devlin pointed to it. "Remember what Leonardo used to do? Mirror-writing. If he wanted to obscure something, he wrote it backward. You had to hold the text up to the mirror to decipher it. Later, it was common practice for some Europeans to start a letter normally and then, when they ran out of room, turn the parchment sideways and keep writing, right over what they had written before. And, of course, you could do both those things, backward. Sentence, retrograde, inversion, and retrograde inversion.

"Cryptography's a complicated thing, as we all know. But, at root, it's not. It's simply a way of communicating with people you like while making the subject of that communication opaque to people you don't. That way, if it falls into the wrong hands, they can't read it. And the rest, as they say" — Devlin gestured around the room, embracing the entire Raven Rock complex in his unspoken metaphor — "is commentary. So let's see what the dancing men have to say." He pretended to consult the book, although ever since he had fully deciphered their message, he had memorized it in its entirety.

What he was about to do he wanted to do for a long time: he was about to face the past, and jerk it back into the present with a vengeance.

"It's a hell of a thing to discover at my age that everything you've been told about who you are and where you came from is a lie, but life is full of little surprises. I won't bore you with the details, but — and Army can confirm all this to you later, Mr. Secretary — for years I believed that the general here and my mother were having an affair, that my father found out, that they all met up in Rome to sort things out and it just so happened that it was our bad luck to be in Leonardo da Vinci Airport that Christmas in 1985 when Abu Nidal came calling, and both my parents were killed."

"I saved your life," growled Seelye.

"Don't rush me," snapped Devlin, totally in control, "especially since the next part stars you, yourself, and you."

Neither of his superiors had anything to say. "But the reason for the meeting turns out to be quite something else. It wasn't about my mother at all — oh, you may have been fucking her, but that wasn't what brought you all together. It was . . . well, here, Army — why don't you read it? It's just a simple substitution cipher, and you're the head of the freakin' NSA."

Devlin tossed the book to Seelye, who stared at the dancing men with dull but visible comprehension. He didn't need to read much. He closed the book gently, quietly, and left it sitting in his lap, one hand resting on the dried blood of Devlin's mother.

"I put her picture up on the wall for your sake," said Seelye. "It was one of the ways I protected you. Even if . . . if anyone suspected that you'd survived, the last place they'd look for you was in an agency where your mother had been proclaimed a traitor."

"Now we're getting somewhere," said Devlin, approvingly. "Protect me from whom?"

"From him," Seelye exhaled.

"Say it out loud."

He had him. Seelye knew that every conversation in this office, just like every conversation in his own office at Fort Meade, was recorded. There was no way out.

"From Emanuel Skorzeny. He wanted to kill you. He still does."

Rubin was incredulous. "And *that's* what this is all about?"

Seelye shrugged helplessly.

Devlin answered, "Don't worry, Mr. Secretary, it gets better. A man like Skorzeny never does anything twice when he can do it once. He's making a move — a big move, and I'm just a bonus at this point. The problem is — tell him, General."

Seelye was beaten and he knew it. "The problem is, we don't know what he's planning. In less than a week, he's ten times richer than he was before . . ." The professional in Seelye was starting to reassert itself. "But we feel, we all feel, that what's past is just prologue to what is to come."

"Which is?" said Rubin.

Devlin took a deep breath before answering. The book of dancing men lay on Seelye's lap. He glanced down at it as he began to speak.

"When I was a kid, just before the Rome Airport massacre, I overheard a conversation in Munich." He didn't need to bother looking at Seelye. "You were there, Army, along with my parents. I couldn't quite piece together everything you were saying, especially since I didn't know some of the languages then, but it turns out, it's all in here."

Devlin picked up the book. "In late 1985, the world's most dangerous terrorist was planning an attack on the Radio Free Europe office — that is to say, the CIA station — in Munich. This came after a series of bombings in Berlin and in France. He was the world's most wanted man, and yet he operated with near-impunity from bases in Budapest, Baghdad, Aden. You know who I'm talking about?"

"Carlos the Jackal," said Rubin.

"Right. Better known as Ilyich Ramirez Sanchez. The man you were supposedly after — right, Dad?"

Seelye blanched, but stayed silent.

"It's okay. You were playing a double game against two men better at it than you were." He looked at Seelye. "Was Skorzeny a CI, a confidential informant, or just redoubled?"

"Neither," said Seelye. "He was playing me, just like he played everybody."

Devlin nodded. "You knew that Skorzeny was working both sides of the street, operating as an honest if rapacious businessman aboveground, while doing his damnedest to destabilize European society by financing a loosely allied collection of bad guys: the IRA, the Red Brigades, the Basques, Abu Nidal, the PLO, you name it."

"He was working with all of them," admitted Seelye, "the whole 'terror network,' as Claire Sterling called it."

"And everybody laughed at her when her book came out," said Devlin. "But she knew the KGB tried to whack the Pope through a Bulgarian cutout and a Muslim Turk shooter and she was right. She knew that the terror groups may have been rivals, maybe even hated each other, but the enemy of my enemy is always my friend. And so they worked together, doing well by, as they saw it, doing good."

Now it was Seelye's turn to nod as Devlin continued. "And Carlos was his main man. It's really brilliant when you think about, and so very postmodern. Capitalist, communist, patriot, internationalist — what's the difference? If you're smart enough, and brazen enough, and rich enough, you can get away with it. And that's what Skorzeny's been doing, ever since. He made a monkey out of you and the only way you could deal with it, the only way you could cover your professional shame, was to take my parents off the board and cast yourself as the hero."

"Carlos is doing life in prison in France. Has been for years," said Rubin.

Devlin ignored him. He rose and loomed over Seelye. "Did you know about Rome?" he shouted, his voice rising. "Well, did you — you son of a bitch?" The accusation was bitter, but it felt good; it was a long time coming. It felt cathartic.

"No!" shouted Seelye. "I might have told

534

him your family was leaving. I didn't know anything about Abu Nidal. I didn't know what they were planning for Rome and Vienna." He looked around the room for absolution, but found none.

Devlin was not satisfied. "I think you did, Army. I think you did. But it almost doesn't matter. Maybe you just lucked into it, but either way, they were gone and your operation was off the hook. So same difference."

"And I've had to live with it every day since then. I did what I could for you."

"Yes, you did," said Devlin. "You made me into the man I am today. *Ecce homo* . . . And that's why you dangled me in front of Tyler when Edwardsville came around. You were ready for it. You knew how to play Tyler's emotions. And you knew that, if you got real lucky, you could kill three clichés with one stone: save the kids, flush out the bad guys, and get rid of me. I don't blame you — that's the play I would have made." Devlin laughed bitterly. "It's just that Tyler turned out to be smarter than all of us. I guess that's why he's the president and we're sitting in a mountain, five hundred feet below the surface of the earth."

Seelye jumped to his feet, his face a mask of rage. Thank God the room was soundproof. "I saved your *fucking life.* And I'm still saving it! Don't you understand?"

If there had been a clock on the mantle, they could have heard it ticking in the silence that followed. But nobody had ticking clocks any more.

"What are you talking about?" said Devlin.

"He's still trying to kill you. He knows you're still alive. I tried to cover your tracks, but he's too smart. He's been researching you, spent a fortune following the trail. It's taken him years but he's patient. And he won't rest until he eliminates you. Not just kills you but humiliates and destroys you. You're an affront to him."

"And now," said Devlin quietly, "I'm an obstacle too." He placed the PDA between his two superiors, punching some keys to strip away all the textural white noise to reveal the three dancing men beneath.

"Misdirection, just as I said from the start. Sure it would be great for him to get me, great to blow the cover off the entire Branch 4 operation, great to give our enemies even more fuel for their hate-America fires. But that's just the means to an end."

He hit two more keys and now the dancing men were upright. Devlin took charge. "This came from Milverton today." Another key and they began dissolving . . . into letters of the alphabet. Letters than spelled: EMP.

"Good God," said Rubin, softly. "A good thing SDI is fully operational on both coasts."

"Against weather balloons?"

"What?"

"That's what we found in the hold of the *Stella Maris,* Skorzeny's 'humanitarian' ship that sank at Long Beach. But there were no nukes on board, no explosives, nothing. Just weather balloons."

"And he raised hell about it," said Rubin. "Demanded that — oh, Jesus — that, in recompense, and in exchange for not making a run on our currency, his other ship, the *Clara Vallis,* be given every courtesy . . ."

"When does she make port?"

"Tomorrow, late in the day. Baltimore." Seelye lunged for the secure phone. "We'll blow her out of the water right —"

Devlin grabbed the phone and set it back in its cradle. "No. Leave her alone. Start circling her now and she'll get that bird in the air. Not optimal — the balloon needs to be over land for max damage — but close enough for government work."

"What are we going to do?" asked Rubin.

"We're going to go for the feint once more. There's a reason Skorzeny wants me

537

to tango with Milverton in London."

"It's a trap," said Seelye.

"Of course it is."

"He wants Milverton to kill you."

"Duh. And the feeling is most definitely mutual. So I want carte blanche, no questions asked. I want what I want and I want what I need and I want what I don't know about yet and I want it all yesterday, today, and tomorrow. And one thing I most definitely want is access to French airspace — low-flying stuff, beneath radar, EZ-in, EZ-out if the frogs don't get their panties in a bunch. There will be some damage, but we'll try to keep it to a minimum — small arms fire, maybe a Sidewinder or two."

"That might be —" said Rubin.

"Who's in charge here? POTUS or Foggy Bottom? Tell Tyler I get what he's been up to. He'll do it. Plus, I want the Branch 4 death sentence on me lifted. Deal?"

"Deal," said Rubin. "I'll personally guarantee it with the president."

"One more thing. I want you to make it right with those FBI families and make sure they're taken care of. For life."

"Done."

"Especially that girl I killed. And keep the lid on Hartley's death for as long as you can. In the meantime, we have to let Milverton know that everything is still hunky-dory."

Using Hartley's Watergate phone number as the origination, Devlin punched in the number that Hartley had called and put the instrument on speakerphone, so they could all hear the cutout clicks as the call was rerouted. He let it ring once and then hung up.

"He'll suspect something," warned Seelye.

"Of course he will," replied Devlin. "That's his job. But he'll do worse than suspect if he doesn't hear from Hartley pretty soon. Right now, it's just a dropped call. The next call he gets from me is going to come in person. One last thing —"

"Name it," said Rubin.

"I want my mother's picture down off the Wall of Shame. I want her files erased from the NSA/CSS system — don't fuck with me on this, because if you don't do it, I'll know. I want my father rehabbed and given a star at Langley. And I want your resignation, General Seelye, whenever I ask for it."

Devlin turned to Rubin. "Good-bye, Mr. Secretary," he said. "You'll never see me again." And then he really was gone.

After he'd left, Rubin looked at Seelye with a mixture of contempt, disappointment, and disgust. "Why didn't you tell him?" he asked.

"Tell him what?"

"That there is no death sentence. That there is no other member of Branch 4. That, in fact, he *is* Branch 4."

"It's on a need-to-know basis," said Seelye. "And he doesn't need to know. Not now, maybe not ever."

■ ■ ■ ■

DAY SEVEN

■ ■ ■ ■

Always remember the dictum of Heraclitus, "Death of earth, birth of water; death of water, birth of air; from air, fire; and so round again."
— MARCUS AURELIUS, *Meditations,* Book IV

CHAPTER
FIFTY-THREE

Ville-sous-la-Ferté, France
Emanuel Skorzeny drank deeply of the air.
This was not his favorite part of France —
except for the champagne, it was nobody's
— but if he closed his eyes and projected
himself back a millennium, he could appreciate what its Cistercian founders might
have seen in it. Troyes was the nearest town;
Chaumont was closer, but there was nothing there. Paris itself lay 235 kilometers to
the west/northwest. At the speeds Pilier
drove, a little over two hours. It was close, it
was convenient and, best of all, absolutely
unfashionable. Especially his piece of it.

"Is everything ready?" he inquired of
Pilier. Visits to the country needed to be set
up in advance, even for him. There were
security arrangements to be made, money
that needed to change hands, preparations,
especially when he was bringing guests.

"I think you will find the arrangements

satisfactory, yes, sir," he replied.

"That goes without saying," said Skorzeny with some asperity. "Competence and trustworthiness. That's what I pay all my people for."

Not for the first time, Skorzeny wondered if he could trust M. Pilier. For one thing, the man had no taste in music. When Skorzeny requested that a private orchestra be prepared to perform a certain piece for strings alone, Pilier had looked at him in puzzlement. As if a cultured man could profess ignorance of such a masterpiece! And then he remembered that Pilier was of the younger generation, the postwar generation, the ones who had learned to despise their cultures, to hate their societies, to root for the man with the knife, even when the knife was at their throats.

The bomb throwers of 1968, of the May uprising that had toppled De Gaulle were, forty years on, the men and women who had been running the country for decades. Now aging themselves, they were long past the age where they qualified for the generous pensions and benefits of the welfare state they had, in part, created. Filled with self-loathing, obsessed by a "fairness" principle that could never be fully realized, they had turned France, and much of western Europe, into a land in which women declined the rigors and joys of childbirth in order to realize their potential as incomplete men. One generation and out — who knew it would be that easy? Two generations after the defeat of fascism, Europe had turned into a suicide cult.

Poor stewards of a thousand years of glory, it was time for them to go.

Although standing here, on a small hill above Vallée d'Absinthe, above the town where Bernard had built his great Abbey, he could still feel the resonance of what once had been. Bernard, who had preached his Crusade, founded the knights Templar, battled Abelard, suckled at the teat of the Blessed Virgin Mary herself and drank the holy breast milk, died and was buried, only to be exhumed after the dissolution of the monastery during the French Revolution and reinterred in Troyes Cathedral. A man who, like Skorzeny, had lived long enough to witness the death of his own civilization. Despite everything that separated them, his kith, his kin.

Here, in what the Romans called the *clara vallis,* the sheltered valley that had preserved the knowledge of the ancient world and had passed it on, from Bernard to St. Malachy, to the Irish monks and wandering scholars, to the *goliards,* the Minnesingers, the troubadours, to the emerging West, he felt right at home.

"Do you know how a parasite operates on the nervous system, Monsieur Pilier? How it destroys the organism benignly?"

Always with the questions. "Yes, sir. It's a Trojan horse, a poisoned pawn, a triumph that turns to tragedy, a pleasure that turns to pain —"

Skorzeny clapped his hands together, like a child. "Indeed. It burrows, it wheedles, it infects. And every time its victim looks in the mirror, what does she see? That which she wants to see — herself, her former, beautiful self. Not the patch over her damaged eye. Not her inchoate rage against the man she cannot have. *O don fatale!*" He turned to Pilier. "You know the reference, of course?"

"Verdi, I believe, sir."

"*Don Carlos.* Princess Eboli and the fatal gift which, as we might say today, keeps on giving."

"Life is full of frustrations, sir," said Pilier, noncommittally.

Skorzeny caught his tone, and its possible subtext. "Then let us take up our residency." They got back into the Citroën limousine and moved off.

Skorzeny looked out the window as they approached the ancient building. "It's magnificent, isn't it?" he said.

From the outside, it was hard to imagine what it once had been: the ancient monastery of Clairvaux, dating back to the twelfth century. Today, it looked more like an eighteenth-century chateau, flying the Tricolor over the main entrance — a relict of the Enlightenment, concealing the bones of the civilization that had made it possible.

What would St. Bernard make of his Abbey today? Contemporary reports of the monastery back in the Middle Ages depicted a place of quiet contemplation, of living in harmony with nature. Scholarship and silence were the watchwords. For more than six hundred years, the Abbey had stood, its fortunes shifting with those of Christendom, until it was swamped by the rising tide of secularism and anticlericalism that culminated in the French Revolution. The monastery was closed, appropriated by the state, and fell into ruins, eventually to rise again.

But it wasn't a chateau. And it was no longer an abbey.

"What of Miss Harrington?"

"In transit, sir."

"You're certain?"

Pilier hated to see the old man like this.

Abject. Supplicative. Needy. It was his one weakness. *She* was his one weakness.

"She received your text message."

"You're sure she's on her way. With the policy?"

"I see no reason to —"

"Do you think me a fool, Monsieur Pilier?" blurted Skorzeny, as they approached the massive fortress. The question was not entirely unexpected.

"If I may be so bold . . . yes, sir, I do."

In the backseat, Skorzeny flinched. "May I ask why?"

"Because you don't need her, sir," replied Pilier. "She's a destabilizing element. Something even you can't control. You've always warned me against that sort of thing. Against that sort of woman."

"We learn from our mistakes, Monsieur Pilier," said Skorzeny with some asperity. Pilier realized that he might have gone too far.

"Here we are, sir," said Pilier.

And there they were, passing through the barbed-wire fence and pulling up before the main gates. The perfect setting for his mood. The perfect setting for what was about to happen. The perfect refuge from the end of the world:

Clairvaux Prison.

Once a cell block, always a cell block.

The guard waved them through on sight. No matter how many times he was here, Pilier never got over an involuntary shudder. Clairvaux Prison was home to some of the toughest convicts in France. It had a high population of violent Muslim immigrants, who had gone from being warehoused in the Paris *banlieues* to being warehoused in the French penal system with nary a stop in between. It was home to murderers, rapists, armed robbers, the lot. Even terrorists; in fact, one very famous terrorist in particular.

Ilyich Ramirez Sanchez.

Skorzeny's quarters, made in arrangement with the French government, were hidden away at the back of the complex. Here, he was as secure as the most high-security prisoner, fully protected from the outside world and from any malevolence it might want to visit upon him. But there was also a strange peacefulness about the place. His suite of rooms looked out at some of the ruins. Even across a distance of nearly a thousand years, he could see the outlines of what had once been the fish ponds, so important to a Cistercian monastery. The monks were great gardeners, great tillers of the soil, great husbanders of natural resources, great foresters. They were men of peace.

"And yet their Abbot preached the Second Crusade," muttered Skorzeny, giving voice to his innermost thoughts as Pilier unpacked his things and laid them out on his bed.

The fact that Skorzeny kept secure quarters in a prison was not as fanciful as it might seem. Conscious of the abbey's place in French history, the government was excavating and restoring the ruins of the old abbey, so there were nonprisoners living at the site. There was even a short concert series in the fall, at the Hostellerie des Dames, where the music included works by Mozart, Ravel, Debussy, and, of course, Messiaen.

"The musicians are ready?" asked Skorzeny, breaking the conversational silence.

"Everything awaits your presence."

Skorzeny glanced at his watch. He was one of those men who still wore a watch. Pilier read his mind. "She'll be here any —"

A soft buzz on the telephone. It was the guard at the front gate. Pilier put down the receiver and said, "She's here."

Skorzeny was still looking at his watch. Pilier waited a decent interval and then coughed quietly. "I said, Miss Harrington is here."

"Excellent," replied Skorzeny, although the tone of his voice signaled anything but pleasure. He tossed one more glance at his watch, as if calculating something. "Is everything in order?"

Pilier had no idea what he was talking about. "Yes, sir. The musicians —"

"I don't mean the musicians. I mean the *Clara Vallis*."

"On schedule, sir, with no trouble from the authorities. In fact, they're being quite cooperative."

The doorbell buzzed even more softly than the telephone. "I'll get it," said Skorzeny, moving with uncharacteristic swiftness toward the door.

Pilier had no fears for his boss's safety; anybody who got this close had to pass three multiple layers of security, including a weapons check. Skorzeny opened the door. Framed in it was Amanda Harrington. Pilier had to admit she was a fine-looking specimen of womanhood. He could see, almost feel, what attracted Skorzeny so powerfully to her.

Standing next to her was a girl of about twelve. From the dull look in her eyes, Pilier could see that she was sedated. She held Amanda's hand limply, like a rag doll. In return, Amanda was clutching the girl's hand tightly in hers, as if she were afraid it would just slip away and never return.

"My dear Miss Harrington," said Skorzeny, "may I say you look lovelier than ever." His eyes fell upon the girl. "And this must be your charming daughter." He leaned down a bit and looked the girl in the face. "What is your name, dear?" he asked.

If the child heard him, she showed no signs of it. In any other context, the silence might have been embarrassing, or at least awkward. Finally, Amanda jogged the girl a little. "Tell Mr. Skorzeny your name, darling," she commanded, gently. "Go on."

A small light came back in the girl's eyes as she registered Amanda's order. "Emma," she said at last. "Emma Gard—"

"Emma Harrington," corrected Amanda, who looked at Skorzeny. Neither of them had embraced, kissed or even shaken hands. "The adoption papers —"

Skorzeny motioned for Amanda and Emma to step inside. "Are in progress," he said. "Isn't that right, Monsieur Pilier?" Pilier had no idea what the old man was talking about, but pretended he did.

"Yes, sir," he said. "In fact, I was in touch with our London solicitors earlier today and everything should be ready within . . . within a fortnight."

"That's too long," said Amanda curtly.

"Would you like a drink?" asked Skorzeny, which was Pilier's cue to head for the bar.

"Let's get Emma to bed first," she said. Skorzeny indicated one of the back bedrooms. Amanda swept Emma up in her arms and whisked her away.

"She seems agitated," observed Skorzeny. "Perhaps with some reason."

"What do you mean, 'adoption papers,' sir?" asked Pilier. "This is the first that I've . . . Who is the girl?"

"My insurance policy," replied Skorzeny. "Against untoward events and harmful visitors. Now, please mix Miss Harrington her favorite martini, if you don't mind."

Pilier was shaking the martini when Amanda emerged from the bedroom. The look on her face was cold. "I've given her her medicine," she said. "She should sleep for quite a while now. It's been a long day."

Amanda took the martini from Pilier without acknowledgment or thanks and downed it. "What the hell is going on?" she said, suddenly, angrily. "Why the urgent summons from London when you know perfectly well that I have work to do. Your work. For the Foundation. In the middle of an international crisis, I really don't have the time for —"

Skorzeny cut her off. "Why don't you shut up?" he said.

The brutality of his tone caught her by surprise. She was just wondering what it was all about when she felt the martini kick in. Except it wasn't the martini, it was whatever Pilier had slipped into it. Some kind of drug. The glass slipped from her hand and shattered on the flagstone floor.

"That's better," said Skorzeny.

Pilier escorted Amanda to a chair and set her down into it. Her eyes were open, but she couldn't move.

"You're probably wondering what's happening to you. Please, don't be afraid. The condition is not permanent, and there is no lasting damage. You will find it hard to speak, so just nod your head to my questions and everything will be fine. Do you understand?"

Amanda nodded, almost imperceptibly, but it would have to do. She cursed herself for falling for it. Her suspicions had been right all along — the old man thought they were trying to kill him at the London Eye. And maybe Milverton was. She had nothing to do with that.

Then another thought hit her. Maybe Milverton had somehow planted the notion in Skorzeny's mind that she wished him dead.

That she was tired of his importunities, and would shed hardly a tear if something happened to him. That with Skorzeny dead, she, more than anybody except perhaps that creepy Pilier, would have access to all the money until the lawyers kicked in, by which time she could be long gone. After all, she'd got what she wanted out of the deal.

She'd finally got her child.

"Were you trying to kill me in London?" There it was. She shook her head, no.

"Don't lie to me. I will have independent corroboration of everything I ask you, and if you lie to me, it will go very hard with you. Very hard, indeed. Do I make myself clear?"

She nodded.

"Very well, then, I repeat. Were you trying to kill me in London?"

There was no way to answer the question. If only she could say something. She tried to move her lips and tongue, but no sound came out. She hoped the desperation she was feeling was somehow reflected in her eyes, hoped that the old man would see the flash and understand, take pity on her. But she also knew that was a forlorn hope.

"Are you cheating on me? Having it off with Milverton, that rotter? Plotting against me?"

Amanda tried, but she couldn't. Couldn't move, couldn't answer. Whatever fate he had in store for her, she had to accept it.

Skorzeny turned to Pilier. "I think we are ready for our concert now," he said.

"Very well, sir." He picked up the phone and spoke softly to someone. Amanda could hear his voice, barely, but couldn't make out any words. "On their way," said Pilier, hanging up.

Skorzeny looked at Amanda, sitting paralyzed in her chair. "The great composers," he began. "How they reinforce our every emotion. Speak to places in the heart we did not know existed. That is the power of music."

Workers poured in, setting up folding chairs in semicircles. They finished quickly. When everything was ready, about twenty musicians, both men and women, each attired in formal dress, entered and took their places: a string orchestra.

"What will replace our culture when it's gone?" continued Skorzeny. Pilier got the sense he was speaking more to himself than anybody else at this point. "What will replace Michelangelo and Leonardo and Bach? The bray of Madonna or the wail of the *muezzin?*" He was lost in thought for a moment. "Better, perhaps, to end it all now, and spare us the agony of having to eat our own entrails as we die." He turned to the orchestra. "You may begin."

From the opening strains, Amanda knew what the piece was: *Metamorphosis for Strings* by Richard Strauss. A late work, one of his last, a threnody for the German civilization he and his music had once exemplified. It had all the glorious radiance of his early works, but none of their expansive joy. This was the work of an old man, composing his own funeral music. As if to underscore the point, near the end, he even quoted Beethoven's funeral march from the "Eroica" Symphony.

It was music to accompany the end of the world.

The last mournful strains died away. There was no applause. As one, the musicians rose and filed out of the room. In her delirium, Amanda might have imagined that one of the violinists, a woman, gave her a searching, sympathetic look, but there was no way she could communicate with her. She could only hope.

They were alone. Skorzeny sat slumped in his chair, his mind still on the music.

Amanda's mind was on the music as well, but in a different way. She had no doubt what was going to happen to her. She was never going to leave this horrible place alive, never going to realize her dream of taking her new daughter, who would learn to love her in time, and moving somewhere, anywhere, as long as it was far away. Never going to realize her dream of leaving Emanuel Skorzeny and all he represented far behind.

Amanda's turmoil was invisible to Skorzeny. Not that he would have cared. He was long past caring.

"It was all so simple, until you . . . what is the word you young people use all the time . . . *fucked* it up. I do mean that literally. After all I did for you. Sacrificed for you. *Risked* for you."

She twitched and tried to blink her eyes, to communicate in some way. It was no use. Her strength was failing her. Just when she needed it most.

"It's over. Don't you see? All of this. A cathedral turned into a prison. A culture turned into a cesspool. A continent into a sewer. An entire civilization into a *souk*. And so, rather than being pissed on . . . I piss on it. 'I am become Death, destroyer of Worlds,' as both Oppenheimer and the Bhagavad Gita famously said. I am the day after Trinity. And which of them was stronger — the Indian poet or the American scientist?"

She couldn't even move her head to

acknowledge the question.

"Once upon a time, I should have said the poet. That is how much I believed. That was how I was raised. With civilization failing and falling all around me, I still *believed.* Do you understand?

"But now, even I no longer believe. During the last century, Europe tried twice to commit suicide. Both times America saved it from its own worst instincts — the second time, just barely. We celebrated America for her selfless sacrifice. We created a worker's paradise of 'social democracy.' Six weeks' vacation, unlimited medical insurance, abortion on demand — why have children if they were going to interfere with your lifestyle? With the rights of women, Western society's proudest achievement. Other cultures, lesser cultures, scorned us, laughed at us, and . . ."

He stopped, looked at her, then kissed her one last time. "They were right." He fussed with something in his pocket. "What was it Louis XV said? *Après moi, le deluge.* Or was in Madame de Pompadour? No matter: the sentiment still obtains."

Amanda tried to mouth some words. Skorzeny pretended to put his ear to her lips.

He had played his hand perfectly, calling forth the shade of someone he once thought dead, but knew in his heart had never died.

His old friend and rival, Seelye, had covered his tracks very well. "Scrubbed" him, brilliantly.

Which is why everything he'd ordered Milverton to do had been leading to this very moment. Flushing the specter out from the shadows, whipsawing him around the Western world as he ratcheted up the stakes. Keeping him so involved in his own personal vendetta that he would never see the big strike coming. The one man he had to rid himself of, because in him Seelye had created the only person who could stop Skorzeny's magnificent *Götterdämmerung*.

Amanda struggled mightily against her own body's self-imposed bonds. There were so many things she had to say, so much to plead for, to live for. But she couldn't even move a muscle. She realized it was useless. She stopped struggling. It was over.

"If only you hadn't betrayed me. Did you not realize that my eyes and ears were everywhere? In your house, in your phones, inside his vaunted ranks of computers? I may be an old man, but certain principles never change. And spies are among the immutables."

Her mouth managed to form the word, Why?

"I can understand him. He is a man, like

me. He has the same desires that I do. The same lusts. A will to power. The will to live. But what, my dear, is your excuse?"

She tried to move her head, but she couldn't.

"I should have thought better of a woman," he said.

She didn't know whether to believe him, that the effects would wear off. She didn't know if she would ever wake up again, ever see Emma again. She felt herself slipping away . . .

When she was quite unconscious, Skorzeny signaled to Pilier. "Inform Mr. Ramirez Sanchez I will see him now," he said.

CHAPTER
FIFTY-FOUR

London

By the time he got to Camden Town, Devlin was as ready as he was ever going to be. CSS had few functional ops in Britain, but SAS and DoD communicated regularly. Devlin liked the SAS guys. They were tough. They were a throw-back to the Brits of yore, the guys who set out to make the world England and damn near succeeded. There was, after all, something to be said in favor of an intact gene pool. When you kill off the best, the brightest, the bravest . . . and leave only the losers, the weak, the objectors, the physically and mentally unfit . . . well — what would Darwin say?

He checked his messages. Maryam was in place. His hunch, her research. She was a woman of many talents.

Once more, Devlin marveled at the chance that had brought them together. On the surface, she was just the kind of woman he should avoid, if not kill. Her fortuitous appearance in Paris when he was first stalking Milverton, her forbearance through the long silence that followed, her reappearance on the plane to Los Angeles . . .

And yet perhaps it was time for a play not in the playbook. Maybe it was time to trust your instincts instead of the probability charts. Whoever had sent her to Paris to track him, whatever the reason she had waited so long, however she had managed for their paths to cross again on the way to LA — it didn't matter.

Could he trust her? Of course not.

Was he going to trust her? Absolutely.

Because, for once in his life, he was going to experience the joys of an absolutely unconditional relationship. Even if it cost him that life.

A "22" masquerading as a cabbie picked him up at Heathrow. The London weather was, as usual, miserable, cold, damp, and raw. "What's the Bulgarian bride's lucky number in *Casablanca*?" Devlin asked, leaning in the window, as if he were giving the driver his final destination.

"Twenty-two, black, gov'nor," came the reply.

Devlin got in. "Louis," he said, "I think

this is the beginning of a beautiful friendship."

"I know it is, sir," said the cabbie. "I can feel it in me bones."

"Damn right you can," replied Devlin.

A Glock 31 with a 17-shot magazine was in the back of the cab. Enough to do the job, if he did it right. No knives, though. Oh well. He had the element of surprise and that, plus superior firepower, should be enough to take the job on.

Number 22 Buck Street was not the sort of place a tourist would stumble upon. It was a dead end between Camden High Street and Kentish Town Road, lined with ramshackle dwellings, some of which had been squatters' dumps back in the 1970s, now rehabbed but still unstylish.

The driver dropped him off at the corner of the Camden High Street. A short walk.

Devlin pretended to pay him: twenty-two pounds, on the nose. The cabbie pretended to accept.

"Why?" said Devlin as the driver put the car in gear and made ready to drive off.

"Why not?" said the cabbie. "The malfeasance of one diminishes us all." He smiled. "But the death of one . . . fuck 'im if he can't take a joke." And then he was gone.

The house wasn't much to look at from

the street, but that was what he would have expected. They were men who lived in the shadows, would always live in the shadows, and only briefly emerge into the sunlight. But this wasn't going to be one of those times. This was the day that one of them would no longer see the sunlight, ever.

Devlin had retroplanned. What would he do in these circumstances? The FBI team had penetrated even his defenses, but that was thanks to Milverton's man on the inside. He had nobody inside Milverton's OODA loop. There was just one true thing he knew: Milverton was human. Devlin could take this guy out, if he was smart enough and strong enough and brave enough.

What was the attacker's rule of thumb? Three-to-one odds. Overwhelming force, overwhelmingly applied. He was two guys short.

Too bad. One-on-one — plus the element of surprise — would have to do.

Not the basement: too easy. Not the skylight: too easy and too hard, simultaneously. Nor the windows. Assume everything rigged, first principles, what is the thing, in and of itself?

The front door. Easy in, easy out. Everybody had to eat, meet, greet. The safety of the antechamber was the most delusory safety on earth.

He was going to ring the doorbell and see what happened. First principles.

He rang it.

If he were Milverton, he would have been watching himself on the CCTV. Just another deliveryman, FedEx, DHL, the Royal Mail, whatever.

He rang it again. Tried to look ready for his close-up.

Still nothing.

He rang it a third time. The Glock was burning a hole in his pocket.

Footfalls, maybe. Steps, certainly.

The door started to open, slowly, cautiously.

Showtime.

This was the moment of maximum vulnerability. When Milverton most suspected whomever was at the door. When he was most ready.

The door opened. A crack —

And now they were face to face.

Milverton didn't look so formidable in his knockabouts. Devlin's hand stole toward one of his firearms, but Milverton just stood there in the doorway, no sign of alarm on his face, no sign of recognition either, just that same icy calm demeanor. Milverton's hands were at his side, empty. This couldn't be this easy —

The door opened wider.

"I've been expecting you," said Milverton, "so why don't you come in and we can get this over with?"

Devlin tensed —

"Don't worry, I'm not going to kill you on my own fucking doorstep. Just don't make me stand here with the door open. Do you know what it costs to heat a house these days?"

Devlin stepped across the threshold and Milverton closed the door behind him.

The house was typical for this part of town: lived-in, comfortable, threadbare — the home of a careless intellectual or a Monty Python character.

"Drink?" asked Milverton.

"Little early for me, thanks," replied Devlin.

"Then sit down and let's talk, before we get down to business."

Devlin took a seat on a well-sprung sofa. "It can't be this easy," he said.

"Of course it can," replied Milverton, "when you want it to be."

"But your own man gave you up. A fellow SAS officer."

"Who still works with me from time to

time. I sent him to pick you up." Milverton smiled and Devlin could see the tips of his canines. "It's nice to stay close to HQ, here in the old neighborhood."

Devlin instinctively inventoried the weapons he had concealed on his person. Milverton picked it up at once. "Don't worry, the Glock's for real, and in good working order. I couldn't very well invite you all the way across the Atlantic and into my home and not give you a sporting chance. Not after all we've been through together, now, could I?"

"What do you want?"

Milverton chuckled mirthlessly. Devlin could practically see the man's scalp through his close-cropped blond hair as his head bobbed involuntarily. He thought about —

"Don't even think about it," said Milverton. "Even you aren't that good. Neither of us is . . . you know, the thought just occurred to me, that we don't know each other's names. Our real names."

"Guys like us don't have real names," said Devlin.

"Do you even know yours? No, let me rephrase that," said Milverton. "As a wise man once said, it's a wise man who knows who his father is." He looked at Devlin directly. "What's your wisdom quotient these days?"

"Fuck you."

"Neither witty nor wise. But I assure you that there is a man on the Continent who would pay dearly for that information."

"Emanuel Skorzeny."

"That's what most people call him, yes. But, as you just so brilliantly noted, blokes like us don't have the luxury of real names. We're shadow people, 'little noted nor long remembered,' as your Mr. Lincoln once said. But we do what we can. And, like everybody else, we try to save our sodding arses."

"What do you want?"

"Isn't it obvious? I want you. That's why I invited you here. Fag?" Milverton held out an open packet of Players.

Devlin shook his head.

"I find it calms my nerves," said Milverton, lighting up. "Nasty old habit I can't seem to break."

"Where's the little girl? Emma? You took her, didn't you?"

"You liked that bit with the chopper, did you? I was rather proud of that myself, although I was surprised you went for it so easily. Unworthy of you, really . . ."

"The little girl?"

"Oh, she's quite safe. Better off than she ever would have been in that dreadful American burg."

"Her mother wants her back."

Milverton took a long drag on his cigarette. "I would say that's up to you, now. Which is another one of your current disadvantages . . . Do you trust her?"

"Trust who? The kid?" Throughout their enforced conversation, Devlin had been sizing up Milverton's own weaponry, which he had concealed on his person as skillfully as Devlin had concealed his hardware. He had also scoped out the internal security measures, the redundant systems. Basically, he was screwed.

"No, not Emma. The pretty little sand nigger I almost killed in Paris," Milverton was saying. "The one who picked you up so inexpertly. That was when I realized that you weren't as good as your reputation, and frankly, nothing you've done since has persuaded me otherwise."

"Maybe today's my lucky day."

"I think not. You're sure you don't want a drink? I hate to imbibe alone. In fact, I insist."

"Bottled beer, then."

"Very good," said Milverton, rising. "Please don't get up — the motion sensors are activated, and . . . well, you know. That 'X'tal vision' really does work, doesn't it?"

Devlin was trying to decide whether to call Milverton's bluff as the SAS man returned bearing two bottles of Grolsch. "Don't worry — one hundred percent purity guaranteed," said Milverton as he returned. Nearly simultaneously, they each flipped the metal switch that popped open the sealed top of the beer bottles, which both, satisfyingly, *whooshed.* "Happy days," said Milverton.

"How do you want to play this?" asked Devlin.

"Simple," replied Milverton. "I want you to give yourself up. To give me everything I need to get Skorzeny off my back."

"To sign my own death warrant."

"That's your problem. Frankly, I don't care what happens to you. I still owe you for Paris, and I just know that you're itching to find out which of us is better. That's something I'd welcome too, but it hardly seems critical at the moment, does it?"

Milverton took another swig of beer. "At the end of the day, I'm a businessman, and right now I'm doing business with a very nasty man whose money and resources command a great deal of my respect. Still, I am eager to get this particular transaction over with, and what happens to my current employer after that . . ."

And then Milverton did something that caught Devlin completely by surprise: he gave him a sympathetic, man-to-man look, unaffected and unadorned. There was no fear in it, but there was some vulnerability. Imagine that, the "worst man in London," vulnerable. Or at least honest. "In the end, we both want the same thing, don't we?"

"A woman . . ." said Devlin. "And that's why you're offering me a deal."

Milverton shook his head. "No. There's no deal. It's strictly take it or leave it. Skorzeny's been looking for you for a long time, and my job is to deliver you to him."

There was nothing to lose. "Where is he?" asked Devlin.

Milverton laughed. "He's in France, at his 'country house.' You know what a history buff the old bugger is, and he's taken it into his head that the safest and most discreet place for him to be at the moment is in the monastery of Clairvaux."

"The *Clara Vallis*. Latin for Clairvaux. At least he hasn't lost his famous sense of humor. You know, the one that nearly broke the Bank of England." Devlin didn't mention he'd already figured that out, and had acted accordingly.

Milverton flashed anger. "England is finished," he barked, "and I'll thank you not to rub it in . . . anyway, what happens after I deliver you to him is none of my business."

"You mean, you don't care if I kill him."

"Shit, as they say, happens. I'm offering you a swap — your life for your country's. If you refuse, I give you an EMP blast that will cripple your country for . . . for long enough for your enemies to finish you off."

"What about the little girl?"

"Unfortunately, she's not part of the transaction."

"Then let's get this over with, then," said Devlin.

"Not until you answer my question," replied Milverton. "Do you trust the bitch? I don't see why you should. She was on to you in Paris before I was. She's good. Very good." Milverton took another swig of his beer. "You know, for a professional, you're a bit of a nancy boy, emotionally speaking. You don't even know her real name, do you?"

Devlin decided to ignore the question. In fact, come to think of it, he didn't. "The bomb. The EMP. Launching it from a ship — on a weather balloon — on the open seas. That is very clever."

Milverton laughed again, this time for

real. "We try." He rose, walked over to a desk, and opened the lid of a laptop. "No, don't get up. It isn't safe."

The laptop sprang back to life. Milverton touched a few keys, then spoke into the laptop's mic. "Whither away," was all he said. Then he turned back to Devlin. "The *Clara Vallis* is still safely beyond American territorial waters, and the weather balloon is now well and truly launched. All that remains for me to do is arm the package and in a few hours an EMP blast will ripple across the eastern United States and that, as they say, will be that. Which is why my offer's sell-by date is getting shorter by the minute."

The room's sensor controls, Devlin knew, would be on the laptop; he'd have to disable it to fight safely, but not destroy the hard drive . . .

"It's showtime, O my brother. The pity is, we'll neither of us ever get to know each other on, shall we say, a real first-name basis." Milverton punched in the arming codes. The only way for Devlin now to stop the bomb was to get to that laptop, to force Milverton to give him the rollback codes. But first he had to disable it, to give himself freedom of movement. Right.

At that moment, Devlin's phone rang.

He didn't move, but only looked at Milverton, who nodded. "Maybe it's your girlfriend."

Carefully, Devlin pulled the BlackBerry out of his breast pocket. It was still ringing. "It's her," he said.

"Well, bloody talk to her," urged Milverton. "Never let it be said that I was not enough of a gentleman to allow the condemned a last tender moment. Who Dares, Wins."

Devlin pressed the Talk button, at the same time he hit the "Sym" key. "I'm having the nicest chat," he said into the phone as he electronically swept the room. "I think a vacation in France would be lovely. Yes. Some historic little town tucked away in a valley where we can drink absinthe and make love. . . ."

He was right: the motion sensors were being controlled from the laptop. Blind the laptop and he just might have a chance. Let's see just how good he was.

Milverton laughed and signaled for him to wrap it up.

"Good-bye, Maryam," he said. "Wish me luck."

Milverton let out a chuckle. "Very touching. And now, for the last time, I ask, what is she to you?"

Devlin realized he was serious. "I don't know," he said.

"Then you're fooling yourself. She's a dream, the dream of the prisoner in the condemned hold. You think that this time it's going to be different, but when they string you up and drop the trap, you'll realize as your neck snaps that it was all a fantasy. Blokes like us, we spend our lives not trusting anybody but ourselves and our weapons, and then some skirt comes along, the one with our name on her arse, and down we go. Happens to the best of us. And you and I . . . we are the best."

Now or never.

Devlin leaped, rolled, firing four shots from the semiautomatic Glock as fast as he could. No time for niceties, just marksmanship. The laptop's LCD screen shattered. He was that fast.

So was Milverton. The return fire nearly took his head off. Then the lights went out. That much he expected. The strobe light, he didn't. Like a seventies' disco, but brighter and more blinding. Illuminating the target, which was him.

He charged, hit the sofa, and flipped it over, ducking beneath it as the shots rained down. Mentally, he calculated the trajectory. Milverton was slightly above him, on a stairway, seizing the high ground, firing down. His temporary refuge was now a killing field. He had to get out of there.

Frontal assault. It was the only way.

He managed to get just enough purchase, just enough leverage, to shove the sofa in Milverton's general direction. The motion caught his eye, then his aim, then his fire.

Big mistake.

The Glock still had plenty of ammo left.

The whirling strobe died first. Then he put a perfect multi-round shot group where his senses and his experience told him Milverton would be.

He was wrong. Milverton was that fast.

Milverton landed on him from behind, clawing, tearing, scratching. Devlin was knocked to the ground by the impetus.

Knives. He had none. And Milverton, he knew from experience, would have several. The first order of business was to protect himself. The killing thrust would come almost immediately. He rolled . . .

And took it right in the shoulder. Deep, slicing through the trapezius, the supraspinatus, and the head of the triceps. More than deep enough.

He was prepared for the pain. He welcomed it.

For it froze Milverton's knife hand, just

long enough . . .

He came up firing.

He could hear Milverton groan as his insides were shredded. It would take him an agonizing while to die.

Which meant he was more dangerous than ever.

No time to relax. Dead wasn't dead until dead was dead.

He shot him again. He could hear the man's agonized breathing, then a scrabbling as he moved, clawing his way toward something.

Toward the computer, its shattered screen casting off sparks. But it was still dangerous — as dangerous as Milverton.

In his pain, a vision of the dying FBI agent came to him. The woman, whose name he never knew and never would know, her face turned to his, her last question on her lips: "Who are you?"

Another unanswered question.

Ahead, he heard a crashing. Of things swept away, to the floor. Of desperation as Milverton lunged for the laptop. "You're too late!" came the voice in the darkness. Big mistake.

His last shot followed the voice trail, striking Milverton square amidships. He fell.

Time to end this.

Devlin dove, landing hard on Milverton's back, full force. He could hear the spine break.

"Get it over with," said the paralyzed man lying beneath him. The pain must have been agonizing. Devlin could feel the involuntary twitching, as the body's neuromuscular system shut down. It would not be long now.

"No luck," he said. "I'm not that nice a guy."

"Who are you?" begged Milverton, still clutching the laptop beneath him.

Devlin popped another clip into his weapon. "The codes. I need those codes."

"Fuck you!"

"Not interested. You're done. You've never done a single worthwhile thing in your whole life. Now's a real good time to start."

Whether he had touched his conscience or whether it was the beating of the wings of the Angel of Death, Milverton suddenly softened. "Trade," said the dying man.

"Trade," soothed Devlin.

"Save her . . ." Milverton released the laptop.

"If I can," said Devlin, grabbing it. "The codes?"

The light was going out in Milverton's eyes. "Bernard, Malachy . . ." he whispered. The pain must have been excruciating, but the SAS man was a tough guy to the end.

Devlin patched the laptop into his PDA and punched what had to be the codes: 1146–1139.

Bernard. Malachy. The years of the Second Crusade and the Malachy prophecies. Things that obviously meant something to Skorzeny. What the hell were they dealing with here? A madman, yes, but a special kind of madman. A madman whose battle was not with the world, but with God.

He had been right all along: the "terrorist" angle was just a smokescreen. St. Bernard, St. Malachy, the passage from *Revelation* that Milverton had quoted to the President . . . There was an apocalypse coming all right, but it didn't have anything to do with the Hidden Imam or the Second Coming.

Milverton was telling the truth. The message flashed:

OVERRIDE SEQUENCE. ABORT Y/N?

He had time. Just enough time. He looked back at Milverton.

"Where is she? Where's Emma?"

He could just barely hear the words. "With her."

He took pity on him.

Devlin turned the sofa upright, lifted Milverton off the floor, and laid him down, gently, on the couch. "Die in bed, O my brother," he said.

He tossed the flat, took everything that was useful, including the hard drive, set the charges — SAS could pick up the rubble later — and downed his beer.

There was a picture of a beautiful woman on Milverton's desk. At last he understood what had happened to Emma.

He memorized the face and laid the picture over Milverton's dead heart.

CHAPTER
FIFTY-FIVE

Clairvaux Prison

Emanuel Skorzeny got into the elevator that would take him down to Level Seven, the most secure part of the prison. It was the French equivalent of the Supermax facility in Colorado, reserved for the most dangerous inmates in the country.

Ilyich Ramirez Sanchez, the notorious "Carlos the Jackal," was lying across his bunk with his back to the cell door, smoking a cigarette. France having succumbed to the antismoking hysteria that had swept the West, it was against the law to smoke in any public building, which included the prisons. But when cigarettes were outlawed, only outlaws would have cigarettes, and Carlos was living proof of the proposition.

"What's up, Manny?" Carlos asked him in English, without preamble. He still had a very strong and pronounced Latin American accent.

582

Skorzeny hated to start a conversation without preamble. And he really hated it when Carlos called him Manny. "How are you today, Monsieur Ramirez Sanchez?"

Carlos rolled over and deigned to look at him. It infuriated Skorzeny that he, one of the most powerful men in the world, had to take such insolence from a man like Ramirez Sanchez, but there it was. Luckily, this would be the last time he would have to spend in the man's company. Even though they'd known each other for decades, they were business associates, not friends. "I don't hear no noise."

"This far underground, and this far away, I doubt that even your keen ears will pick up any sound. You'll certainly hear the reports, however."

"You'd be surprised what I can hear way down here," said Carlos. "Anyway, I never had nothing against the Americans —"

"That's because you're a mercenary, not an ideologue. Even with a name like Ilyich."

"I want to fuck up the Arabs. For what they did to me."

"Perhaps you should have thought of that before you kidnapped the OPEC delegates in Vienna. You made some powerful enemies back then."

Carlos snorted and chain-lit another

cigarette. "Look who's talking. When word of this gets out, your life ain't going to be worth jack shit."

Skorzeny smiled. At last, he had this churl at a disadvantage. "Of course word is going to get out. It's supposed to get out. It's my ship. I learned a long time ago that it is far better to be feared than loved. And the increase in my investments —"

"Easy for you say," said Carlos, looking bored. "Even if you richer than God, nobody fucking loves you. Don't you know the old song? 'Money can't buy me love.' I think that was the Beatles."

Skorzeny was to remonstrate with this savage that somebody indeed did love him, that she was waiting for him, desiring him, lying in his bed right now . . . but this was no time to lose focus.

"Anyway," continued Carlos. "There are plenty of Arabs in here. North Africans, Algerians. The place is filthy with them."

Carlos rose and padded over to his crude shaving mirror. It wasn't a real mirror, of course, not one made of glass. More like a reflective surface, embedded in the wall. He put his hand on it and pushed —

The sound of voices, wafting from somewhere. Spooky.

"This used to be the cellars of the old abbey. Where the monks could hide out, get drunk, fuck around, whatever. But they built it so they could hear what was goin' on upstairs. 'Whispering galleries' or some shit like that. Amazing what those medieval guys could do with no electricity. You can hear a fish fart in the pond. Anyway, I pay off every month for the authorities to leave it alone."

Skorzeny could hear the voices quite clearly now, rough voices speaking in French, Arabic, Urdu, Chinese, Vietnamese . . . the mother country's violent progeny. "You're a powerful man, Monsieur Ramirez Sanchez."

"Yeah, well," said Carlos, "look where it got me. . . . Anyway, what you want? I guess if you're here, the shit really is about to hit the fan."

Skorzeny wished he had some water in which to wash his hands. Just being near this man made him feel unclean. "I wanted to tell you" — here he was, off-balance again — "that it's been a pleasure doing business with you. What we've done together, this day —"

"Or else you scared of something."

Skorzeny despised it when anyone interrupted him, but there wasn't anything he could do about it. His power was useless here. "The only thing I fear is the beating of the wings of the Angel of Death, and I intend to postpone that as long as possible."

Carlos sat back down and looked Skorzeny over. "Yeah, well, from the looks of you, that won't be all that long. You still scared of that kid whose parents you killed. You and those Arabs."

This was hitting uncomfortably close to home. "We all . . . took part in that conversation. You, me . . . the American." Skorzeny was referring to Seelye.

"And that's why he fucked you. 'Cause you fucked him. Everybody guilty, and everybody gotta pay. Way of the world. Me, I'm already doing it. You got a ways to go."

Skorzeny tried to control his rising anger and anxiety. "You're wrong. That boy is dead. If he wasn't then, he is now. Our plan is going to work —"

"What's in it for you? More money? Ain't you got enough?"

"Revenge is what's in it for me. And altruism."

Carlos laughed in his face. "That's a good one. You keep telling yourself that."

"Euthanasia, then," said Skorzeny. Why was he on the defensive?

"That's a big word for murder, Manny."

That did it. Skorzeny actually raised his

voice: "How many times do I have to tell you —"

"What'you going to do about it, baby? Have me killed? One word from me and every porch monkey in this joint gonna be looking to fuck you up. So why don't you shut up and listen for once in your sorry-ass life?"

This was getting out of hand. "Listen to what?" demanded Skorzeny. He had better things to do than to sit here and —

"Listen to this," said Carlos, holding up a hand for silence.

The voices had stopped. That much he could tell. Skorzeny strained his ears, to pick up whatever it was that Carlos was hearing.

And then he heard it.

Thwack thwack thwack . . . It was like the beating of wings.

But it wasn't angels. It was helicopters.

"I think you got company," said Carlos, lying back down on his bunk. "It was a real pleasure doing business with you, Manny. Have a nice day."

CHAPTER FIFTY-SIX

Clairvaux Prison

"Eddie Bartlett" brought his MH-60/DAP Black Hawk down low and fast. The United States didn't have bases in France any more, not since de Gaulle had withdrawn from NATO, but American ships still put into port in the south of France and so he had come aboard the USS *Heliotrope* near St. Paul-de-Vence, where the Black Hawk was gassed and good to go.

There was no flak over French air space. Not that he had expected actual gunfire, but usually the French got a serious wedgie whenever the Americans looked crossways at them. This must be a very special occasion.

He put the whirlybird down right on target, in the middle of the yard, which had been cleared in advance. God, it felt good to be flying one of these babies again.

He had two passengers: Hope and Rory

Gardner. But he was thinking about Jade. She always wanted a helicopter ride. "When you're all better, honey," he thought to himself. Then the two of them would go up and spread Diane's ashes over the Pacific.

There — there was the woman he'd been told look for. It had to be her. But who was that with her? A girl.

"Oh, my God!" screamed Hope. "Oh, my God. EMMA!"

The rotors were whirring for a fast take-off. The woman on the ground couldn't hear her.

"It's her! It's Emma." Hope threw her arms around Danny's neck and hugged him. "You found her! You —"

A bullet smashed into the side of the Hawk.

Danny leaned out the side of the helicopter, motioning for them to run toward him. The girl started to run — unsteadily, groggily, but she was running.

Rory saw his sister. "Come on, Emma!" he shouted.

Several more bullets pierced the Black Hawk. Who was shooting at them?

"Get down!" shouted Danny.

"Come on, Emma!" shouted Rory again. This time, she might have heard the sound of her brother's voice. She looked up. She stumbled and fell.

A bullet pinged off the main rotor. A sniper, for sure. But where was he?

"Emma!"

Rory jumped from the chopper and sprinted across the yard.

"Rory!" screamed Hope. Danny grabbed her before she too could jump. Then he reached for a weapon —

— a Brügger & Thomet TP-9 machine pistol. One of the ghetto gang-bangers' machine pistols of choice. But unlike those clowns spray-painting the side of a Burger King in Baldwin Park, he knew how to use it.

Still, who was he supposed to shoot at? Danny scanned the yard. No guards to be seen.

WTF? Rory had stopped running.

He was gesturing, gesticulating. Not at anybody in particular, but at the heavens themselves.

"Come on!" he was shouting. "Shoot me! But let her go! She's my *sister!*"

Rory was dead. That much Danny knew. The fatal shot would come any second now . . .

Nothing.

Emma staggered into her brother's arms.

Nothing.

Danny made ready to take off. The rotors whirred faster now.

Besides, there was still that other woman on the ground. Who the hell was she? He was supposed to grab the kid and get the hell out of there as fast as possible.

Fuck that noise.

He didn't want to take off. He wanted to fight. It was payback time.

The Brügger spat suppressing fire.

The Black Hawk started to rise.

Come on, kids, goddammit. Come on!

The first thing Skorzeny saw was Amanda, lying where he had left her.

But no Emma. No Pilier.

He was still standing there, in his private quarters, when he was hit from behind.

Punches, raining down, like the Lord's burning wind. Two blows, one each, to the kidneys. Something cut his legs out from underneath him. Falling, he lashed out with a kick.

Another punch, this one more painful than the last. Skorzeny fumbled for one of his pockets. For the canister. He cracked it. A simple vial, like the vial they had given him when he was a child. In case the Russians caught him. Or the Americans. Death before dishonor. *Meine Treue ist meine Ehre.*

My Faithfulness Is My Honor.

He managed to roll over as the capsule cracked. Struggled to his feet, a handkerchief over his mouth. He thought he could hear Carlos laughing at him, mocking him, from his cell in Hell.

The man fell back. His mouth, too, was covered. The cyanide had failed.

Only one chance now —

Rory and Emma ran for Danny's chopper. And then the gunfire began again. Not directed at them. Directed at *him*. And this time, it meant business.

Smart, very smart. Wait for them all to get on board. Then take them out.

Too close quarters to use the Black Hawk's armaments. This was supposed to be an in and out, only necessary force.

There — up on the roof. A big, powerful man with a very nasty looking gun. The Brügger & Thomet was not accurate at this distance. He had to get closer.

Danny turned to Hope — "Grab 'em and duck!" he shouted.

She reached . . . reached . . .

Emma first, tumbling into the spinning chopper. Rory still on the ground.

A round punched through the interior. Time for evasive action. Danny got the

Hawk into the air.

"Rory!" screamed Hope. "You can't leave him —"

Another round. This one just missed Hope as she leaned out.

Only one chance. Straight up, as fast as possible.

Hope grabbed Rory.

The next shot missed.

Hope and the kids were thrown to the floor of the helicopter by the G-forces.

Danny threw the bird into a controlled spiral. It would take an ace, a Tom Powers, to hit them now.

Hope threw up. Emma passed out. Rory whooped.

"Hang on!" shouted Danny, throttling back.

Suddenly, the Hawk dropped thirty feet. Danny pulled it out of its dive and rammed it forward.

The sniper was trying to reload. The Black Hawk was closing fast.

The sniper brought the barrel up. Danny was looking right down it.

Shit! He wasn't going to make it.

Skorzeny slid across the floor. The rapidly dissipating gas cloud was between him. His hands fumbled for the release lever, just by the foot of the bed. This was going to hurt, and hurt bad, but at least he had a chance to survive.

He grasped the catch —

Something grabbed at his feet. He lost a shoe.

Skorzeny had to see. He turned. No doubt about it. It was him. The demon child he had sought so long, the one whose parents he had killed, the one whose presence he had sensed all these years, the one who, he knew, would someday try to take his revenge. The one man who posed him real danger. Seelye's revenge.

"I am the Angel of Death," said Devlin.

The slide opened. The old cistern, which he'd had retrofitted as an emergency escape hatch, yawned. He might break an arm, but the drop wouldn't kill him. It was his only way out.

Half his body dove over the side. But the man's iron grip still held him. "You're ruined," he said.

Skorzeny slid a little farther into the well.

"The EMP device has been neutralized. The *Clara Vallis* has been boarded. There's not a country on earth that will harbor you now, you son of a bitch."

Skorzeny wriggled, willing himself away from this monster — a monster he had in part created.

Danny yanked the Hawk to the left just in time. A bullet nicked the canopy and ricocheted off. If he was lucky, Danny would have just enough time to right the helicopter and get off a shot.

He jerked it back to the right. He could see the sniper now. He reached for the machine pistol.

Not enough time. Not enough time. Then —

The rifle dropped from the man's hands. Wounded, the sniper screamed.

Another shot hit him. But he wouldn't go down.

There — the other shooter. The woman.

Time to finish this.

Danny flew the Black Hawk up his ass.

The TP-9 spoke at nearly point blank range.

The sniper fell, bouncing off the roof and plunging to the courtyard below.

M. Pilier's last thought, as he died, was that he finally was rid of Emanuel Skorzeny.

Skorzeny balanced on the precipice.

"Was all this just about money?" said the man, clutching him, clawing him, pulling him back. But the pain from the knife wound was too great. He was losing him.

"When everything else is gone," gasped Skorzeny, kicking out one last time, and catching Devlin in his wounded shoulder, "what else is there?"

As Devlin winced in pain, Skorzeny broke free.

He plunged into the well, and vanished from sight.

Devlin watched the Black Hawk as it soared into the sky. Out the window he could see a broken body. The guards were already dragging it away.

He looked around the room. The richest man in the world, taking refuge in a cell.

In the end, what else was there?

Her voice, from the doorway. "Are you all right?"

He nodded. He was numb.

She rushed to him. "You're bleeding." She ripped away his shirt. He could feel himself fading. "Hold on, Frank," she said.

"My name's not Frank." He managed to force a painful smile. "Who are you?"

"I'm your guardian angel," she said.

■ ■ ■ ■

AFTERMATH

■ ■ ■ ■

Soon you will have forgotten the world,
and soon the world will have forgotten you.
— MARCUS AURELIUS, *Meditations,* Book VII

CHAPTER
FIFTY-SEVEN

Washington, D.C.

They met at the Willard Hotel, where Tyler kept a private suite of rooms, for moments just like this. There was a TV camera there, ready to start videotaping.

Tyler took his place behind a desk that looked just like the desk in the Oval Office. In close-up, nobody would be able to tell he wasn't at the White House. Tyler nodded at his small audience and began speaking.

"My fellow Americans: the tragic events of the past week were organized and set into motion by a plot that reached from California to Washington and across the seas. The late Senator Hartley, at my personal request, bravely drew the plotters out of the shadows. We were able to prevent a major terrorist attack on the homeland, something that would have made September 11 look like a walk in the park. But he paid for it with his life. And we will honor his sacrifice."

"That's good," whispered Secretary Rubin to General Seelye. "Very good."

"Decades ago," continued Tyler, "your government used to deny the very existence of the National Security Agency, or at least refuse to confirm its existence. The old joke was that the letters NSA stood for No Such Agency. Today, we proudly admit that the National Security Agency and its sister agency, the Central Security Service, are among our country's most stalwart defenders in the wars we fight.

"But I can assure you on my honor as president of the United States that there is no other agency, rogue or otherwise. I am sorry if I gave you the impression there was, but for reasons of state, I had to. This is the reality of the shadow war we fight. A war of exaggeration and disinformation. A war in which it's hard to tell friends from enemies, victories from defeats. But we try.

"And so, as we mourn the dead in Edwardsville and Los Angeles and London, let us keep them always in our thoughts and prayers. And let us resolve to fight this war in the best traditions of America, with as much openness and transparency as we can, but always with the best interests of our nation and our world in our hearts. Thank you, and may God bless America."

The camera shut down. The sound went off. Tyler looked away from his Teleprompter and at the people in the room. "Well?" he said.

"Excellent, Mr. President," said Rubin.

"Well done, sir," said Seelye.

"What about you?" said the president, turning to the third man in the room with him, lurking in near-invisibility by the door. "What do you think?"

"I think my job's not over," the shadow warrior said. "I think Branch 4 is still in business. I ended the siege, and I got Milverton. By rights, I ought to be able to retire."

The president peered into the darkness, the video lights still in his eyes. "That's true. That was our agreement."

The man stepped forward, not enough to be fully visible, but enough for Tyler to make out a shape, a form. "But the job isn't finished. Skorzeny is still out there. And so, with your permission, sir, I'd like to finish the job."

"He's still a very powerful man. We can't risk a total collapse of the international financial system."

"Which is why you've let him skate. That was smart. But he'll resurface once he thinks he's in the clear."

"Why?" asked Tyler. "He has enough money. He can just disappear."

"But he won't. He has unfinished business. With the world, and with me. Endtimes craziness. An atheist's apocalypse. This isn't over."

"Permission granted," said Tyler.

"With one condition."

"Name it," said the president.

"That Branch 4 expands by at least one member. Someone I can trust, someone who . . ."

"Someone who doesn't have to kill you just because they know you," supplied Seelye.

Devlin shot him a killer look. "And only I know this person's identity."

Tyler looked at Seelye, who looked at Rubin. No sense telling the truth now, either to Devlin or the president. What had once been a fiction — Branch 4 — was now becoming a reality, whether they liked it or not. The monster was becoming a man.

"Agreed," said President Tyler.

"Thank you, sir."

The meeting was over. The decision had been made. The President started to gather up some things on his desk, then turned back.

"Who are you, really?" he asked, but the

man was nowhere to be seen. Just a voice out of the shadows.

"Call me Devlin," he said.

ACKNOWLEDGMENTS

In a novel about clandestine services and prototype technology, especially involving the National Security Agency and the Central Security Service, there are necessarily those who cannot be publically thanked, but thanks to them anyway.

Thanks also to Gary Goldstein, my editor at Kensington Books; Cristina Concepcion, my literary agent at Don Congdon Associates; Eva Lontscharitsch, my manager at Imprint Entertainment; Neda Niroumand of Vincent Cirrincione Associates; and Jeff Berg, the chairman of International Creative Management in Los Angeles, all of whom contributed invaluable suggestions to help bring Devlin out of the shadows and onto the page.

Thanks to my screenwriter colleague, John Fasano, for his helpful suggestion of the Barrett .50-caliber rifle as one of Devlin's weapons of choice; to Bruce Feirstein, for his friendship; to Bill Whittle, who taught me about the OODA loop; and to the gang at Yamashiro's and FOA in Los Angeles, good fellows all.

Thanks to my friend and fellow Eastman School of Music alum, Deborah Richards, her father, Bob, and her sister, Kate Motley, for showing me around their home town of Edwardsville, Illinois, a wonderful place in which, really, nothing ever happens.

Finally, as always, thanks to my family: Kate, Alexandra and Clare Walsh, without whose love and support none of this would be possible.

ABOUT THE AUTHOR

Born on the United States Marine Corps base at Camp Lejeune, N.C., **Michael Walsh** comes from a long line of American servicemen, including veterans of the Spanish-American War, World War II, Korea and Vietnam. Walsh grew up among veterans and intelligence officers in duty stations around the world, including Washington, D.C., San Diego and Pearl Harbor. His debut novel, *Exchange Alley* was a Book-of-the-Month Club alternate selection upon its publication in 1997. His novel *And All the Saints* was a winner of the 2004 American Book Award for fiction.